THE UNMATCHED SERIES, BOOK 1

UNMATCHED

EMILIA REED

FOX DEN PRESS

Cover design by Book Brush
Editing by Comma Sutra Editorial

*Content note: this story was written for mature audiences and discusses topics regarding sexual dysfunction and cheating. Reader discretion is advised.

For Boones

CHAPTER ONE

Her

He's giving me that look again. I'm parked behind my laptop at the kitchen table. He's over by the coffee machine, leaning against the counter. His shirt is off, tucked into his waistband, joggers low on his tapered hips. His tanned skin gleams with sweat, brown hair damp and curling at his forehead. At first glance, it looks like he's just sipping his water, but I know better. His arms are crossed to show off the curve of his biceps. His forearms hover over the hills and valleys of his artfully carved abs.

His gaze glides up my legs, caressing each inch of skin as if his eyes were his hands—until his jaw tightens halfway up my thighs. I glance down. At the peek of black lace where my robe has parted most of the way up my legs and down between my breasts. His lips open just slightly. He shifts his hips against the counter. And now his thoughts are so loud it's impossible to keep pretending I'm absorbed by my screen. I *have* to raise my head.

Our eyes meet, and his gaze is a searing invitation.

I should cross the room. Kiss him. Let him pull me into the bedroom to act out the wild visions clearly happening in his head. My hands go to the place where the lace peeks out. He takes in a short breath and licks his lips, stepping toward me with fingers outstretched.

Quickly, I tuck my leg under me, pull my robe shut, and tighten the belt.

"Is there any more coffee?" I look past him toward the stainless carafe.

He doesn't move. Not at first. And in the seconds that pass, my guilt sputters to life.

The nightgown was a mistake.

I couldn't find my favorite pajamas last night. The soft, comfortable, blue-striped ones. It was warm in the house and I was tired, so I threw on the first thing I touched when I opened my drawer. A satin and lace nightgown he bought for our anniversary last year—or maybe it was two years ago. I feel pretty when I wear it, sexy even, but I only slipped it on out of laziness. I wasn't thinking about him at all, just that I didn't have the energy to look for anything else. And now I've sent the wrong message.

Anton's face hardens. He pulls the coffeepot out robotically, overfills the mug beside me with steaming black brew, and disappears down the hall.

The bathroom door slams.

I stare at my screen, leaving the coffee untouched. I'm in the middle of payroll. I need to get to the bank, then Costco. I still have to stop by my office and order my mom's birthday gift before meeting Caprice for lunch. And I have a meeting with my contractor this afternoon to check the progress on renovations to the second Pooch Park location.

Anton knows Saturdays are crazy.

Saturdays, I'm off limits.

He'd been snoring down the hall last night for at least an hour before I went to bed. If I'd turned a light on to find something else to sleep in, I might not have woken with his hand resting on my thigh, his stiff, heavy length pressed against my back in his sleep. Maybe he wouldn't have gone for a run when he got up—whenever he does that, he comes back all amped and sweaty and often wants to fool around. If I'd found my blue-striped pajamas, he wouldn't have thought twice when he found me sitting at the table doing payroll in my glasses. Dressed or not dressed.

But, I remind myself, it shouldn't matter what I'm wearing. He should *know* when I need space.

Even if that's most of the time.

A tennis ball lands in my lap. Heartthrob, our brown and white Akita mix, sits in front of me like a perfect gentleman, gazing patiently, optimistically at my hands. The whisk of his arched tail on the tile is the only indicator of his aspirations. I toss the ball into the living room and watch him take off after it while trying to decide just how pissed my husband is. We had sex not that long ago. Last month, I think. No—he wanted to, but I had my period. Also off limits. But sometime recently, I remember we did. We spent almost an hour going at it, and I was sore the whole next day.

Ugh.

Is a month too long?

I hate myself immediately for even asking the question. We're a young, attractive couple. We should be *shagging like bunnies*, as my friend Caprice likes to say.

Heartthrob returns with his treasure, and this time I toss it down the hall toward the closed bathroom door. The shower is running; I could slip in there with Anton. He'd love that. He always says how much sexier everything is when we're wet. I guess? The times I joined him, everything seemed cold and awkward to me. But if I do that, once it's over, I won't have to feel guilty anymore. He'd back off for at least another week or two. I glance back to my computer. Maybe I can just offer a blowjob. I grimace. My jaw always gets sore, it's impossible not to gag, and I can never figure out how to breathe. But he loves that, and if we finish quickly, I might even still have time to run my reports before lunch.

Heartthrob drops the ball at my feet, but this time I ignore him. I get up and head for the bathroom, removing my robe with a sigh before I reach the door. There's a mirror in the hall and I take a minute to check my reflection, looking for blemishes on my skin or coffee grounds in my teeth. The nightgown is flattering. Black satin edged with lace that dips low in the back. My hair is pulled into an unflattering bun, but that won't matter once it's wet. I place my hand on the knob.

My phone rings in the kitchen.

It's not the regular ring. The notes are from a Pitbull song, indicating it's Tomás, my manager at The Pooch Park. Saturday isn't one of our busiest days; he wouldn't call me unless he had to. My heart rate skips. I pull my robe back on and dash for the phone.

"Tom? What's up?"

"Sorry to bother you, Lydia, I just—" He exhales into the receiver. "We've got seventy dogs here, and it's just me and Francie."

"*Seventy?* On a weekend?" I stop, backing up. "Wait, why just you and Francie? Where is everyone?"

"'Sick,'" he says, using audible air quotes. "Maybe it's the weather?"

Out the window, the sun is shining. Flowers are just starting to bloom. People are out mowing lawns. It's the first *really* nice spring day we've had. Of course there'd be a bout of spring fever among my employees.

"Who's supposed to be on today?"

"Josh, Ana, and Francie."

"Have you called anyone else in yet?"

"Kenyon and Darcy, but Kenyon's the only one who answered. His car won't start."

I grunt, checking the clock on the microwave. It's only nine forty-five. "All right, give me twenty minutes."

Relief is palpable in his voice. "Thanks, Lydia."

Before I've even set my phone down, it rings again. This time it's the number for my grooming shop, Ooh La Pooch. I grit my teeth as I answer. "This is Lydia."

"Hi, it's Scarlet," my employee says over at least two dogs barking and a third howling in the background. Heartthrob's head perks up from where he's settled on the kitchen floor.

I stick my coffee in the microwave, trying to guess the emergency. Scarlet is a good manager, but she tends to freak over little things. "What's going on, Scar?"

"We don't have hot water."

The microwave beeps somewhere behind me as my stomach sinks. "What? Are you sure?"

"I'm holding Chanel Bixby, the toy poodle, shivering in a towel. It was fine for our first few dogs. I have no idea what happened."

I cover my face with my free hand. "Okay, look. Um . . . I'll be there in fifteen."

I shove my laptop and payroll sheets into my bag. Ooh La Pooch is ten minutes in the opposite direction from The Pooch Park, but at least I won't be fighting weekday traffic. I dash off a quick text to Tomás instructing him to offer time and a half to any employee willing to come in on their day off. You can't operate a busy dog daycare for long with only two people, but you can't operate a grooming salon at all without hot water.

Heartthrob rises from his bed, tail curled in a semi-question mark, sensing my imminent departure. I scratch behind his left ear. "Don't worry, you can come."

My thoughts flit back to Anton as I gulp the last of my reheated coffee. Our awkward interaction seems like weeks ago, not minutes. I guess it's just as well I didn't make it into the shower. He knows I'm essential to my businesses, but I still feel bad about this morning. I head for my bedroom, vowing to make it up to him. As soon as I have time.

CHAPTER TWO

Him

I SHUT THE BATHROOM DOOR AND TURN THE SHOWER ON hot. So hot I can hardly bear the scalding spray when I get in. I want it to hurt, at least at first. Long enough for me to rage. At the heat, at myself. At her. *How* could I be so stupid?

When I'm good and numb, I slump against the wall and turn it down from a hundred-and-ten-degree punishment to something more like a warm, comforting embrace.

Or as close as I'm getting to that today.

I close my eyes and immediately I'm in the kitchen again, staring at the open folds of Lydia's robe that exposed so much of her flawless skin she wouldn't have been decent anywhere else.

And all I could think about were the indecent things I wanted to do to her.

Take her in my arms, breathe her scent. Pin her arms behind her back to see her nipples perk against the satin. Run the stubble on my chin over the flesh of her ass and thighs.

I hid her pajamas. In my latest attempt at being pathetic.

I'd emptied the hamper by the washing machine and shoved them all the way to the bottom. The shapeless, blue-striped ones she wears like armor between us in bed. What I wanted to do was burn them. In a bonfire. Along with that awful gray hooded sweatshirt she wears every other day. The one that conceals her elegant curves and repels all touch. I wanted to light them both with a match, watch them go up in electric orange flames, then make her sleep naked for the next six months.

Instead, I hid the PJs. Buried them in a dark corner of our basement like some kind of symbolic corpse.

But it worked.

She put on the nightgown. The one I gave her two years ago for our fifth anniversary. She's tried it on exactly once before, right after I gave it to her, and the memory of her wearing it—and what we did afterward—still gets me hard. So I planted it in her top drawer last night. It was a sad, passive suggestion, and like an idiot I actually got my hopes up when I saw it this morning, draped over her thighs.

Until she looked right into my eyes and shut that shit down.

Fuck me.

Or fuck me not, I guess.

The bathroom door opens with a cool rush of air.

I straighten, clenching my fists behind the fogged shower door. The room is eighty percent steam, thanks to me draining the entire hot water heater as fast as possible. But I came in here to be alone. I don't want her to say she's sorry, ask for a "rain check," or talk at all. Especially not when I'm naked and she isn't.

Unless she's planning to join me . . .

I wipe a small corner of the glass clear and exhale. She's come in to brush her teeth. The house only has one bathroom, so I guess she had to if she's going somewhere, but I'm disappointed in myself for being disappointed about this.

"Scarlet just called," she says after she spits. "Ooh La Pooch has no hot water."

I hesitate, warring over how to respond. This is how it's been lately. All the time. We both work a lot, but ever since she started construction on the new Pooch Park, the demands on her time have been surreal. I barely remember the last time we went out to dinner, let alone had sex. Every time we get a few minutes together, she's either distracted thinking about the expansion or some emergency comes up. Maybe I shouldn't care so much about what happened in the kitchen. Even if we got something started, it would be over now anyway.

"That sucks," I grunt. "Guess you better call the plumber."

"Already left them a message. I wish it wasn't Saturday."

She sighs and takes off her robe to hang on a hook, and I wipe the glass again.

It might be humid as fuck in here, but my throat still goes dry. I take back everything I thought about that nightgown. It's so much *better* than I remembered. The satin drapes over her full breasts like her nipples are the only thing holding it up. It dips low in the back, hugging her small waist, then blossoms over her hips and ass like it was poured over them. This is more of my wife than I've seen for the past six weeks.

I'm not just hard; I'm ready to come.

She pulls the elastic out of her hair, and as the soft blonde waves cascade down her back, I imagine stepping out of the shower behind her, putting my hand on the door to stop her from leaving. I would slip the thin black straps off her shoulders, watching her light pink nipples spring free, taut and standing for my attention as the gown fluttered to the floor. I'd wipe the mirror clear so she could see me looming behind her, pressing my rock-hard dick against her bare ass, and she'd grind into me with a smile. Inviting me. Urging me on. When I'd bend her over the counter, she'd be wet and ready, gripping the sink as I plunged into her slick warmth. With each thrust, she'd be begging for more, until at last we'd come together with shouts of long-suffering lust.

A second cool breeze rushes over me.

"Bye! Sorry! Maybe it'll be a quick fix and I'll make it home for lunch!"

The door clicks shut, and I'm standing under a cool stream of water with my dick in my hand, alone.

I PAD into the bedroom wrapped in a towel. The house is still and quiet. She's taken Heartthrob with her, which means she doesn't actually expect to be back anytime soon. Not that she ever comes home early. Outside, a lawnmower starts up, and a couple of kids are playing street hockey. I watch a man and woman jogging, enjoying the weekend together. In here, nothing moves, nothing breathes. I have a whole list of things to do today. Some of which Lydia's been asking me about for weeks. Clean out the garage, fix the slow sink drain, paint the trim in our bedroom.

I like having a project to do, but I thought we'd do a couple of these things together.

I pull on a T-shirt and jeans and head into our shared home office. The spare room we've casually referred to as the someday-nursery. Down the road. When we're ready. Our seventh wedding anniversary was last December.

We're not ready.

I open up my email to find three bills, a lengthy message about business ventures from my buddy Henry, and an invitation reminder from my boss's wife to his fiftieth birthday party. But I'm not in the mood to respond to any of it.

I take out my phone instead, shooting off a text to my brother, Seth, asking for an update on how Mom is doing at the new facility. Then I open my browser to search for a part I need for my bike. Maybe taking it out for a tune-up will inspire me to clean the garage. But when my eyes land on the most recent tab I left open, I go still.

Welcome to Unmatched! Where everyone plays and no one gets caught.

I'd looked it up yesterday out of curiosity after hearing whisperings around the office—mostly from the younger guys—about the hot women on the site. Lydia and I have had our dry spells, this one being particularly long, so I pulled it up thinking it might make a good addition to my media collection. Something to keep me company those nights when she falls asleep early and my dick is wide awake. I didn't realize until I was on it that it was actually a cheating site. A hookup den for unhappy married people.

I close the tab quickly. I might be frustrated at the moment, but Lydia and I love each other. We've been together since college. I definitely wish we got naked more, but she's a busy, successful businesswoman and I have to respect that. I Google the rear derailleur I'd intended to look for and find it in stock at a local bike shop. I'm about to head out the door when my phone chimes in my hand.

LYDIA

Plumber can't even get here before 2:00
Clients pissed. Won't be home for lunch.

My stomach sinks. Honestly, I'm annoyed she even suggested she'd be back when we both knew this would happen. It's what *always* happens. For a hot second, I consider opening up that Unmatched site again and trying to figure out the difference between my wife and the married women who've posted themselves there.

But I don't.

I'm going to fix my bike, go for a nice long ride, and try to forget about this morning. Lydia will figure out a solution and come home eventually. I pick up my keys and head for the door. But then I imagine climbing into bed tonight with her exhausted and disinterested. Again. I glance at the keys in my hand and hesitate. Maybe if I try to solve her problem, she'd be more into helping me with mine.

I sit back down in front of my laptop, do some quick searching, then text her back.

Check the circuit breaker. Also, there should be a reset button on the high-temperature cutoff by the thermostat. Try pushing that.

LYDIA

Already checked breaker. Trying reset now.

Great. Also, text me a couple pics of the water heater and its nameplate?

She does as I ask, and I do a little more troubleshooting while I wait to hear about the reset. I have to give my wife credit. She's clearly stressed, but she doesn't cry or freak out in a crisis. When things like this happen, she just buckles down and tries to find a solution as best she can. I slip my shoes on and head out the door while I wait for her reply.

LYDIA

Didn't work. Already sent bather home.
Going to have to close the rest of today.

As much as I want her home, if she has to shut her doors, she won't be in any mood for fun.

Let me run to Home Depot. There's one more thing we can try.

I'm already in my truck, pulling out of the driveway. The hardware store isn't anywhere near the bike shop, and I try not to think too hard about my change of plans. But if I can manage the repair I just previewed on YouTube, there's a chance I could turn the day around—for both of us. After all, when Lydia's happy, I'm happy. And, I think with only a slight twinge of guilt, if I save the day, maybe she'll want to thank me later between the sheets.

CHAPTER THREE

Her

Anton exits the bathing room, shirt wet and clinging to his chest, covered in dog hair and grime. He places a rusty-looking piece of metal on the desk in front of me with a wide grin. "Congratulations, you're back in business."

"Really?!" I set the phone down and leap out of my seat. "I was about to start canceling afternoon appointments!"

"No need." He gestures to the corroded part. "The new heating element is working, but you might want to replace the whole water heater soon. I think that thing was installed when we were still in elementary school."

I wrap my arms around him, nestle my chin against his neck, and squeeze. "Thank you. So much."

His hands come up around me, his fingers tracing along my spine, until I catch Scarlet smirking at us in one of the shop mirrors and blood rushes to my face. Anton frowns as I let go and step back.

"Any time," he says. "Especially if it means you won't be stuck here till eight o'clock."

"It means everything." I beam. "Seriously."

Scarlet heads straight into the bathing room with a Havanese and a miniature schnauzer, trying to get caught up on the few morning dogs we didn't reschedule before we're hit with afternoon appointments. Our new groomer, Daniela, shaves the feet and face of a patient black standard poodle across the room as the bell above the front door jingles.

"Hi, welcome to Ooh La Pooch!" I say to the woman walking in. "Is this Aspen?" An adorable red English cocker spaniel puppy zooms in circles at the end of her leash. She puts her feet up against the half door separating us when she hears her name, trying to get close enough to sniff me.

"Yes, this is her first time getting groomed," Aspen's tastefully dressed owner says with an air of wary enthusiasm. "How long will it take?"

I go over the basics of a puppy's first grooming with the new client while Anton busies himself collecting his tools. He's great with his hands and has helped out quite a bit behind the scenes at both of my businesses, but talking to customers is definitely not his thing. He stops to wipe his face with his shirt, inadvertently showing off his eight-pack abs, and Aspen's owner stops speaking midsentence. Anton doesn't seem to notice, but my heart does a weird little flop in my chest. Sometimes I forget I'm married to someone who could double as a romance novel cover model.

The new client heads out the door just as Anton grabs the last of his things. "Guess I'll go home and take another shower," he says as I pluck a tuft of white fur out of his hair.

"Thank you again, Mr. Richie." I rise on my tiptoes to kiss his cheek. "You saved the day."

"Maybe our night too?" he says, nudging my knee with his leg. "Can I ask you out, Mrs. Richie?"

"I . . . uh . . . that sounds nice?" I smile, fidgeting with my necklace —Heartthrob's paw print shrunken down and pressed in silver—a gift from Anton for my last birthday. I am truly grateful, but I can't quite meet the sudden heat in his eyes. My mind is swirling, trying to figure out how I'm going to help the girls with the backed-up appointments, make it to a meeting with my contractor about the new space, and still stop by Pooch Park to check in with Tomás and finish payroll. I doubt I'll have much left in me this evening beyond pajamas and ice cream, but

I don't want to disappoint him. I squeeze his hand. "I'll text you before I head home."

Anton flashes a smile, gives the cocker puppy still dancing at the end of her leash a gentle pat, and says goodbye to Heartthrob. He exits the shop just as my cell phone rings. I scoop Aspen into my arms, trying to answer the call as she covers my face with kisses.

"Hey, I'm here at Taco Den. Are we still on for today?" Caprice says. I glance at the clock and curse under my breath. Scarlet starts up one of the dryers behind me, and I lean my other ear against my shoulder to block the noise, raising my voice.

"I'm so sorry! Had an emergency at Ooh La Pooch. Can we rain check?"

"Again?" she says with a hint of annoyance. I bite my lip hard, trying to remember how many times we've already rescheduled.

"Thursday. I *promise*. Foothills Coffee on your lunch break? I'll be there."

Caprice sighs and chuckles into the phone. "Guess I can get some work done there either way."

I cringe, hating that my friend knows to make backup plans when making plans with me, but also appreciating her for it. "You're the best."

"I know."

"You still going on that date tonight?" I ask, setting the puppy on a grooming table and rewarding her with several treats while she sniffs the new setting. I switch my phone over to Bluetooth and grab my headset so I can speak hands-free.

"With the professor guy? Yes, good memory!"

I grin, running a brush gently through the little cocker's coat, getting her used to the sensation. "I want to hear how it goes."

"Maybe I'll fill you in Thursday. Hope your day isn't too nuts. Say hey to Anton."

We hang up as I finish trimming Aspen's nails and reward her again, then I take her back to the bathing room. Scarlet has rotated back out to the front of the shop, so I'm able to give the puppy a quick, efficient bath without having to make small talk. As I towel her off, Heartthrob wanders into the room, nudging his nose against my butt. He spent most of the morning sleeping in one of the open kennels, but I now realize he hasn't been out to pee since we got here.

"I'll take you as soon as I get this little one dry," I tell him.

In reply, he curls his tail over his back and unearths a hairy tennis ball from the corner, rolling it around his mouth with the same hopeful look he gave me this morning after Anton stormed out of the room.

I close my eyes, wondering how I'm going to handle things at home tonight. If I can make it back before eight, Anton and I could at least have a late dinner together. It has been a while since we went on a real date, but thinking about all the effort of dressing up and finding somewhere to go at the end of the day just makes me tired. Maybe he'd accept a snuggle on the couch instead of an evening out. That actually sounds really nice. We haven't had much time to simply chat and be together. But even as I picture this, I remember the look in his eyes as he left the shop. The heated one he gets when he *really* wants to fool around.

With a sigh, I realize I'll need to offer up more than just conversation this evening. Especially after what happened—or didn't happen—this morning. I've brushed him off too many times lately. And he did literally swoop in and save my day with his super handyman skills. I guess it's the least I can do, even if I am exhausted. I bite my lip, stomach twisting first with guilt over my lack of enthusiasm, then a hint of resentment that I have to feel bad about it at all.

All of this will be better once the second Pooch Park location is open and running. I'm usually busy, but it has been next-level trying to keep everything running *and* get it off the ground. After we've gotten through hiring and officially opened our doors, I'll be able to take a step back and rest a little. Have more fun. Then we can have some real date nights, and both of us will be less frustrated. Hopefully by June—September at the latest. We just have to make it through the next few months.

I put on a pair of ear protectors to dull the hum of the dryers and approach the puppy with the machine set to low. She's nervous at first, but I hold her firmly and securely and coo at her, taking my time, introducing the rush of air at her short little tail and working forward as she gets used to it. Hair from various corners of the room flies into the air as I do this, finding its way into my mouth and clothes. I had already worked up a low-level sweat in the warm shop, and now I'm saturated with the smell of wet dog. Mentally, I add taking a shower to my list of required tasks when I get home. It's hard enough getting myself in the mood without worrying about dog hair stuck in my bra.

I power the dryer off to Aspen's immediate relief and wrap her in a towel. The little English cocker wags her butt as I stop and pull my phone from my pocket. After some deliberation, I send Anton a kiss emoji and tell him I'm excited for this evening. Because I want to be. And if I say it enough, maybe I'll even start to feel it.

CHAPTER FOUR

Him

HEARTTHROB TROTS INTO THE HOUSE AT NEARLY EIGHT P.M. with Lydia behind him. He makes a beeline for the dish I set out for him in the kitchen while she stumbles through the door. "What a day," she mutters. "Sorry I'm so late."

I don't say anything, watching from my place on the couch where I've been parked waiting for her the last two hours. I'd left Ooh La Pooch feeling optimistic after repairing the water heater. I found the part to fix my bike, went for a ride, even had a stroke of inspiration when I came home and decided to book us a little getaway. Nothing over-the-top, just a long weekend in the mountains. Lydia's had so much work stress lately, I thought it might help.

But pretty soon it was five o'clock, then six, and I hadn't heard from her at all. Two hours ago, I texted asking if everything was okay, and she answered, "Home soon." Now here she is, waltzing in at eight o'clock like I've been in some stasis where I don't exist unless she does.

"Thought you were going to text on your way home?"

"Oh." She's removing her shoes, but her motion slows, and I'm pretty sure she swears under her breath. "I'm sorry. Guess I thought I'd get home faster if I just didn't stop."

She slips out of her awful gray hoodie, revealing a snug blue T-shirt and jeans. There is nothing special about this outfit, but the way it hugs her body distracts me, drawing my eyes over the curving lines of her hourglass figure, momentarily taking the sharp edge off my mood. Her hair is up again in its regulation bun, though more of it has escaped now, making me think of how it cascaded over her bare shoulders this morning. Or was that some other time, further back in the past?

"Anton?"

I look up, tracking back to the present. She's gazing at me with a tired smile. "You still want to go out? Or maybe just order in?"

My fingers curl against my palms. I am freshly shaved and dressed to go, but I don't have to guess her preference. I rub my hand over my face, then glance at the clock, searching for the easiest path. "Sure. Yeah. We can order in if that's what you want."

She exhales, walking by me toward the hall but staying easily an arm's length away. "Oh, good. That sounds perfect."

And now, selfishly, I'm kind of sorry I bothered helping this morning. If I were a better spouse, I might ask what else happened and give her a chance to unwind. But I guarantee I've heard it all before. If not the water heater, then another thing went wrong at one of the Pooches—our nickname for both her businesses. Someone didn't show up. She had to fill in. Everything else fell behind. Sometimes the details change, but I'm tired of the story. She comes home like this so often that I might even be suspicious she was having an affair if I wasn't a thousand percent confident she has less time or interest in sex with someone else than she even has for me.

But as she reaches the bathroom door, I remind myself of my last-ditch effort and call out.

"I booked us a vacation."

She stops, not immediately turning around. "What?"

I rise from the couch, trying not to notice the stiff set of her shoulders as I approach. "You've been working so hard. I thought we could both use a getaway. Nothing big, just a long weekend. We've never been to Strawberry Hot Springs."

She turns to look at me as I move close. "Where is that?"

"In the mountains, near Steamboat. Only about four hours from Denver."

Her mouth is tight. "And it's a place you go . . . sit in hot water?"

This query is so ridiculous I can't help laughing. "That's pretty much what people do at a hot springs, yeah. Sit and relax. This place is supposed to be beautiful."

She narrows her eyes. I'm not sure if the hot springs itself or the vacation in general is what she's struggling with, but I'm starting to second-guess my plan. Again.

"Okay," she mutters after a moment or two. "I guess that might be nice. Later in the summer or something, after Pooch Two is open. Things will be easier then."

"Actually, we have a reservation next weekend." I step closer with a shy smile. "They had a great romance package for Saturday and Sunday nights."

Her jaw drops. "*Next* weekend?"

"Yeah . . ." I say slowly, my misgivings taking more shape. "I figured Tomás would have things covered if we left around noon. And Ooh La Pooch isn't even open Mondays."

"Yeah, but—" Lydia blows out a sharp breath. "I have—I just wish you would've—"

Something makes her stop and look at my face. I can't even pretend to conceal my frustration at this point.

She holds her palms up in front of me. "You know I have an appointment with Mark every Saturday to touch base on construction progress."

"Yeah, but can't you miss one? Or reschedule for a different day?"

"I've already canceled once. I can't keep doing that. And today I was late because of the whole water heater thing." Her voice is rising. "But besides that, I just—I need time to prepare for something like a vacation. Payroll is on Saturdays, that's when some of the food orders are due, and—"

"You know what? Never mind."

I turn away from her to let Heartthrob out the back door, dismay hot in my throat. I've bent over backward trying to help her, help *us* today, but she's clearly not interested, and now I'm done. Hopefully she'll go take her shower and leave me the fuck alone.

She follows behind me instead, hovering in the kitchen doorway. "Wait, what do you mean 'never mind'?"

I clench my jaw. "You're right. It's too much trouble," I say, staring out the back door, watching Heartthrob roll in the grass. "We'll stay home."

For a second, I'm sure she'll walk it back, pretend she didn't just fight me tooth and nail about booking a romantic getaway. But then I hear her footsteps recede. The shower turns on in the bathroom, and the door closes. Idly, I wonder if she even locked herself in. Just in case I had any lingering romantic aspirations.

I take out my phone, punching the screen to cancel the hot springs and order food. After we eat, she'll say she's tired and either head straight for bed or suggest we watch a movie and pass out on the couch. It is Saturday night, after all. Either way, we'll sleep together for yet another night—literal sleep, lying next to each other in the dark, not touching—wake, and repeat. Tomorrow it'll be the same, and the next day, and all next weekend, ad infinitum.

If I really get lucky, though, she'll send me another kiss emoji.

Pizza is the last thing I want to eat after spending the day imagining us out at one of the new Mediterranean tapas places or a farm-to-table steakhouse, but it's the easiest thing to order. When it arrives she comes down the hall wearing a stretched-out tank top and an old pair of yoga pants, her hair tied in a towel. So strategically un-sexy, it's like she's doing it on purpose. Mechanically, I carry the box to the dining table. We sit across from each other, picking up slices, chewing and swallowing. I don't taste anything. Maybe I should talk, but I'm afraid of what I'll say. And anyway, all I can think about is how I spent the day. Troubleshooting her problems, trying my hardest to fix them, then waiting foolishly for some kind of reward. And, I shouldn't forget, planning an unwanted, inconvenient vacation getaway.

"How's your mom doing?" Lydia asks.

I blink a few times, caught off guard by the new topic. I had been prepared for silence, or for her to fill the air talking about the Pooches. Maybe a play-by-play of drama between the groomers or some story about a customer at the daycare. But her full attention is on me, brows knit with concern.

"Better," I say.

We both know this is a lie. My mom will not be getting better. But when I finally pinned Seth down today, he told me the bedsores had healed and she'd been less combative with the new staff.

"Great," Lydia says quickly. She opens her mouth to say something else, then closes it again. She knows how bad things were a few weeks ago. How many hoops Seth and I had to jump through to get Mom into better care. Lydia and my mom used to be close—really close—so it stings that she doesn't manage to say more than this now.

Heartthrob is already snoring in his bed, and though it's not even ten o'clock, I decide I've had enough and follow his lead. "I'm beat. Think I'll go turn in."

"Uh . . . me too," she says, jumping up from the table. "That sounds good."

This makes me hesitate. But I'm confident she'll disappear into our office before reaching the bedroom. That's her favorite way to avoid me. She'll go "check on something" for work, then wait to come to bed until I've fallen asleep. I toss the leftover pizza in the fridge and head down the hall, taking my time in the bathroom brushing my teeth.

I nearly do a double-take when I enter the room and see her in our bed, resting against the pillows, covers drawn up like she's waiting. For me? I fumble taking off my watch and spend an extra moment straightening my shoes, completely on edge.

I slip under the sheets in my boxer briefs, noting the fact that she's still fully clothed in the anti-sex getup, but I take some satisfaction in the knowledge that she hasn't found the striped pajamas. On the rare nights we go to bed together, we usually turn away from each other toward our screens. It's familiar and safe, so this is what I do now, and she takes up the same position facing the opposite way. I exhale, allowing myself to relax a little, settling in with the driest economic news I can find and willing myself to get drowsy. The sooner I fall asleep, the sooner I get to my five a.m. alarm and can leave for the gym.

But Lydia shifts next to me, rocking the bed a little, and the next thing I know she's crossed the miles between us, burrowing under my arm. I lay stock still, holding my breath, trying to figure out what to do. She's spent the last hour signaling *stay away*, so I'm not sure what's going on, and I'm afraid to get my hopes up. Several minutes pass and then she withdraws, flipping over, turning her back to me again.

Shit . . . should I have touched her? Made a move? I couldn't tell what that was about, but now it feels like a missed opportunity. She shifts again, clearly getting comfortable under the covers, and I focus back in on my phone until I become aware of a light pressure against my hip. Lydia's backside pressing against me. I glance down, deciding she must be cold. It's not super chilly, but she often jokes about using me for warmth. I stay where I am, letting her take my heat if that's what she wants.

Until she moves again.

With her back still to me, she reaches behind her, finding my free hand under the covers. I clutch my phone in my other hand as she takes my fingers in hers, guiding them to rest on her hip. After placing them there, she pulls away. My heart beats in my throat. There's no sound but the two of us breathing. Several minutes pass, but I don't know what this is. Am I supposed to do something? Then, maybe as an afterthought, she reaches out again. She takes my fingers another step, guiding them beneath the layers of her yoga pants and cotton underwear until she's placed them against the bare skin of her ass. Her hand retreats again, leaving mine squeezed just inside her pants. And then she goes still. As still as the dead.

All this time, she hasn't said a word, but now her message is awkwardly clear: *access granted*.

I'm being given permission. To touch her, climb on top of her, do what I need to do. I know because I've been here before. Last time, it was after I'd worked myself up to cup her breast on the couch after we'd finished a movie. When she didn't turn away, I confused my relief with excitement, not realizing till later that she'd never turned toward me or reached for me either. She just lay back and spread her legs. Not sure how to proceed, I asked if I should continue. She'd said, "Of course," and helped pull down my pants, then let out a few unconvincing moans while I fucked her for fifteen minutes. So dry and unaroused I actually got a friction burn on my dick.

It's the same message this time. Not an invitation so much as a concession. Since this is something *I* want, I can let myself in and meet my needs. She doesn't even have to be present.

My throat burns.

I pull my hand out, away, launching in reverse across the bed. When the edge of the mattress doesn't feel far enough, I throw off the covers, shuddering, and storm out of the room. I slam the door behind me, stalk into the living room, and grab my keys. The night air hits my burning skin as I open the front door, and it's only then I realize I'm standing barefoot in my underwear.

I clench my fists. There's no fucking way I'm walking back into our room after *that*, but my options are limited without my wallet or clothes. And where would I even go if I could leave? I close the door and pace the living room, my body shaking. With revulsion. With shame. I work my ass off at the gym, but I might as well not bother for all the desire my body produces in my wife. I've bought her negligee, brought home flowers. I've tried both seduction and giving her space. I love Lydia, and the frustrating thing is, I know she loves me too.

It's just clear she doesn't *want* me.

CHAPTER FIVE

Him

I SINK TO THE COUCH, PHONE STILL CLUTCHED IN MY HAND. My heart slows as my fingers move to unlock it and open the browser. I don't know what I'm searching for. What the internet could provide that would change anything this evening. I wind up typing: *No sex for months*. Because we might not be there yet, but I don't need a fortune teller to see where things are heading.

The search engine pulls up "10 Signs Your Wife Doesn't Love You Anymore," "What To Do When Your Sex Life Is Over," and "Why Men Deserve Sex." I grunt and keep scrolling, but pause farther down when I spot an ad with a familiar logo. It's actually pretty discreet. A white letter U inside a gold ring. I click before I can stop to think, and then I'm staring at the landing page I'd been so ashamed to open . . . was that just this morning?

Welcome to Unmatched! Where everyone plays and no one gets caught.

I glance down the hallway, but our bedroom door remains closed. Lydia would've come out by now if she wanted to talk. And honestly,

I'm relieved she hasn't. I just need some space to move on and forget everything about today.

Except. I'm too keyed up. My gaze falls back on the screen in front of me. To an image of a long leg peeking out of gold satin, stretching down to a pair of discarded wedding rings.

I don't need *this* site. I could just pull up some porn and take care of my needs. I might not be willing to treat my wife like a fuck doll, but I could still use some release. I have some go-to amateur feeds composed of real couples that I prefer over the "professional" accounts. I used to feel bad looking at them, like getting off watching other husbands fuck their wives somehow counted as infidelity. But honestly? It made me feel better, having somewhere to turn when Lydia was too tired or too busy. Like I could hold out for the next time because what we had still felt like enough.

Except it hasn't lately.

It's not like we used to have crazy wild sex or anything, but it sure felt less forced, and definitely more frequent. She used to smile when I reached for her, not pull away. Lydia's always been a bit shy, but it was fun to coax her out of her clothes and get her to play along. We probably had sex at least once a week during the first couple years we were together. Not as much as I would've liked for sure, but when it happened, it felt like everything, and I'd forget the wait in between. Until it became more like every other week. And then maybe once a month. And now . . . here we are, inching toward seven weeks.

I've been telling myself that happens to everyone. It's just marriage. After a while, relationships change, sex goes on the back burner. But two people who love each other will still make it happen.

I never expected complete disinterest.

Now, staring at the Unmatched screen for several minutes, I close my eyes and realize how much I *miss* Lydia. I want to touch her skin, breathe her in. I want to march back into our bedroom and be welcomed into our bed. Fall asleep with the heat of her body curled into mine. Wake up and enjoy being together rather than worry about to-do lists or responsibilities. We took vows seven years ago to hold, love, and cherish each other. But that feels like something we never do anymore.

The image on the landing page shifts, and now it's a beautiful blonde beckoning someone to follow her through a door. I tilt my head. It wouldn't hurt anything just to browse. Satisfy my curiosity.

I would *never* cheat. I'm not that kind of guy. But I have to admit, even a compliment from a stranger might be a nice ego boost this evening. If I download the app rather than go through the browser, I can just delete the whole thing once I'm finished. That seems reasonable. I won't input any real info and won't send or reply to any messages. I'm not trying to get in trouble; I just want to fill the empty space where Lydia should be.

I bury the app three screens deep inside two separate folders named "business" and "utilities." But I can't get past the welcome screen without creating an account with an email and password. After some deliberation, I type in an old Hotmail address I haven't used since college. Then I'm prompted to select my relationship status: *married.* I clench my jaw, filling out some basic stats after that.

Sex: Male
Age: 31
Height: 6'1"
Weight: 185lbs
Race: Caucasian
Eyes: Hazel
Hair: Brown
Build: Athletic
Interest: Women

My heart pounds as I type that last line. As if downloading the app wasn't already a clear admission of what I'm up to. I click submit, ready to start browsing the unhappy married people of the world. But then I'm prompted to fill out another section about things I enjoy and what kind of "experiences" I'm looking for. This requires a bit more thought than just filling out black-and-white stats. I enjoy not being cock-blocked and getting to have actual, mutually enjoyable sex. I have ideas about things I might like beyond that, things I've fantasized about doing, but I don't really know since I've never felt like I could try them with Lydia. After a few minutes of deliberation, I tap out something like *enjoys long walks on the beach*, except with sex. Not really award-winning content, but this is a throwaway profile anyway. I'm willing to bet the other guys on this app haven't done much better.

To complete the account setup, I have to add a picture, and this makes me hesitate longer than anything. I might be here to enjoy the scenery and fish for compliments, but uploading my face isn't quite the same as giving a list of generic stats. I'd be screwed if anyone who knew me scrolled by and noticed. I realize after a minute that anyone who finds me on a cheating site might not want to draw attention to their presence either. Maybe that's insurance enough?

I take a bunch of selfies first, but in every one of them I look either stupid, angry, or bored. So I dig around the photos Lydia and I share until I find one of us taken at a wedding we attended last year. Someone had cracked a dumb joke, and I'd laughed, which made me look a thousand times more natural than any of the poses I just tried. Lydia is next to me in the image, but I manage to crop her out without it looking too weird.

When I'm finished, my thumb hovers over the green button at the bottom of the page that says **Upload and Post to Community.** My breathing shallows. I scroll up, reading over my entire profile again until I'm satisfied that it's an accurate portrayal of who I am.

Except . . . it's not.

I set the phone face down on the coffee table and rise from the couch.

What the fuck am I doing?

Lydia and I have our problems, but I love her. We love each other. She runs two businesses and is opening a third—she *is* really busy—and as frustrated as I am, I'm also proud of her. She's worked hard to get where she is. I have a straightforward office job as a financial adviser in a big firm, nine to five, Monday through Friday. It's demanding, but nothing like what she deals with.

I guess I'm just not sure where we're *going*. Maybe that's what's bothering me. I wander down the hall, back toward our bedroom, but stop in the doorway to our home office. I stare at the four walls, the window, and the little closet, trying to imagine the space transformed. Belonging to a child. Could Lydia be there for a kid if she can't even be here for me? How could we even *start* a family if we hardly sleep together?

I slump against the doorframe. I just don't know what to do. I've come on to her, romanced her, bought her sexy clothes. I've tried approaching her in the morning, the evening, middle of the day. But lately she's *always* either too tired or too busy. I almost feel like I should request an appointment for sex. Which is both ludicrous and sad. But how else can I get her attention without it turning into what happened tonight?

I turn my head to look at our closed bedroom door, then wander back toward the living room and sink to the couch.

She keeps saying things will get better after the next business opens. Maybe she's right. Maybe I'm an impatient jerk, and I just need to sit tight until we can "resume" intimacy.

I stare at my phone on the table a long time before picking it back up. It's been seven years. I guess I can wait a few more months? But I need *something* to occupy me. A distraction from the impossible-to-ignore fact that no one here is getting laid. Or even going on a dinner date. Or functioning at all like a married couple.

The green **Upload** button glows back at me.

I think of my boss, our friends, my brother finding out, and my dead heart pounds to life.

I can't do it. I hit the red **Delete** button and hang my head.

But then an alert comes on the screen: **Are you sure you want to delete the information you've added?**

My hand shakes.

Just making a profile isn't technically cheating. Yes, it will create a digital record of my feelings—every urge and frustration I've had for months and years—and put it out there for anyone to find. But that isn't the same as climbing into bed with someone.

I just . . . want to be *seen*. Desired. That's all.

I press **No,** then hit the green button. The screen loads, and now it's official.

I'm Unmatched.

CHAPTER SIX

Her

Thanks to ridiculously light lunch traffic, excellent parking karma, and some favorable planetary alignment, I find myself around the corner from Foothills Coffee a full eight minutes before I'm supposed to meet Caprice. Just enough time to check one more thing off today's to-do list. I grip the steering wheel, glance once more at the clock on the dash, and hit the "call" button on my phone, working my mouth into an enthusiastic smile.

"Happy birthday, Mom!"

"Oh! Thank you, sweetheart!" my mother says, muffling the receiver to speak to someone in the background. "It's my daughter. No, the other one, with the dog business."

I roll my eyes and shut off the engine. My mom loves to tell her friends about her two successful daughters. Both of us are entrepreneurs with our own businesses. Though I suspect she finds my sister Celia's position as CEO of a mindset and life coaching company a bit flashier. After all, it doesn't regularly involve dog hair and poop.

"I don't want to pull you away if you're celebrating," I say quickly. "Did my package arrive?"

"It did, thank you. You know I love my films. That was such a sweet gesture."

Her tone seems sincere, so I exhale. My mother is inherently difficult to buy for, but I thought I did okay this year with a "100 Classic Movies" scratch-off poster, a couple of theater passes, and a big popcorn selection. Her favorite films are from an era when all the men were heroes and all the women were there to be kissed. Maybe because our dad hadn't stuck around to do either. But when we watched those films growing up, she always made sure Celia and I were paying attention.

"And," she says, her voice suddenly injected with excitement, "It looks like I'll be getting another special delivery today!"

Clearly I'm supposed to get the significance of this statement, but despite racking my brain, I draw a total blank. "Did you end up ordering that new couch?"

She laughs. "No, silly! Your sister is in labor! I get to be a grandma for my birthday!"

Oh.

Yet another thing my older sister has done better than me. Not only does she have a perfect job and live in a perfect house, she also married the perfect man (a doctor, in case that's not obvious), and the two of them immediately set about giving Mom the one thing that was apparently missing from her life.

"Is it time already? I thought she wasn't due till May."

"End of April. But baby decided to come a little early!" Her voice sounds like she's sitting on a cotton candy cloud.

"Well, keep me posted on . . . what they have." Celia and Adam decided not to find out the sex of their baby, which, after being the first to produce an heir apparent, is the second most annoying thing ever. It just made sending a gift for the shower that much harder.

I make a mental note to text my sister later. Something congratulatory. Though I guess I can count on my mom to let me know when it's official. I glance again at the clock on my dashboard, collecting my purse and sunglasses off the front seat. If Mom's in a hurry to get back to gabbing about her impending grandchild with friends, I might still get to Caprice on time.

"You'll be first to know after me." She chuckles, and I prepare to say our goodbyes, but then she pivots the conversation so fast I hardly know what's happening. "So, when will you be coming to visit?"

"Oh . . . uh . . ." I throw open the car door somewhat hastily, climbing out into the shadow of an apartment building on South Broadway. When my mother isn't fawning over my sister or gossiping with her church friends, she's plotting ways to get me on a plane to Ohio to see them. "I'm not sure. You know, I'm so—"

"Busy," she finishes.

A horn blares at me, and I glue myself to the side of my car in the rush of traffic. "Well, yes."

That, and going home seems to shine a spotlight on every tiny thing I've managed to get wrong since puberty.

"Excuse me, I'll be back in just a moment," Mom says away from the receiver again, and now I wish I had gotten her voicemail. She comes back in my ear with a barely hushed tone. "I know I shouldn't make comparisons, but if your sister can run her business and have a life, so can you. You haven't been here since her wedding."

"That was only last year, Mom. It's just really hard to make time to—"

"And when are you and that husband of yours going to start making me some grandbabies too?"

I nearly fall into traffic. "*Mom.*"

She snorts. "You two have been married seven years. What's the holdup?"

I stagger to the sidewalk, my face surely glowing like a traffic light.

"You—you have a grand-dog," I stutter, wishing I'd come up with something not completely inadequate. Anton and I have discussed this. We do want to start a family. We're just waiting for the right time. "And you know, we both go to these things we call our *jobs.*"

"So do Celia and Adam." She sniffs. "Didn't stop them from getting busy."

I gasp, the corners of my eyes suddenly pricking with tears. She can't know how close this hits right now. How I was so tired the other night, but I *did* try to get something started. How Anton stormed out on me and spent the whole night on the couch. How we haven't spoken about it since. But I'm not about to mention any of that to her. Because she might say something like "I told you so."

"I'm just trying to help, honey. You don't want to wait too long."

"I'm only twenty-nine!" I jam my credit card into a parking meter and stop to collect myself. Anton always tells me I need to set better boundaries, that I feed into her too much. I just can't help it when she starts digging at me like this. It feels like I'm back in high school being grilled on keeping my legs closed and my body pure. Except now I guess the message has reversed. "Anyway, this is between me and Anton."

"Is something going on with you two? You haven't put on weight, have you?"

"Mom, *stop.*"

She lets out a long sigh. "Sweetie, I just want to see you happy like—"

"Like you and Dad?" I snarl, because now I can't help myself. My father walked out when I was four and Celia was ten, and sometimes I think I understand why. "Babies definitely brought you two closer together."

"Oh!" Mom's voice drifts back into its cottony state. "I just got a text from Adam. Celia's already at ten centimeters, and he says she's absolutely glowing!"

I roll my eyes, trying to imagine my sister giving birth without a hair out of place.

"Hope it's beautiful," I say through my teeth. "I've got to go."

"Motherhood will suit her so well," Mom says wistfully. "You're both already much more capable than I was."

Nope. Not even dipping my toe into that subject. "Happy birthday, Mom." I pull the phone away from my ear, my attention shifting to an incoming text from Tomás. "Let me know if it's a boy or a girl."

"Goodbye, my little canine executive officer." She laughs, amused by her own wordplay. "I'll send pictures of your new niece or nephew soon!"

"Sorry I'm late. Thanks again for rescheduling," I say around a bagel shoved in my mouth. I set down my mug at one of the few outdoor tables on the back patio at Foothills Coffee off Alameda, firing off a text to Tomás before I sink into the chair.

Caprice glances up from her phone, looking slightly startled. "Hey. Sure. It's fine. I uh . . . I know how crazy you've been."

"I admit, I barely remember what day it is this week."

"Thursday . . ." she says absently.

"Right." I force a laugh. "Sorry, I just had the most surreal chat with my mom."

She sets her own phone down, raising her head to look up at me. "Oh? What about?"

I open my mouth, then quickly realize I don't want to bring up the whole baby thing. Or my current situation with Anton. We'll be fine in a few days. Hopefully. "Umm, it's her birthday, and she didn't think I got her enough." I turn my phone face down on the table, hoping it stays silent for at least ten minutes. "So, how are things with you?"

"Good. I . . . I started a new blog series."

"That's exciting," I say, relieved to discuss her life instead of mine. "What about?"

She opens her mouth, then closes it. "I can't really talk about it yet."

I wait for her to give me a little more. Caprice and I have known each other since freshman year at CU when we lived in the same dorm. One of the things I love about her is how direct she normally is, but right now, she just looks kind of uncomfortable. The story she's working on must be big if she won't even hint to me about it.

"Okay." I cough. "Well, how'd it go the other night?"

She looks at me blankly. "Which night?"

"You had a date?" I raise my brows. "With the college professor who likes motorcycles, romantic comedies, and home brewing?"

"Oh . . . that guy." She shrugs. "It was fine."

I wait another minute. This is starting to feel weird. Normally, it's hard to get a word in with Caprice. "Was it seriously that bad?" I narrow my eyes. "Or was it seriously that good?"

She waves me off with one hand. "We just met for drinks. He was nice. Lives up in RiNo, I think. Or maybe by the ballpark."

"My barista here was nice," I say, sipping my coffee. "That doesn't mean I'd want to wake up next to him."

She clears her throat suddenly, glancing under the table. "No Heartthrob today?"

"No." I tap the side of my mug. "He was snoring in the office when I left. Figured you wouldn't miss him." Caprice doesn't like dogs, or any animals that I'm aware of, but she and Heartthrob tolerate each other for my sake. It's odd of her to bring him up, though. And she's still so quiet.

I study her more closely. She's in running gear—no surprise. Like my husband, she often spends her lunches in the gym, biking, or jogging. She's invited me along many times, but I've never found the time. Her light brown skin is flawless, as usual. Dark hair straightened and pulled back, the way she often wears it. Her ever-present notepad sits next to her phone on the table. She's ordered a smoothie and some high-protein egg and fruit plate. Also normal.

"Well, is there going to be a second date?"

She stares at me for a second. "Um, probably not. How are you and Anton, though? I feel like I haven't seen you together in ages."

My head nearly swivels with the direction of our conversation. Why is everyone asking about us? Can they tell something's wrong? As a journalist, Caprice does tend to pick up on subtle details. But her attention often goes in five directions. And if her date was bad, maybe she's just tossing out random topics to avoid discussing it. I'm about to formulate an acceptable non-answer to her question when my phone vibrates on the table. "Hang on, I just have to answer Scarlet about a hiring interview this afternoon." I shoot off a quick text, then manage a shrug. "Anton and I are fine. You know, he goes to the office, does his crazy workouts at the gym. You probably see him more than I do sometimes."

She studies her silverware. "You know, I *haven't* seen him much at the gym."

"When the weather gets warmer like this, he prefers to get outside," I mutter. "But honestly, I can't keep track of everywhere he goes. It's been another level of crazy trying to get The Pooch Park's second location figured out."

"That has been taking a while. Is everything still moving forward?"

"Yes, finally." I grin, eager to talk about this at least. "They're working on the wiring this week. Then they can move on to drywall, and I should get an update Saturday on when we might be able to open."

She bites her lip. "But you guys still make time for each other, right? Date nights and all that?"

"What? Yeah, of course." I sip my coffee, annoyed she keeps returning to this. She knows I've been putting everything into expanding my business. Then again, she's not into dogs, so I guess it's not as exciting for her. "I mean, I know I'm busy, if that's what you're saying. But Anton gets it. He's cool with it."

"Is he?"

"Huh?" I raise my head.

My phone rings, and I swear under my breath when I glance at the screen. "Sorry. I *have* to take this. One sec."

I've been waiting two days for my shampoo distributor to get back to me. The salon is super low on oatmeal bath, which is essential for certain dog breeds with sensitive skin, but there's a problem with the manufacturer, and it's been out of stock for weeks. Caprice picks at her food, avoiding my gaze while my distributor informs me that he won't be able to get my particular brand of shampoo for the foreseeable future.

"I know it's not your fault, Steve, but therapeutic baths are our most requested specialty service. I need *something*. Just email me some alternatives, okay?"

I hang up and set the phone back down.

"Sorry. Never own a business," I say with a tight smile. "Now, what is all this about? Did Anton say something to you?"

"I was just . . ." Caprice wipes her forehead. Her skin looks gray.

"Are you okay?"

"Lydia, we need to talk."

"I thought that's what we were doing," I say, going for a chuckle and not quite succeeding as uneasiness grows in my gut.

She sets her coffee aside. "I've been working on a new blog series."

"You said that before. What's it about?"

She swallows hard and looks up at me. "I shouldn't be telling you this."

"Telling me *what*?" I sit back in my chair, anxious to find out what's going on. "Did Anton say something about the second Pooch Park?"

"It's not that." She gives her head a tiny shake. "You know how there are dating apps people use? Like, *married* people?"

"Married people dating? That sounds like good material." My skin prickles. Apparently we're changing subjects again. I take a bite of bagel and tap out a quick text to Tomás about employee hours.

"Right? I thought so too."

She sits up in her chair, her voice slightly sturdier. Caprice needs to feel like she's really onto something before she can write about it. So, if she's excited about a good lead, I'm happy for her. Even if this conversation is all over the place.

"Well, I can't wait to read the series. I'm sure you'll expose the underbelly of Denver's cheating society."

She swallows. "Yeah, there's this one site, Unmatched, that I'm particularly interested in. It's seventy-five percent male, many of whom live in Denver, and they all use aliases."

"I'm sure they would if they're not complete idiots." My mom sends a GIF that says *It's a Boy!* on a group text, and my phone immediately blows up with congrats from aunts, uncles, and cousins. I swallow hard and turn it face down again.

Caprice rearranges her silverware. "Well, I made an Unmatched profile so I could do some covert browsing . . . some of the guys on there seem downright familiar."

"Ooh, you're going undercover? You'll probably sting some local celebrities. Maybe a few politicians. This sounds sensational!" I grin at her, then my phone starts vibrating on the table. I reach for it, knocking back the last sip of my coffee, which has gone cold.

"Lydia—"

"I really should take this," I say through my teeth. "Scarlet's had nothing but problems since last week."

"*Lydia.*"

I pull my hand back at her tone. She's staring right at me with this look like she just ran over my dog. I reach under the table for Heartthrob before remembering he's not there. The tips of my fingers tingle.

The ringing stops. I fold my arms and stare at my friend, who looks every bit like she's about to throw up.

"Caprice, what is it?"

"I'm sorry," she whispers, dropping her gaze to her hands, then back up at me. “I logged onto Unmatched, and I . . . I found a profile for Anton.”

CHAPTER SEVEN

Her

"You must be mistaken," I manage to say after several moments. I swallow hard, fighting a rising thickness in the back of my throat.

"I wish I was." Caprice pulls out her phone and taps the screen.

"Anton looks like a lot of guys," I say. "You said yourself they all use aliases. The pictures are probably fake too. I'm sure it's just some dude with similar features 'cause he would never—"

She holds her phone out to me.

There's a picture of a man on the screen. But I don't reach for it, not yet. I keep my hands in my lap, moving air in and out of my lungs like a machine. I need to stay in this moment for five more seconds, before I have to see that face and think. My phone vibrates with what must be a lengthy voicemail from Scarlet, but for once I don't care who didn't show up for work, which customer complained, or what kind of crisis might've happened with the plumbing. I'm too busy trying not to imagine my husband's golden skin and rock-hard abs under another woman's hands.

Caprice clears her throat. "Username: MountainMan3; Age: 31; Height 6'1"; Eyes: hazel; Hair: brown."

She lists these details like they mean something. Like they don't describe *any* average thirty-one-year-old white guy looking to cheat on his wife.

"Enjoys: Intimate mornings on the beach, naughty afternoons in a hotel bed. Looking for illicit experiences out of town to—"

"*Stop.*" I slap my hand against the table.

"Lyd." Her voice softens. "Look, I don't want to hurt you. But I don't want *him* to either."

She rests the phone on the table in front of me, and despite the warm day, I shiver. Then my eyes focus on the screen. On a handsome smiling face with a square, clean-shaven jaw. The lines around his mouth so familiar I could draw them with my eyes closed. My heart sinks as I recognize the photograph, though at first I can't remember where it's from. There's something odd about the way it's cropped, the way he's crammed over to one side. It's clearly not the whole picture, but I'm not sure what's missing. He doesn't look into the camera, but there's a smirk on his face. The kind he gets when he's amused but doesn't want to admit it. Like someone told a stupid joke and he couldn't help but laugh. I stare at him for a second, at the trees in the background, the collar of his shirt—and then I know. The pic is from my sister's wedding last year. And if you looked at it and thought something was missing, you'd be right. Because I was right on his arm when it was taken, laughing at the same joke.

He's cut me out of the picture. Literally.

I have a framed copy of this photo in its entirety in my office at The Pooch Park. Anton wears a suit every day for work, but since I spend my days with dogs, it's rare I get to dress up, and I loved how we looked together. Him in a suit, me in a form-fitting blue cocktail dress. I wasn't a bridesmaid, so I wore something I actually liked. We looked like the ideal couple. Young, attractive, successful.

Happy?

I had thought so.

I study the cropped version again, and in a moment of fatalistic clarity, I can see why he chose it. He looks great in the shot. Sexy, mature, and ready to pounce. It would've been the ideal profile picture if my head hadn't been resting on his shoulder.

The screen of Caprice's phone times out and goes black in front of me.

I don't look up. I don't want to see the expression my friends will wear when they feel sorry for me. When they think I've been cheated on.

Caprice puts a gentle hand on my arm. "Look, a friend of mine knows an attorney and—"

"*What?*" I blink at her.

She pulls back, sitting straighter in her chair. "Lyd, he has a profile on—"

"It doesn't mean anything." I pause, trying to rein in the shrillness of my voice. "Not necessarily."

Her mouth presses into a thin line. "Sure. Look, why don't you just take some time to process? You probably shouldn't do anything right away."

I shake my head, absently bringing my empty mug to my lips. Is she just assuming we'll *divorce*? Anton and I could never split up. I mean, okay, we have our problems, but we have a solid foundation. One unverified online profile hardly means our marriage is over.

Is it?

I close my eyes. When we got married straight out of college, my mom said we were too young. She warned I wouldn't be enough for him, that he'd get tired of me just like Dad. But all our friends said we were the *forever* couple. The ones who were supposed to make it. We've been together ten years, married seven, and had So. Much. Promise.

But we couldn't hack it . . .

No.

He couldn't.

I ball my fists, moisture welling in my eyes. I hate the possibility that my mother might've been right.

Caprice clears her throat. "Had he said anything recently? Did you know he was unhappy?"

I stare at her, trying to make sense of her question. Did I know? How could I possibly have known? I open my mouth to make this obvious point, but a twinge in my gut stops me before I can say it out loud. Anton hasn't *said* he's unhappy. But he slept on the couch all night Saturday, and we haven't had much conversation outside of the changing weather, what to eat, and of course, the Pooches.

"I . . ." My face heats, my voice coming out a whisper. "I've been a little preoccupied . . ."

Her brows knit with sympathy. "Of course. You're busy. Anyone who knows you can see that."

I shake my head, thinking back to Saturday night. I *had* tried. We didn't wind up going out because I was tired, but I still came home and rallied. I jumped in the shower right away, washing off all the dog hair and grime. Even though I still had a million things I needed to do for work after we ate, I put all of that aside and followed him to bed, figuring I'd give him a happy surprise. I never really know how to get things started, but I was assertive, reaching out for him in the dark. When I guided his hand inside my pants, inviting him to explore further, I thought he'd be excited to slide my clothes off and take care of the rest. We've done it that way before. He slips in from behind and we do it on our sides. It's actually more comfortable for me that way, not so intense. He can reach around and grab where he wants, and it's easy to fall asleep after.

But that isn't what happened.

He got up and left instead.

A tear tracks down my cheek, and Caprice grabs my hand. "Lydia?"

I meet her gaze for the first time since I became *the friend whose husband cheats* and her face is everything I dreaded it would be. "I tried," I say, fighting to breathe through a rapidly clogging nose. "I've been trying."

Caprice's grasp tightens around mine. "Hey. No *way* are you going to blame yourself for this. No married person gets to just date other people when things get hard. Whatever else has been happening"—she waves her phone in front of me—"*this* is on him."

I hear her speaking, trying to say something comforting, but before her words even reach me, my doubts drown them out. He booked us a vacation. Planned a whole getaway at that hot springs place in the mountains. But I panicked about work and refused to go. Okay, if I'm honest, I guess I panicked a little about his intimate expectations too. Is that what triggered all this? What if I'd said yes instead? Would any of this be happening now?

My phone buzzes with a text. Not from Anton. Just Tomás asking if I'm still picking up donuts for the staff meeting this afternoon. I drag my gaze back to Caprice, my voice croaking. "I need to get back to work."

She frowns. "Are you sure that's a good idea? Maybe you should—"

"What else am I going to do?" I snap with venom that isn't meant for her. Honestly, the thought of having to speak to my employees or interact with other people at all makes me nauseous right now, but not as much as the thought of going home. "I'm sorry. I just need to do something normal . . . maybe not think about this for a while."

She presses her lips together and nods. "You want to stay at my place tonight? Clear your head? I've got Netflix and ice cream."

"That sounds nice," I say. "Thank you."

She clears our dishes, offering to drive me back to work in my car since she ran here, and I let her. She even takes me through the line at Dunkin' Donuts. I hug her as she drops me off, thanking her again and vaguely processing her saying she'll come get me after we close.

But as I approach my business, I slow. I'm not the same woman I was the last time I walked through the front door. That woman had a bright, secure future with a faithful husband who would always love and cherish her. She left for work and went about her daily life knowing she'd return home, climb contentedly into bed with him, and start it all again tomorrow. Now, that woman is gone.

I don't know who I am anymore.

I avoid looking at Tomás or anyone else on my way into The Pooch Park, dropping the donuts on the counter and making a beeline for my office. But as soon as I step through the door, I'm overwhelmed by eighty-five pounds of fur and slobbery kisses. Which is somehow exactly what I need. I sink to the floor, shaking and burying my face in my dog's neck, letting Heartthrob try his best to heal the hole in my heart.

CHAPTER EIGHT

Her

"I NEED TO DO SOMETHING," I SAY AS SOON AS I CLOSE THE passenger door of my car.

Caprice assesses me carefully before pulling out of my empty parking lot. "I'm not sure you should do anything until you've had a chance to sleep on this, hon."

I shake my head. Anton was all I could think about this afternoon. I barely functioned through my staff meeting or any of my phone calls. I hardly even registered the pic my mom sent of my new tiny little nephew. My mind just kept spinning around whether this whole thing is just about the hot springs or—my gut twists every time I consider—it goes deeper. If what Anton did was inevitable or if I could've done something to prevent it. And despite my anger, I keep getting stuck on that second possibility. Either way, I don't think I'll be able to sleep until I know what I'm going to do about it.

"Do I confront him?" I fidget in my seat, still unable to come up with any approach other than just screaming at him. "How do people deal with this sort of thing?"

Caprice raises her eyebrows, pursing her lips as she navigates west, crossing Colorado Boulevard. It's a gorgeous evening, sunny and serene, though it looks like a bank of clouds will roll down from the mountains with the sunset, promising an evening shower. "According to my research, you have a variety of options. Personally, I'm in favor of moving out while he's at work and having him served with divorce papers. Though, if you want to get creative, we could probably hack his Unmatched profile and change it to say he has STIs and a tiny dick."

I frown.

"Too much?" she asks.

I shake my head. "It isn't tiny."

She nearly runs a red light, slamming on the brake at the last second, pitching poor Heartthrob halfway into the front seat. He braces himself on the center console and licks her cheek, as if questioning her ability to drive the vehicle.

"Ugh, get your stinking dog out of my lap, Lydia!"

"Heartthrob, off!" I say, and he quickly retreats. "Um, sorry . . ."

She grumbles, wiping the side of her face with her sleeve. I reach back and give his ears a rub when she's not looking.

"I appreciate you letting him tag along."

"The dog might be smelly, but he's currently higher in my esteem than your stupid husband."

I exhale. "Yeah, mine too."

We drive in silence the rest of the way to her apartment building. Caprice recently upgraded to a studio in one of the newer high-rise towers southeast of downtown. She's close to everything, and while she doesn't have a ton of space, she has the most amazing views of both the front range—the literal purple mountains sweeping above the city to the west—and Denver's glimmering skyscrapers to the north. She's also steps from Washington Park, one of my favorite green spaces, with two lakes, sprawling lawns, and several jogging paths. I keep Heartthrob on a close leash as we follow her through the plush lobby and up the elevators to the tenth floor. Once inside, he makes a circuit of her apartment, sniffing over a few things, but quickly loses interest. Maybe because Caprice doesn't have pets.

I unroll a portable dog mat and lay it by the front door. I already fed and walked him, but he must be so confused that we haven't gone home. A lump forms in my throat when I think about it too. I point to the mat and he takes my cue, circling twice and settling down.

Caprice pulls a couple of foil-wrapped burritos from a brown paper bag. "Here, I picked up Illegal Pete's on my way to get you. Potato and green chile okay?"

"Thanks." I accept a plate and sit next to her on one of the barstools at the kitchen counter, though my stomach protests as I stare at the food. After listening to her chew for a few minutes, I look down at the counter and say, "I don't want to get divorced."

Caprice sets down her burrito and grabs a couple bottles of water from the fridge, handing one to me. "You could try therapy?" She doesn't even try to hide her curling lip.

I twist my fingers in my lap. "I just wish I knew how serious this is. How far he's taken it."

"Lydia," she says dryly, waiting for me to look up. "What is there not to know? He made a profile on a dating site for married people. He told other women he wants to spend 'naughty afternoons' with them."

I close my eyes, a wave of heat passing over my face. "But what if it's just a profile? Maybe he hasn't actually . . ."

What *has* he done?

I'm bombarded with images of his bare skin against someone else's. Embracing a woman who isn't me between his muscled arms and chest. Kissing her. Whispering to her. Penetrating her.

I shudder. "He can't be sleeping with someone else, for God's sake. He's only ever slept with me!"

Caprice pauses, her drink halfway to her mouth. "I think I knew that, but I really didn't need to *know* that."

I rest my head on the counter, my thoughts racing back to the weekend, to our non-encounters in the kitchen, in the bed. My whole body flushes hot. If I'd just kissed him and said I'd go to the stupid hot springs, done anything else right, would his "dating" profile even exist? Or has this been going on longer? We've been avoiding each other for days now. What does he do while I'm gone? Who is he with?

What if he already loves someone else?

I sit back in my chair, staring into nothingness until Caprice's voice finally reaches me again.

"Lydia. If he's stepping out, throw his ass out the door."

I look up at her. The world seems thick and foggy. "You think I should?"

"You're *not* going to just ignore this and look the other way."

"No." I shake my head. "I don't think I could."

My phone lights up with yet another baby-gushing text from my mom, but instead of looking at it, I open my thread with Anton. Normally, we text all the time, but we've only exchanged a handful of messages the past few days. He asked me a question about our taxes, and I'd answered, then there were a few lame comments about the weather. I scroll up to last week, before the water heater and the hot springs and the tension, to some bantering we did about politics and a lively meme-filled discussion about whether or not kale belonged on our grocery list. I'd sent him a silly picture of Heartthrob wearing my glasses the day before that, and Anton had made a joke about him making an efficient secretary. My heart aches as I read back over our conversations, feeling foolishly nostalgic for that everyday back-and-forth. Now it's tempting to type out:

Found your Unmatched profile. Did you cheat?

But as much as I want to straight up ask, I'm also afraid. What if he doesn't answer? What if *I* come home to an empty house and I never see him again?

I guess I've figured out one thing. I need to confront him in person, look into his eyes, and get an answer.

But I don't know where to start.

I tap out a message telling him I'm working late, which feels totally resentful but also completely believable. Then I switch over to the browser and plug in the Unmatched web address. It won't let me past the landing page without an account.

"What's your login?" I ask.

Caprice glances over my shoulder at the screen, doing a double-take. "You want to torture yourself more?"

"Can I have it or not?" I point to the site in front of me. "Or should I just make my own?"

"No, don't do that," she grumbles. "You don't need to get yourself in trouble." She tears a sheet of paper out of her notebook and jots down:

Username: LonelyGirl8
Password: 1nFiDel!ty

She hands me the paper with some hesitation. "I was sort of kidding about changing his profile. We'd need someone to hack his account if you really want to do that."

"I'm just looking," I mutter.

I go to Anton's page first, glancing over the stats and reading the description again. I've endured an undercurrent of nausea ever since I first saw it, but looking at it a second time, nothing new pings. It honestly seems sort of generic. I click away to the favorites tab on Caprice's profile. Here, I find a cache of men. Some of the profiles clearly use stock images, others appear more genuine, and there's at least one besides Anton I think I recognize, but I can't say from where. A few of their descriptions are overtly filthy. One or two might pass for gentlemanly if I didn't know what they were there for. But most are honestly boring. *Looking to cheat. Tired of my wife.* My queasiness increases. I'm not sure what I'm after, but the more I scroll through, the less any of these assholes stand out.

I tap my finger against my lips and go back to the main page, clicking on "Ladies" in the search instead of "Men."

This doesn't pull up thousands of results like the dudes, but apparently there are enough unscrupulous women in the area to generate several pages. My lip twitches as I scroll, wondering if my husband has looked over each of these same faces. Darkly, I try to guess which ones he might've clicked.

There's "Isabella," the alluring Hispanic woman. Or maybe he'd prefer "Rachel," the busty redhead. Or hit a little closer to home with "Madison," the blonde. My free hand curls into a fist in my lap. None of their profile pictures are very clear—they're either highly filtered, the camera is centered on their cleavage, or they're peeking through a mane of hair—but they all strike me as genuine. Some of their descriptions claim they're frustrated in their marriages too. Some of them just don't seem to care and want to break the rules. I suppose any one of them could be with my husband right now. Solving his problems, if not their own.

I push my dinner plate farther away on the counter.

Caprice is next to me, scrolling on her phone, jotting things in her notebook.

"So, this blog series you're working on," I say, my voice coming out dry and hoarse. "Are you going to, like, name names? How are you going to find out who people are?"

"It'll be an exposé, yeah. The website is really just a starting point. I have a PI friend who's helping me track some of the dudes down, trying to get photos of them sneaking around. It's actually kind of stupid how easy some of them have been to find."

"No kidding."

She presses her lips into a grim line. "Anyway, a lot of dirt can be found online, but I've had to get creative to find out what happens beyond the site. I've gotten in touch with some of the women, offering them anonymity in exchange for their narratives."

"You are good," I say on an exhale.

She grins. "I'm also considering going undercover. I've already got the profile, obviously, but I might be able to take it to another level if I pose as one of the girls and see how much I can get some of these guys to say and do."

I furrow my brow at her. "That sounds dangerous."

"I'm not actually going to meet any of them in person." She laughs, waving away my concern. "There's a chat feature on the site. I can do messages, phone calls, or even video. I just need to draw them into an exchange where they think something's going to happen so I have more to report on."

"Okay, good."

"I can't confirm it yet, but I suspect I've found at least four political figures and several high-profile businessmen."

"Wow." I sit back on my stool. "And you're okay knowing you're going to piss off some powerful people?"

"It's why I got into journalism." She sniffs. "Anyway, nothing's going to happen to anyone who doesn't deserve it."

I look back down at my phone, navigating to the list of favorite dudes and seeing them in a somewhat different light. Now they've become a list of victims—just not the kind you feel sorry for. I pause when I scroll past my husband's face, thinking over Caprice's plan, an idea forming in the back of my mind.

"Look, I don't want this to get messy for you," Caprice says, flipping through pages in her notebook. "I'm going to talk to my lawyer friends and try to feel out if we've got enough on Anton with just his profile for you to take him to court. There's a chance we'll need to dig deeper, though, figure out more about what he's done. I can ask my PI—"

"*No.*" The sharpness of my voice startles me, but suddenly my brain is churning.

"Okay . . ." She looks up from her notes and gently asks, "Are you thinking you might be open to forgive him?"

I shake my head quickly. My empty stomach roils, and now I'm glad I haven't eaten. "I—I just want to do it myself."

She furrows her brow. "Not sure I follow?"

I sit up straighter, the details coming together as I speak. "You want an exposé? I'll get it for you."

She purses her lips, but her eyes tell me to continue.

I fold my arms over my chest. "If someone's going to get their hands dirty looking at the dark corners of my marriage, it's going to be me."

"Lydia." She covers her mouth with her hand. "I was *never* going to write about you and Anton."

I curl my lip. "If he's been unfaithful, I give you permission to. Anonymously. But I don't want some other person finding that out and telling me. I want to be the one to confront him myself."

"How are you going to do that?" she asks, raising a skeptical brow.

I grab my phone, pull up the generic Unmatched profile she created, and start inputting my own details.

Sex: Female
Age: 29
Height: 5'7"
Weight: 140lbs
Eyes: Blue
Hair: Blonde
Build: Curvy
Interest: Men

When I'm finished, I hand the phone to Caprice with a trembling hand and sit back in my chair. "All I need now is the right profile picture. What do you think?"

Her eyes widen as she reads. "Lydia, this is . . ."

"Brilliant?" I ask.

"*Don't* call yourself curvy, " she says.

I frown. "Uh, well, I've got mega hips and boobs."

"Yes, you do, but curvy means something totally different to the men on here." She edits my profile briefly and keeps scrolling.

I wrinkle my nose, looking over her shoulder. "I'm not 'athletic.'"

"You're more athletic than curvy to these guys, trust me."

"Fine. What about the rest?"

She clears her throat and reads aloud. "'Bored, unfulfilled wife looking for discreet out-of-town adventures with fit, early-thirties male. Preferably on the beach, but let's get started between the sheets at a nice hotel.' Nice nod to his profile. 'If we hit it off, you can spank me for being naughty—'" She looks up from the screen, lip curled in curious surprise. "*Spank* you, huh?"

I thought it seemed racy and daring when I wrote it, but my face burns with her looking at me that way. "Maybe I'll skip that line . . ."

"No. If you want it, keep it." She hands the phone back to me with a look I've never seen. Like I'm someone she hasn't met before. I can't tell if she thinks this is a good or bad thing, but it's exactly the reaction I was shooting for. "I still don't get it, though, Lydia. What are you going to do with all this?"

"What else?" I ignore the hot prickle of my skin, pressing my mouth into a hard smile. "I'm going to cheat."

CHAPTER NINE

Him

Nine messages. Since the moment I signed up on Unmatched, nine women (supposedly, I guess) have checked out my profile, liked what they saw, and reached out. I haven't replied to any of them, and I don't intend to. I'm sticking to my rules. But it's been weirdly validating. Like walking into a bar and having nine separate women come up to tell me they want me, and knowing I could go to bed with any one I pick. Except I'm safely behind my phone, staying out of reach and out of trouble.

It's been exactly what I needed, though. A distraction to get through a very tough week. Lydia and I used to always spend Sundays together since I'm off and both her businesses are closed. We'd go hiking in the foothills, ride our bikes around town, or just stay home and cook ourselves an elaborate lunch. This Sunday was a low point, waking up in separate rooms. And over the last four days, things haven't really improved. I've left early every morning for the gym, and she's been working late into the evenings. We're back to sleeping on separate sides of the same bed, but we haven't talked about what happened or why.

We've barely spoken at all.

As I leave my office Thursday, I can't take it anymore. I decide to shoot her a text. I just want to ask how she is. What her day has been like. If she misses me as much as I miss her. I take my phone out of my pocket, but then my confidence wavers. Maybe I'll ask what she wants for dinner first. That's more neutral. But as I unlock the screen, I find thirty new messages on a group text I have muted. I open the thread, worried something serious is going on, and I'm immediately bombarded with *It's A Boy!* GIFs declaring that Lydia's sister has given birth and congratulating their mom on becoming a grandmother.

My appetite disappears. I'd forgotten Celia and her husband were expecting. Lydia shared the news months ago, not long after we attended their wedding. But she and her sister aren't close, so it hasn't really come up since. For some reason, though, this announcement feels like a punch in the gut.

Like they're doing something right. And we're doing it all wrong.

MARION

Finally! Someone came through with a grandchild!

I roll my eyes. I can tolerate my mother-in-law, mostly because she lives in another state and I only have to speak to her on holidays. But Lydia isn't afforded that luxury, and trying to help her negate interactions with her mom is an ongoing battle. Every time we come back from a visit, Lydia goes on some brutal diet, brings up going back to school, or finds some other way to second-guess her existence. After Celia's wedding, she buried herself even deeper in work, which I hadn't thought possible. I can only guess how she's feeling now.

Then Marion sends a picture of herself in a glittery T-shirt that says *World's Greatest Grandma*.

I swallow hard and remove myself from the thread.

Maybe I'm just in a shitty mood, but it seems like you'd have to qualify as a halfway decent mother before labeling yourself a superlative grandparent. I guess what bothers me more than that is knowing *my* mother would have earned the T-shirt and then some. She could have grandma'd circles around Marion.

And because the universe loves to punctuate pain, my screen lights up at this moment with a call from my brother.

I swipe to answer and immediately say, "What's wrong?" figuring I'll spare him working up to it.

"Anton. Nice to hear your voice. How's the weather there in Denver?"

"What happened?" I ask, even as it dawns on me that I'm the one who wants to be spared.

"Relax, man. All sh—di—wa—bi—som—" he continues speaking, but his voice breaks up so badly I can barely make out the words. Downsides of Mom's new facility. The reception inside is terrible. I'm about to hang up and wait for him to call back when my brain fills in the blanks.

"Wait. What do you mean all she did was *bite* someone?"

"Apparently it happens." His voice is clear again. "But the staff here have been amazing, okay? No one is blaming her or pissed at us. They've changed some of their precautions, but they're still doing everything to give her the utmost care."

I rest my head against my steering wheel. And only as my pulse throbs against the leather do I realize how hard my heart is pounding. A month ago, Mom punched a staff member at the old facility, and I had to fly to Dallas to help Seth deal with the situation. They'd decided to keep her restrained since no one there wanted to handle her, and her physical condition deteriorated so much we had to pull her out.

"You're right. That does sound better." I sigh.

But it doesn't seem like the right word, knowing what we used to have. She was one of those moms who never forgot a birthday. Who decorated for every holiday—even the ones most of us forget. She went to our soccer practices, drove us to music lessons, and sent us monthly care packages after we left for college. Now, she attacks the people who tend to her and can barely recognize her own sons. In darker moments, I wonder if dementia wouldn't have come for her so early if Dad hadn't died so young. Maybe her brain would've been okay if she hadn't had to weather his car accident when we were still in elementary school and figure so many things out on her own. Maybe we wouldn't be dealing with any of this if he'd just stayed by her side and grown old with her.

Lydia lost her dad too, but he walked out when she was little, and to hear Marion tell it, they were better off because he did. My parents loved each other *so* much. Mom acted like Dad hung the moon, and he orbited around her like she was the sun. They had the kind of marriage most people only dream about. And honestly, when I first met Lydia, it's what I thought I'd found.

"So, I'm headed out," Seth says, starting up his car in the background. "Going to shower the nursing home smell off, then go find a woman to bury myself in and forget this day ever happened."

"Sounds . . . refreshing," I say, careful to keep my voice even. It isn't lost on me that we have similar short-term goals. But while Seth seems to find what he needs in the arms of strangers, it feels like Lydia and I have become strangers in our own bedroom.

"Exactly," he says. "Say hey to Lydia and your pooch."

I end the call and navigate on autopilot to the nearest takeout place I can find. A Cuban restaurant Lydia loves. We used to eat here on the patio all the time, hanging out into the evening, but I actually can't remember the last time we did that. I get the food to go and make my way home, trying to convince myself we'll spend the evening together, that she'll come home when I need her just this once.

AT SEVEN O'CLOCK, my phone pings with a text.

LYDIA

Working late, don't wait on dinner.

I glance toward the kitchen where I ate an hour ago. Where her food sits waiting in the fridge. I don't reply. If I hadn't driven by and seen her walking Heartthrob outside Pooch Park on my way home I'm not even sure I'd believe her. I thought about pulling into the lot and asking if she wanted help with supply orders or bookkeeping. I would have without hesitation last week. But something changed between us Saturday night. I'm not sure if it's her fault or mine or if we're both to blame. But today I get the distinct sense she is at work hiding from me.

Since I came home I've tooled around, sorted through mail, and taken out the trash. But once her message comes through, I sink to a chair and stare at my phone, trying to come up with any reason not to open up Unmatched. It's been burning a hole in my pocket all evening, tempting me to check for messages or at least re-read old ones. I suppose it wouldn't hurt to look. Maybe browse a few profiles. Kill time until she comes home, we go to bed, and . . . sleep.

I've barely had the app open fifteen minutes when a new message alert pops up. I purse my lips. This has never happened in real time.

LONELYGIRL8

Hey, sexy. Looking for some fun?

At first, I don't think much of it. It's similar to the nine other generic messages I've received. A line sent to attract attention, gauge interest, but nothing stands out about it. I suppose it could even have been sent by a bot. But when I click on LonelyGirl8's profile, something stirs in my groin. Her pic is the kind I can get off to. Mostly tits—sizable ones at that. Not the kind you touch with just your fingers, but big enough to grab by the handful. Like Lydia's. The rest of the image is similar to others I've seen on Unmatched—face somewhat obscured, but clearly pretty. A come-fuck-me expression peeking out from behind a sweep of long, dark blonde hair. My brain doesn't need much more. I can already imagine wrapping that hair around my fist while I fuck this girl from behind.

Lydia doesn't like to let her hair down during sex. Says she doesn't want it to get sticky.

I read over the profile info quickly. This girl checks all my favorite boxes as far as looks, and honestly, her description reads a lot like my own. *Bored, unfulfilled wife looking for discreet out-of-town adventures with fit, early-thirties male.* Sounds familiar. Skimming over the rest, she clearly has ideas about sex on beaches and in hotels that jibe with my own.

But it's the picture that really does it for me. The hair, the tits, the playfulness—she reminds me of a fantasy version of my wife.

I put the phone down, adjust my pants, and slowly exhale. When I set up this account, I promised myself I wouldn't send or respond to any messages. And I haven't so far. But this is definitely the most I've been tempted. With Lydia at work—ignoring or avoiding me for the fifth night this week—it's hard not to be. But here is a woman I could almost pretend is my wife, inviting me to touch her, showing off more of her body than Lydia's been willing to share for months. Not out of some sense of duty or obligation, but because she longs for intimacy as much as I do. Because she actually *desires* me.

I run my hand through my hair.

It couldn't hurt to reply, see what else she says. Just this once.

CHAPTER TEN

Her

I SPEND WAY TOO LONG TRYING TO GET MY UNMATCHED profile picture right. At first, I was just going to paste in some provocative image of an anonymous woman I found online, but nothing I tried seemed to fit. One girl's hair wasn't the right color, I didn't like another one's smile, there was something strange about the last one's boobs. It takes me a while to admit that I'm actually jealous of all of them. These random, anonymous women I'm trying to use to seduce my husband.

I want Anton to desire *me*. My image.

As messed up as that sounds.

After studying some other ladies' profiles, I realize I can pull it off if I'm careful. Many of the pics those women use make their features hard to decipher. Maybe out of shame or fear of discovery, or maybe they just aren't that pretty. It would serve the asshole men right.

I end up using a selfie I took in Caprice's bathroom, posed to maximize cleavage and bare skin, with my face turned away, obscured behind the cascade of my hair. The shape of my jaw can be made out, a hint of my overall profile—enough to tell I'm probably nice looking—but not the details. I mess with filters until it doesn't resemble me anymore. My hair a different shade of blonde, my skin more tan. But it *is* still me.

And now it's perfect. Time to put my plan into action.

LONELYGIRL8

Hey, sexy. Looking for some fun?

At first, I hold my breath, not sure he'll even answer. Yes, he created the profile, but maybe he was only curious. Maybe he stopped there. If he just put it together, he might not have even had a chance to use it. Or . . . he might have already found someone to hook up with. He might've found several someones. Twenty minutes pass, and I'm swinging between relief and dread when a subtle alert sounds and a surge of adrenaline rushes through me.

MOUNTAINMAN3

Yes. Are you?

A wave of nausea hits me. I clutch my hand to my chest too late. It's already torn open. A sound escapes my lips, somewhere between a gasp and a cry. Caprice looks up from her laptop, alarmed.

"Lyd? What's wrong?"

I open my mouth, trying to say words, but clamp it shut and just look at her, a tear rolling down my cheek.

She comes to peer over my shoulder, her eyes widening when she sees the screen. "MountainMan3? God, you're messaging *Anton*?"

"Who else?" I croak.

"I thought you said you were going to cheat!"

"I am!" I cover my face with my hands and whimper. "With him."

Caprice gives me a long, hard look, then her eyes soften with a measure of sadness, or maybe pity, I've never seen directed at me. I look away, dropping the phone into my lap, but she snatches it up and starts swiping the screen.

"What are you doing?" I ask, my nose already clogged.

She doesn't answer right away, grabbing her notepad and jotting down a few things. Finally, she looks up, wearing her determined journalist face—though still with a hefty amount of sympathy. "When you said you wanted to get your hands dirty in the dark corners of your marriage, I didn't realize this is what you had in mind."

I shrug, too heartbroken to admit I actually thought he might not answer.

"As far as I'm concerned, you have two choices," Caprice continues. "You can delete this whole thing now, forget about it, go home and call a lawyer." She worries her lip. "Or . . . you can see it through."

I raise my gaze to meet hers.

"I don't need an exposé," she says gently, holding up the phone so I can see Anton's profile pic. "But if you can lure him in, I'd love to help you nail his balls to the wall."

I stare at my husband's smile, my brain again filling in the missing parts of the image—my arm linked with his, like a ghost outside the frame. A happy couple who ceased to exist the moment he cropped me out. I look at Caprice and swallow. "Let's do it."

She nods with a grim smile, taps out a message on my screen, then hands it back so I can send it myself.

LONELYGIRL8

Of course! What are you into?

I grit my teeth, hit the button, and let out a long exhale. I'd be okay waiting a good hundred years before I have to see what he says, but he responds almost immediately.

MOUNTAINMAN3

Your tits, mostly.

My jaw nearly hits the ground. I'm curled in the corner of Caprice's couch, but I have to set down the phone and walk to the window. Anton would never speak to a woman that way. Let alone use the word *tits*. He's too caring, too sensitive. Too feminist.

I glance at Caprice, whose lip is curled in resigned distaste.

"Maybe it isn't even him," I say hoarsely. "It could be some dude who stumbled on our picture online, even some jerk friend or coworker." My brain seizes on this. That *has* to be what's happening. Some repulsive guy out there found my husband's picture and is using it to attract women. *My* Anton's probably at the gym. Or at home, having dinner alone. Waiting for me to join him.

I glance at the clock. It's after eight. But then my phone pings again.

MOUNTAINMAN3

I'd like to slide my dick between those tits and come all over them. My wife won't ever let me do that.

And just like that, the walls close in.

All the air escapes the room.

Because I'm sure it's him.

I've never understood this particular fascination. I mean, guys like boobs, I get it. But what's exciting about covering them in a sticky mess? Honestly, I thought he'd slipped the first time he did it. The second time, he shot me in the eye and my vision was blurry for an hour. I was sure I'd get an infection. After that, he asked if I minded him coming on my chest, and I said I did. He never tried it again, and I thought that was that.

But now he's asking some "other woman" if he can do it to her.

Like it's somehow important to him.

My limbs suddenly feel heavy. I'm not sure I want to keep the conversation going. It was one thing to create an Unmatched profile. Pretend to be someone else. Vent a little of my anger and frustration. But now that we're talking, now that he thinks I'm *LonelyGirl8,* a married woman with nothing better to do than have sex with someone else's husband, this is starting to feel too real. I'm not sure I'm ready to see this side of Anton.

Caprice holds her hand out for the phone. "Do you want me to . . ."

I shake my head, biting my lip. Hard.

If he's texting me now, he must not be with someone else. Maybe he hasn't gone through with it yet. I need to play along if I'm going to catch him. I take a sharp breath, trying to channel my inner hussy.

LONELYGIRL8

Ooh, just thinking about that turns me on.

MOUNTAINMAN3

Yeah? What else do you like?

My cheeks burn. The corners of my eyes prick with tears. I remind myself he's talking to *me*. Not someone else. It's *my* picture, *my* stats. Then I lie through my teeth.

LONELYGIRL8

I love sucking dick.

MOUNTAINMAN3

Tell me more.

LONELYGIRL8

I want to suck your dick and let you come all over my tits.

MOUNTAINMAN3

Fuck. You're getting me hard.

I close my eyes and let out a shaky breath. This whole conversation makes me want to go home, throw him out of the house, and take a long shower. But I've got him on the line now. I just need to reel him in. I glance at the description in his profile again: "Naughty afternoons in a hotel bed." Okay, you dirty asshole.

LONELYGIRL8

After that, I want you to throw me across the bed and spank me 'cause I'm naughty.

There's a lag in his reply. A long enough pause that I start to wonder if he got interrupted at the "gym" or wherever he really is tonight. Caprice disappears into the bathroom, and then my phone pings again.

MOUNTAINMAN3

You like that?

LONELYGIRL8

Oh yeah, it gets me hot.

There's another lengthy pause, then he finally answers.

MOUNTAINMAN3

Sorry, that doesn't do anything for me.

I suck in a breath, my pulse pounding in my ears. His profile said *naughty*. Isn't spanking what people who use the word "naughty" like to do?

I look up as Caprice exits the bathroom. "He doesn't want to spank me!"

"Say what?"

"I—I had him. It was working. But then I brought up spanking, and he's not into it."

I show her the phone, scrolling up through the messages. Her hand comes up to cover her mouth, and when she glances at me, I feel my face redden. "Okay, so back off. Not everyone digs that kind of thing."

She says this like she speaks from experience, but I'm way too embarrassed at this point to ask. And I don't want to leave Anton hanging too long.

LONELYGIRL8

If you're not into it, no big deal. What else do you like?

MOUNTAINMAN3

How about butt play?

My eyes bulge. He doesn't want to spank, but he's into *that*? I bring my hand to my cheek and stare at Caprice. She rolls her eyes, plucking the phone out of my grip, and types:

LONELYGIRL8

Have to admit, I've never done it. But I LOVE trying new things.

MOUNTAINMAN3

Excellent.

She hands the phone back to me, and I want to gag. *Butt* play? I don't need to ask Caprice what that means, but at the same time, I don't feel like I really understand it either. My face is on fire as I try to imagine exactly what my husband is suggesting he wants to do—and where he wants to do it. Certainly somewhere he'd never dare try to explore with me.

My stomach turns over. I guess maybe that's the point.

I do some deep breathing, trying to collect myself enough to continue the conversation. When I'm finally centered, I straighten and poise my thumbs over the screen. I don't think we're going to wine and dine at this point. Maybe it's time to clinch the deal.

LONELYGIRL8

Sounds like we could have fun together. Maybe we should meet.

MOUNTAINMAN3

Maybe . . .

LONELYGIRL8

You're in Denver too, right?

A minute passes, then two. I chew my lip, wondering if I jumped ahead too quickly.

MOUNTAINMAN3

Listen . . . I think you're hot. But I've never done this before.

I gasp. My hand rises to my throat, my eyes filling with tears. I knew it. I knew he couldn't have gone through with it! We were each other's *firsts.* You can't just go try out somewhere new when you've never left home. Not easily, at least. But I didn't realize until he said it how much I needed this to be true.

Unless it's a lie? My stomach sinks all the way back down to my toes. What about this whole situation isn't wall-to-wall lies? He's hardly texted me all day, but he's sitting in our home, flirting with what he thinks is another woman.

"Lydia," Caprice says, laying a gentle hand on my shoulder. I'd nearly forgotten she was there. "Look, I want to catch him and all, but are you sure this is how you want to do it?"

I close my eyes. She might be right. I've already opened the door to a world of hurt. Chances are, if I pursue this, that's not going to improve. But every time I imagine him touching someone else, I just feel sick. If it's not me Anton hooks up with, who will it be?

I look at Caprice, nod slowly, and turn back to the screen.

LONELYGIRL8

But you want to. That's why we're both here.

MOUNTAINMAN3

I'd just like to get laid.

My eyes sting, thumbs hovering over the screen.

LONELYGIRL8

Then let's make it happen. Where should we go?

There's a lengthy break in the conversation again. I pace back and forth between the couch and the windows, waiting to see what he says. Caprice goes to her freezer, pulls out a pint of ice cream, and brings back two spoons.

Finally, a message pings.

MOUNTAINMAN3

Sorry . . . I don't think I can do this.

My chest lightens. I breathe in for the first time in what feels like an hour. I wait for him to follow up, say something else to clarify, but nothing comes.

"Dickhead," Caprice mutters over my shoulder.

I set the phone down and turn to face her, hands clasped in front of me. "He doesn't want to do it!"

She grunts.

I turn in a circle, feeling floaty, almost cheerful. Certainly better than I have since lunch. "I knew he couldn't go through with it. This is . . ." I search for the right word. "This is great."

Caprice looks from me to Heartthrob, who's raised his head like he's following the conversation, and folds her arms. "What about this is great?"

I check my screen again, holding it up so she can see his final message. "He isn't going to cheat. He *can't*. Because he loves me."

"He didn't say that."

"He didn't need to. If I don't matter, what's to stop him?"

She opens her mouth, closes it again, then drifts to her laptop at the counter, biting back whatever else was trying to fight past her lips. I set the phone down and start collecting my things. I pack up my computer and a stack of papers from The Pooch Park and finally grab Heartthrob's leash. He stands and stretches, wagging his big arced tail.

"Thanks for dinner," I say. "And putting up with us tonight."

"You're going home?" She raises her eyebrows, processing what I'm doing.

"Well, yeah."

She slides off her stool. "Lydia, don't take this the wrong way, but can I just point out that while you've been 'working late' tonight, he's been home discussing *butt play* with another woman?"

I nearly drop my bag trying to get it over my shoulder. "He's never touched anyone but me," I say to the wall.

"If you believe that."

"Look, you've never been married. Maybe you don't get it," I snap, wincing immediately at the flash of hurt in her eyes. Not so long ago, Caprice was engaged, but we try not to talk about that. "I'm sorry, I'm sorry." I squeeze my eyes shut, taking in a shaky breath. "I just—I need to do this, Caprice. I need to go home and see if we can still make things right."

She huffs, but when I open my eyes again, she shakes her head and wraps me in her arms, giving me a hug I didn't realize I desperately needed. "Fine. I support you. I think your husband's a jackass, but you do what you need to do."

"Thanks," I whisper.

"If you change your mind, you can always stay here. My door is open," she says, pulling back and glancing at my dog. "Even for him."

That's a seriously generous offer, and I want her to know I'm grateful, so I manage a small smile. I place my hand on the doorknob but can't quite figure out what comes next until Heartthrob nudges me with his nose, and somehow I pull it open.

"Maybe you guys should at least consider counseling?" Caprice suggests as I make my way into the hall.

"Probably," I say, moving toward the elevators. Therapy would have to be better than divorce.

But as I exit her building into a sprinkle of spring rain, each step shakier than the last, my confidence plummets. Heartthrob jumps into the backseat when we reach my car, excited to be going home. But I sit for a long time staring through the raindrops on my windshield, wondering what will happen when we get there.

CHAPTER ELEVEN

Him

I STARE AT MY BLANK PHONE SCREEN, MY FINGERS ACTUALLY trembling. I can't believe how far I let that go, how close I came to ruining everything. In some people's eyes, I'm a cheater already. I broke my own rules, went looking for trouble—and dear God, did I find it. A girl with all of Lydia's sexiest features, out there ready and willing to let me fuck her six ways to Sunday. Who I could message right now to say I've changed my mind.

It's nearly nine p.m., and Lydia still isn't home.

No one would have to know.

But when I imagine pulling my clothes off with LonelyGirl8, touching her skin instead of my wife's, my insides burn.

I shove the phone deep into my pocket, afraid to unlock the screen again. I want nothing more than to wait up for Lydia, sweep her into my arms as she comes through the door, and carry her off to the bedroom.

Instead of climbing into bed together and politely avoiding her tits, her back, or—God forbid—brushing my dick against the globe of her ass. Everything would be different if I could act out the fantasies I just shared with a stranger, with her.

If she showed the remotest interest, I wouldn't need the stupid app.

I pull out the phone again. *Not* to open the messages—I just want one more look at the woman who truly seemed to want me. I don't trust most of what's posted on Unmatched, but after our exchange, this girl seems more genuine. I click on her picture and it's even better than I remember. She's clearly beautiful, seems adventurous, and *God*, those tits. They're almost as nice as Lydia's.

I stare at her, trying to fill in the blanks, wondering what she does for work. What she's into. Her profile says she's married, but what brought her to the app? It seems ludicrous that anyone could ignore a woman who looks like this, but it also seems insane that my gorgeous wife completely hates sex.

After ten minutes or so, I hear Lydia's car pull into the driveway. It's still too early to be asleep, but I flip the TV on, lock my phone, and shut my eyes anyway. I don't really feel up to attempting pleasantries. She's been gone almost twelve hours, and we've barely exchanged two texts. I have no idea what kind of day she's had, and she doesn't know what mine was like either. It's like we're becoming strangers inside and outside the bedroom.

The door opens, and Heartthrob runs in and sniffs me. He probably wants me to play tug or toss the ball in the yard, but I roll to face the back of the couch and he gives up, settling on his bed in the corner with an old forgotten bone.

Lydia comes in behind him, carrying a bunch of stuff from the sound of it. She has to walk right by the couch on her way to the kitchen and my whole body tenses as she hesitates next to me. There's an intake of breath like she's going to speak, and I just pray she doesn't. I don't think I can carry on a conversation with my wife right after exchanging messages about another woman's tits.

I pretend to snore, burying my face in an old blanket. It carries scents of flowers and French vanilla, of *her*, and instantly the moment—hell, the entire last few hours—is sabotaged by memory. We brought this blanket the first time we went camping together. It was Memorial Day, and since neither of us is actually from Colorado, we thought it would be a good weekend to go to the mountains. We borrowed a tent and some other gear from friends, but the temperature plunged, and it snowed overnight. We kept from freezing by huddling naked together under this blanket inside the tent.

I can nearly taste the sweetness of her hardened nipples beneath that fabric. Feel the softness of her warm curves under my hands. She was hesitant to make love outdoors, but that was a huge turn-on for me. We spent the whole night in each other's arms, and it was one of the best I can remember.

We've gone camping many times since, but she always stays firmly in her own sleeping bag.

My fist tightens around my phone. With a few swipes of my thumb, I could get my rocks off with a woman as frustrated as I am. But lying here, curled into this blanket, my dick is at half mast for my wife standing next to me.

Or maybe just her memory.

I breathe through my mouth, cutting off the scents and recollections buried in the fabric. Lydia exhales and continues into the kitchen. I listen as she makes a cup of tea. Unloads the dishwasher. Sets up the blender for my protein smoothie tomorrow morning. My heart softens a little. She does make some little gestures for me. Eventually, she visits the bathroom, then shuts herself in our room, closing the door between us with a secure thud.

I actually think about going in. Getting naked and crawling into bed with her. Searching for some reason not to reopen Unmatched. Maybe she'd be naked under the covers too. Maybe she's in there now, just waiting for me to join her.

I don't move. I've gone in with those hopes hundreds of times, and that's never what happens. Instead, I set my phone alarm so I can get out of the house before she's awake. Then, as a reward to myself for *not* reaching out to LonelyGirl8, I pull up my favorite porn feed. The amateur one composed of real couples, not that terrible mass-produced crap. I drift off to GIFs of naked wives who resemble mine, flashing their tits and fucking their husbands with great big smiles.

Outside, the sky is just beginning to lighten. I tiptoe out of our bedroom, my shoes tucked under my arm. I managed to sneak in and get dressed in the dark without waking Lydia, and there's a fifty percent chance my socks even match, but just as I pull our door closed behind me, my phone chimes loudly in my pocket.

EVA WALLACE

Hey! You and Lydia are the only ones I haven't heard from. You two coming to Carl's party tonight?

I wipe my hand over my face. I'd meant to RSVP over the weekend, but I was in such a foul mood by Sunday it must've slipped my mind. I've been at Vesper Financial Advisers for five years, and I enjoy it there. My boss, Carl, essentially lets me handle my own clients and do things the way I want, but about twice a year his wife Eva finds some excuse to institute "mandatory fun," and his fiftieth birthday is her latest effort. The last thing I ever want to do on a Friday night is spend more time with my coworkers, and normally I might find an excuse to skip out. But yesterday Carl mentioned, rather pointedly, that the owner of one of our biggest accounts will also be at this party. An account he's talked about putting me in charge of, and admittedly, one I really, really want.

For a second, I consider just going by myself. I'm too ashamed of how I spent the previous evening to even say good morning to Lydia, let alone invite her to a social event. But I actually can't imagine going without her either. Lydia's good at parties. When she walks into a room, everyone looks at her instead of me. She laughs at the right times, asks the right questions. Plus I've never gone to one of these things by myself, so it would be weird if I showed up alone. People might ask questions. Ones I'm afraid to answer out loud.

Before I can figure out how to reply to the text, the bedroom door opens. Lydia starts when she sees me, wrapped in her robe and clearly only half awake. Heartthrob bounds down the hall beside her.

"Morning," she says, not quite looking my way. She navigates around me, careful not to let our bodies touch, even with both of us fully clothed. On her way to the coffeepot, and then work, as always. I received an invite to an early meeting today, and I'm already crabby about having to skip the gym. But I can't go into the office without resolving this stupid invitation. I clear my throat before she reaches the kitchen.

"There's a party for Carl Wallace tonight. I told Eva we'd go."

It comes out as an order rather than an invite, making me sound like a dick. But I'm afraid of giving her the option to say no.

She turns, letting her gaze slide over me, taking in my suit and the shoes still gripped under my left arm. Ages pass, and she says nothing, her expression completely blank. Then, with a strike of terror, I wonder if she *knows*. She couldn't—but what if, somehow, she found out I was messaging another woman last night? A woman who invited me to do all manner of things with her naked body. A woman I have been trying to forget ever since I woke.

My lips part. I try to ready some excuse, only what the hell is there to say?

But then she runs her hands through her hair and sort of smiles. "His fiftieth, right? Sounds like fun. What time?"

Somewhere deep in my gut, a tiny cache of tension releases. She doesn't know. She can't.

I haven't completely fucked up our marriage.

"Invitation said seven," I say, letting out a slow breath.

"Great. I'll pick up a gift and be ready by six thirty."

She continues past me into the kitchen, and I follow, watching her go about making coffee, turning on the blender, feeding Heartthrob. The things she does every day. Her movements are light; nothing seems out of the ordinary. But that whole exchange just felt a little too easy.

"Are you sure? You've worked late a lot this week."

For just a second, she seems to pause. "I have." Then she shakes her head, pours my smoothie into a to-go cup, and puts the drink in my hand. "Just catching up on some things for the new location. I'm definitely overdue for an evening out."

Her phone rings, and she wanders out of the room to take the call, which, from the sound of it, is an employee out sick. I stand where my feet are planted, heart thudding, trying to decide if it's my own guilt nagging at me or if something's truly off.

Maybe she's just . . . trying?

A little burst of warmth spreads through me, probably quicker than I should allow. A week ago, I couldn't even talk to her about a vacation, and now she's ready for a party at the drop of a hat. I'm not sure what's changed, but it's easier *not* to think about it. Because this feels like the Lydia I miss. The one who used to love any excuse to dress up, who I love to *see* dressed up. And the more time we spend together, the less I want to open Unmatched.

"Sounds good." I slip my shoes on and toss a ball to Heartthrob. And before I lose my nerve, duck in to kiss her cheek. "See you tonight."

CHAPTER TWELVE

Her

"So, over here, we ran into an issue with electrical," my contractor Mark says, pointing out a tangle of wires protruding from the ceiling. "All of this needs to be upgraded. But there's another problem that isn't actually inside the building. I think it's the line from the pole. So we're going to have to talk to the city about that."

"How long will that take?" I ask, wrinkling my nose.

He looks at me like I cracked a joke. "They'll get to us when they feel like it."

"Okay, but after that, everything else is in place? When can you guys start the finish work?"

"Drywall will go in pretty quickly. We'll get that done in about a week. But we can't even start that until the wiring is resolved."

I let out a breath, reminding myself to inhale again. "Keep me posted."

One of Mark's guys calls him over, and at the same moment, my phone rings. I duck out the back door into what will eventually be a large outdoor play yard full of Astroturf, ramps, tunnels, and wading pools. Only right now it looks like a big muddy mess.

I swipe to answer the call and nearly drop the phone into a dirty puddle when I see the screen. Celia is trying to video chat. I've been so preoccupied worrying about my business and my marriage that I completely forgot to congratulate my sister on giving birth. I smooth my hair quickly, then raise the screen to my face.

"Celia, hi! It's a boy!" These idiotic words leave my lips before I can think. I had meant to say something along the lines of *Congrats! I'm so excited to have a nephew! I might be a terrible sister, but I plan to be an excellent aunt!* But apparently my voice had other ideas.

"Yes, yes he is," she says coolly, not bothering to point out how stupid I sound. "I thought you might want to meet Gabriel Edward Cohen."

She angles the camera down to a sleeping, wrinkled little face in her arms. I hate to admit that most infants look the same to me, but I try to make the appropriate "awwww" sounds and say something about how tiny he is the way other people gush over babies.

Then I pause, my brain backing up a few seconds. "Wait, Gabriel *Edward*? You named him after Dad?"

"Uh, no—not really," Celia says abruptly. "Adam's family has a tradition of naming babies after both grandparents, but obviously we're going to call him Gabriel, after Adam's dad."

Even so, color me stunned. My memories of Dad are pretty foggy. He left before I turned five, but Celia was ten, and if there's one person in the world who hates Edward Stanton as much as Mom does, it's her.

"Well, um . . . he seems sweet no matter what you call him. I'll have to come out for a visit after I get my second daycare up and running."

"Oh, how are things going with that?" she asks, peering closer at the phone like she's trying to see where I'm standing. Quickly, I angle myself so her only view is the brick wall behind me and not the mess of construction. "I thought you were hoping to launch in the spring?"

"No." I grit my teeth. "Everything's going great. We should hopefully still open by June."

She arches a well-manicured eyebrow, which draws my attention to the fact that she looks stunning, as always. Her skin is flawless, her blonde hair styled. Definitely not the picture of a brand-new mom. She doesn't even look tired. "Well, you know Lydia, if you ever need to chat about—"

"I'm good!" I interrupt, because the last thing I want is for my sister to start life coaching me. The only thing worse would be if Mom was here to join in. "And actually, I was just about to pop a gift for little Gabriel Edward in the mail, so I had better run. I'll try to make it out for Thanksgiving."

"You and Anton both, I hope."

"Yes! Both of us. Definitely," I say, as if my blood wasn't already boiling without having to think about my husband. "Enjoy motherhood. It looks good on you!"

"Bye—"

I end the call before she can finish her farewell and drum my fingers on the dirty bricks, trying not to envision a perfect holiday spread at her house in November. The table set like a magazine, her family in matching outfits, our mother doting on Baby Gabriel. And me there . . . alone?

I came so close to calling Anton out last night when I got home. He clearly wasn't asleep. It would've been so easy to just stand there and tell him I *knew*. Or even better, send it in a message from LonelyGirl8, just to heighten his shame. But when I walked in, I was just so relieved to see him there. Not at some hotel, or worse, in some other woman's bed. And I can't think what would have stopped him if he didn't still have feelings for me.

We could still make this work.

AT SIX THIRTY SHARP, I step out of the bathroom and walk carefully down the hall. I had just enough time to shower, do my hair, and put on a little mascara after rushing home from work. I hope it's enough. Since I don't get much practice in heels, I'm afraid I might fall right out of these pumps if I move faster than a saunter. But considering the party and who's throwing it, cocktail attire seemed like my only choice.

Anton waits by the front window. Even though he wears a suit every day to work, I stop now, trying to view his figure the way another woman would. Taking in his broad, square shoulders and narrow waist. Imagining the set of washboard abs beneath his crisp white shirt. I stand straighter and suck in, trying not to feel too mismatched since the only weightlifting I do involves hauling dogs into bathtubs. But in the mirror, at least, I looked pretty good. I went with the blue dress I wore to Celia's wedding—the one from the photo Anton cut me out of on Unmatched. Passive-aggressive? Most definitely. But after last night, I couldn't help myself.

I hadn't expected to see him in the hall this morning, hadn't had time to sip my coffee and process what he'd done. The profile. The messages. The things MountainMan3 said to LonelyGirl8. What he said he wanted from her. Accusations were on my lips the moment I laid eyes on him. But when it came time to speak, I found myself playing along. I'm not sure why. Maybe I wanted to pretend we were the same couple we'd been a few days ago. Weeks. Maybe years.

And isn't that what he's doing too?

He'd said he couldn't go through with it. He'd stayed home. And this morning, he asked me on a date.

He turns his head as I enter the room, and suddenly I'm all too aware of his eyes scanning my figure, lingering on the cleavage at my neckline. His lips seem to form a word he doesn't say aloud. I wait for any sign that he makes the connection between the dress and his cheating profile picture, but he just steps toward me, eyes glowing.

"Wow. You look . . ."

I rest one hand on my hip and run it up to toy with my hair, which I blew out smooth, making note of the way his gaze tracks my motions. Like his thoughts and desires are somehow tied to my body's movements. Like I could crush him, or crush him *to* me just by biting my lip. It's a strange, heady feeling. I have felt so powerless the last twenty-four hours, I'm not sure what to do with it.

But then he takes a step forward, hands rising toward me, and an alarm goes off inside my brain.

I step back, the Unmatched messages burning fresh in my mind. What *he* wants is clear. But I can't say the same for me.

"Ready to go?" I say, examining a speck of nothing on my skirt.

In my peripheral vision, I watch him flounder. And for a second, I even feel bad. He came home, *to me*, and now I'm toying with him. But I'm not exactly ready to run into his arms.

"Uh, yeah." He plunges his hands into his pockets and pulls out his keys.

I give Heartthrob a kiss on top of his head and a frozen Kong full of dog food, then I grab Carl Wallace's birthday present—a personalized leather-wrapped desktop Bluetooth speaker—and follow Anton out the door.

"Thanks for picking up a gift," he says halfway to the car. "I'm sure you chose better than I would've."

"That's why you married me," I say, though the words come out a bit sharper than I intend.

He doesn't answer, opening the passenger side of his truck for me like he has since the day I met him. It took me a while to get used to that; he's always said his mother would expect it. I frown, thinking about Sharon and how she'd feel about her son's Unmatched profile.

"It's nice going out for a change," Anton says, climbing into the driver's seat next to me. "I've missed you, Mrs. Richie."

I shoot him a glance. If anyone's been *missing* here, it's him.

Except . . . I know that isn't true. We could've gone out Saturday, couldn't we?

I drop my gaze to my lap. "I keep saying it'll get easier—"

"When Pooch Two is open," he mutters. "Yeah. You do keep saying that."

I bite my lip, tension spooling in my chest. If he wants to sling guilt trips, I've got a hefty one to hit him with.

But then we stop at a light and he turns to me, placing his hand over mine. "Thanks for making the time tonight."

He lets go so he can drive through the intersection, and I soften a little. He hasn't sent any more messages to LonelyGirl8—I checked—but that doesn't mean he hasn't been on the app. Maybe he's found some other girl he likes better. Someone who didn't turn him off by bringing up spanking. I steal a glance at him, my cheeks heating at this thought. Or maybe last night was just what he needed to remember he has everything he needs right here.

Eva and Carl Wallace live south of Denver, all the way down near Castle Rock, in a newly built house that could hold four or five of ours inside it. We've been there one other time for a Christmas party, and it didn't seem like a bad commute, but tonight, when we're both clearly struggling with conversation, the thirty-minute trip seems to drag.

Deer scatter in the yard when we pull up to the Tuscany-meets-American-suburbs house. All the windows are lit up, and as I exit the car, I can tell there's music playing inside, but out here on the gravel drive, it's pretty quiet. I pick my way carefully over the pebbles toward the double front doors until I realize Anton's still in the truck, gripping the wheel. I frown, looking back at him. He's always hated work social events. The fact that we're here at all tells me this one must be important to him. And despite everything else churning through my head this evening, a wave of sympathy surges through my chest. I want to make this easier for him.

He notices me waiting and slams the truck door, quickly coming up beside me. The ground is uneven, and as I wobble toward the front porch, I am seriously regretting my choice of shoes. The faux stone front steps seem a million miles away. We finally make our way up to them when my heel goes out from under me. I let out a gasp, pitching toward the porch, but just before my knees hit concrete, Anton's sturdy arm swoops around my waist. He steadies me, bringing me upright into the circle of his arms. His earthy, clean scent inundates my nose as he ensures I stay on my feet.

"Th-thank you." I look up into his face to find his eyes burning into mine. "Guess I wore the wrong shoes."

He loosens his grip, stepping back to let his gaze travel down the length of my legs, and grunts. "I really like those shoes."

His voice is thick, his hand hot against my skin. My pulse pounds, and suddenly I'm very aware of the short hem of my dress and the cleavage I have on display. I bring my fingers to my lips, avoiding his eyes. This is what I wanted—his desire, his lust. For *me*, not for someone else. I should do something. Lean in to kiss him. Give him some reason to realize I am who and where he wants to be. But every time I think of making a move, all I want to do is pull away. Just like before I ever knew about Unmatched.

"Lydia," Anton tries to get my attention, my name laced with something that sounds a lot like longing.

My eyes cloud. I don't know what to do. I don't know what I want.

Why?

I raise my head, staring past him at the door, hoping I'll figure it out before I take my next breath. His eyes track my movements, careful, assessing. He leans in, his lips part, and in a moment of panic, I reach toward him—and right past him, pressing the small round doorbell beside the polished wood doorframe.

An elaborate set of chimes announces our arrival to everyone inside. I meet his eyes and smile, air rushing out of my lungs. "Don't want to be late for the party."

CHAPTER THIRTEEN

Him

Eva Wallace throws open the double doors of her house, wearing a black dress, her dark hair piled on her head. "It's the Richies! I'm so glad you could both come!" My boss's wife yells over an upbeat song that was popular several years ago. She's your typical middle-aged white socialite in diamond earrings and a professionally brightened smile, but she is also genuinely kind.

I watch as she and Lydia exchange air kisses, which is great because I need a second. A moment ago, I was ready to hightail it home without stepping foot inside this party. Something had seemed to shift between Lydia and me, and I just needed to get her in the car, back home, and naked in our bed. Until she ended it before I could blink.

Eva turns from my wife and folds me in a too-affectionate embrace. I keep my arms at my sides, but over her shoulder, I notice Lydia watching my discomfort, hiding a smile. She goes through these motions with zero effort, but she knows I fucking hate this stuff.

"Lydia, I love your dress. You two are *the* cutest couple," Eva says over the music and chatter. "The catering staff have everything—champagne, hors d'oeuvres. Come on in and make yourselves at home!"

"Thanks, it's so great to be here." Lydia smiles, handing over the wrapped gift. I forgot to ask what it was, but the charmed look on Eva's face makes me sincerely grateful she made the effort.

Eva waves to someone coming up the walk behind us and Lydia takes my hand, pulling me through the front door. We make our way into the great room, my wife greeting my coworkers and their significant others like she's actually excited to see them again. Maybe she is. That, or she deserves an Oscar for her effort. She remembers names I struggle with, asks them about kids, vacations, and illnesses that weren't even on my radar, and every one of them lights up when they see her. We've been struggling so much with each other at home, I'd nearly forgotten how fantastic she is with other people. I manage some minimum discourse, but everyone's so happy to talk to Lydia, I mostly stand back and let them.

"You're the one who owns the doggie daycare, aren't you?" A woman from HR says, draining her champagne flute. Dog owners especially love talking to my wife. "I wish your place was closer. I need a more convenient daycare on my way to and from work."

"Actually, we're opening a new location pretty close to the Vesper office," Lydia says.

"Are you really?" The woman's eyebrows pop up. "When?"

Lydia bites her lip. I expect her to start gushing about the upcoming launch. Instead, she looks uncertain. "Still waiting on a firm date from my contractor, but we're hoping to have our grand opening by the end of June or maybe July."

July? I try to catch her eye, but she looks away. Last I heard, the new branch was supposed to be underway by spring. There was some kind of end in sight. July is months away.

"Another business? Will that make three now?" Carl Wallace joins the conversation, greeting Lydia with a friendly hug. I straighten, smoothing my hair into place. My boss is a big Black man just starting to gray at the temples, with sharp eyes and a warm, booming voice. My wife beams and leans into the hug. And that's when I remember he and Eva have their wheaten terrier groomed at Ooh La Pooch. No wonder Lydia was so willing to come tonight. "Your wife's productivity puts us all to shame, Anton."

I shrug, putting on a practiced smile. "She either has to keep growing the business or turn people away. I'm just going to watch her take over the world."

Lydia meets my eyes as everyone chuckles. She's heard me say some rendition of this line before. It's my go-to endorsement of her as a business owner, but some layer of bitterness might have slipped into my tone.

"I'd love to know more about this dog stuff. It sounds so fun," a woman says, coming up behind Carl. I swallow when I see it's Myra Alvarez, owner of the accounts I'm hoping to be put in charge of.

"Lydia, this is my friend Myra, one of our clients and a very good friend." Carl smiles broadly. "Myra, this is Lydia Richie, Anton's wife, the multi-entrepreneur."

"I didn't realize Anton was married." Myra glances at me and winks, turning back to Lydia. "Your husband is such a charmer. And so knowledgeable. Now, tell me about your favorite dog breeds. I'm considering getting a new pooch."

I stand by, watching Lydia hit it off with my potential client while I try to think of something to say that isn't about finance. They discuss dog temperament, security versus companionship, and are just getting into a back-and-forth about breed size when Eva comes over, spurring a lively discussion about whether hypoallergenic dogs are a real thing. I listen for a while, grateful for the way Lydia shines in the spotlight, but when it becomes clear no one is in a hurry to discuss accounts, I excuse myself to find a drink.

Caterers are wandering around with trays of champagne, but my head is starting to throb so I roam toward the back of the house, looking for a plain bottle of water. Eventually, I stumble upon Carl and Eva's enormous kitchen. It's the kind that looks like it was designed for a professional chef, but judging by the way everything sparkles like it's brand new, I suspect they mostly order takeout.

The only drinks in the fridge are sodas and champagne, so I reach for the pantry door, confident I've seen Eva carrying around Vitamin Water or something like it before. But when I pull it open, I'm startled to find a couple inside—a woman with light brown skin in a short yellow dress and a white guy with his hand snaked under the hem, gripping her ass. They're locked at the lips, and he issues a low groan as her hand twists in his hair.

"Oh." I clear my throat. "Sorry, excuse me."

I go to close the door, my face heating a little even as my eyes linger where they're joined. Until the guy notices me and says my name in a familiar faint British accent. "Anton?"

I hesitate, glancing back into the space full of cereal and canned goods. My friend Henry Hill untangles himself from the woman I now recognize as Annabelle Wallace, Carl and Eva's daughter, who is interning with her dad this year. She's super cute, but super *young*, barely out of college. I've known Henry long enough that it doesn't surprise me to see him with her, though. He's a lot like my brother.

"Henry." I nod to them like we've run into each other on the street, not tucked away next to a sack of potatoes. "Annabelle."

"Hey, Anton," she says with a giggle, her fingers drifting inside Henry's suit jacket.

"I . . . didn't realize you two knew each other," I say.

"We were matched up for singles this morning on the tennis court." Henry grins at Annabelle, who looks like she wants to nibble his ear. "Two sets in, she'd crushed me, and I found myself invited to a party."

I stifle a laugh as he smooths his clothes and leads Annabelle out of the pantry. Henry likes to network, and often has fun with it. He isn't directly in finance, but hooking up with Annabelle Wallace is probably more strategic than he makes it sound. Still, it's hard not to notice the way their hands never seem to leave each other. Even out in the kitchen, he's stroking the inside of her elbow while she keeps toying with his hair. Both of them seem ready to dive back into each other. I can't remember if Lydia and I ever used to act this way.

"Where's your wife?" Henry asks, and I freeze for a second, wondering if he can tell the state of my thoughts just by looking at my face. "I wanted to talk to her about my sister's dog."

This relaxes me a little, though the dog talk is unexpected. Henry comes off as a bit of a snob with his accent, designer suits, and impeccable hair. I'm pretty sure he's too neat and meticulous to ever own a pet. But we were roommates in college, and I happen to know under the flawless surface, he's a decent guy.

“Uh, she’s out there.” I wave in the general direction of the rest of the house.

“I thought you looked miserable.” Henry chuckles, knowing all too well social events are not my scene. “So, you’ve abandoned her to do your schmoozing for you?”

I shrug. “Don’t know what you mean. I’m the life of the party.”

He rolls his eyes. “Listen, I need her help. Or my sister does. Her puppy is ruining my life.”

“Send it to daycare,” I say, promoting the Pooches on autopilot. “Lydia’s opening up a new place close to your office.”

“Another one already?” Henry’s brows shoot up. “Your wife is on fire.”

“Yeah, she is,” I mutter, spotting a case of water bottles and ducking back into the pantry. As I wrestle one free of the plastic, I see Annabelle reach for Henry outside the door, pulling him to her lips. My hands lose coordination as he cups her breast, and she presses her leg between his.

When I finally step out with the water, she pulls away with a gasp. “Let’s get out of here,” she whispers, tugging on Henry’s arm. “C’mon, I’ll introduce you to my dad on the way out. Then let’s go to your place. Nice to see you, Anton!”

Henry winks at me as she leads him into the hall, and I wave. But it’s like their passion lingers in the air, and I’m hit with a sudden, heady desire for my wife. To touch her skin, feel her curves, stoke a fire between us. That can’t be something only other couples get to have.

Clutching the water, I head back to the great room, my pulse urging me on. There’s a new hire trying to impress a girl from IT in the corner. Carl and Eva are smiling at the center of the room, arms around each other as Henry charms them and their daughter. And then I spot Lydia, looking like a perfect hourglass in that sexy blue dress. I swallow hard. Will she let me peel it off tonight? Yank down the zipper and toss it to the floor? I start toward her until someone places a hand on my arm.

“Anton,” says Myra Alvarez. “Carl and I were just talking about you. He couldn’t stop praising how innovative your account strategies have been. I’m looking forward to working together.”

Pivoting my thoughts from undressing my wife back to finance feels like trying to stop a speeding train, but I meet Myra’s deep brown eyes and manage a smile. "I—I have some thoughts already on how to improve your portfolio. Maybe we can sit down and go over them next week."

"That sounds marvelous." She follows my gaze to Lydia across the room with a warm smile. "I remember when I used to watch my wife just the way you're looking at yours."

I snap my eyes back to hers, my face heated, but she just laughs.

"It's obvious you and Lydia have a special bond as well."

I frown. Did Lydia say something to make her think our passion was mutual? Or does she see something I've been missing? The mere thought shortens my breath.

"Of course, that was before the kids, our careers, an international move, and middle age. It's hard to keep romance alive twenty years in, but our relationship is strong. We manage."

This makes me pause. *Do* Lydia and I have a bond like that? I used to think so, but we can't even manage to take a weekend away together. It's hard to imagine where we'll be in twenty years.

I swallow hard. "What, ah, what would you say is your secret?"

"Excellent sex." Myra sips her champagne, eyes twinkling. "And we never speak about work in our bed."

I straighten, unprepared for such a frank answer, but as I think about what she said, my stomach tightens.

Together, we watch Lydia excuse herself from her conversation and disappear down a hall. Myra turns to me and pats my cheek. "You two go enjoy each other. I'll set up an appointment about my boring money next week."

I hesitate, but she steps away with that instruction, and somehow I'm certain of what I need to do, if totally unsure how to proceed. I catch up to Lydia outside the open door of what must be Carl Wallace's study, judging by the heavy-looking furniture and bookshelves. She turns when she hears my footsteps, and her face lights up, sending a surge of affection through me. Suddenly, I'm confident. We both feel this. It's always been there. What we have *has* to be special.

"Anton! I was just coming to find you," she says, and her tone is so warm, I decide to make a move.

Rather than reply with words, I reach for her, pulling her into the quiet study as I press my lips to hers. She's clearly surprised, but as I push her against the back of the closed door, she opens her lips to mine, reaching up to pull me close. I shut my eyes, allowing myself to relish the moment, breathing in her vanilla scent. My hands drift down her waist, over her hips and ass wrapped up like a present in this dress, until my fingers slip beneath the hem.

She jerks slightly when I make contact with her skin. "We can't do that here," she says with a nervous giggle.

"Why not?" I mutter, dipping down to lay kisses along her neckline. "There's a lock on the door."

"It's your *boss's* house," she says in a playful but slightly higher voice.

"Then let's go home." I breathe into her neck, pressing evidence of my growing arousal against her hip. "We don't even have to do that—let's get a hotel right here in Castle Rock."

She doesn't reply right away, pulling me back to her lips, sliding her hand into my hair. I take it as a sign that she's considering, that she can't deny she's as turned on as me. I slip my hand farther up inside her dress, tracing the edge of her panties.

But then she twists her hips away, and my hand is forced out from under her skirt. She places her own hands gently but firmly on my chest. "We can't get a hotel. We have to get home to Heartthrob."

I stand there staring at her, her sweet taste lingering like a ghost on my tongue.

She must read my expression because she quickly says, "Let's plan something, though. A getaway where I can leave him with Tomás."

"Like a weekend at a hot springs?" I can't help it. My voice is sharp as a knife.

She opens her mouth, then has the humility to frown.

I exhale. "I can't keep doing this, Lydia."

"Doing what?" she asks, smoothing her dress, looking everywhere but at me.

I grab her hand and bring it to where my hard-on presses painfully inside my pants. "I *need* you."

For a second, she stares at me, her hand lingering on my cock. And I'm so desperate this is almost enough to make me come. But then she jerks away like she touched a hot stove.

"I—I need to go."

"Lydia—"

I reach for her, but she's out the door so fast I barely say her name before the latch clicks.

Pinching the bridge of my nose, I slump into a deep leather chair to adjust my pants. Myra was obviously wrong about us. I might be overflowing with lust for my wife, but she is clearly *not* interested in me.

On my boss's desk, there's a photo of his family, his wife and daughter smiling at his side. I stare at this and think about the photo of Lydia and me—the one I cropped her out of to use online. And then, deep in the pocket of my pants, my phone vibrates. I pull it out and glance at it, just to make sure it isn't Seth with some update about Mom. But when I see the screen, my mouth goes dry.

You have 5 unread messages on Unmatched

I thought I'd turned off notifications. I glance at the door, listening for footsteps or voices. Then I tap the screen to open the app.

Five new messages from four ready-to-fuck women. At least one of them appears to be a bot, with some cut-and-paste note about cannabis sent twice. The others seem real, but the messages are all the sort of generic stuff you see in porn ads: *I'm hot tonight. Let's fuck at my place. Can you make me cum?* I click on their pictures one by one, and they do look beautiful, but nothing really stands out and makes me want to reply.

I click back to the inbox, scrolling to the message exchange with LonelyGirl8. It's not like we had a super in-depth conversation, but she at least felt like a real person. One willing to do things Lydia would never dream of—starting with getting into bed with me.

Just reading through the thread brings my cock back to life. I click her profile, re-reading her stats and turn-ons, then enlarge the picture to admire those big, glorious tits again. Tits I was invited to not only touch, but do all manner of things to. I bite the inside of my cheek, trying to recall why I chickened out.

Then my gaze falls to the gold ring on my left hand.

I think of what Myra said about keeping romance alive over the years. But what if it was dead to begin with? I love Lydia, and I know she cares about me, but can we go on like this? Playing the happy, successful couple at work and at parties, but never in the bedroom? What would we be to each other in a decade?

Roommates? Friends?

I guess she might be asexual—but what does that mean for our marriage if I most definitely am not?

I get up, pacing out a circuit of the room. If we go the next twenty years without any sex, I'm not sure I'll still *want* to be friends. Let alone share a home. Or a bed. But what if Unmatched presents an outlet? A solution to make it tolerable? Without her having to submit herself to unwanted sex just for my sake and without me having to feel bitter or finish myself off in the shower. What if I had someone to turn to for the *one* thing Lydia can't give me? Someone with a similar need. Who doesn't want to change their whole life either, but just sort of . . . add to it? On the side.

When I think of the possibility, the future seems a little less bleak. Maybe without all the sexual tension, Lydia and I might even have fun like we used to. Not in bed, but other places, doing other things. We could go to Rockies games, out on dates. Maybe she'd even be willing to go camping if there was no expectation of sex with me. It seems unconventional, but maybe not really. People have had lovers outside of marriages for centuries. And I'm not looking for love—*I love Lydia*—I really just need sex.

I hold my breath for the entire time it takes to type my message and hit send.

MOUNTAINMAN3

I've been dreaming of your tits. If you're still interested, I'd love to meet.

CHAPTER FOURTEEN

Her

THE GLASS SLIPS THROUGH MY FINGERS. BUT FOR SOME reason, I see rather than hear it explode when it hits the floor.

"Oh." My hands drop to my sides. One empty now, the other still clutching my phone. "Oh, I'm . . . so sorry. How clumsy of me."

The woman who's been chatting to me in equal time about both dogs and my "cutie husband" places a hand on my shoulder. "Are you all right? You just went really pale."

"I'm—yes. I'm sorry." I can't seem to find any other words.

Eva Wallace comes over, followed by a caterer with a dustpan. "No apologies necessary. It was an accident. You didn't cut yourself, did you, Lydia? Has anyone seen Anton?"

"No, but—" I close my eyes, unable to chase away the message burned into my memory. Nausea rises in my throat, and I bring my hand to my mouth. "Excuse me, I need to use the bathroom."

There are whispers behind me, but I don't hear what any of them say. I'm too focused on getting out.

Once I duck inside a plush powder room near the kitchen, I turn the lock and look at my phone with a shaking hand.

MOUNTAINMAN3

I've been dreaming of your tits. If you're still interested, I'd love to meet.

Exactly the words I thought I'd read. I had to see them again to be sure.

I close the lid of the toilet and sit, pressing my head into my hands. My heart still pounds dully, despite the fact that my chest feels like it's been ripped open. He'd said he couldn't cheat. And I was so sure he wouldn't. That he'd considered it, but decided our love was stronger than his lust.

Apparently it wasn't.

I worked so hard to charm his boss, clients, and coworkers tonight. But when he pulled me into that room and started practically undressing me—suggesting we get a hotel, like some hookup on that app—I couldn't help it; the brakes just came on.

I shut my eyes, his urgent voice replaying in my head: *I can't keep doing this, Lydia. I* need *you.* Then he'd placed my hand on him. Like he expected me to smile and lay down right there on the floor, spread my legs, and invite him on top of me. At a *work* party.

A single hot tear rolls down my cheek as it occurs to me that my mother might've been right—maybe we are like her and Dad. My stomach roils at the thought. *No.* I just needed space to regroup. To get in the right headspace, somewhere private. We could've gone home, like Anton suggested. Maybe talked it through. Probably still had sex.

But he couldn't wait.

And now I just want to keep hiding in here rather than face all the people telling me what a cute couple we are. Because it's either come out breathing fire in front of them or smile and continue pretending we're totally meant to be.

Something Caprice said echoes faintly through my mind: *You're* not *going to just ignore this and look the other way.*

I ball my fists, because she's right. What if this isn't even the first time? He might have already cheated—*been* cheating on me. For months? Years? My stomach twists. Maybe Unmatched is just the latest tool he's trying out to get laid. He might be playing coy with Lonely-

Girl8, acting innocent, but it could just be a strategy. Maybe he's adept at getting women to come to him.

I wipe the tear away, rise to my feet, and stare into the mirror over the sink. This isn't how I imagined the evening going. Though it's not how I imagined my marriage playing out either. I can't decide if I'm stupid or naive. Maybe a little of both. Either way, I only see one choice ahead of me.

Time to return to Plan A.

I unlock my phone and craft my words carefully.

LONELYGIRL8

I'm so excited. Let's make it happen.

It isn't long before a message pings again.

MOUNTAINMAN3

Okay. But I don't want to meet in Denver.
How about Colorado Springs.

LONELYGIRL8

Understood.

MOUNTAINMAN3

Can you get away Monday night?

My mouth sours. That's bold. What's he going to do, schedule a last-minute "business trip?" I swipe over to my calendar, and my stomach clenches. It's so soon—only two days away. My head pounds. I'm not ready. I need more time. But then I think of having to go home and climb into bed next to him, pretending everything's normal. Like the last week hasn't been hard enough. Suddenly, two more nights seem like forever. I want this over with. I type a truth:

LONELYGIRL8

Yes. My husband will be away then, so I'll be
lonely for sure.

There's another long pause. Outside the bathroom door, I hear voices and a growing commotion. My phone vibrates again.

MOUNTAINMAN3

Do you mind if I ask . . . what brought you on Unmatched?

My heart skips. I wasn't expecting that at all. And it doesn't seem fair for him to ask questions *I* want answers to.

LONELYGIRL8

What if I asked you the same thing?

My pulse throbs through my clenched jaw.

MOUNTAINMAN3

Never mind.

MOUNTAINMAN3

How about the Hyatt on the north end of CO Springs? 6:30pm?

I flinch, relieved to follow him away from that particular topic. But now he's led me to something worse. Anton and I have stayed at that hotel. The year after we got married, on the way back from visiting his mom and brother in Texas. A blizzard came up out of nowhere an hour from home, and we decided to stop and spend the night. There's nothing really special about the place. It was clean, had a pool, free breakfast. But I remember we made love there because he said the snow turned him on.

I glare at the messages on my screen. That's one of the happier memories I can come up with in the entire history of our sex life. But he wants to take another girl there and make new ones?

LONELYGIRL8

Hyatt works. I'll Google it.

There's another pause. Another span of seconds ticking away.

MOUNTAINMAN3

To be clear, this is JUST a meetup to fuck. No strings.

LONELYGIRL8

Isn't that the whole point?

MOUNTAINMAN3

Exactly. I can't wait to get my hands on those luscious tits.

My lip curls, and I'm about to shoot a reply when someone taps on the door. "Lydia? Are you all right?"

I lock my phone quickly. There are several voices outside, but I think that was Eva Wallace, owner of the bathroom I'm holed up in. I can't imagine having to give her any kind of explanation when I am literally seething. But at the same time, I've got to figure out some way to get out of here. Home. To my dog.

"I—sorry, must've been something I ate." My voice comes out convincingly ill. That wasn't hard at all.

"Oh no. Don't worry, hon. Someone went to find—"

She's interrupted by a firm knock on the door. "Lydia?"

His deep voice sends my stomach buckling, and now I'm afraid I really might throw up. I lay my hand flat on the door, glance at the tiny window behind me, and consider trying to open it and climb out.

"Sweetheart, what happened?" Anton says, trying the doorknob. And my heart nearly cracks from the very real concern in his voice.

I slump against the wood, trying to envision all the ways this could go. There aren't many. And pretty much all of them require me to open the door and face him in front of an audience. There's a rustle of bodies and murmurs, and suddenly I can picture my husband out there, prickling, surrounded by all those nosy clucking coworkers. His illicit sex plans interrupted by his ailing wife. For just a moment, I savor the idea of his situation being almost as torturous as mine.

And then his voice comes through the door again, right by my ear. This time firm and clear. "Lydia, come on. Let's go home."

I find my reflection in the mirror and manage to swallow my panic. Then I turn the knob.

I hold my hand over my mouth, keeping my eyes on the floor as I swing the door open. I try not to flinch when Anton's arm drapes protectively around my shoulders, guiding me slowly into the hall. At the same time, I'm grateful for him shielding me from the world. The music is still playing elsewhere in the house, though it seems a bit softer now. There are still plenty of people crowded in other rooms and, to my relief, only a few fussing around us. Eva Wallace, Myra Alvarez, and a couple other women who either witnessed my dramatic flight or are just curious about what happened.

"I've got you," Anton whispers, and I want to shriek in his ear that it's the other way around, but instead I let him guide me toward the doors amid a flurry of whispers from his coworkers.

Must be sick.

Suddenly turned green.

Ran for the bathroom.

As we near the exit, I hear one voice speculate a little too loudly that I might be pregnant, and I nearly laugh out loud.

Anton turns to Eva as we leave. "Thanks, Eva. For the party, and your kindness."

"Of course. Always nice to see you." She lowers her voice. "I hope you feel better soon, Lydia."

And then he's helping me down the steps, much the way we arrived. Keeping a firm, steady arm around my waist, which is actually useful when my heels hit the gravel. We reach his truck and he opens the door, helps me in, and then he doesn't seem to know quite what to do. He stands there, hovering, not saying anything, and it's all I can manage not to whip out my phone, wave his messages in his face, and yell. But it seems the stomach flu ruse worked better than I expected because he leans in to feel my forehead, studying my face, looking distressed.

"What happened? Do you want to go to urgent care?" he asks in a low voice. And for a moment, I just want to sink into his arms, bury my face in his chest, and cry.

"No," I whisper with dry lips. I buckle my seatbelt and curl into myself. "I'll be fine. I—I just want to go home and go to bed."

CHAPTER FIFTEEN

Her

Neither of us spoke on the drive home. Anton put on some low instrumental music and glanced at me, looking concerned, but otherwise left me to stare out the window. Thank goodness. I was having a hard enough time just sharing the same air. When we got home, he took Heartthrob for a walk and left me to take a bath. He was gone at least an hour, but I heard him come home and head into our room ten minutes ago. Which surprised me. I thought for sure he'd sleep out on the couch again. But maybe he's making an effort to appear normal. Avoid suspicion. He's doing a better job of it than me.

I sink to the edge of the tub, unlocking my phone for the first time since I saw *MountainMan3's* last message. There are several notifications I'd ignored once I saw the one from Unmatched—a missed call from my mom, some texts and emails from employees, my contractor. And randomly one from Charlotte, my business lawyer, asking whether I've ever considered franchising my businesses.

I answer most of the messages despite the late hour, quipping to Charlotte that I'll have to let her know if I ever get the second Pooch Park off the ground. I grant a day off to my bather and tell my contractor he *has* to use the non-slip flooring, but I wait on my mother.

It's too late to call, plus I'm not sure I can hold it together if she brings up my sister or her baby or anything that reminds me of my own failed marriage. I'll see what she wants in the morning.

I'm about to put the phone away when I notice a new notification from my shared calendar with Anton.

Business Trip - Phoenix
Monday April 17 - Tuesday April 18

My stomach lurches. My palms go clammy. I don't know why this hits harder than anything else this evening—any of his other lies. But for some reason, it seems like a direct slap in the face. I swipe back to my messages.

Sorry it's late. Can you do me a huge favor?

TOMÁS

What's up?

I need to go out of town next week. I'll be gone Mon/Tues, but back by Wednesday, I promise. I wanted to ask ASAP in case that's a problem.

TOMÁS

Not at all! Anton finally convince you to do the hot springs thing?

My lip curls. He told Tomás about that?

Will you be okay if I'm gone? Can I have Scarlet call you if she has issues?

TOMÁS

Of course. We'll be fine! You guys deserve a nice getaway.

A metallic taste fills my mouth.

Thanks, Tom. You're the best. 🩶

I make a mental note to give him a healthy raise at his next review. If the guy wasn't happily married—and gay—I might divorce Anton and marry him.

Okay, no, I wouldn't.

Except I guess maybe the divorce thing is going to happen.

I put my robe on and go to the door. I've delayed as long as possible, but I just need to suck it up and get in bed with Anton, if that's where he is. *Only two nights*, I tell myself. I'll work late tomorrow. Sunday, I'll make an excuse to hang out with Caprice. But I have a lot to do before Monday night.

I turn the knob and lean into the hall, listening. There's no sound—no television and no snoring. I take a hesitant step out, then instead of hanging a left into our bedroom, I head straight down the hall. We bought this house five years ago. It's tiny, but has been just right for the two of us—and might've been for three, I think as I pass our second bedroom. Though that little dream is disappearing now. I've never been someone who desperately wanted babies, but despite my conversation with my mother, I've always envisioned kids as part of our future. Taking them to school, going on family trips. Having a reason to make magic on Christmas morning. In a way, my mom is right. I'm twenty-nine. If Anton and I split now, I guess there's a real chance none of that will ever happen. I might not meet someone else and get that ball rolling again in time.

And what would that even be like, waking up with another man? Going about my whole life with someone who's currently still a stranger? Would he be as handsome as Anton? As interesting to talk to? Anton and I met my second semester of college, and not to be cliché, but it truly felt like I'd found my missing "other half." We were finishing each other's sentences after only a month. I never had to explain my frustrations with my mom and sister or the career goals I couldn't quite define until I got into the pet industry. He just welcomed me into his family, cheered me on, and was basically everything anyone might desire in a spouse.

But I guess maybe I wasn't.

I step carefully down our steep basement stairs in the dark. When I make it to our little laundry space, I reach into the overflowing hamper next to the washing machine on a hunch, digging until I find my blue-striped pajamas at the bottom. They're wrinkled and smell a little musty, but when I pull them to my chest, the gallop of my heart seems to slow. I hadn't even realized how hard it was beating.

After slipping them on, I walk carefully back up the stairs and through the kitchen, pausing outside our bedroom. Now I can hear it—not a snore, but deep, regular breathing. My shoulders relax a bit. I tiptoe into the room, past Heartthrob snoozing in his dog bed, and over to my side.

Anton's outline is visible in the soft moonlight through the window, and for a second I convince myself everything that's happened this week was just a bad dream. I sink to the mattress, where I can see the sharp outline of his jaw that I used to snuggle close to and trace with my thumb. My throat tightens, and despite all the anger I am currently channeling, I find myself wondering where things went wrong. *How* I wasn't enough.

But then I think of the "business trip" on our calendar and how he probably fell asleep thinking about the busty woman he met online. Blood roars through my ears. I bunch the covers in my hands, and suddenly I can't wait for Monday night. As if he can hear my thoughts, he shifts position, rolling toward me. I hold my breath, waiting for him to open his eyes and catch me looking. Wondering what he would say. Or if he would say anything at all.

When he doesn't move again after several minutes, I slip under the duvet, keeping as far as I can toward my side of the bed. Grateful for the comfy striped pajamas between us. Except now I'm hardly sleepy. I pick up my phone, thinking it will serve as a distraction. Instead, I wind up doomscrolling stories about women catching their husbands cheating. Ladies following men and their lovers to motels or coming home midday to find them in their own beds with someone else. Ugh. The more I read, the more relieved I am that I intercepted Anton's booty call. I'll be able to confront him without actually having to see him with someone else.

Still, it feels like something's missing from my plan.

I've set up the date. I'm going to meet him at the hotel and have my "gotcha" moment when he arrives to find me there instead of his stupid fantasy girl. But how can I catch him *and* make him feel sorry he's losing me? Make him regret giving up on us without giving me more of a chance?

My Google ads are homing in on my troubled life, offering me suggestions for everything from online therapists to erotic novelties, which puts a sour taste in my mouth. I swipe to clear my cache, make some attempt at erasing this evidence of my unhappiness. But then a familiar business name catches my eye: Allure Lingerie. The high-end intimates store in Cherry Creek. Vaguely, I remember Anton saying it's where he got that black lace nightgown. He's asked over and over if he could take me there to pick something out for myself, but the idea always made me uncomfortable. It seemed embarrassing to go in together, too obvious—to buy something for *sex*. Besides, I'm more of a T-shirt bra and jeans type of girl. I feel weird in fancy underwear.

But maybe that's just what I need for this situation. I've already pretended to be the girl he thinks he wants. Why not dress up like her too? *Embody* her as I catch him "cheating" and tell him how screwed he is. The more I think about it, the more excited I get about this plan. There's no time to order online, but I click on the Allure website, browsing to get ideas before I go into the store. There's a whole "boudoir" section of the site that's exactly what I'm looking for. Nothing I would ever in a million years have even tried on—till now. Maybe it's sad that this is what's going to get me through the door of the shop at last, but it's a little poetic too. I find a few styles and favorite them, doubting they'll look as good on me as they do on the models, but hoping for the right effect.

Then I pull up Unmatched on my phone, gripping it with clenched hands, and send a reply to MountainMan3's last message. *I can't wait to get my hands on those luscious tits.*

LONELYGIRL8

I can't wait to get my hands on you.

When I'm done, I turn off the light and snuggle down into our bed, trying to imagine his face when he enters the hotel room and sees *me* dressed up like his fantasy girl. Deep down, part of me still hopes Anton will change his mind Monday, and I'll wind up spending a night in Colorado Springs alone.

But if he does show, if he forces me to go through with this, I plan to be everything he's hoped for *and* dreaded.

CHAPTER SIXTEEN

Her

I UNCLIP HEARTTHROB'S LEASH AND PICK UP MY PURSE, glancing at the clock. Anton was up and out of the house hours ago after a brief, stilted exchange where I assured him my stomach had made a miraculous recovery. I guess that was enough for him to head to the gym like always. Normally on a Saturday, I would be at work by now, but the lingerie store doesn't open until ten, so I decided to run some errands and take the dog for a walk since I'm leaving him home today. But it feels like I'm playing hooky.

My phone rings as I'm heading for the front door, and I cross my fingers it's not my contractor calling with yet another setback on the new space. I can only take my life falling apart one piece at a time. But it's not him, it's Charlotte, my lawyer. "Lydia, I'm glad I caught you."

"Hey Char, how are things? Did you get my email about the franchise question?" I cradle the phone between my ear and my shoulder, doubling back to the kitchen to give Heartthrob a treat before I leave.

"Yes. Though I had been hoping for a more serious reply," she says gently.

I bite my lip, recalling my flippant wording. "Um . . . sorry, it was kind of late when I sent that."

"I know you've got your hands full."

"Well, to give you a real answer, I have honestly never considered turning either business into a franchise. I don't think I'd even know how to go about that." I pause, considering for a second. "Why do you ask?"

"I'm just trying to get a sense of your plans for both Ooh La Pooch and The Pooch Park moving forward," she says. "An attorney has been poking around, asking me questions."

"What kinds of questions?" I ask, frowning.

"Mostly general stuff. They won't tell me much, so I'm not giving them much. But it sounds like someone may be interested in an acquisition."

I snort. "Wait. Like, someone wants to buy one of my businesses?"

"Yes. I figured you wouldn't be interested, but thought it was worth at least proposing the franchise idea."

Heartthrob sits patiently in front of the pantry. I give him a sweet potato chew and lean back against the counter. "Who is the interested party?"

"I'm not sure yet," Charlotte says in her easy, matter-of-fact way. "The attorney's from out of town, and as I said, they're pretty tight-lipped. I told them to bring us an actual offer and we could chat more."

My shoulders release. "Oh, okay, so this isn't like a real thing I have to deal with?"

"No, not yet," she says in her most reassuring, motherly tone. "Don't get too excited about it at all. People ask questions like this all the time and nothing comes of it. Just stay focused on what you're doing, but keep in mind that you're successful, and people see that. So maybe start thinking about what you want down the road."

I let out a grateful sigh. I have enough on my plate right now. I can barely fathom what it's going to be like trying to operate three business locations instead of two. Or what's going to happen with my marriage after Monday. I have a feeling I might want to throw myself into work even more very soon. A lump rises in my throat. For a second I wonder if I should ask Charlotte for advice about dividing assets, but she's not even the right kind of lawyer. And while I'm sure she could give me a referral, my chest tugs when I think about putting that into words just yet. Some hopeful, stupid part of me wants to see what happens first.

"I'll give the future some thought," I promise in a shaky voice. "But yeah, I've only started to build my businesses. If they do call back, you can tell them I'm definitely *not* selling."

It's just shopping. For clothes. In a store.

This is what I tell myself as I walk through the doors of Allure Lingerie in the posh Cherry Creek neighborhood. I hold my head high, trying to appear confident, like I belong, but as soon as my eyes hit the tasteful white furniture and elegant gold racks of bras and underwear, I imagine my mother suggesting what *type of women* probably shop here.

"Hello." A tall, beautiful Black lady approaches me.

I glance up, and my mind goes blank. Apparently so does my face.

"You look like you could use some help," she adds.

I take a step back toward the door, wondering if I can pretend I walked in by accident. There's dog hair on my shirt. I don't have on any makeup. I can pretend I was looking for something else—an art gallery, a *church*.

But as I'm about to hightail it back out to the sidewalk, the woman smiles. It's not a knowing, derisive smile like I expect in a store like this, but an attentive, professional one. I glance again at the racks of frilly undergarments. If I'm going to pull off my plan, I need all the help I can get.

"Yes . . . I do need help," I admit, figuring I should stick as close as I can bear to the truth. Buying lingerie doesn't make me a cheater. I just need to look like one. "My anniversary's coming up. I'm looking for something to um . . . spice things up?"

"Ah, yes. I think I can guess what you're looking for," she says, extending her hand. "I'm Georgina. I own Allure."

"Nice to meet you. I'm . . ." For a moment I consider offering a fake name. To buy a bra. "I'm Lydia."

I follow her to one corner of the store. Everything is plush white and pristine, and thankfully hardly anyone else is in here. Classical music plays in the background, and the light coming from a few well-placed crystal chandeliers is soft. A younger salesgirl offers me champagne, which I turn down because, hello, it's ten a.m., but also, I'd feel stupid drinking champagne in a T-shirt and leggings.

I think I spot one of the items I picked out online—something white and complicated, with laces and boning and lots of satin that reminded me of weddings—and I start to move toward it. But Georgina turns the other way, selecting a little black bra made of the sheerest fabric I've ever seen. If someone could have designed a bra made of nothing, this seriously comes close. It looks like it's held together with frills and air.

"We just got these in. They're very fun, with beautiful detail, and of course there's a matching panty."

I cringe. If there's a word out there worse than *tits*, it's got to be *panty*.

I examine the "panties" front and back, only I find there *is* no back to them at all. It's not like a thong—there's nothing in the middle at all—just a delicate lace border around a wide gaping opening where apparently all my cheeks will spill out. What is even the point of that? I can't bring myself to look at Georgina. I'm positive my face is redder than the satin thongs she's standing next to.

"That certainly is . . ."

"Why don't you try it on? It does leave a lot to the imagination." If she winked at me, I would've walked right back out the front door, but she doesn't. She's placid and professional.

"Um, okay, sure," I say, because at this point I feel like trying it on might be the fastest way out of here.

"Wonderful. Do you know your size?"

"Yes, 34C."

She wavers, taking another look at me. "Do you mind if I just measure to be sure? Some of our brands don't fit like others."

"Okay . . ." Really? I haven't been measured for a bra since my mother took me down to some awful store in the mall when I was fourteen. I've always been that same size. It's never changed.

We step back into a dressing room, and after five long, cold, topless minutes where I hold my arms up, down, stand, and bend over, Georgina straightens with her tape measure, looking satisfied. "I'm thinking . . . 30F."

My jaw drops. "I beg your pardon?"

She smiles. "Many women who come in here discover they're wearing the wrong bra size."

"But I'm not . . . there isn't any such thing as a size *F*," I say, crossing my arms over my boobs.

"It's not as common in the US—we can't seem to get past our Ds—but European bras are sized with a more logical system. Let me find you a couple of things to try on . . . besides this." She hangs the sheer set on a hook by the door.

I say nothing as she disappears. The woman is nuts, and now I wish I'd just gone to the mall, or even Target. There is no way I'm actually that many cup sizes bigger.

She reappears a few moments later with a couple more lacy-looking numbers, but she's also holding a gloriously simple nude T-shirt bra. "Try this one first and see what you think."

I press my eyes closed as she exits, then reach for the nude bra. It's molded, and the band is so small the cups look like freaking hot air balloons. I glance at the UK 30F on the tag and roll my eyes, ready to confirm that Georgina's crazy measurements are off.

It's so snug around my ribcage I can barely latch it on the first hook, but when I scoop myself into the cups the way Georgina instructed, I'm shocked to see them totally filled. I stare at the mirror, turning sideways to the left and right. My breasts are up high, front and center, in a flattering position I've never seen them in before. The cups are rounded and pretty, and the whole thing is actually *super* comfortable. I grab my T-shirt, slip it back on, and I'm stunned. It doesn't even look like the same shirt. My waist appears longer and slimmer, giving me more of a real hourglass shape. I have never looked like this in a bra.

I stick my head out of the dressing room and find Georgina returning with a couple more simple bras. "Oh, lovely! Do you mind if I take a look?"

She has me remove my shirt, lean forward and jiggle, then straighten. Nothing pops out the top or needs to be rearranged like I am used to doing with my old bras. I can't remember ever feeling this way in my underwear—supported and secure.

"Yes." She beams. "That's much better."

"I think I'll take this one," I say grudgingly, but also eyeing the new sets with more optimism. "And I guess I should try on what I actually came in for."

She leaves me with an array of satin, lace, and bows. I reach for the made-of-nothing set to eliminate it first. Even in the right size, I'm positive it's going to look ridiculous. I take a minute to figure out what goes where since the structure of the bra seems like a suggestion at best, but I finally figure it out and even pull the "panties" on over my big, comfy, full-coverage nude underwear.

My face goes scarlet in the mirror. A phrase Caprice uses—*sex on a stick*—comes to mind, and I blush even harder. I may have needed a lot of imagination to consider this set, but very little is required once it's on. My nipples are completely visible through the sheer black fabric, and the way the bra is structured, my breasts look like two floating snow globes, my bare skin rising and falling above the neckline with each breath. It plunges in the middle, giving me gravity-defying cleavage I wouldn't have thought physically possible. And the panties. Oh my God. Even over my wide cotton underpants, even with certain vital areas missing, they flatter my hips and ass and suggest nothing but sex, sex, sex.

They're perfect.

More than an hour after I walked in, I step out of Allure Lingerie wearing my new favorite nude bra, feeling more attractive than I have in months. I carry a bag with two delicately wrapped fancy bras and panties. Which, I have to admit, *do* seem totally different from the cotton bikinis I call underwear, making them perfect for the next step of my plan.

A small flash of regret flutters through me that I only bought this lingerie as a means to end my marriage. The delicate fabric makes me feel so sexy and feminine, it seems a bit of a waste. But I want Anton to see *everything* he's losing when I wear it. Everything he thought he could find elsewhere. I never want him to forget how good I looked right before I told him I want a divorce.

CHAPTER SEVENTEEN

Him

MONDAY. TODAY'S THE DAY.

I went to the gym extra early this morning. Skipped coffee in favor of a smoothie. Listened to classical music all the way to work. Nothing will settle my nerves. My overnight bag is packed and waiting in my truck—toothbrush, razor, condoms, change of clothes. I took a remote office day tomorrow. Even invented a quick trip to Phoenix that I put on my shared calendar with Lydia.

But when my brother called with an update on Mom's bloodwork halfway through my commute, I nearly rear-ended the person in front of me. I keep swinging back and forth between excitement and wanting to throw up. There is apparently a vast difference between fantasizing about an affair and actually going through with it.

At least I didn't have to look my wife in the eye today. I left for the gym before she was up. She sent a text wishing me a safe trip, but I couldn't bring myself to answer. I am either about to do the stupidest or the best thing for us. I'm just not sure which.

"Morning, Riya," I say to our receptionist as I pass through the doors of Vesper Financial Advisers.

"Hi, Anton. How's your wife?"

I trip over my own feet, nearly dropping my briefcase and phone. I straighten and stare at her.

"She feeling better?" Riya asks, brows drawn.

Oh. Faintly, I remember her being among the gaggle of women outside the bathroom at Carl's house. She saw that Lydia was sick and knew we had to leave. Which makes sense. She cares. She's concerned.

I don't have a bright red "A" emblazoned on my forehead. Not yet.

"Uh, yeah, she's much better now, thanks." Actually, she made a full recovery the next day, miraculously in time to get to work. "Just a stomach bug, I guess."

"Glad to hear it."

She gives me a funny smile, and I nod, continuing past the conference rooms and down the hall, greeting a few other coworkers. I avoid their gazes and questions, assured Riya will bring them all up to speed, and breathe a sigh when I reach my office. The room isn't huge, but it's my own space with a door that closes, which is a far cry from the cubicle I started in. My desk is just the way I left it Friday—neat, with only a few files I left out for today. There's a pen holder, a box of tissues, and a framed photo of Lydia and me on our wedding day. With a weight in my stomach, I angle it away, facing the visitor side of the desk.

"Anton, glad I caught you," Carl says, appearing in the doorway. "I'm heading into a meeting, but Myra's coming in this morning, and I want you to take care of her. Nothing crazy, just an account review, and she wants to discuss setting up a 529 plan for her nephew."

I jot a few notes on an empty pad of paper, then smile at him. "I'd be happy to help. Thanks for your confidence, Carl."

"I know she'll be in good hands," he says. "Myra already liked you, but she pretty much insisted you take her account after meeting your wife. She said Lydia helped her decide to get a Havanese, and she wants to book all her grooming with Ooh La Pooch."

I chuckle reflexively. "Can't say I'm surprised."

Carl grins. "How's she feeling, by the way?"

"Much better, thanks," I say easily this time.

"Glad to hear it," Carl says, glancing at the photo on my desk. "Eva thought . . . well, I'll be sure to let her know she's okay now."

He disappears and I close the door, my gut twisting with a mix of gratitude toward Lydia for doing exactly what I'd hoped she'd do at the party, guilt over what I'm planning to do tonight, and the ongoing resentment that I'm in this position at all. I made myself sleep in bed with her all weekend. She may have recovered from whatever happened at the party quickly, but she didn't exactly turn to me hot for sex. I stayed on my side of the bed, and she stayed on hers. She even managed to resurrect her sex-repelling pajamas. Which was all kinds of weirdly affirming. Nothing in our bedroom is going to change. People like Myra might assume our private life is one thing when the reality is something else. If we're already living one lie, does it matter if I add another?

I open Unmatched on my phone, pulling up the most recent message from the woman I'll finally meet tonight.

> LONELYGIRL8
>
> I can't wait to get my hands on you.

My dick twitches. I close the app and set the phone aside. I need to focus on work, but the thought of squeezing tits I'm actually allowed to touch and plunging my cock into a wet, turned-on pussy has my pulse pounding throughout my body. I adjust my pants and turn the wedding photo back around in an effort to stay on track. And it works, maybe a little too well. Seeing Lydia on my arm, beautiful in her wedding dress, infuses me with more than a flicker of regret. Because even after years of being frozen out and frustrated, driven to find an outlet somewhere else, I still wish I could just go home tonight and fuck my wife.

Right before six thirty, after the longest workday of my life, I park in the back of the Colorado Springs Hyatt and walk around the building. It seems stupid to be paranoid sixty miles from home, but I feel better not leaving my truck out front. I check over my shoulder as I go, not even sure what I'm looking for. Nothing is familiar. Everything feels foreign and wrong. Which is how it should be, how I want it. But as I approach the main doors and a man comes out, my eyes widen. It's our next-door neighbor, Matt Devore—oh my fucking God. I turn away, looking for some place to hide where he won't see me entering a hotel in another town without my wife. Or should I just run to my truck and drive straight back up I-25? I'm frozen in my tracks, unable to do anything but stare as he comes toward me, but then his phone rings. He answers, and I look closer as he passes. It isn't Matt. The guy doesn't even look remotely like him.

My stomach is sick with self-loathing. There have to be few more disgusting scenarios than a husband meeting a woman who isn't his wife at a hotel, yet here I am, about to do just that. If I go in, there's every chance I'll get laid by a woman ready and willing to let me fuck her in ways that would absolutely horrify my frigid Lydia. And despite some off-the-charts anxiety, I can't deny I'm excited about that. On the other hand, if I leave now, I won't be an asshole. Well, not as big of one. I could just forget this whole scenario, stay faithful, and drive home with fucking blue balls.

My phone vibrates in my pocket.

LONELYGIRL8

Excited to see you soon . . .

Like a jackass, I let my dick decide.

I head through the front doors. We stayed at this place once, Lydia and me. Got stranded in a blizzard five years ago and barely made it here before the highway closed. I picked it for tonight because I knew it was an okay place, but I'm not expecting the wave of nostalgia that hits me when I walk in. Everything inside is exactly the same. The leather chairs and wood paneling. The smell of coffee and fresh fruit in the lobby. It's nothing extraordinary, just a generic hotel like a bunch of others, but we actually had a nice night here. It was earlier in our relationship, but something about being snowed in, cut off from work and everything else, made it romantic, intimate. We spent the night naked in each other's arms, taking pleasure in touching each other, and nothing felt forced. We just enjoyed being together. Or at least, I did.

My chest tightens as I approach reception. "Uh, hi, I have a reservation," I say, clearing my throat. "The name is Smith."

The girl behind the desk types on her computer, and I swear she's smirking. Everything feels so obvious. *Sure, Mr.* Smith. *Wink-wink.*

She glances up. "It looks like your wife already checked in."

"What?" My blood runs cold before I realize she doesn't mean Lydia, but *Mrs. Smith.*

She nods, going into well-practiced instructions like this is completely normal. Like my entire evening hasn't just been thrown off. "You're in room 212. Here's your key. This also gets you into the pool." She points to a small map of the property. "The business center is around the corner. There's a shop here in the lobby if you need any personal items or snacks. Breakfast is complimentary, served from seven to nine a.m." She sticks the plastic room key into a paper sheath and hands me the materials. "Do you have any questions?"

I swallow hard and take them from her. I have about a million questions, but none of them are for her.

"Uh, no . . . that sounds perfect."

"Enjoy your stay." She glances up, taking me in head to toe as if she's seeing me for the first time. She hesitates on my biceps, then my jaw, and licks her lips. I'm not stupid, I know women find me attractive—at least women who aren't my wife. The girl glances away toward the elevators, her cheeks pink, and again I get the sense she knows exactly what I'm up to. Who's in that room upstairs, waiting for me. But then an elderly couple shuffles through the doors, and she turns away to help them.

I carry my duffle bag up to the second floor, pulse pounding in my ears, key card gripped in a sweaty hand. I'm not sure how my "date" got here before me. I was counting on getting here first. To have time to prepare. But somehow she's already in there, waiting for me, and I need to be ready when I walk through the door. Adrenaline makes the thirty steps to the end of the hall feel like a thousand, my brain flashing back and forth the whole time between memory and fantasy. The firm, full globes of my wife's magnificent breasts swinging as we fucked in this very hotel. The promise of a pair of tits nearly as nice waiting for me behind the door. Tits that, as soon as I touch them, will permanently change me. Brand me an adulterer. But also give me permission, I guess, to enjoy myself. Maybe even do this again.

I press my hand against the door frame.

It's not too late. I can still walk out and go home.

To flannel pajama armor and a chafed, neglected dick.

I wave the key card in front of the knob, and with a click, the light turns from red to green.

CHAPTER EIGHTEEN

Her

I CHECKED IN RIGHT AT FOUR O'CLOCK, THOUGH RECEPTION tried to give me a hard time. Anton made the reservation for Mr. and Mrs. Smith, as we agreed, but stupidly used his own credit card. Since the name and address on my ID matched the card—Mr. and Mrs. Richie of 1101 E. Columbine Place—the girl at the desk let me check in, but I'm pretty sure she shouldn't have. When I leave, I'm going to slip her a nice tip.

My husband is predictable. He won't leave work until exactly five, and with traffic, he'll be lucky to show up by six thirty at the earliest. This gives me plenty of time to get ready.

Once I get into the room, I shower and shave, making sure to fill the air with a bold citrus perfume. Something I would never, ever wear. I put on a lot of makeup—also out of the ordinary. I don't know if it will matter once he gets a look at me, but I'll feel silly wearing over-the-top lingerie if I don't dress my face up too. I add a wig borrowed from a friend who works in a costume shop on Colfax. My profile picture on Unmatched made my hair look darker, and if I'm trying to embody Anton's hookup, I'm taking it all the way. Briefly, I consider removing my wedding ring and paw print necklace, but quickly decide they're staying on. Finally, I slip into the lingerie that looks *and* feels like a suggestion of sex. The room is a little cold, and my nipples stand out against the sheer fabric, adding to the overall effect.

Anton better drool.

At exactly six thirty, with nothing much left to do, I send him an Unmatched message saying how excited I am. Just in case whatever morals he has left are giving him second thoughts. I haven't really considered what I'll do if he actually stayed home, but I guess I'll worry about that if it happens. I put on some music using the bedside Bluetooth speaker, draw the curtains, and turn the lights way down—just enough to illuminate my figure on the bed. He won't see much detail until we're close. We've barely spoken the last two days at home—I was too busy seething, and I guess he was preoccupied fantasizing about *tits*. But I've been careful. I don't think he's suspicious at all, and I want to keep it that way till the last possible second.

I can't wait to see the look on his face once he knows he's fucked.

There's a sound in the hall, and my whole body tenses. I force myself back into a leisurely position, but it's hard with my back to the door and my lace-framed ass pretty much presented on a silver platter.

He's out there for sure. I hear him fumbling with his key.

This is it.

I try to remember to breathe.

The door opens with a click and a rush of cool air. And though he doesn't say anything when he enters, I can tell I'm no longer alone. He lets the door slam shut behind him, and when he locks it, the sound of the deadbolt seems to echo through the hotel. For a moment, I panic, doubting it's really Anton behind me, wondering if I've made the biggest mistake of my life and set up this whole crazy scenario with a stranger after all. What if *I'm* the one who's here cheating?

But then he clears his throat, and I pick up the familiar scent of his clean, earthy cologne.

I exhale. And now it's all I can do not to turn around and hurl the lamp at him across the room. I didn't realize until this moment how much I was hoping he wouldn't show up.

"Hello." His voice is low and gravelly. And . . . was there a hint of surprise? My fingers tighten along the edge of the sheet. He can't know it's me. I've planned everything too perfectly. We've been married seven years, but I don't have any identifying marks, and it's too dark for him to really see.

"Hello," I whisper in my practiced faux-southern accent. "I've been waiting for you."

I don't turn around. My heart pounds. I keep expecting him to figure it out, switch the lights on and yell at me, or just leave, but he does none of these things.

"Wow," he breathes. "You are . . ."

His voice comes closer. He's clearly taking in every inch of me, but he trails off midsentence.

"I'm ready," I say through my teeth.

Behind me, he hesitates. Then I hear him remove his shoes and shirt, and unbuckle his pants. As they fall to the floor, I can picture his figure, tall and powerful, abs rippling down to his narrow hips. All taut, lean muscle from working out like it's his second job. And then, of course, there's the rest of him, also standing tall, I have no doubt. Just as robust, and big enough to make anyone gasp. I say a silent, insincere apology to all the legit Unmatched girls he didn't connect with. *Sorry, bitches, this one's still mine.*

He's close enough now I hear him swallow, but he doesn't speak.

Is he actually nervous? Jackass.

The bed dips behind me, and I suck in a breath. I sense the heat of his hand near my hip, but he doesn't make contact. Not yet. Just hovering. "Can I . . . ?"

My throat tightens. For a second, I can't speak. That's my husband. Always such a fucking gentleman.

"Please," I whisper, realizing too late that I forgot the accent. I quickly add, "I need you."

Half a second later, his hands are all over me. Gripping my flesh. He takes a fistful of my ass and squeezes hard, then runs his other hand down the length of my thigh, gently parting my legs on the way back up. His fingers drift toward my center, which I realize with a sudden flash of mortification, is growing moist. I clench my thighs—I don't mean to, it just happens—blocking him from going any further, from making that discovery through the open middle of my panties.

Unfortunately, this is the same way I've shut him down countless times at home, and he hesitates. Quickly, I arch back, grinding against his hand. He responds with enthusiasm, hardly missing a beat. His fingers change direction, tracing the edge of the lace encircling my hips and waist. His other hand runs along my back, snaking around to explore my newly designated F-cups. One of his thumbs brushes over the tip of my nipple, and we both shudder.

"You can't be real," he whispers, and my mouth tightens into a bitter smirk.

He traces his lips along my arm, my chest, focused solely on my body in the dim light. But I can tell by the trajectory that his mouth is seeking mine, and that seems like a bad idea. I try to turn away, avoid him again, but this time his grip tightens in a way that's commanding, unfamiliar. He slips one powerful hand around to grip the back of my neck and holds my head still, so all I can do is brace myself for his lips.

And they burn.

Scorching against my flesh, he traces kisses along my jaw, sampling every inch until he zeroes in and closes his mouth over mine. His tongue plunges past my lips, and despite every hurt swirling through my head, I find myself opening to him, tasting and sucking him like I don't want to let him go.

He inhales deeply, then pauses. And I can tell something's wrong. His hands are no longer moving; his whole body has frozen. Something's finally occurred to him, and my charade falls away like an unused wedding veil. Our lips part. I raise my gaze, meeting his eyes for the first time since he entered the room, and somehow I manage to speak.

"Hello, Anton."

One moment, he's holding me in a heated embrace against his nude body. The next, he nearly throws me across the bed in his effort to get away. I land face down on the blankets, and by the time I sit back up, he's backed into a chair across the room, his discarded shirt clutched over his groin.

My instinct is to cover myself too. To reach for my clothes or one of the robes hanging in the hotel closet. But I resist. I've never understood female superhero attire. Wonder Woman. Xena. Even Sailor Moon. Fighting battles with their legs and breasts barely covered, wielding little more than swords or wands, defending the world from injustice while standing nearly nude.

Except now I think I get it. Now I understand the power of the costume.

Straightening, I thrust my chest out, kneeling on the bed as I reach up to remove the itchy wig. I pull a few pins, toss it aside, and let my own light blonde hair spill down over my shoulders.

I take a deep breath and meet his gaze again. I'm not sure what kind of reaction I thought I'd get. Defiance? Repentance? A cocky *fuck you*? The look on his face isn't any of those things.

When I peer closely, it almost looks like he's hurt.

We stay this way for several moments. Awkward seconds tick by, my chest just as tight as his fists. I wasn't prepared for whatever this is I'm feeling, and I guess he wasn't either since neither of us seem to have the first clue what to say.

What *is* there to say now?

"Lydia," he finally whispers, and that one word is so loaded with emotion it nearly knocks me down.

I look away, clearing my throat. "I've got a lawyer," I lie. "I think you'd better . . ."

Of course this is where the words trickle away. Where my semi-nude superhero confidence crumples. He'd better what? I came here ready to look him in the eye and throw him out, put an end to the last ten years of whatever we had. But the warmth of his embrace still lingers on my skin, keeping me from speaking all the words I've been practicing in my head.

I want a divorce. I want you gone.

I want you to hold me again?

Anton growls. He rises, throws down the shirt, and comes to stand by the bed, hovering naked over me. Suddenly I wish it was five minutes ago—no, maybe five years. I wish this was a game we decided to play back in that blizzard and everything didn't feel so much like the end.

"I'd better what?" he says, low and stern in a way he's never spoken to me. He's always so deferential, ready to listen and support. Find the quickest way to help. But the way he's looking at me now—I get the distinct impression he's not considering what he can give, but what he'd like to take. And I'm surprised when this thought leaves a tingle between my legs.

I shake my head. "I . . . I think this needs to be over."

His eyes sear into me. He rakes his gaze over my body, along the curve of my calves and down to my painted toes. He doesn't move from his position at the edge of the bed, but I find it hard not to squirm as he continues, studying each piece of me like he's taking inventory. Edging up my thighs, the curve of my hips, even my arms resting in my lap. He pauses on my nearly exposed breasts, lingering on one and then the other with hungry ownership before finally settling on my open lips.

"What if that's not what I want?"

My skin prickles. I straighten, trying to find the strength to meet his gaze again when the inside of my chest feels like it's about to go nuclear. I lash my arm out, gesturing around the room. At the generic hotel sixty miles from our house. At his naked, perfect body—still clearly aroused for someone else—and the lingerie I bought so he would think I was her.

"What the fuck *do* you want? Because it's obviously not me."

He doesn't speak right away; he just stands there staring, every beautiful muscle in his body tensed, eyes blazing. Until finally, he sinks to his knees next to me.

"Lydia. *You* are all I've ever wanted."

CHAPTER NINETEEN

Her

My eyes fill with tears.

It's been five days since my lunch with Caprice. Five days since a single page on a website sent my marriage crashing down around me, since I got on this rollercoaster of emotion, shooting between hope and revenge. So far, I haven't really given myself the space or permission to truly cry, but I can't now either—I'm still not ready for that.

I take a deep, trembling breath and blink them away. "Don't give me that bullshit."

"It's the truth."

"Oh, absolutely, *MountainMan3*."

He leans in, voice shaking even as he reaches for me. "Come on, Mrs. Richie—"

"Don't you mean *LonelyGirl8?*" I swat his hand away, my face absolutely burning. "How dare you call me Mrs."

Heat rises in Anton's eyes. His gaze dips to the delicate space between my breasts, then to where my traitorous nipples challenge the sheer fabric. He licks his lips. "Because you're my wife. And you being here is the best thing that could've happened tonight."

I cross my arm in front of me, but he grabs my hand and pushes me back into the pillows, descending on me with a kiss so deep it's like winter melting into spring. I can't escape the musky, earthy scent of him, his desire growing thick once more against my hip. Unfortunately, I also can't shake the image of him here in this hotel room with who knows how many other women.

I pull back and shove him away with all my strength, which isn't much of a match for his, but he stops immediately. "Don't *touch* me," I say.

He recoils like I've slapped him, and for a moment he just sits there, staring at his own hands. I wonder if he actually feels ashamed. Will he brave the truth, or is he coming up with another lie? Finally, he blinks and pulls back. And as he does, all the heat from moments ago melts away. A chill settles over the room.

"Okay," he says in a ragged voice. "If that's what you want."

I fold my arms over my chest in an effort to regain my confidence. "How many others have there been? Did you bring them all here?"

"You're the first," he says. "The only."

A lump forms in my throat. That's what I've thought since college —that our first times were together, and there's never been anyone else. I swallow hard. "Why should I believe that?"

He shrugs, raising his gaze to my face, eyes not straying anywhere on my body this time. When he speaks again, his words come out cool. "Is it going to matter if you do?" He rises from the bed, crosses to the chair, and slips on his boxer briefs.

I hesitate. "Wh-what are you doing?"

"Getting dressed." His voice is flat and emotionless.

"Why?"

He pauses at this admittedly ridiculous question, then continues gathering his things. I don't know why that came out of my mouth, why my stomach tightens more with every article of clothing he finds. Why I suddenly wish I'd said and done everything leading up to this moment differently.

"I'll move my stuff out this weekend," he says. "We can start the paperwork before that. I see no reason to make this uglier than it already is."

He takes his shirt off the chair, slips it on, and turns away as he does the buttons. I stare at his back, stiff and straight, at the well-carved curve of his ass, and try to imagine what he'd take from our house. What things are his? Which are mine? How could he even tell?

He pulls on his pants, tucking in his shirt while I sit on the bed, now very underdressed for the somber occasion. I pull a blanket across my lap, envisioning myself getting up for work next week, alone in our home. Not texting him during the day with silly GIFs or asking what he's doing for lunch. And then I think of Heartthrob. Who will keep him? Is there shared custody for dogs? I picture his eager face rushing in after work, looking for Anton to play, and finding the house empty. Dear God, it breaks my heart to think about our poor disappointed dog.

As Anton locates his shoes, nearly dressed, a sense of dread pools in my gut. Maybe it's guilt, which is stupid. Or a healthy dose of remorse. Maybe it's what he said—about only wanting me. But I'm overcome with this horrible feeling, like once he walks out the door, that will be it. I'll never see him again.

And even though I came here with every intention of ending our relationship, suddenly I'm no longer sure that's what I want.

He picks up his keys. Duffle bag. Reaches for the door handle.

"*Wait—*" I say, rising from the bed. The blanket falls away, landing around my ankles.

Anton stops, hand on the knob. Lingering an eternity, presumably waiting for me to say something else, to do something.

"Why?" he finally asks when I don't speak. He doesn't turn to look at me. But there's something in his tone that wasn't there a second ago. Regret? Maybe disgust. I falter, unsure if it's meant for me or for himself.

"I—" I stammer, trying to figure out what I want to say. "I don't want you to move out."

He lets go of the knob and turns to stare at me. Goose flesh rises on my arms. "*Why?*"

I open my mouth, but I'm still having trouble understanding myself.

He gestures to me, the wig on the floor, the entire hotel room. "If you don't want to be rid of me, Lydia, what was the *point* of all this?"

I press my lips together. It's a legitimate question. But I don't know the answer anymore. I was so sure of myself as I lay in wait tonight, driven by hurt and betrayal. Ready to catch my no-good, cheating husband in a salacious act. So how come, now that I've pulled it off, I'm second-guessing? Why, instead of feeling glorious, is a voice inside me screaming not to let him go?

You *are all I've ever wanted.*

Do I really believe that? Or am I just afraid?

In a shaky voice, I whisper, "Have you really never"—I swallow past the burning in my throat—"been with anyone else?"

His jaw tightens, but his chin dips in a nearly imperceptible nod.

I drop my gaze, trying not to shiver as I stare at my hands. "Then why did you come here tonight?"

There's a long silence. In which I become too aware of everything in the room. The tear in the carpet by the closet. The drip of the bathroom faucet. The forced air blowing cool under the curtain. The way he's dressed and I'm not. Like we aren't a married couple and this is some other kind of transaction.

He takes a shallow breath. "Lydia, it's been—"

"Ten *years*." I gesture between us, trying to emphasize the length of our relationship as the reason we ought to try harder, but my voice comes out so small it seems to punctuate the opposite.

"Yeah." Anton nods, his voice raw. "And I'm lonely as fuck."

I open my mouth to protest. That's ridiculous. We're together all the time when we're not both at work. It's not like we live separate lives. We're home every night, in the same bed, and we *just* attended the Wallace's party—though, of course, we both know how that ended. But I close my mouth because deep inside, I know he isn't talking about socializing.

I look down at my breasts, wrapped in lace and ribbon like matching gifts. "You're talking about our sex life."

He lets out a short breath that almost sounds like a laugh. But when he returns my gaze, his face is stern.

"Maybe it's something we could work on." I try to make it sound like I mean this, but my throat is so dry. "I . . . I'm just not sure something that lasted ten years should end in one night."

He levels me with a look that says we both know it has *not* been just a night, and I have to swallow hard around the lump in my throat.

"Lydia," he says, his voice quieter, tired. "What do you think we could work on that hasn't changed over the last decade?"

"I don't know." I bite my trembling lip. "Maybe . . . I can do better."

I meant to say *we*, but that's the way it comes out.

His eyes widen. "*I'm* the one who put myself on a fucking cheating app."

"You sure did." My voice breaks as I acknowledge this, but ever since I saw his stupid profile, I haven't been able to keep from thinking *I* could've done things differently. Maybe if I hadn't worked quite so much, or I'd gone with him to the hot springs.

My mind screams, *but I've been busy.*

While my heart whispers, *I've been avoiding him.*

A knot forms inside my chest.

"Look . . ." Anton wipes his hand over his face. "I'm sorry. This was an enormous mistake. I'll do things however you want." He raises his head to look at me. "But I can't go on the way it's been."

His words ring through the air, vibrating into my body. He's right, of course. Neither of us can. I just wish I had some kind of guide telling me what to do next. Is he a cheater, or isn't he? Can you move forward with someone after they've broken your heart, or is this really the end?

I nod. "I . . . I need to do some thinking."

"Me too." He looks around with a slightly dazed expression, one I'm probably also wearing. Like we each had ideas about what would take place in this hotel room—only this? This definitely wasn't one of them.

I sink to the bed, pulling the sheet across my lap.

And since neither of us seems to have anything else to say, he turns back to the door. "I'll see you at home."

CHAPTER TWENTY

Him

It's a miracle I don't get a speeding ticket between Colorado Springs and Denver. My foot is like lead on the gas pedal, my mind flashing between all the ways I anticipated the night going and how it actually played out.

The worst part is, now that everything is said and done, I can't decide who I'm angrier with—Lydia or myself.

What she did took guts, I'll give her that. Finding me on the app, luring me in with messages, then pushing to hook up at a hotel. If I'd been at all suspicious, I might've figured it out. Shut the whole thing down, deleted the app, and laid low. But that profile picture she took? *Fuck*. That didn't exactly help me think with my upstairs brain.

And if I'm totally honest, part of me is grateful she did it.

I can't deny why I drove to Colorado Springs. I was ready for some action, and I'm pretty sure I would have gotten it if not for my wife. But now that it's behind me, I'm so *glad* I didn't. Because as awful as I feel barreling up the highway after being caught by my wife with my literal pants down, I'm not sure I could've driven home to face her at all after fucking another woman.

In some ways, it's like she saved me from myself.

That, or she's trying to kill me.

And holy fuck, no woman I met online could have compared with how Lydia looked tonight. It was all I could do to keep from ripping that bra off just to bury my face between her breasts. And once I knew it was her, that actually made it worse—I wasn't a cheater having an affair anymore; I was a man with his own *wife*. I wanted nothing more than to bend her over the side of that bed, tear those backless panties down her legs, and fuck her guilt-free, nice and slow. In the ten years we've been together, she's never worn anything like that lingerie, and I've *tried* to make it happen. Hell, I doubt we would've ended up here if she had.

Maybe that's not fair.

But it doesn't matter. Because even though she wore it, enticed me with it, she *still* pushed me away.

I grip the wheel, searching for the headlights of her Toyota in my rearview mirror. She would have had to dress and pack up, but even if we'd left together, at the rate I'm going she'd be several miles back. I'll beat her home by a good fifteen minutes, and I'm still so mortified by everything that happened tonight, I'm tempted to just throw some stuff in a bag and leave before she gets there. I could spend a few nights with Henry. Find a place of my own, hire some movers to go back into the house for my stuff. Can you ghost on a marriage?

Possibly—except for one thing.

You're talking about our sex life . . . maybe it's something we could work on.

I guess I'm enough of an asshole to cheat on my wife, but not enough of one to deny her the chance to try.

I can't decide if she's sincere or just trying to punish me, though. Why couldn't we have worked on it a year ago? Or three? The fact that she actually suggested out loud that we could *have* sex fills me with stupid hope, but I really wish it didn't. Because she'll never follow through. Once we're home she might make a halfhearted effort. Wear a low-cut shirt, wave her cleavage in front of me, then invite me to get on top of her for ten minutes as per usual. Nothing's going to make her magically start desiring me. Then she'll get busy at work, go back to avoiding me, and turn me down the next time I'm desperate enough to make a move.

No fucking thank you. I should have walked away tonight when she was most upset. It would've been easier.

And *God*—I showed up ready to sleep with a stranger. Even if she did want me, I don't fucking deserve her.

I step into the house and slam the front door. There's no barking or full-body dog tackle. Lydia must've left Heartthrob with Tomás.

I pace from the living room to the kitchen. It's a small relief we had to drive back separately—I needed the time with my own thoughts—but now I'm all keyed up, wondering what we're supposed to do when she gets here. Where I should be, what she's expecting. It's only eleven o'clock at night. Are we supposed to sit and make small talk? Get into bed? Then what? It figures that after waiting *years* for her to meet me halfway under the sheets, I'm now dreading it. I don't know how to touch her after what I did tonight. I can't imagine she'd ever want to touch me again.

I decide to change clothes just as she pulls into the driveway. She takes her time coming in, and I'm just tying my shoes when she walks in the door.

"Going for a run?" Her eyebrows arch, taking in my joggers and reflective jacket.

"Yeah." It feels like I should say more, justify my actions, but I'm afraid to. I've done enough damage tonight.

"Okay." She seems to want to say something else too, but she just nods after a moment. "Well, I um . . . have to catch up on some things."

My stomach sinks, quickly knotting around her words, despite a simultaneous sense of relief. *Of course.* She's going to work. What else would she do? I almost laugh, but the corners of my eyes start to burn, so I keep my face an impassive mask. This is familiar. I know what to do when she works. I zip my jacket and head out the door without another word.

My calves burn like crazy. It was a longer run than I normally would've taken so late at night, but it was that or come home. After a while, everything that happened today started piling up in my chest—driving sixty miles for an affair, getting *caught*, then my marriage not quite falling apart—until I had to slow to a walk. I drag my feet to our front porch, so tired I can hardly stand, but I make myself take time to stretch, hoping Lydia's gone to sleep. I don't want to have to face her again. I just want to go to bed and pretend this whole day never fucking happened.

When I finally open the door, the house is dark. I step lightly, easing it closed so it won't creak, leaving my shoes by the coat rack. She's not at her desk in the second bedroom when I pass, but that doesn't mean anything. She carries her laptop all over the place when she works, and our bed is less than sacred. As I get close to our bedroom door, I can hear music playing, which is odd. I'll put on a playlist sometimes to relax or try to set a mood. She usually listens to podcasts or news reports, saying she prefers to stay informed. I can't remember the last time she sat back and just played a song.

I head past our door and lock myself in the bathroom. When I turn on the shower, I adjust the spray to make the hot water last as long as possible. Then I just stand there, letting it run down my body, soothing my aching muscles, willing it to cleanse the sin from my skin.

When I'm finally brave enough to leave the confines of the bathroom, I find Lydia curled asleep in our bed. She's not wearing the lingerie anymore, which is both a relief, and if I'm honest, a total disappointment. But she's pulled on a sleeveless cotton nightgown that I have to admit I adore because it shows so much skin. She usually saves it for summer when it's too hot for the striped anti-sex long sleeves. The lights are low, and the music drifting through the room is coming from the small Bluetooth speaker beside the bed. It takes me a few minutes to realize the songs she's cued up are actually the playlist from our wedding. One of the knots in my chest loosens a little.

Her breathing is low and even, and I linger over her, staring at her yellow hair fanned over the pillow, her parted lips, the smooth planes of her face. She still looks exactly the way she did when we first met, if not somehow more beautiful. I pull the blankets up over her shoulders, my hand hovering by her cheek, heart caught in my chest. I wasn't lying when I told her she's all I've ever wanted—*she is*. I just don't think she'll ever feel the same way about me.

I turn out the light and walk around to my side, shedding my towel and slipping under the covers naked, but staying as close to the edge of the bed as I can. I unlock my phone and pull up my alarm app out of habit, my thumb poised over five a.m. when I like to go to the gym. But something stops me from setting it this time. For one, despite the shower, my legs already feel like they're ready to fall off. If I work out tomorrow, it's going to be arm work only.

But another part of me wants to stay in, see what happens in the morning. I'm not delusional; I don't expect her to roll over tomorrow hot for morning sex. Honestly, it would make more sense if she changed her mind and threw all my clothes out the front window. But I keep thinking about the tremor in her voice when she said, *I don't want you to move out.* And the corresponding lump that formed in my own throat. Would she really put in the work we need? Or are we both delaying the inevitable? I hate setting myself up for more disappointment, and it feels like that's what I'm about to do. But I'm curious—and probably stupid—enough to wait and see.

CHAPTER TWENTY-ONE

Her

It takes me a minute to register his weight next to me on the mattress. The heat of his skin beneath the covers. The rhythm of his breath. He's actually here. I'd half expected him to be gone before I woke up. If not *gone* gone, at the very least off at the gym for some killer workout. But it's already six thirty. The sun is up. Either he slept through his alarm, or he never set one.

I sit up, realizing my alarms didn't go off either. I need to look at my messages and check in with my managers. It's Tuesday, which means there's a whole list of things I need to do. I still haven't gone through a stack of references for employee applications. A drain in one of the Ooh La Pooch tubs is running slow and might need a plumber. I have a list of questions to answer for a feature with a local magazine. I need to email my bank about the financing for the new location, and of course, I'm having issues with payroll . . .

I swipe my phone off the bedside table, thumb hovering over the screen as I calculate how long it will take me to get dressed and out the door. But then Anton stirs beside me, flooding my brain with memories of last night, and I'm pulled back into my bedroom, where the walls feel like they're closing in. I run a hand through my hair, drawing my knees to my chest.

I'll do things however you want . . . but I can't go on the way it's been.

I clutch the phone in my hand. It doesn't seem like *he* should be laying down conditions. Maybe I have some things to work on, but he's the one who went to a hotel to screw someone else.

Even as my skin flushes with this thought, my gaze strays back to my husband, flitting over his form like I'm afraid to look too hard and somehow wake him. Why? Because he might reach for me? Because I don't want him to?

My stomach twists.

But what if it hadn't been me with him in that hotel room last night? What if I had wished him a good business trip and gotten up for work this morning, blissfully unaware? What if, while I walked the dog, sipped my coffee, and worked on payroll, he was waking up naked with someone else?

A weight settles in my chest.

It feels like I need to do something. But when I have so many other pressing things to think about, staying in bed, staying home—*just* to have sex—almost feels irresponsible. I wish it could wait till this evening. Or tomorrow. The weekend. Until I realize this sort of thinking is probably how we got to this point.

With a heavy sigh, I put the phone face down on the bedside table. Tomás still thinks I'm on "vacation." The Pooch Park should be okay, at least for the morning. Ooh La Pooch doesn't open until eight. I don't even have to get up to let Heartthrob out.

But . . . what do I do? I glance at Anton's form next to me. Do I reach for him? Speak to him? This seems like something I should understand, but I don't even know where to start. I study his face, turned slightly toward me on the pillow. It could just be the weak morning light, but something about him seems different. In the surface of his forehead, or the angle of his brows. It takes me a minute, but I finally notice there are no lines creasing his face or tightness to his jaw. He looks peaceful . . . relaxed. Younger, even. Like when we first met.

Totally different from the scowling man at the hotel last night.

His breathing hitches, and I freeze as he shifts onto his side. I clutch my hands in my lap. Will he open his eyes? Catch me watching him?

Should I kiss him? Touch him? For heaven's sake, we've been married seven years. *Why* don't I know what to do?

Self-consciousness takes over. What if my breath smells? What if I have mascara under my eyes? I'm probably a wreck, and that's not going to make this go any smoother. I slip out of bed, grab my phone, and tiptoe to the bathroom. Pee. Check myself in the mirror. Fix my hair. Brush away my morning breath. And while I do this, I ask my therapist, Dr. Google for advice.

Turns out there are an overwhelming number of opinions about how to improve one's sex life. Unfortunately, many of them feel one hundred percent beyond me.

Wear sexy lingerie - Been there, done that. He was plenty able to resist.

Watch a sexy movie - I'm not sure whether this means *Fifty Shades of Grey* or actual pornography. Either way, six thirty in the morning doesn't seem like the time to curl up with a bowl of popcorn.

Role play - I cringe, picturing myself dressed up as a schoolgirl and Anton pretending to be the teacher. Ew.

Bring accessories into the bedroom - That's not something we've done before, but I'm not sure where to start. Handcuffs? Riding crops? My face goes pink in the mirror. Who has those types of things, anyway? I know what my mother would say.

Do a sexy striptease - I pause on this one. While the idea of acting like a stripper makes me cringe, taking my clothes off is something I am capable of that doesn't seem totally off the wall. It's not like he's never seen me naked; then again, he's already *seen* me naked. What's exciting about that? So I guess the question is whether I could do it and actually manage to entice him.

I stare at myself in the mirror, wondering if this is even the right approach. Arousing Anton isn't really a problem—quite the opposite. I just need to convince him the *only* person he wants to be aroused with is me.

When I step back into our bedroom, the air has shifted. I can tell he's awake, but he hasn't moved. I'm not sure if he's watching, but I have to assume he is. The music I put on repeat last night still plays low over the speaker, and lucky for me, it's on a slow, sexy song. I take a deep breath and walk purposefully toward the bed, exaggerating my footsteps in an attempt to roll my hips. The way I'm sure I've seen actresses do in movies—women who've either been directed or feel confident in what sexy looks like. The strap of my nightgown falls off one shoulder, and I go with it like it was planned. It seems like a good idea. But once I reach the foot of the bed, I'm suddenly not sure what else to do. I'm only wearing my cotton nightgown and underwear. Can you do a striptease with only two pieces of clothing? I could really use more time to sit and think this through. I raise my hem to reveal a peek at my underpants, then let the gown fall back down.

He's watching me openly now, but I gauge nothing from his expression. There's no clear interest. No heat. He could be watching a vacuum commercial on TV. My face warms. Maybe I should just give up and go make coffee . . . or maybe I need to step it up.

I slide down the other strap of my nightgown, then slip my arms out carefully, keeping my breasts covered for now. His face is still flat, but is he sitting up straighter in bed? The song changes to something faster, but I keep moving. I'm holding the nightgown up with one hand, using the other to play with my hair as I jut my hip to the right. But then I realize my left boob has crept out, exposed in the air. I pull the gown up quickly, then decide that was the wrong move and drop it completely. The material doesn't flutter sexily to the floor like on TV, but bunches up around my waist like a sack. In a moment of panic, I grab it and shimmy it over my hips in a move that I'm pretty sure looks like I'm trying to pull down my pants to pee.

Somehow, I manage to get out of the nightgown and leave my underpants on without falling over, but by the time I straighten, my cheeks are ready to ignite. I cross my arms over my naked chest and turn away from Anton, trying to gather myself as I sway my cotton-covered ass to the beat, afraid to look back at his face.

I feel like I need a brass pole, but all we've got in here is a bookshelf.

With a rush of relief, I remember I'm not through. My thumbs drift to the elastic band of my light blue underwear. They're definitely underpants, *not* panties. Broad, comfortable full-coverage cotton. But I bank on their removal being more exciting than their looks. Keeping my back to him, I slide the fabric down slowly, trying my best to keep swaying in time to the beat. Luckily, I already did some serious frontal trimming in order to wear that sheer lingerie yesterday. My ass is nothing special. It's round enough in proportion to my waist, but I wouldn't call it my standout feature. The second it's exposed, though, I remember Anton's message about "butt play," and I freeze. Every inch of my skin flushes hot, and in some attempt to dash that thought from my mortified mind —and his—I spin to face him.

This is a mistake. Because now we're staring at each other, and I haven't planned my next move. There aren't any clothes left. The song is about to end. And I'm just standing here, my breasts bare, hands clapped between my legs like Eve making a break from the Garden of Eden.

It takes me a second to realize I'm actually scared of whatever happens next.

What does he want that I haven't given him before?

But then he reaches toward me, and I get a small rush of victory. His face is still unreadable, betraying nothing of how he feels, but his hand is moving closer. Maybe I'm doing better than I thought?

I clear my throat. If he's into this, I might as well take it all the way.

"Ooh baby," I say in my best attempt at a stripper voice—*do* strippers ever talk? It comes out sounding forced, like I'm pretending to be some weird little anime girl, but I go with it. "I've been so naughty. You wanna fuck me?"

At last, his fingers meet my skin—but he doesn't grab for my breasts or my ass. He wraps his hand around my wrist with a firm grip. I look up in surprise, and when I meet his gaze, his lip is curled. The look in his eyes is far from aroused.

"Lydia?" he growls. "What the fuck are you doing?"

Reality crashes in with a shiver of bare skin, and now I'm desperate for a robe or even just a towel to cover myself. What *am* I doing? I wish I'd never gotten out of bed. Or at least never left the bathroom. Still, I resume my normal voice and feign confidence. "Isn't it obvious?"

He lets go of my arm and sits back, recoiling into the pillows. "This isn't . . ."

My hands start shaking. I wait for him to say it isn't working. I'm not for him. That he's changed his mind about giving things a try and just wants a divorce.

"This isn't you," he whispers.

I meet his eyes, and the utter distaste in his expression is like a punch to the gut. I swallow hard, forcing down the rising lump in my throat. And when I finally manage to move my feet, I can't get away fast enough.

Asshole. I grab my phone and the first clothes I see—a pair of leggings and a T-shirt tossed on top of the dresser—then bolt for the door.

It's Tuesday morning. If it had been up to me, I would've had coffee in my PJs, started some supply orders, and grabbed bagels for Ooh La Pooch on my way in to work. A *striptease* would've been the furthest thing from my mind.

But that wasn't for me. It was for him.

And it still wasn't enough.

I lock myself in the bathroom, jam the clothes on, and pull my hair into a bun, then I race for the front door. It's not until I'm forcing my feet into my Converse that I realize I don't have a bra, but there's no way I'm going back in our room now. I grab a hoodie, my laptop and keys, and slam the front door on my way out.

CHAPTER TWENTY-TWO

Her

After a therapeutic stop for coffee, I run to Target and buy a sports bra, but sadly, it's no substitution for my new favorite T-shirt bra from Allure. I can tell Tomás is surprised to see me when I walk into The Pooch Park, but as soon as I step through my office door, Heartthrob jumps all over me, and I let myself forget every single dude on the planet who isn't a canine. I spend the morning going over employment applications, working on the dog bakery order, and taking Heartthrob for a long walk. Since I'm not in the mood for lunch, I choke down an energy bar and make the ten-minute drive to check on things at Ooh La Pooch. And it's a good thing I do because Scarlet hurt her back, our second groomer is out of town at a wedding, and our bather, Alicia, needs help lifting two enormous Leonbergers into our elevated steel tubs.

By three o'clock, I've mostly run out of managerial things to do and the only dogs left to be bathed are a couple of toy poodles. I'm also suspicious Scarlet's been talking with Tomás because she has emphasized at least three times that everything's under control and I should go home.

She has no idea.

After organizing the front desk and emptying every trash receptacle

I can find, I say goodbye to Scarlet and Alicia and sit in my car. My phone has been pinging in my pocket all day, but never with calls or texts from Anton. I don't know if he's spent today at the gym, moved out, or is waiting at home to talk to me. And I'm not ready to find out. I'm in no mood to deal with my mother and her onslaught of baby pictures either, but I need something, *someone* I can talk to about the last twenty-four hours. So I dial Caprice.

"Hey. Uh . . . how's your Tuesday?" My voice comes out like a strangled Smurf.

"Did you go through with it?" she demands. "God, you could have at least sent me a text. I was starting to think things went badly."

"Oh." My lip curls. "They did."

She lets out a quiet sigh. "I'm sorry, hon. At least it's over now?"

A sound comes out of my mouth, somewhere between a desperate laugh and a sob, and because Caprice has excellent listening skills, she simply waits for me to speak.

"I—it's not over," I finally say. "Not yet."

There's a pause. And then she switches our phone call to video. I reluctantly accept.

She peers at me through the screen. "I just needed to verify no one was standing behind you with a gun to your head."

I press my lips together, and when she homes in on my face, I wish I could turn off the video again.

"Hey, talk to me. What happened?"

I let out a long breath, studying the bright red tip of my own nose in the corner of the screen. "Well, we were going to give things another shot—"

"Hold on. You need to back up." Her brown eyes bug. "He thought he had a date with LonelyGirl8. You showed up instead, and now you guys are kissing and making up? Did I miss a step?"

I shake my head. "It doesn't matter. I think I already screwed it up."

"Lydia." Her brows draw together. "How did *you* mess up here?"

I look at my lap, my mind churning again through everything that happened at the hotel—from the moment Anton touched me to the moment he left—then back over the awful scenario in our bedroom this morning. But it doesn't stop there. My brain keeps spinning through other moments—at the Wallace's party, at Ooh La Pooch last week, even just random nights in our bed.

I can't go on the way it's been.

"Can I ask you a personal question?"

She raises a brow. "Sure."

"What is sex like for you?" My voice is so low I can barely hear myself.

A flash of confusion crosses her face, but she shrugs. "Um, fun?"

I swallow hard. Caprice and I are both young, healthy women in our twenties. But I'm married, and she isn't. Does that automatically take out the *fun*? Because it isn't the word that comes to mind for me. My thoughts go to things like *tedious, messy, uncomfortable* . . .

"Maybe there's something wrong with me."

"Excuse me?" She narrows her eyes. "How did we get from your husband being a lying cheater to there being something wrong with you?"

So I tell her everything that's been swirling through my mind. What went down at the hotel and the awful striptease this morning, but also other stuff that's been bothering me. How Anton seems to want sex all the time, but it's the last thing I want to do. That I avoid touching him. And when I do give in to him, I wouldn't describe it as *fun*. It feels . . . obligatory.

"So maybe this is all my fault." I frown.

"Can I ask a question before you play the blame game?" Caprice says, ignoring me. "You guys have been together, what, eight? Ten years? Was it always this way?"

I open my mouth to say yes, except that's not true. When Anton and I first met, things were different. I remember getting excited when we touched. Wanting to take off each other's clothes. The first time we had sex was terrible, but it was the first time for both of us with anyone. That seemed like a given. It got easier from there, some times definitely better than others. But I have to admit it used to be different than it is now.

"Maybe not?"

"Great!" she says, looking slightly relieved. "Then you can get back to that—there's hope. But I think you might be approaching this wrong. You don't need to do stuff like a striptease if you're not into it."

"Then what *should* I do?"

"I don't know. Maybe spend some time figuring out what's changed. See if you can get back to what used to work?"

I mull that over. I don't have a lot of faith in my instincts here, but maybe she's on to something. "You sure your passion is journalism? I feel like you could charge a decent rate for therapy."

Her eyes glimmer. "I'm almost finished writing this article. Trust me, your husband's Unmatched bros will be paying my fee."

"Fair enough." My skin stings thinking of the other wives about to discover the truth in their marriages. I wonder how many of them will end up dumping their husbands. And how many will find themselves in some kind of love-tethered limbo like me.

"Don't worry, I'm keeping you and Anton out of it," Caprice assures me. "But Lydia, before you bend over backward to figure this out by yourself, don't forget *he* was the one ready to cheat. He owes you some extra effort too."

My arms are overloaded with cleaning supplies from a last-minute Costco run as I get back to The Pooch Park to pick up Heartthrob, so I don't see the person standing outside until he offers to get the door for me.

"Oh, thank you so much." I glance up and spot a familiar face. "Henry! How's it going?"

Anton's college friend is possibly the last person I expected to see outside my daycare, considering he's never owned a dog, but he gives me a subdued smile and follows me inside. I set the Clorox wipes, garbage bags, and other items behind the desk and straighten up to find Henry peering through one of the interior windows into the main playroom, watching a goldendoodle wrestle with a dalmatian until a cattle dog zooms between them and all three give chase around the room. Over in the smaller dog area, a couple of dachshunds take turns having their bellies rubbed by one of my employees.

"Looks like you're doing a brisk business," he says in his faint British accent. He's holding a leash in his hand, and I follow it down to an adorable fawn French bulldog standing at his feet.

"Oh my goodness—who is this?" I ask, falling to my knees in front of the little pup. She wiggles her butt and bows at the attention, sniffs my outstretched hand, then spins happily in a circle. "Henry, she's adorable!"

"Her name is Carmelita," he says, rolling his eyes. "My sister suckered me into taking care of her while she travels abroad."

I tickle Carmelita behind her big ears until she makes all kinds of adorable snorts, and I laugh. "I bet she'll be lucky if you even want to give her back."

Henry frowns. "Look, she's doing a number on my apartment while I'm at work. Anton said it might help if I brought her here."

I stiffen a little at my husband's name, but there's nothing in Henry's face indicating Anton's let his friend in on the state of our marriage.

"Sure," I say, straightening back up. "She seems pretty young. Two or three days a week here would give her some good exercise, keep her entertained, and wear her out. If you want, I can take her back for a few minutes and see how she does. We like to do a sort of 'interview' with every new dog before they start."

"A dog interview?" Henry's lip twitches, but he hands me the leash. "Great, I'll be right back."

I hand off the little Frenchie to Tomás, who introduces her to the small dog area as we watch through the window. She hesitates at first, looking cautious as the dachshunds and a Westie all come over to sniff her, but she quickly decides this is fun and engages a little beagle mix in a very bouncy game.

I smile at Henry. "Just as I suspected. She'll be a perfect fit."

"Great," he says, looking relieved. It seems obvious now that he's less than thrilled with his new charge. Henry's a good-looking guy, always well dressed, hair never out of place. The few times I've been to his Seventeenth Street loft with Anton, it's looked much the same as its owner. He reminds me a bit of Caprice—not really a dog person.

"How long did you say you're taking care of her?"

"Only through summer. I hope. While Ruby's back in England finishing her studies."

"That's so cool that you can give her a good home while your sister's gone. Carmelita will have a blast here."

Henry sniffs. "What's the pricing like for this, by the way?"

I indicate the fees detailed on the wall behind the desk. I'm not sure exactly what Henry does for work—something with real estate or banking—but he always drives a leased Mercedes, so I doubt it'll be a problem for him.

He studies the board, peers through the window like he's counting dogs, then gives a low whistle. "You make a killing with this, don't you? Just sitting around watching dogs play."

My face heats up. Occasionally, people bring this up. Usually men. I'm proud of my business, but when they make it sound like I'm raking in money doing nothing, it always makes me feel weird. I work my butt off to run this place.

"Just filling a niche," I say with an awkward laugh. "People in Denver *love* their dogs."

He leans casually on the desk. "You have another business too, right?"

"Yep, Ooh La Pooch was my first. It's a grooming salon. And we're actually in the process of opening a second Pooch Park."

Henry shakes his head, looking me up and down in a peculiar way, and suddenly I can't tell if he's impressed that people spend so much on their dogs or that I'm really a successful businesswoman.

"Okay, go ahead and give me the monthly package." He hands me a credit card. "Ruby had better pay me back for this."

I input Carmelita into our system as Tomás brings her back out, still running in delighted circles at the end of her leash. Henry holds it at arm's length until she settles down.

"All set," I say, handing him his new member card and receipt. "You can bring her in tomorrow if you like."

"Great. Thanks, Lydia." He nods and strides for the door. "Tell Anton I owe him one."

CHAPTER TWENTY-THREE

Him

I PACE TO THE FRONT WINDOW, BUT THE DRIVEWAY IS STILL empty. I drove by both The Pooch Park and Ooh La Pooch earlier, saw her car at the latter, and drove back home. I called my brother Seth, went to the gym, then deep cleaned our entire bungalow. I was about to buy flowers or chocolate, but that seemed so cliché I couldn't bring myself to do it. Instead, I ordered from Lydia's favorite sushi place, and it's waiting in the fridge for whenever she gets home.

If she comes home.

I know I fucked up. Possibly even more than yesterday. I've at least added insult to injury.

Lydia performing a striptease was the last thing I expected to wake up to today. I didn't know how to react. At first, I'll admit I was a little excited. Her movements were awkward and kind of stiff, but as soon as her tits swung free, I absolutely did not care. As she continued, though, I started to realize how forced the whole thing was. She wasn't smiling; she didn't make eye contact. Because she clearly didn't want to be doing it. And when she spoke to me in that awful little-girl voice, my dick just deflated. It wasn't till she was gone that I could see her actions for what they really were: a gesture. She may have repelled rather than enticed, but she tried. Really hard.

My phone rings.

"Hey."

"Still not home?" my brother asks, a little surprised.

"Nope," I say, walking by the front window again.

"She'll be back, man." His voice is so sympathetic, I want to end the call and go back to sitting in silence. But at the same time, part of me is afraid to hang up.

"She has the dog."

"Doesn't he always go to work with her?"

"Usually, but . . ." My voice trails off. I don't know how to put this into words. I feel like I blew my chance at everything.

"Look," Seth says. "I've been thinking about what you said this morning. You are an asshole for getting on that app and taking it all the way to a hotel, and I'm glad she nailed you. But she hasn't been prioritizing you or your marriage. You should probably *both* apologize. But after that, I think you just need to get over yourselves and fuck."

"Easy for you to say," I mutter. My little brother, the king of one-nighters, has never had a monogamous relationship in his life.

"Yeah. And still true."

"But she doesn't *want* that." My voice breaks, and I cover my face with one hand. "It's like she wants a roommate, not a husband. Maybe I just need to suck it up and accept that our relationship will never be what I want."

"Anton, don't take this the wrong way, but *Lydia* . . ." he emphasizes her name, then stops, like he's grasping for words. "Dude, she's—I mean those tits alone—"

"You can stop there," I say in a warning tone.

"You know what I mean." He exhales. "Sorry, man, just stating the obvious. Your wife is fuckin' hot. And no way a girl who looks like *that* doesn't want to use what she's got."

I close my eyes. "I'm here to tell you. It's been ten years. She doesn't."

He pauses, probably trying to grasp the concept. I'm one hundred percent certain my little brother's never been turned down for sex. But maybe that's because he's never hooked up with the same girl twice. He sighs, finally admitting he's out of his depth. "You can't live like that."

"No. But she could."

"Okay, look—"

"How's Mom?" I ask, changing the subject.

When we spoke this morning, Seth had gotten a call that she'd attacked one of the staff members at Sunny Cove while they were trying to bathe her, and they'd had to sedate her to get her calm.

"She's good. I went and saw her this afternoon after some of the drugs wore off. She was a lot more peaceful. Even gave me a bit of a smile."

"Do you—do you think I should come out?"

I tiptoe carefully around my feelings. Seth is the decision maker because he's with her in Dallas. He personally deals with Mom, her caregivers, and every issue that comes up. It's my job to shut the fuck up and not second-guess him.

"No," he says sharply. "I think you've got enough shit going on with Lydia. Mom would say the same. She'd want you to stay there and fix things. You know how she feels about you guys."

Felt, I want to say. But we can't seem to avoid speaking about her as if she's still actually with us. One thing I will always treasure about Lydia is that she knew my mom, was even close with her, before the dementia really took over. The two of them were like peas in a pod. Shopping together, chatting for hours. Lydia became the daughter Mom never had, and Lydia, whose own mother is a real piece of work, was happy to fill the role. By the time we got married there were already little signs Mom was struggling, but it took us all a long time—and her nearly burning the house down—to see them for what they really were. To realize she needed care and finally place her in a facility. I still can't believe it some days. Mom is only sixty-four.

"You're a great son, Sethie," I mutter into the phone, trying to make light of my guilt. The fact that I'm not the one there, making sure she's cared for myself. "She's lucky to have you."

"Shut up, asshole. You and Lyd made her happy when it counted. And you're going to keep doing that once you figure this shit out. I'm just the fuckup cleanup crew."

"Thanks for being there," I say, and this time I'm completely sincere. "I know it means a lot to her—and me."

. . .

At ten minutes to seven, Heartthrob bounds through the front door, tackling me with a face full of sloppy dog kisses. And for the briefest moment, I am so grateful. For both of them. His nonstop tail wagging, the way he makes us feel more like a family, the fact that she came back at all. And the possibility that I might not have to spend the night in this silent house, alone with my regrets. I grab Heartthrob's favorite rope toy off the floor, and we circle the coffee table in a vigorous game of tug-of-war, which I let him win when Lydia comes in and shuts the door.

"Hey," I say, straightening. I think I owe it to her to be the first one to speak.

"Hi." She sets her things down by the door, but I can't get a read on her face. Is she still upset? Resigned? Optimistic?

"Do you uh . . ." My voice trails off as I notice the dog holding his leash in his mouth, tilting his head. "Should we maybe take him for a walk?"

"Yeah. Sure."

We head down the sidewalk toward a park a few blocks away. There are flowers peeking out everywhere. The sun has been setting noticeably later, and the air has been warm all week. It's the time of year when everyone starts to get excited for spring, but we shuffle along, barely lifting our feet while the dog makes efficient work marking his territory. It figures—I've been sitting around the house waiting to talk to her all day, and now I just keep opening and closing my mouth like a dumb fish. Nothing ever comes out.

When we reach the far end of the park, we turn back toward home. Her hair is coming loose from its bun, and she pulls out the elastic, letting it fall over one eye the way it did this morning when she stood naked and beautiful in our bedroom before everything went wrong again. My dick stirs in my pants, and I stop right there on the path, suddenly more sure of myself than I've been all day. "Look, Lydia—"

Her phone rings.

She gives me a look that's half apology, half relief, and then she answers the damn thing. Effectively cutting me off right when I was about to set everything right.

"Hello? Charlotte?"

My hands curl into fists, but I stop cold at her lawyer's name. She keeps walking down the sidewalk without even glancing at me. Surely she's not going to discuss a divorce right here? My pulse jumps, all the relief I felt after she came home suddenly evaporating, a heavy dread sinking into its place.

I watch the sway of her hips ahead of me, moving farther away, and my mouth goes dry. Can I even blame her? She caught me red fucking handed trying to cheat. And when she gave me a second chance I never deserved, I blew it to smithereens. I close my eyes, wishing I'd said or done *anything* different this morning. Yesterday. This whole week.

But then it occurs to me—Charlotte's a business lawyer. She's negotiated contracts, written up legal documents, and advised Lydia on a couple employee disputes, but she wouldn't handle our personal mess. Maybe Lydia got in touch with her asking for a referral to someone who would, though. I tug on Heartthrob's leash, increasing my pace until I fall into step right behind her. Close enough to hear her side of the conversation. I'm sure she knows I'm there. We'll see what she's willing to discuss.

"That's not at all what I expected you to say," Lydia mutters.

There's a long silence. We reach the green space along the duck pond, and Heartthrob catches my eye, stretching his paws out in front of him and sinking his big body into a playful bow. I insert a tennis ball into his ball launcher, unclip his leash, and hurl it across the grass. He takes off after it like the whole balance of the universe depends on him.

"I . . . I'm going to have to think it over," Lydia finally says. "I don't know if I'm ready for this."

She turns away. I can't see her face, but her shoulders are tense, and my brain struggles to fill in the gaps. It's nearly eight p.m. Lydia and Charlotte have worked together for years, but I can't think of what could be important enough to call about outside of business hours. Unless it's a personal favor.

Heartthrob drops the ball at my feet, and I throw it again absently.

"Okay. Let me know when and I'll meet you at your office. Thank you again, Charlotte, for everything."

She ends the call, staring at the dog shooting back toward us over the lawn. He reaches her, drops the ball directly at her feet, and she flings it back into the air, watching him take off again. After a couple repetitions of this, she glances over her shoulder, raising her eyebrows like she's surprised to see me.

"So." The corners of her mouth turn down. "How was your day?"

I part my lips. Then press them back together. She's really not going to say a thing about our current situation or the call she just took in front of me?

I clear my throat. I don't know how to have this conversation, but I'm also tired of beating around the bush. "Look, this morning, I wasn't expecting—"

"It was a mistake." Her eyes close briefly. "I had this idea, but . . . it wasn't a good one."

I want to tell her it *was*. She took her freaking clothes off trying to get me aroused. I can't remember the last time she did anything like that. I could've kept my mouth shut and touched her. We could've spent the day in bed together.

"It doesn't matter," I say. Her eyes snap to mine, and I grimace. God, I'm going to fuck this up worse before I fix it. "Um, what I meant is, I was a jerk. I'm sorry."

She holds my gaze for a moment, her eyes clearly stating: *Yes. You were.* Then she shakes her head. "It won't happen again."

My stomach drops. Does this mean we're done trying? Was the call with Charlotte about us after all? What happened to seeing if we can do better? I close my eyes, wishing I could go back to this morning. Redirect her. Tell her, without being an ass, that the whole performance wasn't necessary—she doesn't have to act like someone else. I just want her to *want* me.

Unless. She really doesn't.

Heartthrob tosses the tennis ball at my leg and whines. I open my eyes. Lydia takes the ball launcher, sending the dog racing back across the grass, and as she lowers her arm, the setting sun glints off her wedding rings. She hasn't taken them off. She straightens and looks at me, and as she does a breeze tosses her hair, making her look fresh and carefree and completely alluring. I step forward, holding her gaze, my body absolutely buzzing for her now. I reach out, but she turns her head away again to the dog. And I have to fold my arms and clench my jaw.

Maybe this is a waste of time. Maybe I'm torturing both of us trying to hold on when she's clearly not interested. My brother's right about her being every straight guy's fantasy, but I've done enough frustrated late-night reading to understand there are people in the world who just aren't into sex. If the universe is cruel enough to make my wife one of them, I can't hold it against her.

But I can't live that way either.

I clear my throat, balling my hands into fists. "Lydia, I think—"

"The past few days have been a lot," she says at the same time, staring at Heartthrob's leash.

I raise my brow. Maybe she's reached the same conclusion on her own. Maybe she's already made the decision for me.

"I need some time. I—I don't want to rush this."

No. I bite back the word, but she can't be serious. We can't keep dragging this out. "Ah, look, if we're coming to an end no matter what, let's just be done with it."

Her eyes widen. "What?"

Okay, maybe we're not on the same page. I glance past her toward the pink and red horizon. "It seems pretty clear we're incompatible."

"What makes you say that?"

My eyes dart back to hers.

She shakes her head. "Our favorite hiking trail is to Maxwell Falls. Last summer, we went for bike rides almost every night at sunset, and we had fun. I know you make lasagna when you've been thinking of your mom. You know exactly how to shut down *my* mom before she gets to me. We both enjoy listening to the sounds of crickets more than music . . . we both love dogs," she says, gesturing to Heartthrob. "I don't think it's a stretch to say we enjoy each other."

I sigh. "All of those things are nice, but—"

"You're the only person I've ever *been* with," she whispers, her cheeks turning pink.

I step back, wondering if that was a dig about Unmatched, but her expression suggests she is just listing facts. Still, I have to call it like I see it. "What if you don't actually *want* to be with anyone?"

Her face darkens from pink to red.

"Look, I'm not trying to make this all about sex . . ." I run my hand over my face. "It's just . . . if you take that out, what you described sounds like friendship. Not marriage."

She sits on that for a minute, taking the ball from the dog again. After securing it back in the launcher, she tosses it and turns to me. "I want to be with you. But, I don't know, for some reason . . . this is difficult for me."

Something in her voice makes me pause. "What's difficult?"

She doesn't speak. But with an unsteady hand, she reaches out to touch my cheek.

And my skin comes alive under her fingers. The ache, the desire, floods through my cells as soon as she makes contact. I want to lean in, grab her other hand, and pull her to me. This isn't fair—the intensity of my reaction stirred by the simple touch of her flesh.

Her face is solemn, but when I look into her eyes—the same ones I've stared into the last ten years—there's a glimmer of optimism. It's something about Lydia that has always confounded me, but that I also admire. Her ability to keep pushing when things seem impossibly hard.

"I'd just like to give us another try."

I open my mouth to say *yes*, I am here for all the trying she wants to do. Until I notice how awkwardly she's holding her arm out to touch me. How hard she seems to have to work to maintain this touch. My thoughts drag back to her striptease this morning. The one she clearly forced and neither of us enjoyed.

If it takes this much effort for her to *try*, will it be worth it? For either of us?

"Okay," I say, and before I can think too hard about it, "But let's set a limit—thirty days."

The tennis ball lands at her feet again, but she doesn't move to pick it up.

I wince at the look on her face, but I need to protect us both. "Lydia, if we try, and nothing's better in a month . . . I don't think it ever will be."

She bites her lip like she disagrees, then withdraws her hand from my cheek and nods. "You're right."

It's funny how you can almost feel the absence of someone's touch more than their presence.

I chuck the ball one last time for Heartthrob, and as he runs for it, I close my eyes. It's tempting to resign myself to just wait another month. There's a good chance she'll get busy at work and our relationship will fall by the wayside. Again. I could stick it out, take this time to get our accounts and stuff in order so the end is as smooth as possible.

But the fact that she *hasn't* already moved out, filed papers, even taken off her rings after what I did to her —to us—makes it harder to just give up. Maybe I owe her that much. At least if I do this, I can move on feeling like I tried everything.

I clip the leash back on Heartthrob's collar and we turn together back toward home, but Lydia stops suddenly in the middle of the sidewalk. "If we agree to thirty days, Anton, will you—" She stops, looking up at me with a flushed face. "Do you promise not to go back on that app?"

My throat tightens at the expression in her eyes. At the realization that, after everything that's happened this weekend, she actually thinks I would. "Of course," I murmur. "I promise. Never again."

CHAPTER TWENTY-FOUR

Her

"Lydia." Charlotte greets me, giving my hand a firm squeeze as I enter her office. She's a motherly middle-aged Asian American woman, graying hair cut into a short, no-nonsense bob, her lipstick always a bright shade of pink. Today, she wears one of her power suits in blue, but I notice slippers on her feet and her heels set to one side. Which is one of the things I love about her. "Thanks for coming in on short notice."

I sit in the chair across from her desk and silence my phone, stealing one more look at the screen before tucking it into my purse. I was supposed to meet up with Mark to go over the completed plumbing work in the new space, but we rescheduled for this afternoon. No one has called in sick at Ooh La Pooch *or* The Pooch Park, and Anton is busy at his own office. I almost have the headspace for this meeting.

"So, you said you received an actual contract?" I ask.

When we spoke initially last week, she was only fielding questions from someone interested in the Pooches. I'd almost forgotten the whole thing until my phone rang Tuesday and she told me a formal offer was coming in.

"Yep, I have everything here." She slides a packet of papers to me across the desk. "I know you said you're not interested in selling, but you should see what's on the table before we send a formal response."

Charlotte and I have known each other for years. I found her through the Small Business Administration, and she's had several businesses of her own. At times, she has acted as my mentor as much as she's handled legal questions, so I leaf through the packet out of deference to her more than interest. There are pages of terms, clauses, and legalese. I don't see the point in really reading any of it since I won't be signing. I know it's silly because these things happen all the time, but I'm actually a little offended that someone thinks they could run my Pooches better than me.

After a few minutes, Charlotte clears her throat and gestures to one of the sheets in front of me. "The amount they're offering is there, on the second page."

"Oh, thanks." I fumble with the paper she pointed to, scanning down the text, but as soon as I read the figure the blood drains from my face. "Th-this number here?"

"Yes." She says it with a sort of smile, watching my reaction.

My throat is bone dry, but somehow I swallow.

"I realize this may change how you feel, but there's no rush to decide. I've already told their attorney we need time to consider." Charlotte hesitates, then continues. "If you do choose to accept, Lydia, there are several things I'd want to negotiate. One of them is the price. We should ask for more than this, but I think they'll expect—"

"Wait, more than *this*?" I jab at the second page.

"For two successful businesses and another location on the way?" She nods. "I think if we approach this carefully we could get them closer to . . ." She jots a figure on a sticky note and hands it to me.

The ground feels like it's sinking out from under me, and I'm grateful to be sitting in a chair. It has been six years since I launched Ooh La Pooch, bathing and grooming my own dogs with just one other employee. The Pooch Park came shortly after that, and demand was so overwhelming I began planning the second location almost immediately. I hadn't really intended to become a serial entrepreneur, but there is such a market for high-end pet services in Denver, almost everything I've tried has been successful, and things just keep growing.

But the amount of money in front of me? It could change our lives.

"Charlotte, that—" I close my eyes, forcing air into my lungs. I keep thinking of the very first customer I had at Ooh La Pooch, a five-pound poodle named Coco, and how her sixty-dollar haircut six years ago could somehow turn into this many zeros.

I wonder what Anton will say. He's supported me every step of the way, working with me to develop my logos and branding at first, then helping out nights and weekends to build out and paint the first business space. He's always listened patiently when I've had employee problems and even occasionally helps with repairs like the water heater the other day. I can't imagine even considering this decision without talking it over with him. But then I think about the current state of our marriage, and my hands drop heavily in my lap. How can we discuss the future of my businesses when I don't even know if *we'll* have a future?

I sit a minute, breathing in the cool air of Charlotte's office.

Eventually, she clears her throat, and I refocus, searching the papers on the desk until my gaze lands on the buyer's name: *ABizCorp, LLC.* I furrow my brow. Business names can sometimes be vague, but that sounds like an obvious shell company. Selling out to an eager wannabe business owner would be one thing, but I'm not about to hand over my blood, sweat, and tears from the last six years to some empty passive investment firm. "Do you know anything about who this is?"

She shakes her head. "Not yet, but I'll find out. So far, I've only heard directly from their attorney, but now that they're serious, I can dig for more."

"Okay, yeah." I pull at a loose thread on my sleeve. "I mean, I'd want to know who I'd be selling to—*if* I sell." I shake my head, still trying to grasp the concept of that much money. "I'm not sure what I would even do with myself if I sold."

"With that amount of cash? I'd go to the beach first!" Charlotte cackles. "But seriously, Lydia, you're a clever, successful woman. You could always start something new."

"I guess . . ." My voice trails off as I think of walking away from my little office and all my routines. The supply orders and repairs. My employees. My favorite dogs. Would Tomás and Scarlet and everyone else be upset, or would they understand? "I—I need to think it over for sure."

"No one expects you to make a decision right now," she says. "But we'll need to keep them interested. I already have a list of questions for their attorney. Why don't you go talk this over with that handsome husband of yours over the weekend and see how you feel?"

I force a smile when she says this, only because I knew it was coming. Charlotte's single, in her midfifties, and has always made eyes over Anton. He *does* look like he belongs on the cover of some fitness magazine. And I've seen more than a few lust-filled gazes turn sour when I've taken his arm and his admirers registered me. I spin my wedding rings on my finger, wondering if I'll look at him with longing too someday, walking by at some other woman's side.

"Yeah. Um, if you can buy a little time, that would be great. I think we would like to mull this over together."

"Of course," Charlotte says. She leans forward and meets my eyes. "No matter what you decide, this is a big deal. It's a life-changing amount of money that you're either going to accept or turn down. Take all the time you need."

I nod, thanking her as I exit the office, wondering vaguely what Anton and I would even do with all that cash. Would it make us happier? We could buy a bigger house, nicer cars. Maybe we would go to the beach, or the hot springs like he wanted. Or would something this big simply drag things out between us longer? Becoming more to divide and distribute if we still end in divorce?

My brain is in a fog by the time I stumble in the front door at home. I made mistakes on two dog food orders this afternoon and inadvertently made one of my daycare workers cry. On top of that, Scarlet's back injury flared up, and she had to leave work early. Then one of her clients yelled at me that their dog's haircut was lopsided. At this point I want nothing more than to snuggle up with Anton on the couch and watch a movie like we used to. Just turn my brain off and be comforted by his presence. Or maybe we should discuss the business purchase offer

I've been sitting on since this morning. Except every time I entertain the idea of taking the cash and walking away, giving these problems to someone else, I start to cry.

As I close the door, I'm lured by the scents of simmering garlic, tomato, and onions wafting from the kitchen. I find Anton at the stove listening to something on his headphones.

"Smells delicious," I say. I hadn't expected him to be home at all. He's stayed late at the gym the past couple of evenings, which has been sort of a relief, but here he is making dinner in our kitchen with Heartthrob parked at his heels.

"I was getting sick of takeout," he says, sliding the headphones off one ear.

"Lasagna?" I ask. It's been a while since he prepared his mother's recipe. I study his face for signs that something's changed with Sharon, but the tension in his eyes and across his forehead is unchanged.

He nods in reply.

"Well, my whole day just improved." I smile at him, and he smiles back, but he keeps layering pasta in the pan, clearly distracted by the task and whatever he's listening to. I watch him slide the dish into the oven, then glance at the clock. "Guess I'll take a quick shower if it has to bake."

It's a little warm for my striped pajamas after I towel off, so I go with a camisole and sleep shorts, wrapping up in my fuzzy pink robe for extra comfort. Anton glances at me when I walk into the dining room, and I'm truly relieved when his eyes don't linger anywhere.

"This looks amazing. Thanks for cooking." I grab some plates and glasses and take a deep breath, hoping for simple conversation.

At that moment, my phone rings on the kitchen counter. Great. I reach for it reflexively, sure it's some new fire I need to put out—a bout of kennel cough, maybe bickering employees—until I notice Anton following my movement. He's watching without comment, but there's a familiar wariness in his posture as I grasp the phone. I hesitate. Both my businesses are closed. Maybe whatever this is can wait until tomorrow. I turn the ringer to silent and leave it sitting on the counter.

"Umm, how was your day?" I ask, settling into a chair.

He arches an eyebrow, then takes a bowl of steaming broccoli off the counter and sits too. "Okay. How about yours?"

I'd been hoping he'd share just a *tiny* bit before turning it around on me. It's not like Anton's usually a chatterbox, but our conversation has been especially spare the last few days since we started this dance around the new elephant in the room.

He serves me a square of lasagna, and I try to think of something else to say. I really want to tell him about the meeting with Charlotte, get his opinion on all the pros and cons of selling or *not* selling the Pooches. And all that money. But I'm getting the vibe this isn't the time to talk about work.

"Did I tell you Celia had her baby? A boy. Last week."

He pauses, hovering his fork over his plate. Something passes through his eyes, but isn't there long enough for me to read. "Right. Tell her congratulations. She and Adam must be happy."

I clear my throat. "They named him Gabriel Edward Cohen. After both grandfathers."

His eyes widen. Anton's known my mom and sister long enough that I'm sure he's as surprised to hear this as I was.

"Anyway, I think my mom might be more excited about her new status as a grandma than she is about the kid," I mutter.

His eyes flicker to mine. It's a small thing, but with this show of sympathy, it's clear he's already guessed my feelings about that situation, and I'm grateful for it.

"Is Marion behaving herself?" he asks carefully.

I shrug. "Honestly, I've been avoiding her."

"Good," he says with a hint of pride. "I'm glad you're protecting yourself from her garbage."

"Poor Celia is probably getting the brunt of it." I roll my eyes. "Though Mom made it clear we're next on her grandchild-delivery list."

The words pass my lips before I think them through, and just like that, I've drawn attention to the elephant again. Anton's been wanting to start a family for a while now. Really, since around the time his mom got sick. But present circumstances have left all of that up in the air.

We both focus on our plates, mechanically making the food disappear. I wish I could walk the conversation back a few minutes. "Um, have you spoken to Seth? Is your mom still doing better?" I ask.

Anton pauses, his expression darkening. "Ah, yeah. The new place is better, but . . ." He sighs. "The doctors think she's been having, like, mini-strokes."

I set my fork down and study him. "What does that mean?"

A line cuts across his forehead. "Nothing, really. It's just part of the progression."

I reach out, placing my hand over his, and my skin tingles where we touch. He gives me a sharp look, and I think he's going to snatch his hand away, but his jaw—no, his whole body—stiffens, and he remains as he is.

"I'm sorry," I whisper.

I sit there, wondering if I ought to lean in, offer him a hug or something more than a pat on the hand. His comment about our marriage being more of a *friendship* still haunts me. But I hesitate too long.

He exhales and stands. "Are you done with your plate?"

"Um, yes." I jump up. "I've got the dishes. This was delicious, Anton, thank you. We should really cook more often."

I take the plates out of his hands, washing up the mess in the kitchen while he takes Heartthrob out in the yard and throws a rope toy for him. I take extra time scrubbing all the pots and pans and loading the dishwasher. Once I've wiped down all the counters, the stove, and even the cabinets, I realize it's gotten dark out and my husband and dog are still outside.

There's a window in the kitchen that looks out onto the patio in our postage-stamp backyard. I catch the glow of Anton's phone out there at our little table, and my gut twists. When we agreed to thirty days, he promised not to go back on Unmatched. But we've been spinning our wheels for three days. Would he actually return to it this soon, and practically right in front of me? I peer out the window, squinting through the dark. His back is to me, and I can just make out the screen over his shoulder. My breath pauses as I watch him scroll.

He's reading some kind of article. Not browsing for girls.

I exhale and head to our bedroom. It is the strangest, most uncomfortable feeling, sharing space with someone you care deeply about when it feels like there's some sort of wall between you. Since our conversation in the park, we have gone to bed, woken up, been to work, and returned home three times. The needle hasn't budged on our relationship at all. I look into the mirror above our dresser and frown. Caprice suggested I try to find what *used to work*, but I'm still not sure what that is.

I hear Anton and Heartthrob come inside. The dog runs to greet me, but my husband stops in the bathroom. I glance at the bed, a familiar knot forming in my stomach over what will or won't happen there. I toss my robe on the chair and quickly slip under the covers to at least prepare myself before he comes in. Anton follows a few minutes later, and maybe he thinks I'm already asleep, because he doesn't say anything. I relax at this possibility, which is quickly followed by a flood of guilt. We *agreed* we'd work on our sex life. So why do I just want to roll over and go to sleep?

Anton's as far to his side of the bed as he can probably be without falling off, but he's awake, still looking at his phone. I shift around, adjust my pillow, try to broadcast my consciousness. I suppose I could just sit up and suggest we have sex, but I don't want it to seem forced. On impulse, I reach up and push the straps of my camisole over my shoulders, slipping my arms out and pulling the fabric down. Exposing my breasts under the covers but not leaving me totally nude. Now if Anton reaches over, he'll find a surprise. I smile to myself, clear my throat loudly, and lie still. Waiting, staring up at the ceiling in the dark.

Minutes go by. He doesn't speak. He doesn't move.

But I'm ready.

His phone clicks locked after a little while, and the room goes fully dark. The bed shifts as he moves around, and I tense up, sure that his tits-radar or whatever will tell him I'm over here half naked. Or maybe he'll at least brush against me and put it together. Instead, he just burrows down into the covers without coming any closer.

I bite my lip. Maybe he's not in the mood.

If he was, wouldn't he reach for me? I push the straps back up and roll over too, trying to get comfortable on the pillow. Maybe I can just sleep tonight after all and we'll work on things later. Tomorrow. I close my eyes and try to relax, listening to our mingled breathing. But after a while, to my utter chagrin, I realize I wish he *had* found my surprise. Had wanted to come searching for it. I actually, almost, sort of wanted him to.

A little pang shoots through my chest.

I am definitely doing something wrong.

CHAPTER TWENTY-FIVE

Him

Jessica: Welcome to the *Come And Get Her* podcast. We're your hosts, Jessica and Isabella, two licensed sex therapists here to educate men on how to get ladies *off*. We've got a fabulous show for you this week—Demi Lane visits us again to give us the latest on all her new favorite couples' toys—but first we'll get started with a selection from our mailbag.

Isabella: I'm excited about the mail this week, Jessica! Very often we hear from younger men looking for tips to land themselves a second or third date. But this letter is from an older gentleman and I love what he is asking. Let me read it to you:

Dear Jess & Izzy,

My wife and I have been married for twenty-five years [aww!]. We've been through a lot together, raised a couple of kids, and our sex life, while not amazing, has always at least been pretty steady. Lately, however, it seems like she's lost interest in me. I've tried giving her space, coming on to her, buying her gifts. Nothing has worked. Every time I try to initiate, I get excuses. She's tired. Too busy. Maybe tomorrow. I'm not sure what else to do. I don't think she's seeing anyone else, but I'm not sure how to rekindle the spark. Do you have any advice?

Sincerely,

Cold Embers

Jessica: Oh, Embers. First of all, I just want to acknowledge your courage in writing this email. You must be feeling so alone, but you've reached out for help—and that's what we're going to try to do.

Isabella: Jess, I have a feeling this one is about the big D.

Jessica: For sure. I had the same thought.

Isabella: Okay, so men—listen up, all of you, for a second. Yes, even you guys who are doing everything great and getting laid every night. Congratulations! We're glad you've been following our advice.

Jessica: Now, boys, here's the great big caveat to everything we tell you: People change. Bodies change. Relationships change. And the really big one . . . so does *desire.*

Isabella: I could literally spend a whole episode on that word.

Jessica: Right? [laughs] Okay, so I think most of us here are familiar with the cliché about wives not enjoying sex.

Isabella: Um, let it be noted in the transcript how hard I'm rolling my eyes—this is half the reason our show exists.

Jessica: Absolutely. Okay, obviously, many of our regular listeners know at least ten ways to get a girl off in ten minutes or less—

Isabella: We have *failed* if you don't.

Jessica: But let me tell you something important—you can be a master of the entire fucking *Kama Sutra*, hold the title of G-Spot King, but it will get you *nowhere* if you don't first understand desire . . .

I TAKE OFF MY HEADPHONES AT THE END OF MY RUN, stopping to do some stretching on our front porch. It's the pattern I've been following all week—listening to the podcast while I jog, or at the gym after work. I stumbled on Jess and Izzy purely by accident after Lydia and I awkwardly agreed to give our relationship thirty more days and it felt like a clock immediately started ticking.

I never expected to find a whole beautifully produced podcast explaining all the subtleties of how to touch a woman, how to turn her on, how to get her aroused and bring her to climax. Granted, I haven't had the opportunity to *try* any of it yet, but I feel like I've learned so much—about blood flow, erogenous zones, nipple stimulation, clitoral orgasm vs. penetration—things I have to admit I had been pretty clueless about. I wouldn't say I had no idea what I've been doing the last ten years, but I feel like I have the chance to do so much *better* now.

If I can just work myself up to approach Lydia.

But every night, she's stayed firmly over on her side of the bed, and I've been hesitant to stray from mine. And every time I think about leaning in for a goodnight kiss or even just a hug, I second-guess why *she* hasn't—she's the one who pushed to keep trying, who insisted she wanted to be with me.

Did she change her mind?

Her Toyota pulls into the driveway just as I open the door to head inside. We wave at each other, and I wait as she parks and lets Heartthrob out of the back seat. He zooms across the yard, and I greet him with his favorite squeaky octopus.

"Hi," I say as Lydia follows him inside, and when she smiles in response, I am *sure* this is the moment—I could kiss her cheek, maybe even pull her into an embrace.

But I hesitate too long.

"I picked up stuff for nachos," she says, carrying a grocery bag into the kitchen. "But I think I'll jump in the shower first—avoid dog hair in the cheese."

I nod. The black shirt she's wearing is plastered with white hair, but while her face is tired, she doesn't avoid my eyes. "Sounds good," I say, taking the bag as Heartthrob spins in front of me. "I'll feed this guy and start the oven."

Lydia gives me another smile, plugs her phone into the charger on the counter, and disappears.

I mix up food for the dog, then start searching for something to make nachos in. Down the hall, I hear the bathroom door close and the water come on, and because everything feels desperate, I immediately picture Lydia in there naked. This is torture. Maybe I should just take the plunge tonight with some of Jess and Izzy's tips. But is it worth the risk?

I locate the pan I'm looking for and set it on the counter next to Lydia's phone, only just as I do, a notification lights up her screen.

Caprice_Phipps@DenverEditorial.com

FWD: Till Unmatched Do Us Part—Six Married Denver Men, Busted

Hey Lyd, thanks again for your help on the article. It's live now on the site. See below . . .

My skin goes cold. I step back, nearly falling over a chair as I pull my own phone from my pocket. I hadn't really considered *how* Lydia found my Unmatched profile—the fact that she had was such a nightmare, it didn't seem important. But of course Caprice was the one doing the digging. She's a freaking reporter. Was all that stuff Lydia said about *giving it another try* just to string me along until they could shame me publicly?

I punch in the web address for *Denver Editorial*, and seconds later, I'm staring at the headline right on the main page. My thumb hovers over the screen. But I'm not sure I'm ready to read this. Watch myself get dragged through the mud in front of my boss, coworkers, Lydia's family, our friends and neighbors, the entire city. Down the hall, the water shuts off in the bathroom, and my heart begins to race. I forward the article to my brother and shove the phone back into my pocket. I can suffer the details with Seth later. Right now, I just want to be gone.

I close myself in our bedroom, grab my duffle from under the bed, and start emptying drawers. Underwear, socks, then workout clothes. I don't pay much attention.

The bag is nearly full when I hear a light tap on the door. "Anton?"

I grunt, moving to the closet when I remember I need work clothes.

"Hey, um, are you decent?" she calls. Because God forbid she walk in on her own husband naked, I guess.

I'm exiting our closet with a pile of pants and shirts as she turns the knob and peeks in.

"Oh, hey—" She stops abruptly in the doorway, watching me lay clothes into a garment bag. "What are you doing?"

I zip too many things inside, then grab a pair of shoes. "What I should've done two weeks ago."

Her figure fills the narrow doorway, and even now, my eyes can't help tracing along the edge of the towel she clutches around her body, still dripping from the shower. She frowns, peering at my face. "Did something happen?"

"Why don't you go ask one of the neighbors? Or my boss?" My lip curls. "Maybe they've had a chance to read the news."

"News?" Her brows draw together, her gaze drifting toward the kitchen where she left her phone.

I duck into the second bedroom as she steps away. I'll need my laptop and chargers, but I can come back later for books and furniture. Unless the gloves are completely off now and she decides to dump them on the curb. Heartthrob follows behind me, squeaking his stuffed octopus, unaware of the domestic upheaval. I throw the toy for him as I head for the front door, trying not to think about leaving him behind.

But as I dig my keys out of my pocket, my phone chimes with a message from my brother.

SETH

Yikes, freaking ugly. Lucky you dodged that bullet.

What is that supposed to mean? *Denver Editorial* is a relatively young but respected local news source. By tomorrow the story will disperse to even more major outlets.

Failing to see the luck.

SETH

Did you READ the article, asshole?

I pause, glancing around for Lydia, an uncomfortable feeling creeping into my gut when I don't see or hear her anywhere. I swipe back to the feature, forcing myself to absorb the text on the screen.

Caprice's words are scathing.

As the headline suggests, she tears into six Denver men, although she doesn't actually name any of them—she doesn't have to. From her descriptions, it's pretty easy to figure out at least two of them are well-known politicians, and one sounds a lot like a popular radio personality from a local station. Caprice is an excellent writer, giving just the right amount of detail to paint a clear picture of each guy, so I'm sure the others can be identified by anyone close to them. One is some sort of professional athlete. One is a chef. Another's a banker in his midfifties. All of them are married with families.

But not a single one of them sounds even remotely like me.

I let out a long, whispering breath, my heartbeat quieting enough that I can tune back in to the sounds of the house. Is Lydia still here? Or did I turn my *jackass* up so high she left?

I retrace my steps to the kitchen and find her hunched in a chair, focused blank-faced on her phone screen.

I clear my throat. "I um . . . I owe you an apology."

She raises her head and looks at me.

"Another one," I add in a shaky voice.

She sits back, folding her arms across her chest.

"I saw Caprice's email about the article, and I thought—"

Our eyes meet, and the words dry up in my throat.

"Lydia—I'm so sorry."

The echo of my apology settles between us in the silence, and I slump against the doorframe, hoping she'll understand—I'm not just saying sorry for tonight. I'm sorry for being on Unmatched at all, for going to the hotel, for not being more patient or trying harder. I'm sorry for every way I've betrayed her trust. *Including* tonight.

Her eyes traverse my face, then she glances back at her phone. "I'm not in a big hurry for people to know what you did. It was bad enough dealing with it privately."

I swallow hard, wiping one hand over my face. Of course. Caprice wouldn't have publicly tied me to a social scandal. Anything she wrote about me would directly impact Lydia and the Pooches. If Lydia had wanted, I guess she could have given permission—let Caprice rake me over the coals for revenge. Instead they both protected me. But my head was so far up my own ass, I couldn't think of anyone but myself.

Which is how we got here in the first place.

Lydia stands. She's wearing her robe now, a towel wrapped around her head, posture clearly exhausted. Despite that, or maybe even because of it, I find myself wanting to pull her to me, let her hair down so I can run my fingers through it and down over her hips. Needy for the comfort of her warmth, her skin. I think of Jess and Izzy's podcast and bite the inside of my cheek, realizing I might have blown my chance to try any of those new ways to touch her, bring her pleasure, draw us back together.

But if this was the last straw, if she asks me to leave, I'll respect that. She clearly deserves better.

With a sigh, she gestures at the packed duffle bag still gripped in my hand. "So, now that we've established that *I* didn't betray *you* . . ." She pauses just long enough for that to really sting. "Are you coming or going?"

I furrow my brow, studying her face carefully.

"It's Tuesday. I'm keeping track. We've still got what, three more weeks?"

My mind spins in a circle before I realize what she means. "We, ah . . ." I take a deep breath. "You mean you're still willing?"

She shrugs. I can tell it's forced by the set of her shoulders, but she looks back and says, "Thirty days. We agreed."

A lump rises in my throat. I am the last person who deserves a second, let alone a third or fourth chance. But I'll take every bone she throws. "Okay. Yeah."

Her stomach lets out a plaintive growl, and she covers it with one hand. "I did um . . . burn the nachos last time I tried to make them . . ."

The corners of my mouth rise at the memory. Last winter, on one of the coldest days of the year, we'd had to open every window in the house to get the smoke detectors to stop beeping. Lydia is great with dogs, but she's never really honed her cooking skills.

"I've got it." I set my duffle on the bed. "Let me just unpack."

CHAPTER TWENTY-SIX

Her

"ARE YOU SURE YOU WANT TO RUN THE ENTIRE LOOP?" Caprice asks. "We could split it up, do a little walking and jogging?"

"Nah, if you normally run the whole thing, I'm here for it," I say, gazing down the gravel path through the trees on the north end of Wash Park. I can't remember the last time I actually went running, but after her phone call this morning, I couldn't turn her down. "Have there been any other messages?"

"Just the one so far," she says, glancing over her shoulder. "Thanks for keeping me company."

"Of course." I tuck my phone away, and we take off. Probably at a slower jog than she'd prefer since *I* am not ninety percent legs, but I keep pace. "I'm not going to let some jerk take the shine off your success. Last I checked, there were a thousand comments on the article! Seems like you hit a nerve."

"It's up to five thousand," she says under her breath. "Got picked up for syndication, and now *Bustle* and the *New York Post* want me to write follow-ups focused on cheaters in other cities."

"Caprice!" I turn my jog into a run-skip and nearly fall on my grinning face. "What's it like to hit the big time?"

"On the backs of hundreds of destroyed marriages?" She huffs. "It feels great. I particularly love the personal attacks and death threats."

I nearly stumble to a halt. "You said there was only one."

"Technically, only one actually threatened to kill me," she says, slowing beside me. "There are a handful that promised other unpleasant things."

I'm not even sure what to say. Anton's reaction to her article was intense, and I know too well how torn apart some of the affected families must feel. But no one who "dated" on Unmatched has any right to direct their anger at Caprice. If those people's lives are ruined, they only have themselves to blame.

"You should call the police."

"It's just part of journalism." She gives a passing jogger a wary glance and picks up speed. "It'll blow over soon."

I push forward, a stitch forming in my side as I try to keep up with her past the fire station and fishing pond.

"Do you want to come stay with us or something?"

She looks at me and snorts. "That's some in-depth coverage. Staying in the house of a relationship I ruined."

My face heats. "I—I wouldn't call us ruined," I say thickly, but she goes on like she didn't hear.

"My building is super secure; no one's going to mess with me if I'm at work or at the gym. But thanks for coming with me today. I was starting to go stir-crazy only running on a treadmill."

"Sure. But I still think you ought to—"

"I'll be fine." She says this with confidence, though her voice wavers at the end. "Anyway, what's the latest on you and Anton?"

I press my lips together, listening to the crunch of our feet on the path. It feels like ages since the hotel, since my failed striptease. And our agreement to give things "another try." But that was ten days ago, and I can tell you exactly how much "trying" has happened since.

Part of it's on me. I was filling in for Scarlet at Ooh La Pooch and had forgotten how head-to-toe exhausting grooming every day can be, crawling into bed each night and passing out immediately. But I *was* considering how to approach my husband . . . until I got my period. Nothing like cramps and heavy bleeding to kill a mood before it happens. I told myself I'd make twice the effort as soon as I felt normal again. But the bleeding ended two days ago, and I haven't exactly jumped naked into Anton's lap.

He hasn't made any gestures either, which somehow makes me feel worse. Like he's already given up. But if he was really done, why bother laying down the thirty-day deadline?

Twenty, I remind myself. We're already down to twenty days.

"We've made zero progress," I breathe, the stitch in my side intensifying, slowing me to a walk. "We agreed to try and fix things for thirty days, but it's already been ten. Also . . ." I trail off. I was going to tell Caprice about the purchase offer, about the huge business decision I have to make, but suddenly it doesn't feel right. That's a conversation I need to have with Anton first. "It's just a lot."

"When you say you've made zero progress, what have you tried?" Caprice asks, jogging circles around me to make up for my slow pace.

"I mean, I told you about my awful striptease," I say, jumping out of the way of a mom pushing a jogging stroller.

"Right," she says matter-of-factly, "but what else? Did you use some new toys? Watch some porn? I'm just trying to get a sense of what hasn't worked."

I glance at her out of the corner of my eye, unable to even respond to that.

"Hey, I promise I won't write about it." Her tone is light, but she waits for a real answer.

I put in a burst of speed. "I haven't . . . actually . . . tried anything else."

"Like, nothing new?" she asks, keeping up easily. "Maybe that's the issue. You guys need to spice things up."

"No—" I pant. "I mean—we haven't tried at all."

This time it's Caprice who comes to a halt. And for a second, I'm tempted to continue my sprint down the trail, away from this conversation. But when I think of leaving her by herself in the park with her five thousand internet comments, I slow and circle back around.

"Lydia," Caprice says, stepping off the jogging path. "When was the last time you and Anton had sex?"

My hands fall to my sides as I join her, and I close my eyes. I know we've done it at least once or twice since New Year's. There was that time he got handsy after the movie. But was that the last time? "It . . . it might've been six or eight weeks ago? I can't remember."

"But that means you haven't at all since you guys—"

"I told you, it's hard for us to get started." As soon as I say this, I realize it's not actually true. "I mean, *he* doesn't have any issue, but . . ."

My voice trails off. She already knows all the very worst about me and the state of my marriage. Still, I can't bring myself to say this out loud.

"Lots of ladies need something to get their engines going—that's totally normal," she says gently. A group of joggers passes by, and I feel like every intimate detail we're discussing is written on my face. Caprice pulls me farther from the busy path into the shade of a large tree. "Okay, I think I know what you need."

"What's that?" I say on autopilot, both dreading what she'll say and ready for an easy answer to all my problems.

"Accessories. Something to help you get in the mood."

I scrunch my nose. "Like what?"

"Well, I mean, that's up to you. Maybe a nice negligee, or a game, or a good vibrator—you just have to figure out what works."

My eyes widen, my whole body flushing bright red, particularly at that last suggestion. "Okay, thanks. I'll give that some thought." I turn back toward the jogging path.

"Do you want me to go with you?" she asks.

"Go where?"

"Lydia, your daycare is like, five minutes from Playful Pleasures."

"The *sex* shop?" I can't help it; my voice is totally shrill.

"Yeah. You need to go shopping."

I try to imagine pulling into the parking lot of the two-story *sensual superstore*, let alone walking through the doors. I've driven by it every single day for years, but it has never crossed my mind to actually go in. "Caprice, that's just not a place I would ever—"

"Exactly," she says. "Do you want me to come with you?"

"I—" My words catch in my throat. "*No.*"

She frowns. "Okay, that's cool. I get it. It might be better if you went by yourself. I have a friend who works there, Daphne. She can hook you up."

"You don't understand . . ." My skin breaks into a light sweat.

"I think I do." I can tell she's smiling behind me, but I'm definitely not.

I wrap my arm around my waist, finally landing on what feels like the right words. But when I turn to look at her, they come out too loud and too fast. "Caprice, I don't want to buy sex toys!"

She pauses for a long moment. "Why not?"

"I don't think I need—" I stop, uncomfortable even trying to explain my discomfort. This is not the Victorian era. I should feel like a modern, empowered woman going into a store like that. If I could shut up the little voice in my brain whispering that it's *dirty*. "What if someone saw me?"

"Oh my God, Lydia, you're not buying drugs."

"I don't want to buy anything. I—I just don't want my husband to leave me!"

Neither of us says anything for what feels like several minutes.

When Caprice finally speaks again, her tone is gentler. "I'm sorry . . . you're right. Everyone has different comfort levels. I shouldn't have assumed. It's okay if vibrators aren't your thing."

"Thanks." I exhale, even as I second-guess myself. Again. What if she's right? The thought of buying *sex merchandise* makes me shudder, but what if that's what's missing? Could "accessories" make Anton want to stay with me?

"It's none of my business what you and Anton do," she goes on, leading us back to the jogging path. "Just ignore me—I've already meddled too much in your marriage."

"No, it's okay. I do appreciate your advice," I say quietly, falling again into a slow pace beside her.

She looks at me with a sad smile. "I'm sorry you're going through this."

I focus on the trail ahead of us, trying not to think about the dwindling number of days left on the calendar. "Me too."

"Maybe . . ." She pauses. "Do you think you might be focusing too much on Anton? I was thinking about what you said before, how you thought there was something wrong with you. Maybe the important thing right now is to figure out what *you* need?"

I draw my brows together, watching the sun sink in the sky over Grasmere Lake. "Maybe."

Slowly, we make our way to where the path curves around the southeast corner of the park. "I feel a lot better having you here with me," she says quietly.

Her posture is stiff in a way I hadn't noticed earlier. We pass a couple of guys whose gazes linger on her legs—the kind of attention Caprice would normally invite, and even flaunt. Instead, discomfort flickers over her face, and I wonder how much she's downplayed her situation. "Any of those online assholes wants to mess with you needs to get past me first," I say. "I've got pepper spray."

"Thanks." She laughs a little.

A woman runs past with a gorgeous Doberman pinscher, and I smile. "You could get a dog for protection?"

Caprice rolls her head to look at me, and her expression is so incredulous, we both laugh for real. But as we curve toward the sunset, I reach out and squeeze her hand.

"I'm glad you wrote the article. If you hadn't found out about Anton . . . I don't know. I'm just glad you did."

CHAPTER TWENTY-SEVEN

Her

I DRIVE THREE TIMES AROUND THE BLOCK BEFORE PULLING into the parking lot and steering my Toyota under a tree, as if it might disguise my presence. This is closer than I've made it to walking in the door of Playful Pleasures in two days, though I'm not sure whether I should be proud of that or embarrassed. My conversation with Caprice has been haunting me.

When was the last time you and Anton had sex?

You need something to help you get in the mood.

I glance at the unassuming white storefront, one hundred percent certain Anton and I *need* some kind of help, but also skeptical I'm going to find it at this store. I sort of love imagining what my mother would think if she knew I was here. But I'm also a little terrified of finding something Anton might like. I bet they have all kinds of whips and blow-up dolls and whatever else he's into.

But as I squirm in my seat, I wonder. *Is* that the sort of stuff he likes?

I'd like to slide my dick between those tits and come all over them.

My wife won't ever let me do that.

I meet my own eyes in the rearview mirror, my face on fire as I recall the rest of the conversation about how he didn't want to spank me. But *how about butt play?*

My stomach clenches. I curl my hands into determined fists in my lap. There's no chance in hell I'm letting him do *anything* to my butt. But I'll be damned if he's going to try those things on someone else.

I open my car door. It's probably fine just to look around.

The facade of the building looks a little like a strip club. Two stories of nondescript brick and stucco and all the windows are glass block. There actually *is* a strip club a block away, but also a Super Target. Gotta love this area of the city. I watch a few people enter and exit, convinced I'll be shopping with the most lecherous patrons in town. But all I see is a normal-looking white guy in a plaid shirt, then a couple of college-aged girls. None of them seem suspicious or strange. They all look like they could just as easily be at the mall.

A man and woman head out the front doors together. They're smiling at each other, holding hands. She seems excited about whatever she's holding in a black plastic shopping bag and stops to kiss him right there in the parking lot. The kiss is deep and goes on way longer than necessary, until I start to feel awkward watching. Anton and I don't kiss like that—not anymore. I know we did once. Maybe these two are newlyweds. I'm sure they'll settle down in a few years, just like us. The kiss finally ends, and they break apart, letting go of each other long enough to climb into their car. It's clear no matter what they bought, they're going to be busy tonight.

Maybe this is stupid. Nothing sold inside this store is going to magically save my marriage. But I've gotten nowhere on my own the past two weeks. Maybe Caprice is right and I need some help. Anton clearly wants something more physical, but I don't know how to give it to him.

I adjust my sunglasses and check my phone as I approach the entrance, trying extra hard to look casual. Like I'm just running in for a specific something because I've been here a million times and I'm not at all intimidated by whatever lies inside.

The door beeps loudly when I walk in, and that's almost enough to make me turn right around and run for my car. I take a quick look at my surroundings. I'm not sure what I was expecting—dark, seedy corners and used condoms on the floor? The place is super clean and brightly lit, very much like a mall. Two girls are working behind a counter, there are several display areas, and a set of stairs leading up to a second floor. A few other patrons are wandering around, but it's far from crowded.

I veer off to one side, trying to look casual by a *Fifty Shades*-themed display. There are blindfolds, riding crops, and handcuffs. I examine a ball wrapped with adjustable leather straps, wondering if it's some kind of fashion accessory until I glance at the tag and realize it's a gag. My eyes widen. Would my husband want to use *this*?

A man strolls past me and I step away from the display, not wanting to give the impression that *I'm* into whips and chains. I glance around the store, trying to decide whether to just grab a bunch of leather or zero in on a sale section full of leftovers from Valentine's Day, but then I turn and find myself face-to-face with one of the female employees. She's a white girl with these Bettie Page bangs, a septum nose ring, and some elaborate cat-eye makeup. She also has an incredibly warm smile.

"Hello. Did you need help finding anything?" she asks.

"I . . . no. I'm just . . . browsing." My face is so hot, I think my head might burst into flames. This was a bad idea. If she'd just step aside, I could run out of here, but she's directly between me and the door.

"We have a nice selection of couples' toys," she says, eyeing the rings on my finger. "Do you know what you're interested in, or would you like me to show you some things?"

"I . . . I don't know," I sputter. "Can you just point me toward stuff that most men like?"

I'll buy anything she puts in my hand. As long as it gets me out of here fast.

She taps her lip, and I notice a tattoo of a cat curled on her shoulder. She lowers her voice. "Can I ask a few questions?"

I glance around. The only other patron is the guy I nearly ran into by *Fifty Shades,* but he's on the other side of the store now. "Questions?"

She smiles. Her name tag says Daphne, and I try to remember if this is the girl Caprice said she knew. "What kinds of toys do you already have at home?"

I almost say "dog toys." I have to suppress a burst of nervous laughter, taking a breath and digging my nails into my palms until I can get back under control. "Um . . . we don't really have much."

"Like, just one or two basics?"

I stare at the chunky Mary Janes on her feet, trying not to feel stupid. "Like none."

"Oh, got it." She straightens, but her voice doesn't falter. "Okay, come with me."

She leads me up the stairs, past a display of exotic-looking nightwear, over to a wide table decorated with a variety of items in colorful shapes.

I come to a halt. "Are those—"

"Have you ever used a vibrator?" she asks.

"Well, I mean . . ."

That would be a firm *no.* God, just a second ago I was almost too embarrassed to walk into this store. And now I'm mortified to admit to someone who works with sex toys all day long that I've never so much as touched one. Caprice and several of my other friends have vibrators aplenty—I know because they come up in conversation like toothbrushes and TV remotes—but each of them has also spent long stretches of time single. I have nothing against this kind of "accessory," I'm sure they work great. I just always thought they were more for people flying solo.

"Are you able to achieve vaginal orgasms?" Daphne asks.

"I'm sorry?" I nearly choke answering her blunt question.

She had been reaching for a rubbery purple thing right in front of us, but pauses and withdraws her hand. "Forgive me, I didn't mean to assume. Let me back up. Are you able to achieve *any* orgasms?"

My eyes shift quickly around the room, resting on the table of bright phallic shapes, like I'm in some weird Freudian dream. My voice is nearly a whisper. "Um . . . yes."

"Perfect." She smiles. "Some women can't at all. Or don't know how to."

"It just—" I add before I can think too clearly. "It just takes a while sometimes."

Daphne thinks a moment, then selects a box from the display. "This is a basic rabbit. It should be a good place to start."

I take it from her reluctantly, studying the thing like a science specimen through the clear plastic window. I always imagined vibrators being flesh-colored and veiny, like disembodied plastic penises. This "rabbit" is hot pink and silky smooth. Long enough to fit . . . wherever you need to put it, I guess. But not freakishly large at all when I compare it to Anton in my mind.

"Here, this is a sample." She grabs an identical unboxed item off the table and places it in my other hand. With a flick of her manicured fingers, it starts to buzz in my palm. I hold it away from myself like it's going to shock me, and though she has been entirely professional this whole time, I swear Daphne stifles a laugh.

"It . . . um . . . it really vibrates," I say, in a stunningly original observation.

"That's the idea, yes."

I want nothing more than to set it back down on the table, but it seems like she's waiting for me to ask questions or make some judgment about it. I turn it over a couple times until I find the off switch, and at last I exhale. I couldn't form coherent sentences with that bright pink rod buzzing away in my hand.

"What is this for?" I ask, pointing to a small extension shaped—unsurprisingly?—like rabbit ears sticking out on the side. "Does it go —" I stop midsentence, thinking about the possibilities and wishing I hadn't asked.

"That's for clitoral stimulation," she says, easing my fears, though we *are* standing in a room full of objects meant to go all manner of places. "Most women find it very effective."

I turn it over awkwardly, still gripping the new-in-box version in my other hand. It seems so bizarre that a vibrating piece of rubber would feel good inside my vagina. But now that I think about it . . . even *Anton* doesn't always feel great in there. The first several times we had sex in college, it just hurt. I think every girl expects losing the big V to be painful, but I hadn't been prepared for it to be that way the first three or four times. When I finally did orgasm, maybe five or six weeks later, it was only when I assisted with my own fingers—and it's never happened with him inside me. He has gotten me to climax with his tongue, but I've always felt weird about that, and all of these different approaches require a lot of time and concentration on my part. Last time I think he was down between my legs for close to an hour. I actually considered just yelling a bunch so we could both finally go to sleep.

Besides, getting *me* off isn't what I came in here for.

"This seems nice," I say, handing the "sample" back to her and looking around for some hand sanitizer. "But what I really want is something more for my husband."

"Oh, the rabbit should work for both of you."

I blanch, suddenly forced to consider whether his interest in "butt play" is not about *my* butt at all. "Wait, is he supposed to—"

"He can use it on *you*," she says. "Or he can just enjoy you using it."

My still-warm face ignites again. I bite my lip. That's something I hadn't really considered. On the whole, I've always felt Anton and I were pretty traditional. I spread my legs, he does his thing, then with some effort, I can sometimes come after he's done. But even though we do it together, it's always felt pretty individual. His turn, my turn. We've never climaxed in tandem like people do in movies—I doubt anyone does. And it's hard to imagine *my* orgasm doing anything for him. Why would it? It's just a lot of work to get me off. On the flip side, I have to admit, I've never really been excited to help him climax either, except to hurry up and get the whole thing over with.

I turn the box for the hot-pink rabbit over, wondering how he'd react if I walked into the house and handed it to him. Would he be excited? Or sneer at me the way he did the other morning? Even if he is willing to try, it's not like batteries and pink silicone are going to fix everything.

"Okay, I'll take it. But what else have you got?"

The salesgirl laughs. "How about a blindfold to go with it . . . and definitely some lube."

"Do you think that's enough?" I ask, following her back down the stairs.

She takes a black silk eye mask from the *Fifty Shades* display and grabs a large bottle of clear liquid from behind the counter, then turns to me with narrowed eyes. "Did you have something more specific in mind?"

"I don't know, I just think we might need something more . . . maybe for *him*?" I grimace, eyeing a male mannequin with a chain dangling from its nipples, holding some elaborate whip-looking thing.

"A vibrator, some lube, and a blindfold should give you both plenty to start with." She follows my gaze, then gently adds, "It's generally best to work your way up to the harder stuff."

I clasp my hands in front of me, face glowing like a fire truck. Honestly, I'm a little relieved she said that, but my marriage feels so tenuous right now. I'm afraid to screw up again.

"I just . . . I don't want him to be bored," I say in a low voice.

"Most guys are pretty easy to please. We're the difficult ones. In fact, it might not be a bad idea to practice a little on your own before you try this together."

She gives me a friendly wink, but I bite my lip in horror as I follow her to the register. I haven't touched myself *alone* since the day my mother walked in on me when I was thirteen. I squeeze my eyes shut, trying hard not to remember the appalled look on her face. How she'd made me shower immediately and told me to never do it again. The experience was so mortifying that I didn't let my fingers drift between my legs again until Anton and I were together. But it still feels too illicit to do without him.

Obviously, this woman was raised differently. She's casual about all of this in a way I can't imagine ever being. But *should* I feel differently? If this whole shopping trip turns out to be a failure and I wind up divorced in a few more weeks, maybe I'll want to join the vibrator club after all.

Daphne places her hand on my arm and holds up my purchases. "If you two have never used any of these things, I promise, there's no *way* he's going to get bored."

I watch her scan each item at the counter, thinking over what she said. Especially the part about who's more difficult.

"Thanks for your help." I mumble the words, but I mean them. I didn't realize how much guidance I needed when I walked in, but I'll be grateful if any of the things she picked out do something for Anton and me.

"That's what I'm here for." She smiles and hands me a card with her name. "Have fun, and when you're ready for the next steps, come see me again."

CHAPTER TWENTY-EIGHT

Him

I SHOVE MY FEET BACK INTO MY SHOES AND YANK MY SHIRT over my head with limp arms. I might have pushed a little hard on those last four sets. I lifted heavier and completed more reps than I've tried in several months. My arms and chest will definitely be talking to me tomorrow, but I can't deny I'm satisfied with the fatigued, clumsy feeling in my burned-out muscles. I drink about a gallon of water after I finish, but now my stomach is making noise, and in the back of my mind I host a debate between throwing some burgers on the grill at home or picking up Snarf's on the way there. I grab my bag off the bench and head for the locker room door, but just as I'm fumbling for my keys, I run into Henry on his way in.

"Anton, what's up?"

"Hey, man."

I haven't seen Henry since Carl and Eva's house, at least a million years ago. Before the hotel, before I ruined everything. He stops in the door like he wants to chat, but seeing him sends me back to that night—the decisions I made, the messages I sent—never realizing *Lydia* was the "other woman" the whole time. My appetite disappears, and I lose interest in exchanging pleasantries. I try to just wave and push past Henry toward the door, but he keeps talking.

"Sorry we didn't get a chance to catch up the other day."

I force myself to look at him, managing a shrug. "How's things with you and Annabelle?"

"Annabelle . . ." He flashes a wicked grin. "She was great. Ah, on the rebound, I think. But we had fun. I'm playing a round of golf with her dad tomorrow night."

I roll my eyes. If my brother is king of the anonymous hookup, Henry rules casual business acquaintance sex. The difference being he picks up women in his work sphere rather than bars, but the "relationships" last just as long. On some level I know he does it for the connections and influence, but it seems he also just enjoys himself. I set my jaw. What would that be like, having sex whenever you want, just for fun?

"How's business?" I ask, changing the subject. "You still doing the franchise thing?"

"Not anymore, actually." He leans against the wall just inside the locker room door. "Went out on my own. Bought up a little restaurant chain that was floundering, rebranded, and turned it around. That went so well I'm looking for my next big thing."

"Cool. Good for you." I'm not sure what else to say. I've barely held a conversation outside of work for the past two weeks, and my ability to form casual sentences, let alone pretend to care, is deteriorating.

"Listen, I owe you a big thanks for your advice. I can't believe I'm paying for *dog* daycare, but it has totally saved me from my sister's beast." He gives me a funny glance and scratches the back of his head. "How's Lydia's expansion going, by the way?"

It's a completely innocent question. Henry's known us both since college. He was at our wedding. He's in business. But because my wife has buried herself in work exactly the way I expected she would since we agreed to work on our sex life, her business is pretty much the last thing I want to talk about. "Going great."

"Listen, I wondered—"

He stops short when somebody pushes past us both to get in the locker room, and I seize the opportunity to escape. "I gotta run, Henry."

He looks reluctant, then nods, holding up his hand as I duck through the door. "Okay, let's grab a squash match or something soon."

The girl at the reception desk waves as I head for the front doors of the gym. I think her name is either Sofia or Britney. She's young, and always a little too friendly, but this time as she leans forward, angling herself to ensure I get an eyeful of cleavage, I'm happy to slow down and drink it in. I'm not remotely interested in her flirty smile and batting eyelashes, but I haven't laid eyes on a pair of tits in almost fourteen days —when my "hookup" at the hotel completely blew up in my face—and while my dick has remained downright monastic ever since, my brain is in take-what-you-can-get mode.

I smile back. Not at her, just at her chest. But when I finally tear my eyes away, they land directly on Caprice Phipps across the desk.

Her eyes are glacial, effectively extinguishing any flicker of arousal on its way to my brain. I curse under my breath, but manage a polite nod. She's my wife's best friend, keeper of my sins. And I suppose she could still ruin me with the flick of a few words. Caprice stops, openly glaring at me, and it's clear she saw what I was looking at. I avert my gaze to the screen of my phone, pushing through the doors to the parking lot, hoping I look properly cowed.

As I climb into my truck and start the engine, the latest *Come And Get Her* podcast picks up where it left off on a discussion of orgasm and the different ways it can be achieved. I hit pause, my thumb hesitating over the phone screen.

We're nearly halfway to the thirty-day mark and Lydia still hasn't sent any kind of signal inviting me to touch her, and she sure as hell hasn't reached for me. I'd been so optimistic when I found the podcast, thinking I could do better—find a way to get her to want me. But it's started to feel like a waste of time. I can't blow her mind with orgasms if she never lets me between her legs.

I pull up an email from a lawyer I spoke to yesterday. After days of debate, I decided to have a consult just to put things in place. He explained how we'd divide our assets; that I had a right to half her businesses. But despite his strong suggestions, I said I wasn't interested. I make good money. And Lydia's put more effort into the Pooches than she ever has into our marriage. Why would I want a stake in the thing she's more passionate about than me?

"You're lucky you didn't have kids," the guy must have said at least five times. I couldn't reply to that, so I just nodded.

LYDIA and the dog aren't home when I get there. No surprise. But my skin prickles when I see her empty spot in the driveway all the same. Like she's the one out with someone else. Only we both know the other party in our relationship is her job.

I picked up a couple of sandwiches on my way home because I know she won't have eaten. I finish mine alone in the kitchen, then leave hers on the table where she'll see it. I'm just settling in on the couch for the evening when I hear the front screen door creak open and her key in the lock. My pulse spikes. It's too late to sprint for the bathroom, so I search around for another way to occupy myself. To make it look like I don't care that she'd rather spend her evening working than connect at all with me.

Heartthrob comes to my rescue, running in the door, playful and hungry. I jump up, grab his dish by the back door, and set about preparing his concoction of dog kibble and fish oil, focusing very hard on mixing it up just the way he likes it.

Lydia follows him in, setting her purse and a few other things down on a kitchen chair.

"Got you dinner," I say without looking at her. She could've figured that out herself just by looking at the table, but I decide to go the extra mile to fill the silence.

"Oh, thank you—" she cuts off like she was about to say more, then just stands there, staring at the sandwich like she's not sure what to do with it.

I grunt and move past her, putting the dish down for the dog, then heading for the back door. I can't bring myself to climb in bed when the sun is still up, so yard maintenance it is.

She squeaks awkwardly behind me. "I um thought . . ."

I wait for her to finish whatever she's trying to say. She's holding a black plastic bag in her hands and just stands there, crinkling the material. I reach for the door.

"Do you want to—" she chokes. Then she takes a deep breath and sighs. "I mean, it's been a while since we . . . um, stayed in together."

I close my eyes, trying not to clench my jaw as I realize what she's suggesting. Lydia's version of a "date night" is staying in on the couch, watching some period drama while she tries not to come close enough to touch me. My gut twists because I think I'm supposed to see this invite as effort, but I just . . . can't.

"Look, I'm not really in the mood for a movie," I say, pulling open the door.

"*No.* I uh . . ." She swallows, looking at my feet. "That's not really what I was thinking."

I turn at the awkward tone of her voice. Taking in her strange, rigid posture. The way she fidgets with the paw print necklace I gave her for her birthday. She looks sincere, vulnerable, clinging to that black plastic bag like it's a life raft.

Suddenly I realize. This *is* an actual gesture.

Heartthrob comes and wags his tail in front of me, licking the last of the fish oil off his nose. I look from the dog back to my wife standing there waiting for my response, and I do exactly the wrong thing.

"Dog needs to go out." I grab some waste bags and slip through the door.

She doesn't follow.

Outside, I take what feels like the first clean breath of air I've had in weeks. Then I take another. And another. Only forcing myself to slow when I start to get lightheaded. Through the windows, I see Lydia moving around, but I'm not sure what she's doing.

Maybe throwing my stuff to the curb. Closing the blinds. Changing the locks.

Every time she actually reaches for me, I turn into the biggest ass.

But it's been *eleven* days. What changed? Why now?

I don't think I can take another forced effort. Waving her tits in my face, lying back so I can climb on top of her. Spreading her legs without reaching for me.

But there's a whisper at the back of my mind. An echo of conversation between Jess and Izzy, patiently explaining the way desire works for different people:

Isabella: You know, some of us start with desire—men in particular—they see something they like, and they want it.

Jessica: Straightforward and simple.

Isabella: But for some of us, it's the other way around. Some of us only experience desire *after* we're aroused.

Lydia is no longer visible in the window. Maybe she left to spend the night with Caprice. Maybe she's having dinner in front of her laptop. But I close my eyes, letting myself imagine her the way I do in my fantasies. Naked under the sheets, back arched, nipples perked. Aroused and reaching for me.

My dick stirs. The sky has darkened, but it's not officially night as I move toward the door. Heartthrob pops his head up from where he was sniffing a clump of weeds, running happily inside ahead of me. Tail curled high, nails thundering like a freight train across the hardwood.

I let my lust draw me inside, but in the kitchen, I dawdle. Filling the dog bowl with fresh water, unloading the dishwasher, trying to listen and figure out where she is. The rest of the house is silent.

A peek down the hall toward the two bedrooms tells me she's not at her desk in the little office, and the bathroom light is off. So she either left or she's in our room. Maybe this is our chance. Maybe I just need to go in there and help her *find* her desire.

But what if it goes badly? What if it's the totally wrong thing?

I'm halfway to the bedroom door when a small piece of paper catches my attention, curled on the floor. Just a receipt, probably for takeout or Starbucks, but something makes me pick it up, and when I do, the logo at the top grabs my attention.

Playful Pleasures.

The sex store?

I glance down the hall again, hesitant to trust the feelings stirring inside me. Just the idea of Lydia walking in the door of that place sends blood flowing to my groin. I've been there a few times, mostly for lube —an unfortunate necessity—but honestly? I have a hard time imagining my wife ever crossing the threshold. I stretch the receipt out, scanning over the purchases.

BLINDF - 1 @ 11.99
YOU LUB - 1 @ 12.99
RABBIT VIBE - 1 @ 89.99

My jaw drops. *Lydia* spent ninety dollars on a vibrator?

The sensation in my pants progresses to something more substantial. I try to imagine my beautiful, chaste wife going into Playful Pleasures and making a purchase like that. Talking to a salesperson about her desires, her *needs*. Instantly, I'm hit by a wave of despairing lust. Was she thinking about us when she bought it? Or maybe about life without me?

And *why*, after years of frigid disinterest, would she suddenly pursue her own pleasure? I grind my teeth, trying not to feel bitter. Why couldn't she have done this earlier? Was it my attempt to cheat? Or does it turn her on to think of being free of me?

I swallow hard, forcing myself to stop. Lydia bought herself a *sex toy*. I don't care why; I just want to know if I'm invited. I think of our awkward interaction when she got home, of how she clearly tried to get something going in her own dysfunctional way. And the whole time she was holding that black plastic bag. I grasp the receipt in my hand, wishing I hadn't snapped at her so hastily.

It's dark in the house now. I'm not sure how long I've been standing here, but I can just make out the walls and shapes of the furniture. I glance back at the empty couch, then ahead of me to the dim light coming through our open door.

If Lydia has a new toy, I want to play.

CHAPTER TWENTY-NINE

Her

The back door slams, sending an unexpected jolt between my legs. I hear Anton throw the lock, and then he's shuffling around, doing something at the sink. Moments later, the sound of Heartthrob guzzling water echoes like a metronome from the kitchen, mingling with the clinking of a few dishes and mugs as Anton unloads the dishwasher.

God, he must be dreading coming in here as much as me.

Heartthrob comes down the hall, greets me with a tired tail wag, then circles and curls into his bed. I stare at the empty doorway, wondering if my husband will follow.

The black plastic shopping bag crinkles loudly in my hand, and I resist the urge to run outside, to throw it and everything inside it in the trash. What am I supposed to do, whip out the hot-pink vibrator and just present it to him? *Hey, I know we're having trouble in the bedroom, so here's something I bought for* me. I haven't forgotten what the salesgirl said about it helping both of us. But I can't help second-guessing everything now that it's time to actually use it.

He moves from the kitchen to the living room at a slow pace, and I carry the bag to my side of the bed, my limbs like tight rubber bands. What if he doesn't come in here at all? I listen for the sound of him picking up his keys, opening the front door to leave. He's probably gotten impatient and found someone else on Unmatched over the last two weeks.

Except he promised.

And after a while his footsteps start down the hall.

I look down at myself, and my heart leaps in my chest. I've been so worried about the stupid vibrator, I haven't thought about anything else. I'm still in my work clothes, hair a mess—not exactly super sexy. Before Anton can round the corner, I toss the shopping bag on my nightstand, dash past him into the bathroom, and lock the door.

"I—I just need a moment to freshen up," I call, then immediately grimace. What am I, a character from some old-fashioned movie?

He pauses outside the door, then continues into the bedroom, saying nothing in response. But that isn't surprising. Our conversations haven't been super verbose this week. I turn on the water in the sink just to drown out the sound of my roaring thoughts. My pounding heart. I grab my toothbrush, brush my teeth, floss. Neaten my hair. But unfortunately, without going into our room, I have nothing more attractive to change into. I consider just taking off all my clothes and throwing myself at him nude, but that feels too much like my last few unfortunate attempts at intimacy, the memories of which tie my stomach into knots. In the end, I remove my shoes and bra, but keep my leggings and T-shirt. It's a starting point, I guess.

My phone pings in my pocket as I reach for the door, and I pull it out to see who needs me. But it's just my mom sending a gazillion more pictures of my happy sister and her happy baby. My mind spins down a rabbit hole, and I find myself wondering if Celia enjoys sex. That's not the sort of thing we've ever talked about. I cringe, trying to shake images of my sister and her husband in various positions, then I clench my fists, annoyed that I'm in here thinking about them naked when I should be naked with my husband. I silence my phone and leave it on the bathroom counter.

When I tiptoe into our bedroom, Anton's perched on the end of the bed, head bowed, almost like he's meditating. He's switched on one of the low bedside lamps and put on some quiet music, and I'm grateful there's some sound besides our breathing and the creak of my feet on the floorboards. The black shopping bag rests on my nightstand undisturbed.

I move toward my side of the bed to get the rabbit because I have zero other ideas about how to start, but halfway there my brain finally kicks in. I remember something the salesgirl said about working up to certain things. I pivot, stepping awkwardly toward my husband instead.

He doesn't move, but in the dim light, I can tell he's watching.

I wish he would *do* something. Reach for me. Help me get the ball rolling. But I'm the one who wanted to try. *I'm* the one who's taken so long.

I stop in front of him, excruciating moments passing as I try to decide what to do. Finally, I reach out, hesitating a second before running my fingers through his thick, dark hair. This seems like a benign place to start. He stiffens, but doesn't pull away, breath moving slowly in and out.

With him on the bed and me standing in front of him, his head is about at the level of my chest. I'm not sure if I should bend over and kiss him, or maybe kneel. If I kneel, he might think I'm going in for a blow job, and . . . I guess I could. I've tried them a handful of times, but it never felt like I was doing things right, with all the excess spit and inevitable gagging. From a practical perspective, that also doesn't seem like an activity that would help me introduce the rabbit. So, after a very long cluster of seconds, I reach out and take his hands, guiding them to my sides, slipping them beneath the fabric of my shirt. I've done things like this before, but this time I keep my hands over his and move them together.

I startle at the warmth of his fingers on my bare skin, at the tingle that runs through me as I move them over my hips and along the curve of my waist. We reach the undersides of my bare breasts, and I could swear something changes in his breathing. In the way his fingers move beneath mine. I am no longer guiding them; he's taking control. A tiny jolt of excitement unfurls in my core. He slides his hands higher, exploring the full curve of my breasts beneath my shirt, circling the soft swell and dipping down between, then just lightly brushing one of my nipples. This is somewhere his touch often lingers, and on instinct, I pull away.

But I catch myself, instead trying to focus where he's touching and think about why he's drawn there, centering my attention on the sensation rather than waiting for it to go away. The soft peak tightens, just enough to stand out against the fabric as his hands slide out from under my shirt, and as soon as his touch is gone my skin actually seems to crave his missing heat. He places his hands at his sides, like he's completed the task assigned and is awaiting further instruction. And I realize he's letting *me* lead the way.

I finger the hem of my shirt, debating whether I should just lift it up and cut to the chase. Wave my naked boobs in front of him. But something in the back of my head warns that's too over-the-top again. He didn't go for it when I "stripped" for him, so why would it work now? I bite my lip, scanning over his body. His gray joggers and trainers. His open hoodie and tight athletic shirt beneath, clinging to the broad, toned muscles of his chest.

Maybe my shirt isn't the one that should come off first.

I move my hands over his shoulders, sliding my fingers beneath the fabric of his hoodie, guiding it down his arms until it circles his waist on the bed. I don't realize I'm holding my breath until he pulls his own wrists free of the sleeves. He could have easily pushed me away, like he did the other morning. But he's going along with it, and I exhale, running my fingers lightly over the snug blue shirt beneath. It hugs the shape of him that was hidden by the hoodie. The broadness of his shoulders and the way his torso tapers to his hips. I glide along the smooth, stretchy fabric until I reach the hem, and now it's *my* fingers dipping under, slipping between the shirt and the heat of his skin. I work it up slowly, letting my hands run along every dip and ridge of his washboard abs and over the tight muscled curve of his chest.

And then his arms come up. I freeze, waiting for him to stop me, push me away. But he just pulls free of the sleeves, allowing me to slide the shirt over his head and drop it beside the bed. I pause a moment, taking him in once it's gone. I know I don't stop enough to appreciate my husband as a work of art, but he truly is. He carries at least an eight-pack to some men's six, and you could draw a diagram of the male body's muscles just by sketching the outline of his arms and chest. His neck and shoulders are well defined and don't disappear into each other

—but he is vividly strong. His slightest movements outline the ideal functions of his body.

Unfortunately, studying Anton's perfection highlights how *not* fit I am. I'm no couch potato—I walk the dog, cycle, or swim whenever I can—but I don't have the time or focus to lift weights, and I've never sculpted anything out of my body other than a decent waist-to-hip ratio. I like to rationalize that the few extra pounds I carry help accentuate my curves, but really I'm just lazy. I don't have the inclination to work for the kind of physique he maintains, and I've always worried he'd prefer someone more like Caprice, who's lean and toned from all the time she spends in the gym. Maybe that's our problem. He has always encouraged me to exercise, and I do in my own ways, but never at his level. So I may never be enough for him.

I think of how I described myself as "athletic" on Unmatched rather than "curvy" and wonder if I got it wrong. Maybe I'm *not* what Anton was looking for. Maybe this thirty-day exercise is just me keeping him from his ideal.

Suddenly, I realize the air has cooled between us. I let myself get distracted, let my hands leave his skin, and now I've lost the moment I was trying to build. I steal a glance at his face, his expression unreadable, and I'm not sure what to do. He's just sitting there, not touching me. And I'm not touching him. Part of me just wants to turn the light out and crawl to our separate sides of the bed like always, but again, in the back of my head, it occurs to me that doing that is at least part of how we got here in the first place. The fact that he's here right now, with *me* instead of some stranger, is something. And though he hasn't reached for me himself, he has stayed here with me.

So I make a move.

I grab the plastic bag off my nightstand. "I, um . . . I went shopping today."

As soon as the words leave my lips, I realize it's too early. And now it's too late to take them back.

He raises his head. His mouth remains flat, but there's a hint of something—curiosity?—deep in his eyes, where he can't totally lock it away.

I fumble with the bag, struggling to remove the cumbersome packaging until I finally have the box in hand, and I present it to him like some pink battery-operated trophy.

"The salesperson said—well, I guess you don't need that whole conversation, but she said it would be good since I don't—I mean, well —" I force myself to stop. Take a breath. "It's just something to try. If you want."

I am so thankful that the sun has gone down. In the waning light of our bedroom, my face won't glow quite as fire-engine red as it feels. Anton takes the box out of my hand and studies it. I chew my lip, trying to steel myself for his judgment, for him to hand it back to me and tell me he'll leave me alone so I can have fun without him.

I've kept my eyes glued to the toy ever since I got it out, but I can't take it any longer. I need to know what he's thinking. Only I'm not fully prepared for the searing gaze he hits me with when I look up. His mouth is hard. But when our eyes meet, every inch of my skin prickles with a feeling like I'm about to be consumed.

He opens the box and takes the rabbit out, hand curling lightly around the rubbery shaft as he turns it over, studying its unique curving shape. It looks even bigger and more alien somehow in his palm. His thumb finds the power switch so quickly that I wonder briefly how he knew where to look, but then the room fills with a low electric hum.

My face is already burning hot. But I'm surprised when other parts of me seem to warm at the sound.

Anton switches it back off, and the air seems absent of something as he kicks off his shoes and rises from the bed, rabbit in hand. I swallow hard, trying to decide if it looks like he's holding an instrument of torture or some sort of warped magic wand. We stand there looking at each other, not saying anything, until he finally speaks.

"You should probably get on the bed."

CHAPTER THIRTY

Her

He phrased it like a suggestion, almost a request, but the urgency in his tone nearly melts my insides. I crawl onto the bedspread, think twice, then shimmy awkwardly out of my leggings and underpants, leaving them in a pile beside his shoes. This feels oddly procedural, but also necessary, I guess. I'm not sure where exactly to position myself once I've climbed up, so I just lay back against the pillows, crossing my legs and pulling my T-shirt down in some attempt to cover my nakedness.

The mattress sinks under Anton's weight as he kneels near my feet. He remains shirtless, but I can't help noticing he's kept his joggers on. It bothers me, though I'm not sure why. As if being covered from the waist down gives him some kind of power I don't have. He places one hand gently on my left ankle. "You're going to have to—"

"Oh. Right." I say this without really knowing what he's suggesting. But then I realize he wants me to uncross my legs. I hesitate, no longer confident in where this is going. What's supposed to happen next. He's going to do something to me with this *object* I bought, and I'm going to lie here and let it be done.

And the expectation is, I will enjoy it.

What if I *don't?*

Panicked seconds go by while I consider hiding under the covers. Then, instead, I uncross my feet and part my legs. It's hard not to feel like I'm in my doctor's office preparing for a pelvic exam and Anton's holding a speculum, ready to place it unceremoniously in my lady parts. I try closing my eyes as he positions himself between my legs, but that just makes it worse. Like I'm some kind of car about to be serviced. And now my face is in full-on nuclear meltdown, and I have so much buyer's remorse. I just want this whole scenario to be over as soon as possible.

I brace myself, preparing for the intrusion when he rams the thing inside me. *Insert Part A into Part B, then get off.* Somehow.

But instead, Anton starts running his fingers slowly up my leg. His touch is warm and light, and . . . totally unfamiliar. After a minute I realize he must've set the rabbit aside because a *lot* of his fingers are stroking up the inside of my thighs, and I'm surprised again when the muscles at my core tighten in response. It's not until his beard stubble grazes the most tender skin between my legs that I realize I've lost track of him, my gaze fixed straight up at the ceiling. I gasp at a puff of warm breath against the outer folds of my labia, and I want to sit up and tell him he's forgotten what we're supposed to be doing, that we should be using our accessory. But at the same time I'm completely unable to move.

My legs are spread wide when he descends on my center, his fingers gently parting my flesh until the hot tip of his tongue suddenly darts over my clit, and my whole body shudders. He circles the sensitive nub, traveling round and round until I squirm, and he finally clamps his lips down, sucking firmly until my hips buck in response.

We repeat this dance, his tongue exploring me in gentle swirls, breathing deeply against my flesh until I'm moving with him, slow and relaxed—then he'll ravage my clit when I'm completely off guard. I feel like an instrument he keeps picking up to play, then suddenly putting down.

Until, all at once, he pulls away.

The muscles at my core are so tight, I squirm in his absence, and I'm about to sit up to look for him when I sense a gentle probing at my entrance. Before I can take another breath, he penetrates me—not with the rabbit, but with one long, delicate finger, sliding smoothly in, then back out almost as quickly. I give a silent gasp. He repeats this motion, adding a second digit, and my hips tilt in response, rocking in a slow rhythm. I'm shocked, and honestly a little embarrassed, at how slick I become with each intrusion and removal, and he seems to note it too, spreading my wetness all over my flesh.

And then, that low vibration pierces the air.

This time, there's no pause in his ministrations. One moment his fingers are thrust deep inside me, then they're gone, replaced by a light, humming pressure outside my center. Which could only be the rounded pink head of the rabbit.

"Are you ready?" he whispers in a husky voice, forcing me to pull my gaze from the ceiling.

I drop my chin, and now he's staring at me bare-chested, framed between my naked legs. His expression is so different than I've seen it for weeks—the planes of his face smooth, eyes open, optimistic—I take in a sudden breath. And then I nod.

He dips his head, keeping his eyes locked with mine, slowly pushing the tip of the pulsing pink toy inside me. I widen my eyes once it penetrates, my cheeks flush, and the raw lust that takes over Anton's face forces me to tear my gaze away.

I collapse against the pillows as he starts moving the toy gently in and out, following the same pattern he had with his fingers. It's so utterly different from any time *he* has been inside me. The pink silicone is firm and unyielding in a way his flesh isn't, and the vibration feels foreign and robotic. But the way it fills me is . . . nice.

I'm not sure what I had been expecting. I guess that it would hurt or at least be uncomfortable. But as my husband glides the shaft in and out of my very wet vagina and my muscles clamp around it, I can't deny it's surprisingly pleasant.

My breathing starts to stutter, and I turn my head to the side. This feels good, but I need something more. I'm just not sure what. I run my hands over my chest, now wishing I'd taken off my shirt. I tilt my pelvis slightly, trying to adjust my position, and in the process discover the motion is exactly what I'm looking for. I start rocking my hips, moving in time with Anton's rhythm. The low vibration hums through my flesh, echoing in the air, accompanied by the wet sounds of my arousal, and I don't know whether to feel embarrassed or turned on by all this strange noise.

Then something shifts. I had thought I was already experiencing the rabbit in its full capacity until Anton plunges it deeper. The lower shaft of the toy is wider, placing further pressure on my inner walls even as it continues sliding against them with indescribable friction. This is a lot on its own, but then the "rabbit ears," the strange little appendage I'd nearly forgotten about, touch down on my clit just as Anton turns up the speed of the vibration. And it's too much. I squirm, wanting to pull away *and* push into it more, and then, with almost zero warning, my body begins to shudder and come apart. My legs fall open, every muscle in my core contracts, and my hips buck as shrieks and moans issue from my throat.

Anton decreases the speed of the vibration as I come down from my peak until my body goes still against the bedspread, then he turns the toy off. I lie there for several minutes, the muscles between my thighs still gently pulsing, trying to process everything that just happened. In the ten years we've been together, I've never felt quite this way any time we've ever had sex. Not because I hadn't climaxed . . . it was just never like *that*.

Anton sets the toy on the nightstand, switches off the light, and lies down on his side of the bed. I'm not sure when the sun fully set, but it's totally dark in the bedroom, and I can't really see beyond his silhouette or make out his expression. I wait long moments for him to do something else. Reach over, climb on top of me, get back to business. It's his turn. We might not do this a lot, but we've always been very fair when it comes to mutual orgasms. If you have one, you get one.

Though I have to admit, now that I've come down from my own high, I'm not super motivated to do the exchange. Despite what just happened, I prefer when he comes first. It's harder for me to keep focused after I've climaxed. I'll start thinking about other things—chores I haven't done, problems at work—lose lubrication, and end up sore. But fair is fair. And the woman at the store *did* say the rabbit should help both of us. When more minutes tick by and Anton doesn't move, I take a breath and speak into the darkness.

"Do you want to, um . . ."

My voice trails off before I can finish, the implied question hanging in the air.

"No. I'm good," he says after a minute.

He shifts next to me, and I catch a glimpse of his face in the dim light. But I must've heard wrong. I continue waiting, preparing for him to reach for my breasts or press his hard length against my thigh. But then he pulls the covers back, slips under, and rolls away from me without another word. For a while I expect his hands to search me out, take what's rightfully his, but then I realize his breathing has slowed, become even, and my legs are suddenly cold. I'm still naked from the waist down on top of the covers. I slip off the bed, locate my cozy striped pajamas, and slip into them. Brush my teeth. Clean up a little.

The space between my legs seems to carry a light, unfamiliar hum.

When I return to bed, I ease slowly onto the mattress, careful not to disturb Anton. I half expect him to roll over and grab for me. Wrap his arms around my waist, pull my bottoms down, and finish what he started. After another few minutes I almost *wish* he would. But he doesn't. He lies still on his half of the bed, unconscious and uninterested.

What. The. Hell.

I turn on my side, mimicking his posture, facing the opposite direction. I ought to drift off, relieved, happily off the hook because there's *no* way I'd ever figure out how to do to him what he just did to me.

Instead, I slip my fingers beneath my PJs and down between my legs, exploring the moist, still-sensitive folds. Everything is just barely swollen and tender, but not in the uncomfortable way I'm used to after sex. On the contrary, I'm tempted to keep moving my fingers, search out that pleasure again. It feels like it's still there, pulsing somewhere under the surface, waiting to be discovered and drawn back out. I can't remember ever having this sensation before, though I'm not totally sure why. Did I just need a fancy vibrator all this time?

Or did something change between us tonight?

A heavy, deep-sleep snort issues from my husband's side of the bed, and I withdraw my hand. I might have enjoyed myself as promised by the woman at Playful Pleasures, but Anton didn't.

I squeeze my eyes shut as my exhilaration slowly fades. Because I owe him now.

But the funny thing is, now that I think about it, Anton didn't have that familiar, craving look after I climaxed. The one he gets when I *know* he wants sex. The one he's worn for the past several weeks. All he did tonight was work to get *me* off, then crawl between the sheets and turn away from me. And despite not getting anything himself, the look on his face was almost peaceful. Content.

CHAPTER THIRTY-ONE

Him

Lydia's chest rises and falls, her teeth clacking every so often as she clenches her jaw in a dream. There's a strand of hair I want to brush away from her cheek. If I reach out, I could—we're close enough I can feel her warmth through the sheets—but I'm careful not to move. Definitely not to touch her. I woke stiff with need, my brain swimming with the images and sounds of her bucking and moaning against the vibrator, her pussy dripping with pleasure. I'm desperate to pull her to me, press my shaft against the crack of her ass, wake her up trailing my lips against her neck.

But I hold back.

The hot-pink rabbit lies on her bedside table, a visual confirmation that what I remember *wasn't* a dream. Lydia bought a sex toy, of all things. And I got her off with it—made her scream in a way she never has our entire marriage. She didn't just come against the rabbit, but also my lips and fingers, and it took everything I had afterward not to sink my dick into her slick heat and share the feeling with her.

God knows I wanted to.

But as the minutes ticked by after she came down from her peak and I watched her tremble through the remains of her pleasure, I had to admit, I was scared. To ask for what I wanted, what I *needed*—to pound away all of my doubts and frustrations between her legs.

Because there was still every chance, even after the incredible things I got her body to do, that she'd turn me down. Not overtly, of course. Usually, she'll at least roll over and admit me after I get her off. Out of some obligation, maybe. But it always seems like she's so tired, like it takes so much effort to reach her own climax that there's nothing left for mine.

Last night I just couldn't bring myself to burden her with it.

And now I don't know what this means for our situation. It's been nearly two weeks since I set the thirty-day deadline, and we just had sex for the first time in over two months. Well, technically, I gave and didn't receive. But seeing her like that was everything. I nearly came in my pants as she writhed against the rabbit.

Giving her space to savor the feeling made denying my own need easier. But sometime after we finished, she must've changed into her old pajamas. And now I'm staring at her in them, at the place where the thick fabric gapes a little between the buttons to reveal the curve of one breast, wondering what all of this means.

The alarm I set to go for a run went off ten minutes ago, and if I slip out of bed now I could still get dressed and be out of the house before she wakes. Avoid what's guaranteed to be an awkward morning. Either we'll both pretend like it didn't happen or . . . maybe we won't?

What if I touch her? Would she respond or pull away?

She lets out a sigh next to me and stretches, reaching her arms above her head while her toes peek out from under the sheet toward the closed bedroom door. As she does this, the striped pajamas pull up to reveal the flawless bare skin of her lower back. The tapered area of her waist just above where her hips curve out to shape her ass. The sound that leaves her lips then, coupled with the sight of her arching body and naked flesh, is like a lightning rod to my dick. I glance at the rabbit on the nightstand, and the doubts I had about making a move, about whether she'll respond, seem to melt away. My fingers make contact with her waist. I slide my heated palm along her skin, gliding over her bare curves.

She goes still.

I slow my hand, waiting for her to process, catch up to what I'm doing and respond. She's fully awake now, and she'll have to either turn toward me and acknowledge this thing that we both *can* clearly enjoy—that I'm sure we both need—or pull away from me once and for all.

Neither of us moves. My breath hangs in the air.

Then she sits up. Swings her legs over the side of the bed, scurries down the hall, and closes herself in the bathroom. Without even a glance at me.

The bed goes cold when she leaves. I twist my fist into the sheets, furious with myself for being surprised. For thinking that anything would ever change. Last night was an exception—one of several we've had over the years—but not the rule.

I snatch the rabbit from where it sits taunting me on the bedside table and hurl it across the room. It flies into the open closet door, landing with an unsatisfying, muffled thud amid her shoes and clothes.

Why did she even bother to buy the damn thing? Or give it to me to use?

I've spent the last eleven days learning everything I could to cultivate her desire. Where to touch her and how, ways to tune in to her responses. And I was a damn good student if I do say so, based on how she rode my face just hours ago.

But as these thoughts tumble through my mind, as anger and frustration simmer beneath my skin, my gaze lands on my phone—and my body floods with shame.

I went on an app in search of someone else.

And I'm the one mad at her?

I'm not sure how long I sit with that, lost somewhere between my need and my guilt, but after a while, the bathroom door opens. I look up, steeling myself for her to announce that last night wasn't good enough. She doesn't want me. Can't forgive me. Whatever I deserve.

But something's clearly different when she reenters the bedroom. She's changed out of her awful pajamas, though not into real clothes. All she's wearing is a fitted white camisole and a pair of pale pink underwear. Nothing overtly sexy, but her nipples perk through the thin white fabric, and on cue, my dick twitches under the covers.

"It's um . . . warm already," she says with a nervous laugh, and despite myself, I utter a silent blessing to our stuffy bungalow and the mild spring we're having if it got her out of her sleep armor.

She approaches the bed from her side, gripping her phone in her hand. She keeps glancing at the screen, and I wait, sure she'll start texting Tomás or Scarlet about the latest crises like she does almost every day. But she just stands there, shifting back and forth on her feet. I watch her sneak a glance at me and take a sharp breath, but she looks back at her phone, avoiding my gaze. I clench my jaw, waiting for her to pick up her glasses, leave to make coffee. But then, in one swift movement, she pulls back the covers and slips back into bed beside me.

I am perched on the far edge of the mattress, but she crosses the expanse until her leg brushes mine, and her bare flesh makes absolutely everything, starting with my balls, come alive. It's all I can do not to turn on my side and take her in my arms, pull her to me so every inch of her skin is in contact with mine. I want to snake both my hands beneath that camisole, seek out and tweak the nipples I saw taut against the cotton. I want to remove those pale pink panties and press my shaft against her center, letting the weight of my desire lay thick outside her entrance.

But I lie still.

Lust might be coursing throughout my body, but I'm right back to the same old problem—I can't reach for her. Even though she came back. I know if I do, she'll shut me down somehow.

She is studying something intently on her phone, but suddenly locks the screen and sets it aside. She stares straight up at the ceiling, almost like she's waiting. And I wait next to her, my cock standing at attention, overwhelmed by her nearly naked presence. I think of all the Sunday mornings we've spent in this bed, countless times I've reached for her, hoped for her, and been denied. Maybe after last night, something has to change. Or maybe I've reached a new level of desperate. But she's *here*. Sans pajamas. And just that is enough to pump my dick—and if I'm honest, my heart—full of hope.

We lay there like two bomb technicians afraid to cut the wrong wire or make the wrong move lest we detonate the space between us. Until I realize her breathing has slowed, become calm and steady, like she's gone to sleep. My stomach dips. I clench my jaw and reach for the edge of the covers, ready to toss them back and head for the shower to take care of myself the way I always do.

But then something moves under the sheets. It's just a slight disturbance, like a snake darting through grass. So sudden it's over before I've really processed that it happened. Except then there's a sensation on my thigh. An exploration of fingers, tentative but warm. I freeze, unable to look anywhere but straight ahead. Her hand moves in gentle circles, sweeping up my leg. Before I'm ready, she dips into my crotch to grab my dick, and I gasp aloud. Not because it's unpleasant—just unexpected, it's so fast. She hesitates like she has realized this, and for a second I'm afraid she'll stop. But then her hand begins to move up and down my already painfully stiff shaft, and I close my eyes, afraid to believe this is actually happening. I'm not alone in the shower, or even alone in the dark, but joined with my wife in bed.

Her weight shifts toward the bottom of the bed, and I glance down to see her lips poised over my dick, grinning up at me in the weak morning light. It's a sultry, lustful smile, like she's been waiting all day just to feast on my cock, and it catches me off guard. I've never seen this expression or anything like it on her face. Ever.

The next thing I know, her lips have closed warm and silky over the head of my shaft, and I almost shoot my load down her throat right then and there. I get hold of myself with a groan and sit up. She pulls back, lips open and uncertain, and I quickly shift to the edge of the bed where she can kneel between my legs. She seems to catch on and goes with it, positioning herself in front of my throbbing cock and wrapping her lips around my head once again. She begins bobbing slowly up and down, letting me grow slick with her saliva, and each time I slide deeper down her throat.

I can't understand it. She's given me blowjobs before, but they've always been kind of apathetic. Dry and full of teeth. Right now her mouth is so warm, wet, and willing, I am desperate to thrust into her, but also sure I will lose control if I even tilt my hips. Every move she makes threatens to send me over the edge. But as she reaches down to caress my balls lightly with her fingers, sending a wave of unbelievable new sensation through me, I decide I can wait to figure it out.

I close my eyes, losing myself in the slick confines of her mouth. Her tongue and cheeks slide over me in what has to be some kind of expert new move, and I actually glance down to make sure this really is my wife and she hasn't changed places with some porn star. But no, the long waves of blonde hair and upturned nose most definitely belong to Lydia, and seeing her kneeling there, bobbing up and down with a mouthful of my dick, nearly makes me lose it again.

To get hold of myself, I reach out a desperate hand, grab a fistful of her hair, and twist. She pops off the tip and goes still, unable to move now that I've seized control, and though I'm dying to plunge back between her luscious lips, I hold off just another moment, making sure we both can breathe. My grip, along with my willpower, quickly lessens, and when it does she leans back in, mouth open, pulling against the hair in my fist like she's hungry for more. As her lips seal again over the head of my cock, she looks up at me, and there's something in her wide eyes I've never seen—a hint of pleasure, like she's *enjoying* herself? This is just too much. I twist her hair again and thrust, a tingling sensation shooting up my spine as my balls throb and tighten. Then I groan, exploding into her mouth with a force that's been building for two fucking months.

CHAPTER THIRTY-TWO

Her

I RUN FOR THE BATHROOM.

Unceremonious, I know. But I panicked, okay?

After I spit into the sink, gargle, and rinse, I find myself staring into the mirror, trying to catch up with what just happened. My cheeks are flushed, lips definitely swollen, and my hair is a total mess. I got a little scared at one point when Anton grabbed me—I thought I was going to suffocate or gag for a couple of moments. But I didn't. And when I caught the look on my husband's face . . .

I close my eyes, tuning in to the slowing thrum of my pulse. And as I look up again and glimpse my reflection, there's something new there, almost like a glow.

When I woke to Anton's touch this morning, I didn't know what to do. How to respond. I felt like I owed him—it was *his turn*, of course—but I wasn't sure how to proceed. After my experience with the rabbit, it felt like I should do something different. Try harder. I wished I'd asked the girl at Playful Pleasures for some tips, but since I hadn't, I freaked out and ran from the room to get my phone.

From the safety of our bathroom, I managed to pull up an article titled "The Classic Guide to Blowjobs," which . . . did seem like the perfect response to what he'd done with the rabbit. I've given them before, but never really knew what I was doing, so I took a moment to run over the major points. It seemed pretty straightforward: *focus on the head, make sure not to go too fast, keep him slick and wet, make eye contact,* etc. But the article's number one bit of BJ advice caught me by surprise: *be enthusiastic.*

Huh.

Obvious, and also something I'd never really considered.

So, I went for it, putting on a big smile as I got started, trying to act like having his dick in my mouth was what I lived for. On a basic level, the whole concept of sucking another person's genitals seems so . . . odd. Pleasurable to be on the receiving end, I had to admit, especially after last night, but how could that be fun for the giver?

Except this time was different.

As I went along, grinning and pretending my husband's rock-hard dick was the best thing I'd ever tasted, I started to kind of get into it. I think everyone's heard of those studies where forcing the facial muscles into a smile supposedly sends a message to the brain that can convince it you're happy. Well, maybe the same holds true for blowjobs? I started out simply going through the motions, checking boxes off the guide in my head—with a smile—but the longer I worked at it, the less it felt like a chore. And, if I'm honest, it has *always* felt like a chore. After a while, I even started getting into what I was doing, paying attention to Anton's responses. I was interested to see what his face looked like when I changed position or speed. The way he gasped when I popped off the tip. A little thrill even rose up in my core at the sound of his groan when he came—and not just because it meant we were done.

Now, staring at myself in the mirror after getting him off, I have this giddy sense of satisfaction. My whole body feels weirdly awake and alive. Even though I'm not the one who had an orgasm.

I almost, kind of, want to do it again.

All because I smiled?

After I finish cleaning up, I'm wrapping myself in a towel when I hear my phone playing the theme to *Gone With The Wind*. Scarlet's calling—on a Sunday? My brain shifts quickly into business mode, and I dash back into our room to answer, giving Anton an apologetic wave when he looks up from the bed.

"Hello? Scarlet?"

The distinct sounds of sobbing meet my ear. "Lydia," she says. "I broke up with Trent."

"Oh," I say, trying to come off sympathetic, but this is also weird. Scarlet has worked for me for three years, and while we have a great professional relationship, we don't share much personal stuff. "I'm sorry to hear that, Scar. Do you need to take a few days?"

"No." She bursts into sobs all over again. "I called to let you know I'm moving back to California."

I blink, but she keeps going before I can figure out how to answer.

"I know I ought to give you two weeks," she says, voice quavering with apology, "But my lease is up in a week. I leave Saturday."

Whatever was left of my glowy feeling fades. I wander out of the bedroom, resting my head against the bathroom doorframe. "Your schedule's booked out six weeks," I mumble.

"I have a friend who's looking for a job. She said she'd call you."

I close my eyes. "Okay, give her my number." Decent groomers are impossible to find. I've been lucky to have Scarlet this long. "Is there *any* way you'd consider staying on another month?"

"I'm moving in with my mom. I'm so sorry, Lydia."

After we hang up, I sink back against the wall, trying to wrap my head around how to run two businesses, launch a third, *and* groom a full schedule of Scarlet's dogs. I glance back toward our bedroom. Not to mention make time for my marriage.

When I return to my husband, it's pretty clear the prior moment has passed. Anton's at the edge of the bed, shirtless in his joggers. My heart sinks when he doesn't look up. I bite my lip, watching him shove his feet into his sneakers, realizing too late, *again*, that I made the wrong move. Things were starting to feel different between us for the first time since the hotel. Why couldn't I just stay in the moment? Let the call go to voicemail?

Then again, it's not like I totally skipped out on him. What we did —this morning, last night—that should still count.

So why does it feel like I blew everything?

I pull the towel more tightly around my naked body and sink next to him on the bed, but just as I do, he stands and starts pulling on a shirt. The air seems thin. Maybe there's a storm system moving in. Or the air pressure is simply dropping in this room.

I open my mouth to say something about that. The weather. That's a good, safe, stupid topic. Perfect for everyone from strangers to people married for seven years. But then he grabs his phone and heads for the door. All I want is to tell him about Scarlet, acknowledge what we *did*, and maybe lean my head on his shoulder and cry about how hard everything is. Instead, I manage to blurt something else important.

"Someone wants to buy the Pooches."

He stops, fingers curling at his side, the muscles in his arm and chest standing out with the tension. He looks back at me, and a flicker of something—confusion? surprise?—passes over his face. He still doesn't speak, but he turns fully toward me.

"One second." I hold up a finger and dart from the bed, still clutching the towel around me. I return with my laptop, glasses perched on my nose. Anton tenses at first, until I shove the computer in front of him. I pull up my current business plans for both The Pooch Park and Ooh La Pooch, and my balance sheets for the past two years. Then I click over to the written offer Charlotte forwarded from *ABizCorp, LLC.*

Anton takes the computer from me and settles back against the headboard, scrolling down, his eyes flashing over the text as he absorbs the pages of legal language I have only skimmed. This is something he's really good at; he always makes sure he understands the fine print. I scoot out of the way, nearly losing my towel in the process. He must catch the movement because when I look up, his gaze burns so hot I expect the towel to burst into flames. An echo of sensation from last night heats up in my core and spreads through my body. For half a second, I'm convinced he'll shove the computer aside and pull me back into his arms.

But he doesn't. He clenches his jaw and drags his eyes back to the screen.

"I—I'll go make coffee."

In the kitchen, my chest flutters with a mix of regret and relief. About what happened last night. And this morning. Why things got weird. And finally being able to talk to him about this huge business decision.

I've just poured us each a strong cup of my favorite dark blend when he comes into the kitchen and places the computer on the counter. He takes the mug I offer with a nod, sipping it black while I add cream to mine. I've replaced the towel with my more practical robe, but somehow I still feel naked with his eyes on me. I adjust my glasses, straightening a little, trying to focus all of my attention on the screen, ready to hear his steadfast professional analysis of the offer we've received. He will lay out the pros and cons, maybe plug some figures into Excel, and we'll discuss data projections and other things he understands and can explain much better than me. I will listen attentively, careful to consider everything he says, before I get around to telling him I've already made my decision.

But when our eyes meet, I falter. The lines that recently started crossing his forehead are missing. His shoulders have straightened. And there's a light in his face I can't remember ever seeing.

He glances at the screen, then raises his eyebrows. "Seems like a great deal to me."

CHAPTER THIRTY-THREE

Him

Lydia stares at me. Brows drawn, lips pursed, trying and failing to settle on irritation or overwhelm. It's the same look she gets every year during tax season, always in the home stretch after we've gone over receipts, deductions, and depreciation of assets. She is a really talented employer, manager, and business owner. But she doesn't trust herself when it comes to numbers. Even mind-blowing ones like this.

And she's smart to be cautious. I had to read through the details three times before I decided the offer was legit.

Honestly, I wish I'd had the chance to go running before processing this. I would've liked to clear my head, sort out everything already knocking around my brain about last night and this morning. How she let me use a *vibrator* on her and I literally made her scream. And then she blew both my cock and my mind—before running away to spit in the sink like I'd shot her mouth full of poison. Not the finale I might've hoped for, but I didn't care because everything up to that point was amazing. For the first time in ages, it felt like we'd truly connected.

Right up until she went running back to work.

But even if I'd run twenty miles this morning, I doubt it could've prepared me for this purchase offer with its pile of cash.

Well, it's her money, not mine. But I can't help feeling like it's an opportunity for both of us.

"What do you mean?" she asks.

I hop up to sit on the counter, trying hard to conceal the enthusiasm bubbling in my core. "It's a good offer on paper. But obviously there are a lot of details to consider."

She seems almost surprised. "So . . . you think I should take it?"

I level my gaze with hers. "I would never tell you what to do with the Pooches."

"I know that." She straightens. "But I'm interested in your opinion."

"Okay. Then my opinion is you should sit down and have a discussion with these guys."

She flashes me a look, clearly challenging my casual use of the word "guys." Lydia's worked her ass off to prove herself as a female business owner, and people acting surprised she isn't male rankles her every time. Which is part of the reason I said it.

I bite back a smile as she narrows her eyes. And for a second, everything almost feels right.

Now, despite myself, I'm antsy to touch her again. The expression on her face, coupled with the fact that I know she is fully naked under that robe is making it hard to focus.

I clear my throat. "There's a lot you could do with that amount of money."

"Yes. But there are factors to consider besides just the offer amount," she says abruptly.

"Well, yeah, of course." I know Lydia will have the best interests of her companies and employees at heart, but that can all be built into negotiations. I'm not a lawyer, but I read over every line of the contract and her profit and loss statements, and it's a *good* initial offer. As it stands, she'll make more from this deal than she would just owning the businesses over the next ten years.

But I'll admit I'm having a hard time seeing past my own fantasies at the moment. A bunch of dreams I thought I'd let go of have drifted back to the surface. We could go on a second honeymoon—or a first one, really, since we skipped ours seven years ago to save up for the house. A trip of any kind would be nice, just some time to reconnect. Maybe we could start with the hot springs, then Europe. Bring along her new pink toy and keep up what we've started. I never thought she'd really "work on" sex, but she's proven me way wrong. Maybe we'll keep getting better at it.

The options seem limitless as soon as Lydia has time for *us*. And I can't see a better opportunity than this.

"I have my employees to think about," she says, and I simmer in a moment of irritation, because she never seems to put as much value on *us* as them. Tomás is a good guy. He could stay on with a new owner and probably get a nice raise. I'm not sure what new drama is going on with Scarlet. She's more trouble than Lydia's willing to admit, but she's got a good gig and she knows it. The rest will figure things out for themselves.

"Okay, sure. What else?" I ask, trying to play devil's advocate.

She sinks to one of the chairs across from me, resting her head in her hands. Her robe parts, exposing her naked thighs, and I am dying to push it up the rest of the way.

"I just—I don't—" She stops and presses her lips together.

Something softens in my chest hearing her confidence waver.

"Hey," I say, hopping to the floor. "Maybe we need to back up and appreciate how huge this offer even is for someone who opened her first business with a zero percent offer on a credit card." I smile, reminding us both of the early days of Ooh La Pooch. I gesture to the offer on the laptop screen. "*Look* what you've achieved, Lydia. Most businesses fail within five years—this is unimaginable success."

She blinks at me, her eyes shining a little.

I sink down in front of her and take her hand. "I know this is a huge decision, but I'll be right here with you. Once it's done, you can regroup, take some time to focus on things you haven't had time for. Maybe you could even open another business down the road. Whatever you want to do, I just want you to know I'm proud, and I support you."

"Anton, I—" She looks down at our joined hands, and a tear tracks down her cheek. "Thank you. I can't tell you how much that means."

I give her fingers a gentle squeeze, and my heart nudges open just a little more. When she raises her head, we share a shy smile, and by the color of her cheeks I'm sure we're both thinking about how we spent the last twelve hours. A vivid future unfurls in my imagination, one I could never have fathomed a couple of weeks ago. Where we actually play together on the same team, like a real married couple—maybe even as a family. Something stirs deep within me and I lose myself in the possibilities as we lean toward each other, our lips meeting in a slow, hopeful kiss.

"I've already decided," she whispers against my cheek. "I'm going to turn it down."

I open my eyes, so lost in the vanilla scent of her hair, I must have misheard what she said. "Huh?"

"I'm not going to sell." She pulls back to look at me, a bold glint in her eye. "Like you said, I've achieved so much. I'm not ready to stop."

I flounder, trying to take my next breath. "I uh—that's not actually what I was suggesting."

She tilts her head. "What do you mean?"

"Accepting this offer—selling the Pooches—could change your whole life. *Our* life."

"Well, yeah, obviously. But so could turning it down." A smile plays at her lips. "You just reaffirmed to me—I am already successful, and can continue to be. I guess I've just been so overwhelmed opening Pooch Park II, I couldn't see my own potential until someone else was interested."

"Come again?" I ask, struggling to follow.

"Why let *ABizCorp* take the Pooches to the next level when I can do it myself? I could add boarding or pet sitting to the daycare if I figure out the logistics and insurance. And I've been wanting to add a mobile service to Ooh La Pooch—oh! Actually, I might even be able to offer obedience training!" She turns to her laptop and starts typing up notes.

I clench my jaw, watching her work with an enthusiasm she never seems to have for anything else.

"That all sounds nice." My voice comes out hollow. "But who's going to run it?"

Her brows draw together as she types. "I will?"

"And when Scarlet hurts her back? Or Tomás takes a vacation?" I get to my feet. "What do you do when they're both off, then the new mobile groomer *and* the dog trainer call out sick?"

"I—I would—"

"*You* would fill in. Do it all. Except you can't." My lip curls. "Lydia, I love you, and I believe you can do anything. But you can't do everything."

She stops typing to stare at me. "I don't understand. I thought you just told me to go for it? You just applauded my 'unimaginable success.'"

I rake my hand through my hair. "Look, I mean this in the nicest way possible, but quit while you're ahead. Offers like this don't come along every day."

She stiffens. "I misunderstood. I thought you said you'd support me."

"I *do*," I say, grabbing her hand. "I support you taking care of yourself, doing what's best for you." I look into her eyes, desperate for her to hear me. "But you have to see there's more to lose here than potential growth."

She tilts her head, clearly not following. "I'm currently in the black, even with all the second location startup costs."

"*Lydia.*" I wait for her to look at me, though she flinches when our gazes meet. "The Pooches may be in the black, but our marriage is in the red."

Her mouth opens, but she doesn't speak. I let go of her hand. Heartthrob wanders sleepily into the kitchen, probably trying to figure out why our voices are raised. I hate that I had to put it like that, but I don't know what else to say. I'm not about to get back on Unmatched. I've had enough of that. But does she really expect me to stand by and clap while she puts a hundred and ten percent into everything but us?

"Is this about sex?" Her voice is cool as she rises to her feet.

The back of my throat burns. "This is about *you* and *me*."

"Really?" She exhales. "Because lately it seems like you're only interested in one thing."

My body goes hot. I set my jaw, pushing words out through my teeth. "And what is that?"

"Come on, Anton," she says, her tone suddenly less certain. "I've always thought we had something special, something bigger than most marriages. We've been together so long, it's like we're not just husband and wife. We're best friends."

"Best friends," I say dryly.

She looks at me with a small smile, and my stomach sours.

"Lydia, we're married. If you want to live with a 'best friend,' go get yourself a roommate, not a husband."

I push past her for the coffeepot, refilling my mug to have an excuse to look away. She moves aside, face bright red as she pulls her robe chastely closed. "Maybe you're forgetting what we did last night? *And* this morning?"

"Forgive me if I don't get super excited," I say, a void opening in my chest, "that my wife finally forced herself to touch me for the first time in months."

"See? This is what I mean," she hisses. "Everything is just about sex. It's like I'm never enough for you!"

"Wrong," I growl. "You. Are. Everything. I want *you*. But I don't think you see how out of balance everything is. It's not just sex. You put all you have into work, and there's nothing left. We barely see each other. We don't go anywhere or do anything together. Even when you're around, it's like you aren't there. And now you want to add to that?"

"Look, I know I've been busy, but most of that has been because of the new—"

"Oh yes, the new location. Everything will be better once it opens." I scowl. "Until you start up the next one. And the next."

"I'll take a break in between." She has the humility to blush. "Anyway, things *will* smooth out soon, and then I'll have more time for . . . everything."

My lip curls. "Sorry, I'm not super interested in waiting around until you have time for me."

"What—that's not what I meant!"

I pick up Heartthrob's food dish because he's staring at me like there should be less talking and more attention to him, and I definitely agree. Lydia just stands there, fists balled at her sides, watching me feed the dog from where she sits in the hole she's dug.

"You know, I'm not the only one who isn't perfect here," she finally sputters. "If you were so miserable, you could've said something. But you didn't. You decided to cheat."

I close my eyes, pressing my mouth into a line. "I guess it seemed reasonable since you've been having an affair with your job for years."

"You never said you were unhappy! How am I supposed to know how you feel if you never tell me? You're impossible to read."

"You want it spelled out?"

"Actually, yes," she says. "Because I have been making an effort. *I* bought us a sex toy—which we used—*I* gave you a pretty excellent blowjob. But then *you* got all moody and tried to leave without even saying anything!"

My throat tightens. An image of her flashes through my mind, lips wrapped around my cock. Then another of her running to answer the phone like she couldn't change gears fast enough. I pick up my keys.

"Kind of like you're doing right now," she says.

"Look, Lydia," I say, trying to sound more firm than defeated. "I love you—I always have, and I always will. But if nothing's going to change, I don't think either of us will be happy."

She's quiet for a minute, then lets out a low breath. "And the only solution is for me to sell my businesses? So I can, what, lie around all day waiting to have sex with you?"

I level my gaze at her, unwilling to even grant that an answer.

"Wow. This is not where I thought we'd end up," she says, and her trembling voice forces an uncomfortable lump into the back of my throat. "I've never imagined us *not* together. After Pooch Park II opened, I thought we might even talk about starting a family . . ."

My chest burns. I don't bother pointing out that you need to have sex to make a baby, that children don't raise themselves.

Her frown deepens.

I sigh, dumping the rest of my coffee in the sink. "Look, I want you to be happy, Mrs.—" I stop, unable to call her by the nickname I've used for seven years. "But I need to be happy too."

"The Pooches do make me happy. I can't give that up."

For you.

She doesn't say these last two words, but the room fills with them.

I don't answer. I'm tired of feeling hurt, and I don't want to hurt her more.

I move for the door, forcing my brain to focus on "next steps" to try and escape this moment. I'll make an appointment with the lawyer, look for an apartment. I might need to take some time off work to move. Maybe I'll even talk to Carl about working remotely and long-term travel. I love Denver, but a fresh start might be for the best. A new city.

Or maybe I should just go home to Dallas.

Faintly, as I think of this, over the sounds of our dully beating hearts and gloomy breaths, a melody makes its way to my ears. It takes almost half a minute for me to fully grasp the notes cutting through the air. The ringer on someone's phone. Not Lydia's for once, though. Mine.

CHAPTER THIRTY-FOUR

Her

I'M TRYING SO HARD TO HOLD IT TOGETHER, TO *NOT* CRY, that I nearly fall out of my chair when Anton suddenly darts from the room. For a second, I think he left. Maybe he couldn't take this emotional overload either and went to the gym. Except he was headed toward our bedroom, not the front door. And then I hear the ringing. It cuts off almost as soon as it registers, replaced by Anton's deep, serious greeting.

"Hello?"

There's a long silence after that. So long that I wonder if I actually heard any of it. Maybe he did leave.

I slip out of the kitchen and down the hall, my heart picking up speed.

"What happened?" I hear him say next.

The air is deathly silent when I peer around the corner, hesitant to enter, as if I'm an intruder in my own room.

"Okay." Anton sits hunched on the bed with his back to me, his voice grim. "I—I should be able to get a flight in the next few hours."

My heart sits in my throat, with just enough knowledge to guess what's going on, but not enough to be able to cope. Quietly, I sink to the bed beside him, but I can tell his thoughts are already hundreds of miles away.

"*No*, Seth. Don't give me that," he snaps. "If Mom's in the hospital, I'm fucking coming to be with her."

I let out a long, low sigh of relief. Because while "hospital" isn't good, it's something we all know how to handle; we've been here before. Still, it's an uncomfortable reassurance. Because it's a place we can only end up so many times before we don't anymore.

I squeeze my eyes shut, trying to picture Sharon as she used to be, as I remember her. The ultimate best mother-in-law any girl could have asked for. She'd raised Anton and Seth entirely by herself after their dad died when they were ten and seven. The first time Anton brought me home to meet her after we got engaged, she embraced me so warmly, declaring me the daughter she'd always wanted. A far cry from the visit Anton endured with my own mom, in which she shook his hand then politely grilled him for an hour on his career aspirations.

Anton snarls into the phone. "Then you know better than to argue with me."

He ends the call and immediately pulls up one of his travel apps, searching for flights. I draw my knees to my chest, scanning his face, trying to gauge his turbulent feelings and how I might be able to help. He punches the screen with more force than necessary, but doesn't seem to even register me.

Finally, I clear my throat. "Is your mom—" I stop. "Are you okay?"

He closes his eyes. Anton, Seth, and I all knew when Sharon went into care—first at that horrible place, and then finally in the more capable hands at Sunny Cove—that she would never be "okay" again. Not the way she used to be. The important thing was her safety, but we've all known for a while that things were not headed to a good place. I just don't think any of us expected it would be this soon.

"I'm so sorry, Anton. I thought Sharon—" My voice cuts out. It just doesn't seem fair. She ought to have decades of life ahead of her. Anton and Seth should've had more time to spend with their mom—as her children, not her caregivers. There's so much tradition and family everyone's been cheated out of. Going home for holidays, enjoying pans of her famous lasagna, just being able to call and hear each other's voices. None of that has been possible for a while, but somehow the absence seems punctuated in this moment. When it feels like there's so much more impending loss. Anton looks up, and my eyes brim with tears. "I thought maybe she'd stay with us a little longer."

"Yeah. Well, it is what it is." His voice thickens when our eyes meet. "Seth was trying to tell me not to even come."

"No. You need to go. Your mom needs you." I take his hand, pulling it into my lap and squeezing his fingers, our pulses beating against each other. I guess we're both surprised by the gesture because it's several seconds before we both let go and pull back.

He clears his throat and stands, ducking into the bathroom. When he comes back, he has a few toiletries in his hand and starts digging for his suitcase under the bed. I watch for a minute, and it feels like the whole room has shifted into slow motion. Or maybe only I have. But as the sound of his luggage zipper cuts through the air, I blink, and my body shifts back into action. I kneel at the side of the bed and pull out my own purple suitcase, laying it next to his black one. Then I open the dresser, grabbing underwear, jeans, and shirts, pausing somberly to consider whether I should pack a black dress.

I bump into Anton as we each try to navigate our narrow walk-in closet.

"What are you doing?" he asks, glancing from the clothes draped over my arm to the travel bags on the bed.

"Packing for Dallas," I say, though it seems obvious enough.

He takes the dress out of my hands, shaking his head as he hangs it back up. "No."

I follow his movements, eyebrows raised. "Um. Why not?"

His eyes are cool, closed-off. "Because there's no reason for you to come."

"If Sharon's in the hospital, I'm coming to be with her, to be with —" I was going to say *you*, but the look on his face is so cold I go silent.

He shakes his head. "Please don't."

My eyes burn. My throat feels like it's closing up. "Anton, I need to go, you can't just—"

"I think you've made clear what matters most to you. Stay here. So you don't have to miss work." He moves past me, not looking at me. "Right now, I need to be with my family."

His words hit like a punch.

I step back. Watching. Chest hollow. He continues, going through the motions of folding clothes into his suitcase, and I step back to observe, a heaviness I've never felt creeping into my gut. After some minutes, I finally realize what it is—we both feel like he's packing to leave for good.

Maybe he is.

I can't bear to look at the purple suitcase being left behind on the bed, so I head for the bathroom. Brush my teeth. Walk to the kitchen to let Heartthrob out and set up the coffeepot for tomorrow. All things I do every day with him here. Things I'll still do without him around. He heads into the bathroom to shave, like it's any normal day and we're getting ready to go to our jobs.

I'm standing in my bra and leggings in the bedroom, getting dressed for work because that's a familiar thing I know how to do, when Anton comes in to get his suitcase. He stops and openly stares at me about to put my shirt on, and I wish for half a second that I was wearing the lingerie from the hotel. The whole point of it had been to rub one last look in his face of everything he was about to lose, and I wish I could steal that moment back for myself. I make the best of it now, even in just the plain push-up T-shirt bra, taking my time pulling my top over my head, trying to broadcast that he'll never see these boobs again.

Out of the corner of my eye, I spot a bright patch of pink on the floor of the closet among my shoes. I don't know how the rabbit got there, but I cross the room and pick it up. I carry it to the bathroom, holding it out like it's somehow responsible for what's happening, and then I clean it carefully, a twinge shooting through my lower regions when my fingers brush the "on" button. Anton is standing in the same spot when I reenter with the sex toy. He watches me walk back over to my side of the bed and tuck it carefully away in my bedside drawer. Then I rise and turn to him, trying to school my expression to suggest I'm planning to use it without him after he's gone.

Maybe I will.

Anton shifts, tucking his shirt into his pants, and pulls his suitcase off the bed. He's put on jeans and a hoodie for the trip, casually delicious with a white shirt stretched across his chest. All the ladies between here and Dallas can have a visual free-for-all.

My phone pings with a text from my sister, which I'm actually grateful for.

CELIA

Baby Gabriel got his present from Aunt Lydia! Thank you!

I shift my eyes to the screen, trying to process why she sent me a picture of a stuffed guacamole and chips dangling over a baby until I remember that I sent them. I purse my lips, thinking way too hard about my generic reply.

Anton clears his throat. "I'm going to head to the airport and get checked in."

I glance up, trying hard to make it seem like I'd forgotten he was there, but mostly hoping to keep tears from spilling all down my face. We look at each other in that moment, and while his face is still impossible to read, his eyes aren't the cold steel they were a little while ago. Now they're swimming with sadness.

I don't know if it's for me, for his mom, or just the whole terrible situation. But a feeling deep in my stomach wrenches me into action. I step forward and put my arms around him.

It's just a hug. Something we've done thousands of times before, and arguably appropriate for the situation. But he pauses a long beat before returning the gesture, finally placing his hands against the curve of my back and pulling me lightly against him.

I don't breathe until we each let go.

He checks his pockets for his ID and phone, and I want to say "Let me know when you're there safe," or "Give Seth a hug from me." But I don't. I stand motionless and quiet.

Finally, he turns to leave the room. And as he does, I find my voice.

"Anton, I'm—"

"Please," he says. "Don't."

He wheels the suitcase through the house, and I trail behind because I'm not sure what else to do. Heartthrob trots beside him, nudging his hand as he opens the front door. The dog knows what packed luggage usually means. Anton rubs his head and looks at him, lingering for a moment, possibly conveying *be a good boy. I'll miss you.* Or maybe *keep her safe.* Or nothing of the sort. Then he's out the door, tossing his things in his truck.

I watch from the front porch, not expecting him to look back. So when he rolls the window down, my heart jumps with a stupid thrill. Maybe he's having second thoughts—he wants me to come after all. Or to say he'll be back. That it hasn't even been thirty days, so we still have time to work on things.

He opens his mouth. "I . . ."

I clasp my hand to my throat, suddenly sure he's going to say what married people say when they leave. The three most basic words that will hold everything together while we're apart.

Then he pauses, shakes his head, and raises his hand. "Bye."

CHAPTER THIRTY-FIVE

Her

AN ONSLAUGHT OF BARKING GREETS ME AS I WALK INTO THE Pooch Park, and like every day this week, I am grateful for the din. Tomás raises a hand to wave hello, then presses it back against his ear as he shouts into the phone.

"Sure! We can get Freckles in next week. Which days are you thinking?"

I don't have to check the computer to picture Freckles the English Springer Spaniel. He's a sweet, playful dog who's come for daycare almost since we opened. He and Ginger, a red standard poodle, like to race around the play yard on hot days, splashing through the wading pools. Both of them are also clients at Ooh La Pooch, coming in every six weeks for a bath and a trim. A small part of the loyal client base I've worked so hard to build.

Heartthrob is out playing with his buddies and his favorite staff member, a girl with green hair named Francie. My office often feels like a tiny refuge, and this week it's been a lot more comforting than home. I set my empty travel mug on my desk just as my phone rings, but when I see Mark's name I breathe a sigh, closing the door to muffle some of the barking.

"Hey, Mark. How are things going?" I greet my contractor tentatively, not sure I want to know why he's calling.

"Good news! We finally resolved those HVAC and electrical issues. We should be hanging drywall by the end of the week."

"Seriously?" My voice rises above a monotone for the first time all day. "That's fantastic!" Once drywall is up, we can paint, and everything else should move along quickly. I have a storage unit full of everything we'll need in reception. After the inspectors give us approval, I'll be able to set a tentative grand opening date.

He gives me a couple other minor updates before we hang up, then I sit there with my fingers hovered over my phone, wishing I could share my excitement with someone. Caprice will not understand the delight of drywall. Definitely not Celia or my mom. Actually, this is the sort of thing Anton is great at celebrating. He's always quick to jump on little milestones that prove things are moving along.

I slump into my desk chair. My husband—I can still call him that for now—hasn't texted or called since he left five days ago. Seth took pity on me when I broke down and asked what was going on, and he's been sending updates here and there, but it doesn't sound like Sharon's condition has changed. Or Anton's, for that matter. Seth says he barely speaks and has hardly left her bedside. I feel sick thinking about it, wishing I was there with all of them. But I know I'm not welcome, so it feels like there's nothing to do.

I open my laptop. There's a spreadsheet open on the screen from this morning. Something I need to finish updating in order to run a report for my insurance company. But instead of settling in to crunch numbers, I pick up my phone and text my brother-in-law.

"365 new days, 365 new chances."

SETH

"Don't wait for the perfect moment. Take the moment and make it perfect."

I chuckle. A couple years ago, when Sharon's situation started to feel really grim, Seth and I started exchanging cheesy inspirational quotes. The kind you see on day calendars or in high school guidance offices.

Anton rolls his eyes every time we add to this back-and-forth, but Seth usually manages to top me, so I'm always looking for new ones. The exchange has taken some of the edge off our pain, and I'm especially grateful for it now.

SETH

Things here status quo. Hospital can't keep her, so moving back to Sunny Cove.

Ok, thank you. I wish I was there.

SETH

Want me to punch Anton in the face and tell him to stop being a dick?

No. He's right. I don't belong there. But please let me know if anything changes. I'm sorry, Seth.

A knock on the door draws my attention back to work. It's such a strange feeling, being normal and secure in one place but wishing you were sad and grieving in another.

"C-come in?" I look up, expecting to see Tomás, but Henry Hill pokes his long nose around the door.

"Hey, hope I'm not interrupting?" He glances into the small room.

"No, not at all . . . how's it going?" I manage to inject enthusiasm, though I have to admit seeing my husband's old roommate is doing nothing for my mood.

"Just dropping off Carmelita and wanted to say thanks. She's been coming here twice a week, and my apartment might actually survive till my sister gets back to town."

I smile, and this time even manage to make it genuine. "Oh, that's awesome to hear. She's been having *so* much fun. There's a little dachshund named Turbo she adores playing with."

Henry flickers a smile, then glances again around the little room like he wants to say something else. "Ah, well, give Anton a shout, would you?"

"When he's back from Dallas, sure," I say absently, turning back to my spreadsheet.

"Oh. Is his mum . . . ?"

My throat tightens. I don't think Henry knew Sharon well, but I'm sure he met her at some point and is aware of her condition. I nod.

"I'm sorry to hear that." He leans against the doorway, chin tucked like he's debating something. I look back, ready for him to carry on, return to his business deals or banking or whatever he does so I can get back to my own work. "Listen, Lydia, it's probably not a good time . . ." He pauses. "I really hate to ask when you guys are going through a rough patch, but I'm just curious if you might reconsider my offer?"

"What?" I caught 'rough patch,' and for a second, I was sure he'd somehow heard our marriage is in shambles. Until I stop to think about it. Anton never shares his feelings. Surely he wouldn't have unloaded to Henry about all that and not the situation with his mom.

I knit my brows, trying to figure out what he means.

"Listen, I'm flexible about the terms. I was hoping we could at least meet to discuss before you turned me down." He looks meaningfully at me, then glances behind him toward the play areas and reception desk. "I'd just love to get in on this."

My eyes widen as the information finally clicks. "*You're* ABizCorp, LLC?"

His brow furrows. "Yes, of course."

My skin breaks into a cool sweat as I think of the calls I've been dodging from Charlotte since I told her to turn down the deal. "Um . . . I guess with everything happening with Sharon, I didn't realize."

Henry straightens. "Mind if I come in a minute?"

"Sure, yeah." I hop out of my chair, clearing a place on the little couch across from my desk that's currently holding a Costco-sized package of paper towels. Henry perches on the edge, obviously trying not to get dog hair on his expensive-looking suit.

"So, what can I do to make you reconsider?" he asks. "If you're willing, I'd want to keep you on as a consultant for a time, of course, but that's negotiable." He grins.

I sit up in my chair, wishing my hair was neater. And I was wearing something other than leggings and a T-shirt from one of the more recent animal shelter fundraisers. I've barely even showered since Anton left. I didn't leave the house at all prepared for a business meeting.

"Do you mind if I ask what interests you about The Pooch Park and Ooh La Pooch?" I glance over Henry's spotless suit, his manicured fingers. There isn't a single hair out of place on his head. "Don't take this the wrong way, but you don't really strike me as a dog person. You don't even have a dog of your own."

He leans back on the couch, cool and confident. "I've done my research, crunched the numbers. Your business thus far is impressive. But I think it could be systemized, made more efficient, and significantly expanded."

I frown. I have plans of my own to keep growing, but the way he talks about it sounds sort of cold and soulless.

"Don't think of it like that," Henry says, apparently reading my face. "You and I both know these decisions come down to the bottom dollar." He clears his throat. "And I am offering you a lot of them."

I exhale, trying to hide my irritation. "Yes, um . . . I did give your offer some serious thought."

My chest starts to ache, thinking back on my exchange with Anton.

"I'm sure." Henry flashes a toothy smile. "Did Anton think it wasn't enough?"

"Well, no—"

"I am willing to come up." He raises a sharp eyebrow. "With a few agreements, of course."

Ugh. I feel like I did when I bought my first car. I'd never made such a big purchase on my own, and I remember sitting in the dealership while they threw numbers at me, until I wasn't sure if I got a good price or not. Somehow, dealing with Henry is ten times more overwhelming. Or maybe it's just the numbers he's waving around. If I was really interested, I would set up a meeting with Charlotte and let her handle negotiations. But my answer isn't about to change. If anything, with my marriage on the brink, I need the Pooches—my career—more than ever.

"Sorry, I'm still not interested."

His eager expression wavers a little. "Are you sure? We could hold off further talks until Anton's back, if that would be better."

My neck prickles. I don't get the vibe he's trying to suggest I step back and let my husband decide, but he's toeing the line. "The businesses are mine. It's my decision. But Anton and I did speak about it, and he knows how I feel."

My gut twists as these last words leave my lips. *I think you've made clear what matters most to you.*

Henry's mouth presses into a firm line. "Okay. Well, obviously I'm still game. So if you decide you want to reconsider—"

"How many different ways do I have to say *no?*" I snap. "I'm not interested!"

He stiffens, then rises abruptly from the couch. "Sorry, Lydia. I didn't mean to overstep." He reaches into his pocket, then hands me a glossy-looking business card. "The success you've had with your dog businesses is impressive. I was just interested in taking it to the next level."

"Thank you," I say, showing him the door. "So am I."

I SPEND the rest of the morning trying to catch up on shampoo and bakery orders, scheduling, and reading up on changes to employee health insurance. But my brain is still preoccupied with the knowledge that Henry Hill wants to buy my business. Did Anton know? Is that why he responded the way he did? I want to ask, but I'm afraid if I call, his phone will ring at the worst possible moment. Instead, I keep shifting from one task to another and not actually getting anything finished. Around lunchtime, my mom calls, and I give up on productivity.

"Lydia, I was just thinking—have you ever tried the cabbage soup diet?"

I cringe, not at all in the mood to be pestered about my weight or any other imperfections today. I've been avoiding sharing the news about Anton's mom, hoping for a better update from him first. But I can't put it off any longer.

"Sharon's in the hospital. Some kind of stroke, they think."

"Oh, no." Her tone changes instantly, and I'm grateful for that, at least. "When did this happen?"

"Seth called Sunday night. Anton flew out right away, and he's been there ever since."

"But you're not with him?"

I clench the arm of my office chair, rankling at the surprise in her voice. But there is no way in hell I'm going to discuss the reasons why. "I have businesses to run, Mom."

"Yes, but this sounds serious. What if—"

"Look, nothing terrible has happened yet."

"You don't think this is already terrible?" she says in a low tone.

"Of course I do. But Anton and I talked about it and . . ." I close my eyes. "He told me not to come."

My mother says nothing. Which is pretty much like saying everything for a woman who never shuts up.

"How are Celia and the baby?" I try.

She doesn't take the bait, and I'm about to look for an excuse to end the call because I don't need whatever judgment she's stewing on right now. But then she speaks again.

"When your dad . . ." she starts, then trails off. And now I'm fully alarmed. My father took off when I was four, and we never saw him again. She does *not* bring him up, not unless she has to. "There were times certain things happened when we were young, and I . . . I just wished I'd done things differently."

I don't know what to say. She has always maintained that their marriage had been perfect up until our dad abandoned us, that he'd left her totally blindsided. I am floored by the sorrow in her voice.

"That was a long time ago, Mom," I say carefully.

"Yes. It was." She sniffs like she's dismissing a bad odor. "I just don't want you to get to my age and feel the same way."

I swallow, wondering if the damage has already been done. "I'll keep it in mind."

"Now, I need to chat with your sister." She returns to her normal, directive tone. "She has this idea that just because her husband is Jewish, my grandson shouldn't be christened. You really should give her a call, Lydia."

"I'll leave you to that," I say.

"Keep me updated on Sharon," she says quietly. "I'll be praying for her."

"Thank you."

I end the call and find myself staring at the picture from Celia's wedding. Anton in his suit, me in my blue dress. A tender thread of regret weaves its way through my gut.

I hate when my mother is right.

CHAPTER THIRTY-SIX

Him

"Hey. Uh, she seems pretty settled. I mean, as much as she can be," Seth says. "You wanna go grab a burger or something?"

I can tell my brother just wants out of here. *I* want the hell out of here. But I'm reluctant to leave my chair. I've been in Dallas almost a week, and things with Mom have shifted out of crisis mode, but no one will really say what's next because no one knows. Her vitals remain surprisingly strong, but she still hasn't woken up at all. The hospital couldn't keep her, so she's back in her room at Sunny Cove.

"Yeah, okay. Just give me a minute."

"Sure, man. I'll wait in the car."

He tromps out of the room, and I take my mother's hand. Like I have every day for the last five days. I know she'll be fine—as fine as possible under the circumstances. The staff come in regularly to care for her. They feed and toilet her, and they've been wonderful. But I'm worried something will change as soon as I go.

"I might have to go back to Denver for a bit," I whisper to her. "Sethie's going to be here, but I just have to—" My voice breaks. *Return to work? Get back to normal?* All the reasons I can think of to leave make me feel like the world's shittiest son. But it's worse than that. Because what I'm actually dreading most about going home is facing my own damn problems. "Mom, Lydia and I—"

Her fingers tighten around mine.

I freeze, staring at her face. Nothing has changed in her expression, but her hand stays firmly closed around mine for at least a minute before finally letting go. I'm not sure what to think of this. It could be a coincidence, just a muscle reflex. Her nurses warned us about that. But my distraught brain convinces me there's some significance in her reaction to my wife's name. There has to be.

My mom was so stupid excited when Lydia and I got married. Her own marriage had been cut short after my dad died in a car accident when I was ten, but growing up, she made clear how grateful she was for the brief time they had together. People used to tell us how much she adored our dad, that they were made for one another. She never said she thought the connection between Lydia and me was similar, but it shined in her eyes every time she looked at us.

I never wanted to tell her otherwise.

It feels like we lost my dad a million years ago. I've known for a while Mom would slip away too, but for the longest time I thought I'd be okay with Seth, with Lydia, and maybe one day even a child of our own to fill the family-sized void in my heart.

I squeeze Mom's hand back, then rest it gently on the sheet. "I'll stop in again to say goodbye before I go."

My brother and I don't say much over dinner. We go to some greasy spoon he likes mostly for the beer, and I pick at my burger and fries.

"So, then. When are you thinking of heading out?"

"Maybe I shouldn't," I say. "My boss would probably let me go remote. That way I could be around in case something . . ."

A muscle in his cheek twitches. Otherwise his face doesn't move. "The doctors said she could be like this a while."

"I know. That's why I thought I could stay. Maybe check in on her in the mornings, give you a break. I could even start going through some of that stuff in the basement."

"Anton, I donated most of that shit last year."

"Oh."

Seth had moved into our old house with Mom five years ago, back when she first showed signs of memory issues. It was a good plan for a while; it definitely helped to have someone around to keep the place clean and make sure she was eating and showering regularly. But then she started wandering off, and once we even had to call the police. The night she mistook the oven for a fireplace and nearly burned the place down, we knew it was time to do something else.

I keep waiting to feel as confident about what's happening now.

"Well, still. I can spend some extra time with her."

"Sure. Anything that helps you avoid going back to Denver," he drawls.

I glare at him, then look around for our waitress to ask for the check.

"We haven't talked much about Lydia since you got here," he continues, like he's inquiring about the stock market.

"Nothing to talk about."

"Why was it you said she didn't come with you?"

I sit there, staring at him, but the little shit just stares back, waiting me out.

"It's over." I press my lips together. "There, we talked about it." I signal the waitress.

He dips a french fry in ketchup slowly, like he's really pondering. "Define *over*. Like, the existence of the dodo bird? The Rangers' chances for the World Series—"

"My fucking marriage, dumbass."

He raises his eyebrows. "So, you guys never did end up in the sack?"

This is what I get for sharing details with my brother. But my mind flits to those precious minutes with my face between her thighs, breathing in her sweet scent while she bucked and moaned for me Saturday night. God. That seems like a hundred years ago.

"I got her off." I shrug. "She gave me a BJ."

"Oof. Sounds marriage-ending," Seth says.

My hand curls into a fist under the table. "Can we go?"

"How was it, though?" He tips his head at me.

I clench my jaw, fighting the memory of her slick lips and tongue sliding along my shaft. The way she came at me like she was hungry for it, and I thought I might explode when my tip hit the back of her throat.

"She only did it because she felt like she had to," I mutter.

He winces. "Ooh. So, bad? Like, lots of teeth and stuff?"

I release a hot puff of air and look away.

A slow smile creeps over his lips. "Or was it good?"

I scan the restaurant again. "Where is the goddamn server?"

"So, I'm confused," he says, ignoring me. "You both finally got laid, and by all accounts it was great. She wishes she was here with you. But you're getting divorced?"

I snap my eyes to his face, nearly knocking over my water glass. "You talked to her?"

He shrugs. "You should try it sometime."

"What did she say?" I don't mean to growl, but it definitely comes out that way. I have nearly called Lydia half a dozen times since I boarded the plane in Denver, but I've always stopped because what would I even say?

I miss you.

I love you.

I still want you.

I try to imagine what she's doing without me back home. She's probably happier, camped out in the kitchen with her laptop, PJs, and glasses, making business calls. Maybe she doesn't miss me at all.

Or maybe she does.

The picture in my head changes, and she's alone at home in our bed, reaching for her nightstand. She lies naked across the covers, legs spread wide as she thinks of me, vibrator humming in her juices.

Fuck.

I shift in my seat and check myself. In the ten years we've been together, Lydia has never once indicated that she pleasures herself. That rabbit is destined to gather dust.

"She didn't say much." Seth twirls a coaster in front of him. "Called to check in because she was worried. Said you told her not to come."

I look away.

Seth lays down the coaster. "Anton, this is definitely none of my business, but I don't know if you've got the right read on your wife."

I pound my fist on the table. "Have you not been listening to me for the past . . . what, year? Two years? I *told* you about that whole disaster at the hotel."

"Look, I'm not stupid. You two definitely have your issues. But just in case you're blind, it's fucking clear she loves you."

I exhale and close my eyes, pinching the bridge of my nose. When I look up, my gaze falls on a tiny little girl dashing by our table, giggling with delight. A man about my age follows her, presumably her dad, pretending to give chase. He swoops her up, tickling her as he carries her back to a smiling woman at a nearby table. Something deep in my chest tightens.

"We don't want the same things," I say. "She wants her career, and I want . . . something else."

"How do you know?"

I scowl at him. "We just fucking talked about it."

"Bro, no offense, but you're not the most amazing communicator."

"And you've never slept two nights in a row with the same woman, so maybe you're not the best source of monogamy advice."

"Touché." He shrugs. "Maybe you guys should at least try therapy."

I roll my eyes. "Great, so I can sit in some office with her and a stranger and *talk* about how she doesn't actually fucking want me."

"Dude." He gives me a sidelong glance. "She didn't have to suck your dick."

"That's my point! She didn't do it because she wanted to."

"Are you sure about that?"

I scowl and don't give him an answer.

"Okay. Look, I know Lydia well enough. I feel confident saying she loves you. And you *obviously* still love her."

"That doesn't mean we're meant to be," I mutter.

Seth crumples his napkin and tosses it on the table. "Mom always said you were one of those couples that was going to last."

I open my mouth to tell him to fuck off, but then I think of Mom's face on our wedding day, and this lump in the back of my throat makes me choke. I end up grinding my teeth instead, and maybe Seth can hear that because he seems to get the message.

"Sorry," he says. And it's clear he means it. "I'll get the check."

CHAPTER THIRTY-SEVEN

Her

The absolute worst part of coming home is the empty house. The silence reverberating through every room. The deserted backyard with no one weeding or playing with the dog. The vacant couch with no one stretched out snoring. Even with Heartthrob here, following me around with unusual attentiveness, everything still seems too quiet. Like I've stepped into a vacuum.

I take out my phone when I get home Friday night and pull up Anton's number. Maybe he'd answer if I actually dialed. But what would I say?

I swipe away instead, selecting the number I've called every evening for the past five days.

"Hey. This is your daily check-in. Have you been abducted or murdered?" I ask, scooping food into Heartthrob's dish.

"I am alive and well at this moment, thanks," Caprice says with a dry laugh. "Not even any new threats. I actually haven't had one in . . . three whole days."

"Good," I breathe. "Maybe this has blown over enough you can finally relax?"

"The *Bustle* follow-up drops Sunday, so . . . I kind of think not."

I open the fridge in an effort to feed myself. "Have you considered other areas of journalism? Sports and fitness?"

"Maybe if I hadn't already been fronted payment for the next two articles. Marital happiness is on the decline, and people are eating up the married-dating thing."

I close the fridge and sink to a kitchen chair, thinking of the lists of faces on Unmatched. Anton hasn't been back on the app. At least, not that I can tell. I can't really see him scrolling for girls at his mother's bedside. But I suppose I've been wrong about him before.

"Hey," Caprice says gently. "How are *you* doing?"

I let out a slow breath. "Oh, you know . . ."

"Any word on your mother-in-law?"

I swallow. "Seth says nothing's changed and she could be that way a while. Says Anton hardly speaks to him. I—I just wish I was there. For both of them. For her."

"I'm sorry," she says. "I know this is hard."

I shrug to myself, straightening the napkins in front of me. "You want to hang out tonight? I upgraded my streaming subscription."

"Actually, my brother's on his way here from the airport," she says, sounding distracted.

"Oh." I furrow my brow. "I thought Theo was still overseas."

"Apparently he's on leave, and he just *has* to see me about . . . Um, well, it's complicated. Maybe we can meet up for lunch next week and I'll be able to fill you in."

Something in her voice sounds off, but I pull the phone away from my ear and swipe over to my calendar, figuring she'll tell me more when I see her. "I think I can do that." I grimace. "Though maybe not till Thursday."

She chuckles. "Sure you don't want to reconsider the Pooches offer?"

A pang shoots through my chest. I filled Caprice in about everything—Anton, Sharon, the offer from Henry—right after he left Sunday. The amount of money also blew her mind, but after I explained my business goals, she supported my decision.

"Hey, I was just joking," she says when I struggle to respond. "You made the right choice. Anton's a douche for not seeing that, but you don't need him. I'm excited to watch you blow the top off the Denver pet industry."

"Thanks," I say quietly. Heartthrob finishes licking his empty dish across the floor, and I stand to let him out in the yard to chase a squirrel. "I'm going to go walk my dog. Then maybe binge-watch that new mystery series."

"Uh, not to sound like a broken record, but a trip to the gym might make you feel better . . ."

"Yeah, I think you have said that before," I quip, staring at an old pair of running shoes Anton left by the back door. Caprice has been trying to convince me to drown my sorrows in endorphins, but I much prefer Ben & Jerry's.

"Fine." She huffs. "Wallow, if that's what you want. But eventually, you'll need to do something for *yourself*."

"Chocolate Fudge Brownie is currently doing everything for me."

She pauses, her voice turning more playful. "It's Friday night. Maybe what you ought to do after your lactose delight is take out that new vibe you bought and have a little post-dessert fun."

"*Caprice*." My face flames hot as soon as I process what she's suggesting. "Why would I do that?"

She laughs. "Always makes me feel better!"

"I don't think so," I say, though I kind of sound like a Catholic school nun.

I haven't looked at or touched the rabbit since the day Anton left. Just picturing it reminds me of those last few hours, when everything seemed like it might come together—until it all fell apart.

"You're no fun." She sighs. "Suit yourself."

I pinch the bridge of my nose, watching the dog wander around the yard.

"Be careful this weekend," I say in an effort to change the subject.

"I will literally have a US Marine sleeping on my couch," she says, though she sounds tired. "I'll probably be safer this weekend than I have been for a while."

"Okay, but still. Text me next week, and we'll figure out where to go for lunch. I'm dying to hear why your brother suddenly flew halfway across the country to see you."

"Will do," she says. Then, after a pause: "Hang in there, Lyd."

I STEP out of the shower to find my phone notifications surprisingly empty. No one calling in sick tomorrow, no contractor hurdles, not even my mother questioning my life choices. Without a work crisis to solve, I wrap up in my robe and wander into the living room, ready to lose myself to a TV mystery. Except about halfway into the first episode, I realize my head is just not into it. My mind is wandering. I keep having to skip back and rewatch parts when I can't follow what's going on.

I try to give it a second episode, but when I realize I don't even know the main character's name, I sigh, turn off the TV, and head back to my room. My laptop is on the nightstand, and my first inclination is to busy myself with work. Emails, supply orders, or some task related to payroll. The problem is, I'm already caught up. I guess this is what happens when you start work before six a.m., stay through lunch, and make sure not to go home until after dinner five days in a row. There is literally nothing of any substance left to do until tomorrow.

I guess the single life will be good for productivity. Ugh.

I pick up my phone, thinking maybe I'll download a book or read mindless celebrity news or something, but when I open my browser, I find myself staring at the tab open to "The Classic Guide to Blowjobs." My lip curls as memories flood in from the last time I looked at this site. Was it only a week ago? I'm about to close it when I notice a menu with a host of links, including: "The Classic Guide to Arousal," "The Classic Guide to Sex Toys," and "The Classic Guide to Orgasms."

Curiosity nudges my thumb to explore. More than a few times since he left, my mind has grudgingly wandered back to the night Anton used the rabbit on me. I've had orgasms before, but I've never felt quite the way I did that night, and I'm not sure why. Had we just been lacking a battery-powered pink column of silicone all this time? Or did using it change something else? I have to admit, I haven't been able to forget the look in Anton's eyes when I handed him the box.

"The Classic Guide" claims to educate people on how to give (and receive) sexual pleasure, and while I'm not sure what I could learn here that will help me now, I keep reading.

> *Arousal. For women, touching, kissing, and even talking can* lead *to arousal, which may* then *turn into desire. But it might not be spontaneous the way it is for men. Some women may find that engaging in stimulation, even when they're not feeling it, may actually help get them in the mood.*

I raise an eyebrow. Something about this rings true. If I'm honest with myself, I have always been reluctant to get started having sex. Even ten years in, it's just embarrassing and hard. But there have been times, like last week, when I found myself getting more into it the more we touched. Maybe that's what Caprice meant about getting my engine going.

> *It's difficult for some people to stay present and focused during sex. Letting go of other things on your mind can improve your enjoyment. Stop worrying about what you look like—your partner's just glad you're naked. You don't need to think about doing the dishes. And that work project can wait till tomorrow.*

I lay my phone on my chest and close my eyes when I read this. I can't count the number of times I have literally been under Anton thinking about payroll or going over my weekly to-do list. No wonder I'm bad at it.

> *Get to know yourself: Spend some time with yourself alone, using mindful masturbation. This can be done with sex toys or just your fingers. Get comfortable with your body and learn what you like. Self-love tip: 1/3 of women can only orgasm through clitoral stimulation.*

I scroll through several more pages, stopping when I get to a step-by-step guide to female masturbation. At this point, I have to set my phone aside, pull my robe tight around me, and wait for my face to stop burning. I've never actually touched myself without Anton. Maybe because we met so young and only ever explored sex together. I know lots of people masturbate, and obviously the website I've been reading indicated it's normal and healthy, but something about it has always seemed . . . I don't know. Not exactly wrong. But it didn't seem like there was much point without him.

Then again, when I try to imagine touching myself *with* Anton, I get even more squeamish. Like it's not something I want him to see. Or, if I'm honest, something that embarrasses me.

My eyes flutter closed.

Maybe none of this matters anymore. Anton's far away in Dallas; he's probably not even coming back. And I'm here. Just me.

After crossing the room to close the door, despite telling myself no one's going to walk in, I slide open the drawer of my nightstand and remove the toy tucked inside. The salesgirl suggested I "practice" anyway, so I guess that's what I'm going to do. I pull the drawstring of the black velvet storage bag it came with and pull out the silky pink phallus, examining it in my palm. It isn't as heavy as I remember, but when my thumb locates the on switch and it buzzes to life, I let out an audible gasp.

Heartthrob raises his head from where he's snoozing in his dog bed, and I click it off quickly, then laugh at my own mortification over my dog seeing my sex toy.

I try the power button a few more times, cycling through different patterns and levels of vibration—all of them somehow too loud—turning it over in my hands. I'm not sure why, but the little rabbit ears appendage intimidates me more than the big hot-pink shaft.

Once I've got a handle on the vibrator's basic functions, I skim the lengthy section on masturbation in the "Classic Guide." It actually suggests starting with just fingers before introducing a toy, which is a tiny relief. I set the rabbit aside, pausing to put on some music so all my overthinking doesn't echo through my brain quite so loudly. Then I lean back into the pillows and take a deep breath.

I pull at the belt of my robe, shyly parting the fabric and taking in the landscape. I've never waxed or anything, but I try to keep pretty well-trimmed below deck. Reclining the way I am, my waist seems small and attractively flat. My breasts are pale and full, falling slightly to the sides. One of my nipples is slightly inverted, which my doctor has assured me is normal. Sometimes it peeks out, especially if I'm cold, but I guess it's feeling like the rest of me right now because there's no sign it's coming out. I squeeze gently the way my gynecologist showed me, and it pops up for a second. Tentatively, I touch both nipples, but it just seems kind of clinical, like I'm doing a breast exam or something.

Loads of fun.

Just to be thorough, I reach down, checking for any signs of arousal. My vagina, like most I'm sure, isn't a total desert. But there's clearly not a whole lot of fluid action going on. It seems about as welcoming to my touch as a naked nun. I check the guide again, which encourages using a moist finger to stroke over and around the clitoris. Saliva is suggested as a lubricant, but that kind of wigs me out, so I open up the little bottle from Playful Pleasures. The clear lube is silky and light, and thankfully doesn't seem to smell like anything. I pour a few drops on my fingers, hesitate, then reach between my legs, searching for the sensitive little nub tucked in the folds just above my vagina.

Per the guide, I start making circles on and around it, spreading my legs open a little for better range of motion. *This* actually kind of does something. It's not overpowering or anything, but the sensation is pleasant. Almost like some little bit of me is waking up. I open my legs a little wider and change direction a few times, sliding up and down lengthwise, which is also quite nice. Still not intense, but it feels like things are building, and will continue to build if I keep this up.

The article emphasized paying attention to other erogenous zones like breasts and nipples too, so without removing my right hand, I reach to explore there. Surprisingly, my one shy nipple has decided to come out to play. I give it a light squeeze, and I'm surprised when this time the sensation seems to shoot down between my legs. Almost like the areas are connected. After another minute or two, I realize there's been a shift in my lower regions. Things feel different—my skin flushed and hot instead of tight and clammy. When I run my fingers over the delicate tissues, they're moist and swollen—not a lot, not painfully—just enough to make everything feel . . . well, turned on.

Oh wow. Is *that* what that means?

I glance over at the pink rabbit lying next to me on the bed, and though my whole body is already warm, my cheeks burn a little hotter. I look again toward the closed door, to my dog sleeping peacefully in his bed, then I roll my eyes at myself and pick up the toy.

It hums to life in my hand, and my memory flashes to last weekend when Anton was the one wielding it between my legs. *Are you ready?* he whispered, bare-chested, looking up at me. And then he plunged it into my slick, waiting flesh. I imagine him there again as I lower the toy to my center, urging it gently between my folds. I flinch at the sudden contact but start sliding the vibrator up and down, letting it grow slick with my body's arousal. I find a rhythm the way I'd done with my fingers, and my legs part a little more. My eyes fall closed as I move the toy lower, imagining it in Anton's hands as the tip hums against my flesh, finding its way to my entrance. My center throbs with anticipation as I pause outside, just the way he did.

Something seems to curl within me then, and I thrust my hips, pushing the tip inside, gasping at both the intrusion and what a relief it is. The strange, unyielding shape fills me again, much like my husband, except also completely different. Slowly, I begin guiding the rabbit in and out of my vagina, its slick, wet sounds making me groan as I explore deeper with each thrust. My muscles tighten around the toy, welcoming it like this is everything I've been waiting for, this fullness and friction.

I close my eyes, letting my head fall back on my pillow. My hips buck, and I realize I'm imagining Anton inside me, mimicking his thrusts and attentions. I ache, thinking of his body, hot and strong, joined with mine. And then, with the next rock of my hips, without really preparing myself at all, the rabbit sinks deeper, and its little ears touch down on my wet, throbbing clit.

Suddenly, in my mind, Anton is everywhere. Thrusting inside me, pinching my nipples, sucking my clit all at once. My core tightens and I let out a cry, bucking and thrusting the toy between my legs as my muscles spasm and euphoria rolls through me. I ride the wave, my body's pulses, urging it on and on and on until finally, regretfully, it slowly fades away.

I find the off switch on the toy and go completely still, letting my hand fall to my side in the silence. I open my eyes, and my gaze lands on the bed beside me. The big, empty space where Anton ought to be. I reach out, tracing my fingers over his pillow, until suddenly I grab it, pulling it to my chest. I crush it against my body, breathing in his scent, desperate for his warmth. My body curls around it, still humming from the fantasy of him as I cry into the fabric.

CHAPTER THIRTY-EIGHT

Her

"Hello? Lydia, is that you?"

I take a deep breath, hoping my voice will sound right when I open my mouth. I'm just calling to check in on my sister and nephew, get the lowdown on how they're settling in, making an attempt at being a decent aunt. That is definitely why I'm calling.

I mean, I do care. I hope they're doing well.

But Celia and I never just call each other to chat. So she's going to think I want something. And I hate that she'll be correct.

"Uh, yeah. Hi."

"Hello," Celia says again, sounding about as awkward and surprised as I feel.

"Is this a good time? I don't want to interrupt any um . . . baby things."

At this, my sister laughs. And for once, it sounds genuine, not dismissive or forced. "If you mean endless laundry and diaper folding, I'll let it slide for a bit. Gabriel's napping right now. I could use some adult conversation."

"Oh. Great." I'm not sure what to say next. I hadn't given much thought to anything past dialing her number, which was hard enough. "Are you enjoying being a mother?"

I cringe as soon as I ask this. What new mom is going to say they don't like motherhood? I cover my face with my palm while Celia affirms the obvious.

"Oh, it's the best. I don't sleep as much, for sure, but I'm in love with little Gabriel. Wouldn't trade him for anything. I can't wait for you to meet him."

She sounds like a Hallmark card, and I feel slightly nauseous.

"That's great."

I'm struggling to remember why I called, why this conversation was worth having when I could've just sent a text without all the uncomfortable silence, but then Celia speaks again and inadvertently reminds me.

"Mom said Anton's mother was in the hospital." Her voice is sober. "I'm sorry to hear that."

"I . . ." I swallow past the lump in my throat. "Thanks."

My sister can't know how devastated I am about Sharon, about what's happened between me and Anton. How I feel like everything around me is coming to an end all at once. But I appreciate her sincerity.

"Look, I actually called to ask if I could run something by you. It's, um, a business situation. You can bill me for coaching if you want."

She snorts. "I'm not going to charge my own sister just to answer a question." She pauses, then amends. "Well . . . maybe I won't if you promise you and Anton will come for Thanksgiving."

I grit my teeth, trying not to imagine what the next family holiday might look like. "Fine. Whatever. I'll buy the pies."

"Hah." I can tell she's angling her nose high, like she's won something.

"Okay, let me just get to it. I—I received an offer from an associate interested in purchasing my businesses. All of them. I had initially turned it down, but now I'm having second thoughts."

"Interesting." Her voice rises in surprise. "What kind of figures are we talking?"

I share the number and she whistles. "Not bad, Lydia, considering."

Considering the dog poop? Fleas? She doesn't elaborate, and I don't ask.

"So, out of curiosity . . . If you already declined, what's making you reconsider?"

I miss my husband.

A twinge of pain works through my chest. He hasn't called. Hasn't texted. Hasn't done anything to indicate he feels the same way I do. But I haven't been able to stop thinking about him. Or our argument before he went to Dallas. *I'm not super interested in waiting around until you have time for me.*

My stomach feels heavy. I was awake all last night thinking about everything. The past few weeks, the past ten years. Anton probably spoke more actual words about our relationship the morning he left than he has our entire marriage, but when I really think about it—Unmatched, the thirty-day deadline—he *has* been communicating how he feels. I've been the one avoiding him.

"I'm just worried it might've been a hasty decision. I don't want to wind up regretting it later."

"That's wise." I can hear her clicking around on a computer. "What does Anton say about it?"

"He wants me to sell." The tip of my nose burns. "He thinks I work too much."

"Ah, marital discord," Celia says. And there's a surprising bitterness in her voice I've never heard before. "Well, let's coach you through this. I mean, if you want a real analysis, I'll need to see the proposal, your profit and loss statements for the last several years, etc. But for the sake of this conversation, what are all the immediate pros and cons?"

"Pros of selling would be . . . money, obviously. A change of pace. Flexibility to travel and focus on things I haven't had time for." *Like my marriage.* My face burns. "It might also be an opportunity to pursue other things."

"Like what?" she asks.

"Uh . . . I don't know. Maybe a new business."

"You don't have anything in mind?"

"No. Not at all. All of my plans for the foreseeable future were tied to the Pooches." Unless you count starting my own family?

"Hmm." She types for several minutes, then pauses. "Okay, what about the cons of selling?"

"Giving up my livelihood," I say, a little too quickly. "Lump sums aside, my businesses are profitable. We're not hurting, and I enjoy them. I'm not sure I'm ready to walk away."

"Profitable even with the new place opening up?"

I nod. "Even if we only get half the business of the first location, we'll be fine."

"Look at you," she lilts, not quite under her breath. "Okay, and I can assume the pros of *not* selling would be getting to keep and grow the pet businesses you love, having a stable income, and the cons would be . . . poor work-life balance, less flexibility for travel, and no pile of cash."

And no marriage, I add in my head. "Essentially."

Celia makes a humming sound, then lets out a low breath. "I mean, if it were me, I'd take the money. But if you don't need it and don't have something else you really want to pursue, it still makes sense to hold on to the dog stuff. Especially if it makes you happy."

I raise my eyebrows, surprised. After a minute, my shoulders slump with disappointment. I was sure she'd tell me to sell the business and take the cash—that's what I needed her to say. This feels like the same conversation I already had with Anton. The Pooches do make me happy, but they can't be the answer. Because what I couldn't grasp before, maybe what should have been obvious, is how happy *he* makes me too. It doesn't seem fair that I have to choose—one or the other—our life together, or apart.

Henry's offer is open on my laptop. I still feel bad about our meeting in my office on Wednesday. He was being pushy, but I hadn't meant to snap at him. He could probably sense I'd been impulsive about the decision and was just trying to get me to reconsider. Well, I guess it worked after all because here I am, reconsidering. But I can't bring myself to make the call.

I wish I could talk to Anton about it.

Except I already have.

"Anton never insisted I quit," I say quietly, more to myself than my sister. "I think his point was I'm over-committed."

"Anton's never been a female in business." Celia sniffs. "Who is making the offer, by the way? Is it anyone you know? Think they might consider a counter of some kind?"

I pause, trying to process her suggestion. "What do you mean?"

"It's kind of a long shot, and might not be something you're interested in, but you could see if they'd be willing to hammer out some sort of compromise. Maybe not a full acquisition, but more of a partnership?"

I take a sharp breath. And it's like something clicks in the back of my mind.

I scroll through the offer again. To the section where Henry specified that he wanted me to stay on for a limited time as a consultant. Meaning, stick around and run things because he knows nothing about dog care. And, I'm willing to bet, he really doesn't want to know either. Henry's goal is purely to improve the business and make money.

"Celia . . . thank you." My heart races to keep pace with my mind, but I force myself to breathe, slow down, and extend genuine praise to my sister. "You really are good at what you do."

Charlotte gives me a brief hug as I walk through the reception area of her office. "You look like someone who's been weighing big decisions."

"You could say that," I mutter, following her to a small conference room. "Thanks for working on this so quickly."

She waves her hand in the air as we each take a seat. "This is how these sorts of deals happen. Lots of overthinking and back-and-forth, then suddenly, it's done."

I fidget with my paw print necklace. "We'll see about that."

I ended up being too chicken to contact Henry myself. If Anton had been here, we might've managed it together. Approached him as a team. He could've smoothed out all the things I'd handled badly. But since we still haven't spoken, and because I've already screwed up enough to nearly ruin things, I felt more comfortable letting Charlotte handle the delivery of my counter-proposal.

The door opens, and in walks Henry Hill, followed by another man in a suit and glasses. Presumably his attorney. Charlotte greets them both like the cool professional she is, and I'm grateful for her. I haven't actually spoken to Henry since I essentially stomped on his offer and threw him out of my office. Maybe it wasn't quite that bad, but I do wish I'd handled it differently.

Charlotte gestures for the men to sit, then turns to me. "Lydia Richie, this is Mr. Hill, whom I understand you already know, and his attorney, Mr. Lunter."

"Yes." I extend my arm to shake their hands. "Nice to meet you. And good to see you again, Henry."

He takes my hand with a bright smile. "Glad you were willing to give the deal some more thought."

I blush a little, sure we're both recalling the impulsive way I last spoke to him. "Yes, well, this is a bit different from the deal you originally proposed."

"True." He cocks an eyebrow. "But this might actually work out better."

I exhale a little, hearing him validate my own hopes. Not just for the Pooches, but maybe all parts of my life.

"Mr. Lunter and I have already nailed down the financial details, and that's all in order." Charlotte puts on a pair of glasses, shuffling through the papers in front of her. "But before we move forward, we should discuss how you each envision this working. How do you see your roles as co-owners of Ooh La Pooch and the rapidly growing Pooch Park?"

I take a deep breath, again grateful for Charlotte's wisdom and ability to think with her feet on the ground. All I've been able to do for the past forty-eight hours is rehash Anton's words from the other morning. *You put all you have into work, and there's nothing left.*

"I . . . I want to have more time to focus on certain things. I love the Pooches, and they're both thriving, but I do have a number of balls in the air." I pause at Henry's confused expression. "Sorry, 'The Pooches' is Anton's nickname for both businesses."

"Ah. Cute," he says.

"There are things I truly adore about running The Pooch Park and Ooh La Pooch," I press on. "I love making clients feel their dogs are special to us. I love making my employees feel valued and important. And I *love* getting to play with the actual dogs." Henry nods as he listens, the corner of his mouth twitching when I mention our canine clients. He carefully removes a hair from his sleeve. "The things I don't love about running the Pooches? Processing payroll, staying up-to-date on insurance and employee benefits, figuring out anything to do with our taxes . . ."

Henry sits forward. "I have systems to streamline all of those things. And more."

"I thought you might." I offer a warm smile. "I think I'm ready to not wear every hat myself, but I *love* my businesses. I still want to be involved on a day-to-day level, but maybe not twenty-four hours a day. And I have specific ideas about possible expansion."

"Mr. Hill," Charlotte asks. "Does Ms. Richie's description match up with how you're envisioning this partnership?"

"I believe it does." Henry glances at his attorney, who removes some papers from his briefcase. "We took the liberty of drawing up specifics on the division of labor, so to speak, as well as some financial projections. Lydia and I will be equal partners, but my role will remain more behind the scenes, focused on things like accounting, human resources, website development, and social media, while Lydia continues as the face of the business, and . . ." Henry trails off, waving his hands as if to dismiss something unpleasant.

"I handle the actual dogs," I finish for him, biting back a laugh.

"Yes, preferably," he says.

Charlotte peruses the documents from the other attorney, and we all make notes, going further into the details. Henry asks about the status of the new Pooch Park location, and we discuss whether to hire someone new or promote Tomás to take some of the managerial pressure off me. I tell him about Scarlet quitting last minute, how incredibly hard it is to find decent groomers, and he makes some really great suggestions about how to incentivize the right people to replace her. Then we go into detail on my expansion plans, and I listen as he speculates what might be most profitable. It's actually kind of nice when he offers to run comparisons on similar business models, and I realize all I have to do is focus on the fun parts—what boarding, pet sitting, or dog training might look like added to our operations—without having to slog through their financial viability first.

By the time we leave Charlotte's office that afternoon, we have a tentative agreement. Henry will be buying a fifty percent stake in the Pooches and all related businesses going forward, and I will receive a nice injection of cash. It's not the mind-blowing amount initially proposed, but it's still significant.

I pull my phone out on the way to my car, desperate to call Anton and tell him everything. I have a plan—I *can* strike a balance. I'm making time for both work and pleasure, and I want that pleasure to include him.

My brain catches up to my fingers before I manage to dial. I haven't heard from Seth for two days. That might mean nothing with Sharon has changed, but if it has . . .

I swipe to my browser and start Googling flights. Whatever the situation, Anton and I need to be face-to-face.

CHAPTER THIRTY-NINE

Her

Heartthrob follows me around the house, practically glued to my heels. He's been a mess ever since I pulled my purple suitcase back out and started packing for Dallas. Actually, we both have.

"You'll have fun with Tomás and all your buddies," I say in my most reassuring voice.

He tilts his head like he's unconvinced, and I guess I can't blame him. It's been more than a week since Anton packed his own suitcase and walked out. Heartthrob whined and paced the first twenty-four hours, and he's parked himself by the front window every day since, waiting for his return. They—we—have never been apart this long.

I look into his deep brown eyes, stroking the extra-soft fuzz on his Akita ears. "I won't be gone long, and . . . maybe I'll bring him home with me."

My voice wavers as I express this hope. Heartthrob gives a resigned sigh, and I turn back to the bed to fold the rest of my shirts. My phone lights up on the duvet.

SETH

Shoot me your flight info so I can pick you up tonight.

Nah, don't worry, I'll get a Lyft. Will you guys be at Sunny Cove, or should I come to the house?

SETH

Cove. He sits with her from nine to five like it's his job. I'm glad you're coming.

Does he know?

SETH

Hell no. I'm staying out of this. Just get here so you can kiss and make up.

I manage a small smile. My brother-in-law inherited all the easy communication Anton didn't get from their mom. When I called to feel him out about my plan, Seth was elated. He said if I didn't come soon he'd put Anton on a plane to Denver himself.

When my suitcase is nearly full, I realize I almost forgot the essentials and pull open my underwear drawer. I am about to grab a handful of my usual cotton briefs when a glimpse of lace catches my eye toward the back. I pull out the two sexy lingerie sets I purchased before meeting Anton at the hotel. With a warm feeling in my belly, I slip into the set I haven't worn yet. It's a champagne color, with delicate pink flowers scattered over the sheer fabric covering my clearly visible nipples. It's a bit more structurally complete than the set I wore at the hotel, but seeing it in the mirror still makes me blush. I can't help wondering if Anton will like it—if he even sees it. Or if he'll ask me to leave before he gets the chance.

After a few instructions and a pep talk with my bather, Alicia, about how to open Ooh La Pooch without Scarlet, I drop Heartthrob with Tomás on my way to the airport. I haven't mentioned the deal with Henry to him yet, and I'm worried how he'll react, but Anton is the person I need to talk to about that next. I hope he can see what I'm trying to do—what it could mean for us.

. . .

I NEARLY ABANDON the entire trip at airport security when, of all things, my carry-on starts to buzz. Two TSA agents approach, looking official and insisting I unzip the suitcase to show them what's inside. I had packed my electric toothbrush, and for several seconds I pray to the airport gods that it's the source of the vibration. Because I had also thrown the rabbit in as an afterthought just before I left the house, a vote of confidence for myself that this whole effort might go well. I should've left it at home. I should have at least taken out the batteries.

The vibration was not coming from the toothbrush.

After an extended period of mortification during which the agents relay cryptic messages over their radios through bouts of muffled laughter, they finally decide I'm not carrying explosives and allow me to repack my bag. Though joke's on me when I look for the battery—it's rechargeable. By this point, I'm closer to the terminal than the airport exit, so I power toward my gate, trying not to die of humiliation. I find an empty corner facing a window so I can put my back to anyone who might've witnessed that particular disgrace, and I'm about to pull up my flight status when my phone rings.

"Hello?" I answer, grateful to see Caprice's name.

"Hey, glad I caught you," she says in a rush. "Have you left for the airport yet?"

I pinch the bridge of my nose, trying not to relive what just happened. "Oh, I'm there."

She makes a sound I can't identify. "Okay, um . . . shit, I was hoping to catch you before you left."

I lean forward in my uncomfortable airport chair at the tone of her voice. She knows about the plan with Henry, why I'm going to Dallas, and what my hopes are for confronting Anton. If there's a reason she wants to stop me, it's probably bad.

"God, Lydia, I don't know what else to tell you," she says, blowing out a hard breath. "Anton's back on Unmatched."

My back hits the hard plastic seat.

Out the window, a Southwest Airlines jet barrels down a runway, taking off.

"Wh-what do you mean?"

"I was working on one of the follow-ups to the married-cheating article. I hadn't logged into the site since the first one published, so I was checking to see what had changed. New policies, which guys were gone, who was brave enough to stick around, and . . . his profile's back up. It's active again." Her voice gets quiet. "I'm sorry."

I pull the phone away from my ear, staring at the screen like there should be something I can see. Something tangible. But it only shows the seconds of the call ticking by. What does this information mean? What do I do with it? I had about ten different plans in my head of various ways to move forward depending on how things went in Dallas, but Anton dating other women wasn't one of those scenarios. Seth assured me my husband had been in a rut since he arrived, that he was miserable and would welcome my arrival. But . . . maybe not.

Maybe I'm too late.

"Lydia?"

"Yeah?" I bring the phone back to my ear, watching planes negotiate the busy runway. Trying to figure out if I'm coming or going.

"You want me to come get you?"

I swallow past the lump in my throat. "Let me call you back."

WITH SHAKING HANDS, I navigate my browser to the site with the sultry blonde woman peeking out at me from the screen, beckoning me —someone—for a hookup. I'd deleted the app weeks ago, after that terrible striptease, when Anton promised he wouldn't go on it again. *Of course,* he said. *I promise. Never again.*

At least, not for thirty days.

But this is only day twenty-one.

My skin goes clammy as I log in, click over to "favorites," and my husband's profile appears. Smiling at me, smug, from that same idiotic cropped photo. The phone hits my lap as my face falls into my hands. How could I be so stupid? He's made clear what he wanted for weeks. I don't know why I ever thought it would be me.

Some announcement blares from a speaker overhead. Maybe about my flight. I don't comprehend the words. I manage to raise one hand from where it sits like a stone in my lap, ready to take Caprice up on her offer for a ride. Anywhere. I don't care. But just as I'm about to close the site that has *unmatched* my marriage in every way, I notice something. A small red dot in the corner of the screen, indicating I have unread messages.

Probably it's just spam. Or unsolicited offers from other amoral men. Someone else looking to wreck their home. But something curls deep inside me as I stare at the notification, and I can't bring myself to click away until I know for sure.

There are six unread messages. All sent over the last three days:

MOUNTAINMAN3

You said I'm hard to read. That I never tell you how I feel. And now here I am, typing all the words I should have said into the app that ruined everything. Useless, maybe. But better than not saying them at all, I guess.

MOUNTAINMAN3

Sitting here alone, watching my mom slip away is awful. But it's worse realizing I've lost you too.

MOUNTAINMAN3

I thought maybe if I learned the right skills, I could figure out how to fix us. It felt like we came close the other day. I should have asked if you felt it too. Instead I focused on all the wrong things.

MOUNTAINMAN3

I can't and WON'T ask you to give anything up for me.

MOUNTAINMAN3

I know I've lost every chance I had. And it sounds lame, but if I could do it over, I would. I'd listen about the Pooches, then take you back to bed. Find all the right places on your body to make you reach the stars again. Then sit with you until we figured out how to reach your dreams too.

MOUNTAINMAN3

Lydia, I can't imagine my life with anyone but you.

CHAPTER FORTY

Him

My phone pings in my pocket. I barely hear it, busy as I am counting speckles in the Sunny Cove ceiling tiles. It's an unfamiliar sound. Not a text or email or any notification I can immediately identify. Maybe there's a weather alert or something. I haven't been paying attention to spring in Dallas, but I suppose there could be a tornado watch or something. There are shelters in this building, but I'm not sure about moving Mom. I tear my gaze from the ceiling and dig around for my phone.

You have 37 unread messages on Unmatched

My mouth goes dry.

I hover my thumb to open the app, but then I glance at my mother lying in the bed, looking both too young to be there and older than her years. She's quiet, peaceful, like she's asleep. The same way she's looked for days. Even so, I mutter an excuse out loud to leave the room. I'm not opening up a cheating app in the same room with my mom.

I head outside to the walking path in the Sunny Cove gardens.

My inbox is jam-packed. I don't know what happened. I reactivated my account and sent a bunch of messages to LonelyGirl8 the other day. Out of a mix of sadness and desperation, I guess. It felt more like writing in a journal than something she'd ever see. Didn't make me feel better, but it did help me sleep. But now, scanning the subject lines and usernames, a tight, familiar feeling creeps into my chest.

There's a note titled "Let's have a pool hook up" from *SexyMama2.* Another from *FullFrontalPeaks* titled "Hungry for a lunch fuck." And another that says "I'm your girl" from *KinkyWife01.* I don't open any of them. Maybe I should be happy with all the offers for tits and ass, but after everything that's happened the last few weeks, I can't help wondering what brought them there. If it's because they're sad or hurt. Or maybe looking to hurt someone else.

Ugh. I can't even see hookups the same anymore.

I keep scrolling, my hopes fading as I make my way down the page, until I see a username that halts everything.

I sink to a bench on the side of the path.

LonelyGirl8

The message line says simply: "No subject."

I swallow hard. Lydia hasn't texted or called since I left Denver. I really didn't expect her to after everything we both said; I couldn't either. Which is why I wound up back on Unmatched. Staring at a version of her that—I can see now—she clearly made for me. The unlikely last place we managed to reconnect. When staring at her profile wasn't enough, I started writing.

Never in a million years did I expect her to reply.

But I'd never expected her to be in that hotel room either.

With a shaking hand, I tap open the message.

LONELYGIRL8

Hey, sexy. Still looking for fun?

I stare at the chat window for a full minute, wondering if it's actually my wife. Maybe it's Caprice, or someone else. Maybe the account was hacked.

I want to say, *Is this really you?* But that seems too direct. If she wanted a normal conversation, she could have sent a normal message. Or texted me. But she didn't.

MOUNTAINMAN3

Yes. Though my last date here didn't end so well.

The phone pings again right away.

LONELYGIRL8

Mine either.

MOUNTAINMAN3

Then what brings you back?

LONELYGIRL8

Well, I've been told I have great tits. And I'm lonely.

I snort. Never in ten years have I heard Lydia use the word "tits." This has got to be a sham. I start typing to dismiss whoever this is, tell them where to shove it, but another message comes through before I get the chance.

LONELYGIRL8

Also realized . . . I do want more than just a roommate.

My pulse spikes.

I glance around the empty gardens. Not sure what I'm looking for, but suddenly I wish I was somewhere more private. Maybe it's Lydia on the other end of this app after all. I swipe over to her profile. The pic is the same—fucking gorgeous—I don't know how I could have seen it before and *not* known my own wife. Her stats haven't changed, but the info after that looks like it's been updated. I take a minute to read through:

Sex: Female
Age: 29
Height: 5'7"
Weight: 140lbs
Eyes: Blue

Hair: Blonde
Build: Curvy
Interest: Men

<u>What I Enjoy:</u>
Tall, dark, and athletic for days. Must love dogs. Willingness to communicate needs.

<u>Experiences I'm Looking For:</u>
Less work, more play.
Figuring out what turns me on.
Figuring out how to get you off.
Trying out new things.
Learning about my body.
Learning about *your* body.
I think I could get better at this.
I *do* want you. I miss you.
I love you.

It's been an hour since Lydia's last message. Since I read through all the updates on her profile. I sat in the garden at Sunny Cove until the shadows started to grow long, trying to figure out what to say. How to respond. I even typed out half a dozen messages, but wound up deleting them all.

I have questions. Things I definitely want to say. But nothing feels right from seven hundred miles away.

Back in Mom's room, I wait for Seth to pick me up, take me home, and feed me, like he's been doing since I got here. Mom always used to insist that I needed to look out for him since I was the big brother. But lately, in his own way, Seth's been the one caring for what's left of our little family.

Maybe he'll know what I should do.

A light tap on the door draws my attention. I turn my head, expecting to see my brother or one of the staff members coming in with Mom's meds, to check her vitals, or change her position.

Nothing prepares me to see Lydia silhouetted in the doorway.

Seth is at her shoulder, but once she enters the room, he fades back into the hall.

For a minute, my jaw hardens, and I just sit there. I'd told her not to come, but every day, sitting here with my mom, it's felt like something was missing. And the minute Lydia walks in, I know immediately what it was. A low ache spreads through my chest. I rise from my chair.

I was stupid, thinking I could leave everything behind in Denver.

Her gaze flits to me, then to my mom in the bed. She whispers, "Is she sleeping?"

I glance at Mom, but don't nod or shake my head because I don't actually know.

After a moment of hesitation, Lydia comes toward the bed. She's ditched her leggings for an actual pair of jeans. Ones that, even in this somber moment, I can't help noticing hug her ass like they were made for her. She's wearing her favorite gray hooded sweatshirt that hides her curves, but instead of cramming her hair into a bun the way she does most days, she's let it fall in loose waves around her shoulders. She isn't wearing any makeup as far as I can tell. There are shadows under her eyes, and her lips are pale. She looks tired. She looks beautiful.

She moves to the opposite side of the bed, and I can tell she's taking inventory of how things are different, the way I did when I got here. I had come for a brief visit last Thanksgiving, before we pulled Mom out of the old facility, but Lydia and I haven't been to Dallas together in more than a year, and Mom was in a totally different place back then. She'd just started to become combative about certain things, but we were able to enjoy a few peaceful moments. Lydia sat by her side reading *Winnie the Pooh*, and Mom rested her head on the pillow and smiled at her the whole time.

Lydia pulls up a chair now and speaks in a soothing voice. "Sharon, it's Lydia. I'm here with Anton."

I glance at Mom's head on the pillow. I just want her to respond. Turn her head, move her hand again, something. But she stays motionless. Maybe she is asleep.

Lydia's gaze flickers to mine across the bed, and I see her expression changing, grief shining in her eyes. A knot of guilt registers in my core.

She genuinely loves my mom. I should never have told her she wasn't welcome.

"I'm glad you're out of the hospital," she says in a thick voice, turning back to the bed. "You have some beautiful flowers and stuffed animals." She glances around the room, then reaches out and strokes Mom's fingers with a trembling hand.

I can barely swallow.

"Heartthrob sends slobbery kisses," she whispers, barely audible. "And Seth assures me Bruno is getting all the sardines he can handle . . ." Her voice trails off like she's not sure what else to say.

We stay like that for a while, the three of us. Lydia sitting in silent reverie, Mom motionless in the bed, me backed up to the window. Until I can't take anymore and I walk out the door.

It's too bright in the hall. The walls are too many colors. People are smiling too much. Moving with too much spring in their steps. I drag my feet toward the exit, past a silver-haired couple shuffling together down the corridor, alert and alive. A staff member swaps jokes with an elderly man, something about bananas. I'm nearly to the doors when I hear Lydia call my name, but I don't stop. I need out of this cheery, horrible building.

When I get outside, it's almost worse. The early evening sun is still bright, the spring air warm and fragrant with hydrangeas—my mom's favorite flowers. I charge down the sidewalk toward the parking lot, but before I can even try to find where Seth is parked, Lydia grabs my arm and plants herself between me and everything.

"*Anton.*"

I look into her wide blue eyes, forehead lined with concern. She pulls her hand away, uncertain, severing our touch, and it's like there's nothing left to hold me up.

I crumple into her right there on the sidewalk.

After a while, people start to eye us curiously, so we shift to a bench under a tree.

She doesn't speak. Just studies me, glancing over my unshaven chin, the muss of hair that needs a wash, and the rumpled shirt I've been wearing for three days. I've barely left my mother's side enough to eat, let alone maintain my appearance, but now that Lydia's looking, I wish

I'd at least showered. Out of nowhere, my mind flashes back to those hours back home before Seth called. Before she and I talked about the Pooches. I wonder where we might be now if nothing else had happened. If we'd just stayed in our bedroom, taking pleasure in one another.

"I should've come sooner," she whispers.

I glance up at the Sunny Cove windows and shrug. "It's not like she—"

"No, Anton. For *you*."

CHAPTER FORTY-ONE

Him

It's getting dark out. The streetlights have just come on, but since this is Dallas and not Denver, there's no bite to the temperature with the sun going down. It only takes ten minutes for Seth to navigate through the neighborhoods back to Mom's little ranch house. He does his best to make small talk, asking Lydia about her flight, but when he inquires about the Pooches, we both go silent, and finally he just turns on the radio.

We pull up to the curb in front of our childhood home, and Seth hops out, leaving the engine idling as he retrieves her suitcase from the trunk. Lydia climbs out of the back seat to meet him on the front walk, giving him an earnest hug as he hands over her luggage. For a minute, I just sit in the passenger seat, staring through the windshield with my hands in my lap, not sure if I should be grateful or annoyed they get along so well.

Seth opens my door and waits for me to climb out. "Think I'll go find myself a nightcap."

I narrow my eyes, pretty sure I know what he's thirsty for. But I also can't blame him for wanting to make himself scarce.

"Night," I say, peeling myself out of his SUV.

The air is warm and calm as he drives away, and I shuffle up the walkway behind Lydia. Definitely not watching the sway of her gorgeous hips in those jeans.

She pauses at the stoop and opens her mouth like she wants to say something, but closes it again. Taking a step back, she puts a friendly distance between us, like strangers on the street.

I bite my lip, unlocking the door and holding it open. Lydia reaches for her suitcase. I don't know what she packed in there, but when she struggles to heft it off the stoop, I grab the handle, relieving her of the burden. Lydia hesitates, with an uncomfortable glance at me. "Um . . . if you'd prefer, I can book a hotel."

Her voice rises like a question at the end, and I freeze on the doorstep. Mom's two-bedroom ranch isn't exactly huge. Seth's in the master bedroom, but I've been crashing in the room we shared as kids—the same one Lydia and I have stayed in together every time we've visited.

I raise my head to stare at her, the word "hotel" ricocheting through my mind, lighting up memories of her lace-framed ass and the heated texts of a fantasy girl who doesn't exist.

The instant our eyes meet, I can tell she's having the same flood of memory.

She opens her mouth, face flushed. "I just thought—I mean, I wasn't sure whether—"

"You'll stay here."

My words come out gruff and commanding. No room for argument or debate, just directive. And I know if my brother had stayed, he would tell me I'm an ass or just punch me in the face. I flex my fingers, waiting for Lydia to object. But thank God, she doesn't. She studies me, arching one eyebrow the way she does when she's trying to strategize. Then she nods slowly, and I carry her suitcase inside.

Mom's old orange tabby cat, Bruno, greets us with a broken-sounding meow as soon as we walk in, and Lydia goes right to him, rubbing him gently behind the ears.

"Seth been taking good care of you?" she asks, and it's a second before I realize she's talking to the cat.

Bruno struts along the back of the couch, wailing a string of lies about being underloved and undernourished. Lydia takes him at his word, walking straight to the pantry in the kitchen. It doesn't take long for her to find the giant stock of sardines my mother has always kept and my brother now maintains just for the mangy cat's benefit.

"That's better, isn't it?" she asks as he devours one of the headless silver fish off a plate.

"That's his third one today," I mutter, opening the fridge for some sweet tea. Mom always used to brew it herself, but Seth is lazy and buys the bottled kind that never tastes quite right. Remembering my manners, I hold one out to Lydia, though she's never been a fan. As expected, she wrinkles her nose and declines.

I retrieve a glass for myself, watching her out of the corner of my eye. She's removed her hoodie and is studying a snapshot Mom stuck on the fridge years ago of Lydia and me embracing at the top of Quandary Peak in Colorado. It was our first fourteener—mountains over fourteen thousand feet high that you can scale in a day. We had plans to climb more, or at least I did, but that had to be five or more years ago and we still haven't summited a second.

"Remember that?" she says with a wistful half smile.

I look more closely at the image. We'd driven to the mountains for the weekend, taking a much-needed break from the work grind right after she got Ooh La Pooch up and running. You can hike to the summit and back in half a day, but above ten thousand feet, it was a more strenuous hike than either of us was used to. Once we got there, it felt amazing standing on top of the peak, looking out at the entire world. After we'd made it back to our campsite that night and were curled up in our tent, I'd reached for her, ready to cap off a fantastic day by making love deep in the forest. There was no one around for miles. But she'd shut me down, rolled over, and pulled away because "someone might hear us." Some raccoon, fox, or bear that might object to the sounds of animal pleasures, I guess.

She raises her eyes to mine when I don't answer, and her smile fades.

But as I think about that trip some more, Jess and Izzy's voices start whispering through my head, and I wonder if I could've approached her differently. Made her feel more comfortable, relaxed, instead of turning away and giving up.

"What are you really doing here?" I ask, clearing my throat. I know she wanted to see Mom, but after our exchange on Unmatched, I'm more confused than ever. I just need to know what's going on.

She straightens. "I needed to come."

I can't help noticing she has her phone gripped in her hand, ready to answer any Pooch demand at a moment's notice, like always.

"Shouldn't you be at work?" I say, somehow unable to dial down my inner jerk.

She opens her mouth, a strange look crossing her features. "Actually, I *am* also here for a business meeting."

My shoulders slump involuntarily. I should've known. I clench my jaw, wishing I hadn't asked.

"With you," she says, stepping toward me.

I raise my head.

"Anton, I—I decided to reconsider the deal with ABizCorp." Her eyes are bright, filled with an emotion I can't process.

I let her words sink in, drifting around my mind, trying to find a meaningful shape. She's going to sell the Pooches? After everything she said back in Denver?

"Why would you do that?"

"Because it makes sense." She sets her phone face down on the counter without even glancing at it. "You were right. I've been working too much. I haven't been balancing things well."

I stare at her, my throat tightening.

She lowers her voice. "After you left Denver, I—"

"No." I cut her off, realizing what she's trying to do. "You made your choice. I'm not going to watch you sell what you've worked for, what you love most, just for . . ."

I can't look at her and finish the sentence, so I turn toward the bedroom to get my running shoes, wishing she'd gone to a hotel after all.

"I'm not selling," she says quietly. "*ABizCorp, LLC* belongs to Henry Hill. We're forming a partnership. Dividing the workload. Creating balance."

My feet slow. Her footsteps follow behind me.

"I *want* you, Anton," she says, the choice of words hitting me in the chest. "And after I saw your messages on Unmatched . . . I think you still want me too."

I stop in the doorway to my childhood bedroom, my heart pounding.

"You said if you could do it over, you would." She comes around in front of me, placing a hand on my arm. "Did you mean it?"

I raise my head, locking her eyes with mine, afraid I'll find a placating gaze. The one she puts on when she's giving in, resigning herself to let me have what I'm after. But something's changed. Her eyes radiate a heat that sets my skin aflame.

"*Of course* I would." The words rip out of me.

Her hand slides from my arm to my chest, and I close my eyes, her fingers scorching through my shirt.

"I don't think I know my own body very well," she whispers, so quietly I can barely hear. "I don't think I ever have."

Slowly, cautiously, I touch the tips of my fingers to her thigh, dragging them up over her hip until they dip along her waist under her T-shirt. Every part of her is already so familiar. "Would you like to?"

A soft rose pink blooms over her cheeks. "Yes . . . I think I would."

"I wouldn't mind getting to know some places better," I say, my guard beginning to crumble as I nuzzle her hair.

Even in the dim light, I see her face grow a deeper pink.

I pause. "But only if you're comfortable."

She swallows, not looking up. "For a while, I wasn't sure." She traces my abdominal muscles lightly through my shirt. "It didn't seem like being . . . with you . . . could ever feel good."

My stomach knots. My hands go still. "Lydia, there are some people who—"

"But when I got the rabbit," she continues, fingers dipping beneath my shirt. "I started to think I was wrong."

I suck in a breath. My brain immediately overloads with images of her exploring her own pleasure, sprawled across our bed, hot-pink vibrator slick between her legs. I am hard instantly.

I pull her against me, murmuring in her ear. "And how do you feel about it now?"

"Like I want to learn more," she breathes.

Gently, I slide my hands beneath her shirt, caressing her skin until my fingers make contact with what feels like a lacy, delicate bra. A fiery pulse in my groin punctuates my own arousal, but quietly in the back of my mind, Jess and Izzy whisper: *now bring her into the moment with you.* I let my fingers explore, running my thumbs over her nipples until Lydia lets out a small gasp.

"And you're *sure* this is what you want," I say, tracing my lips over her collarbone, her sweet vanilla scent *almost* enough to drown my doubts.

She doesn't respond with words. Instead, she does something spectacular. She brings one hand to my waist, slips into my pants, and starts to stroke me. Before I even realize it's what I want. I am already so hard; my cock turns to steel under her fingers. I back her up until she hits the wall, and I grind into her hip, feeling utterly primal. She wraps her other arm around my neck, and my hands are everywhere under her shirt, pushing the fabric up. Our eyes meet, and I pause, searching for any sign of reluctance. In answer, she locks her lips warm and sweet over mine. I slip the shirt the rest of the way over her head, and then she's standing in just her jeans and the most tantalizing bra I think I've seen—aside from the night at the hotel. Its champagne color is almost invisible against her skin, nipples showing clearly through sheer fabric that makes her breasts look like they're floating.

Her lashes flutter and she looks at me like she's where she's always wanted to be. "I want to keep learning . . . about *both* our bodies."

CHAPTER FORTY-TWO

Her

ANTON LOOKS LIKE HE MIGHT DEVOUR ME WITH JUST HIS eyes when my shirt hits the floor, instantly validating my decision to change into this bra. I pull his shirt off in turn, taking a moment to run my hands over his skin, showing my appreciation for his rock-hard abs and chest. If anything, this intensifies his gaze, sending an unexpected thrill between my legs. He tackles my lips with his, and in response, I attempt to wrap my leg around his waist. Which sets us unfortunately off-balance. We stumble into the bookshelf, nearly knocking a collection of young adult novels and several baseball trophies to the floor.

"Ouch," he mutters, but there's a spark in his eyes, and if he's in pain it sure doesn't show. Instead, he pivots us toward the more accommodating bed. My suitcase lies where he'd left it on the navy blue bedspread, but he yanks it to the floor and out of the way with one hand, laying me gently in its place.

Our lips meet again, and then he pulls back to gaze at me, but as he does, there's another uncertain flicker in his eyes. I think I understand. Because staring up at him like this, I feel it too. This moment, this scenario, is familiar. Obviously, we've stayed in this room, in this very bed, dozens of times. I was never comfortable being intimate in his mother's house before. But that's not it.

It's our positioning. Him, looming over me, me lying under him. We're both thinking about how this has gone in the past. Me bracing myself while he pushed inside my body, my mind drifting away to my Costco shopping list, employee issues, or the sink of unwashed dishes. Whatever I could focus on while waiting for the experience to be over, rather than remaining present and letting myself sink into the moment with him.

But this time, instead of checking out and pulling away, I make a point of holding his gaze. I reach up, running my fingers through his hair, keeping us in constant contact. Trying to stay attuned to the cues from his body, his breaths, his movements. How his mouth seeks mine and he seems to lean into every touch—but also, the way my own body responds. How my skin tingles when he draws his fingers along my waistline, and something tugs deep in my core as his eyes meet mine. It's overwhelming, trying to take it all in at once, but I notice an immediate difference. We haven't even taken off our pants, but there's a connection between us I've never felt, like we're moving as one instead of two separate parts.

His lips are tracing along my jawline, fingers working to undo the button on my jeans when we both register the sound. A low, steady hum quietly fills the room. He pauses to look up at me, his expression still warm, but his brows draw in. I shrug in response, my mind preoccupied with the heat of his skin and woodsy scent. Until he sits up, and I see where his gaze lands. My suitcase, discarded on the floor.

His eyes return to mine, and as my brain finally processes the hum—no, the *vibration*—I feel the color rise in my cheeks.

"Lydia," Anton says with a raised brow. "What have you got in the bag?"

My breath catches. This is almost exactly what I was asked at the airport. I'd thrown the rabbit into my carry-on just before I left the house. A little burst of optimism that we might end up in a moment just like this, where we could revisit its pleasure, continue what we started back home. But later, I wished I'd never packed it. This vibrating bag has nearly done me in today.

Anton studies my face, his expression hovering somewhere between craving, amusement, and concern. "Is something wrong?"

"No, I just ran into some trouble with that at airport security."

His eyes widen at first, but as he processes, the corner of his mouth tugs a little to one side. "You did?"

I don't think I can bear for him to laugh. Not after the TSA agents stood there sniggering at me. I cover my face with my hands, sure it's the shade of a traffic light by now. A flashing red one.

But then a pair of gentle hands pull my fingers away. I can tell he's right in front of me. I'm afraid to peek at his face, but when I finally steal a glance, I'm caught off guard by the smoldering look in his eyes.

"Tell me what happened." His voice is low and gravelly.

"They—they made me turn it off."

"How?"

I glare at him. I am literally dying re-living this mortification, and he wants me to rehash the details? But then my eyes drop to his lap, where his arousal is obvious.

Is he enjoying this?

I moisten my lips. "They asked me to open the zipper and show them where the sound was coming from. Like they thought I had a bomb."

His eyes meet mine with the same searing gaze they held when I handed him the rabbit back in Denver, and I get the distinct impression he wishes he had been at the airport to watch me do this. A hot feeling surges through me as I kind of wish he'd been there, too.

I cross my legs, my breaths coming faster.

"Perhaps you'd better show *me*," he says.

I swallow hard, reaching for the suitcase zipper and sliding it open just the way I did this afternoon. My fingers drift over the smooth fabric of the black satin nightgown I packed, then close around the soft, silky silicone. I fumble with the switch to turn it off, then hold up the hot-pink toy for his inspection, just as I did for those merciless TSA agents.

"Definitely dangerous," Anton whispers. "I'm going to need to confiscate that."

He holds out his hand, and I place the rabbit in his palm like it's something forbidden. I wonder briefly, is this role playing? Is that what we're doing now? This day has spiraled so far out of my comfort zone, but I'm surprised to admit I'm kind of enjoying it now.

He leans in and whispers, "I bet you turned on the entire security line." I close my eyes as he traces his tongue along the lobe of my ear. "Those TSA agents might dream tonight about you unpacking your suitcase—but I'm the one who gets to play with your toys."

And just like that, my body ignites.

His free hand slides between my legs, stroking my center through my jeans with the tips of his fingers until I groan, pressing my hips forward. I fumble to unfasten my button and zipper, and he follows my lead, yanking the pants down my legs until I'm sprawled on the bed in just the sheer bra and panties.

He stands over me for what feels like a full minute, staring like he's drinking me in. My eyes drop to the erection straining against his joggers, and a pulse of excitement shoots through my core.

Then he finds the power switch on the rabbit, filling the too-silent room with the sound of electric sex once again. He traces kisses along my cleavage and touches the vibe to my nipples, rubbing it where they show clearly through my bra until each of them tightens—even the reluctant one—and I gasp, arching my back. He brings his fingers to my center, rubbing the same way he had through my pants, only it's ten times more powerful through the delicate fabric. I buck against his hand, trying to mitigate the intensity, but it's too much, and I leap up before it becomes too consuming.

Anton looks startled, like he's afraid he did something wrong, so I quickly kiss him to let him know I'm just changing things up. I place my hands on his chest, letting my fingers delight in the rippling muscles beneath his skin. Our eyes lock again, and I trace down toward his waist, holding his gaze as I slide his pants down to free his rock-hard cock. I take it in my right hand, briefly exploring between my own legs with my left. I don't even need to check past my panties, which are already soaked. My vagina has that hot, swollen feeling I remember from exploring with my fingers at home. I have no doubt about my head being in the game, and here's a physical indicator that my body is definitely turned on.

I sink down to kiss Anton's thick, throbbing cock. Briefly, I think of the "Classic Guide," how it instructed to "look enthusiastic" about putting a man's dick in your mouth. And I do smile, but it's more for myself this time around, because this feels almost effortless. My body and my mind are one, and I *want* to suck him off.

I flick my tongue over his tip several times—another instruction I recall—then sink my lips down around his shaft, making sure to keep it slick with plenty of saliva. I start moving up and down, sliding him a little deeper into my mouth each time until he's teasing the back of my throat. Anton groans, which amps up my excitement, but then I take him a little too deep, and I gag. I pull away for a second, swallowing and making sure I can breathe. I hadn't expected that, but after a quick glance up at the look of rapture on his face, I decide I'm okay and ready to try again. I open my mouth to take him once more, but as I do, he pulls back, placing a finger under my chin, raising my face to his instead.

His lips descend on mine, and next thing I know, he's fumbling with the back of my bra. I let the straps slide off my shoulders, but he seems to be having trouble, so I reach back to assist. With one hand, I release the clasp and my breasts spring free, the delicate lace and mesh sliding down my arms. Anton immediately replaces the cups with his hands, closing them hot and urgent over my breasts, squeezing each one lightly but firmly before again teasing my nipples, tugging and kneading them gently, sending little lightning bolts of sensation shooting to my core. I arch my back, seeking more, and he lingers there, squeezing and pulsing, pushing my breasts together—my *tits*, I think with a deep blush—pressing his face between them, seemingly losing himself in my cleavage.

After exploring every inch of my chest with his mouth and tongue, he travels south, keeping his hands firmly cupped over my breasts. His lips roam down my stomach and over my navel until I feel the trace of his hot breath against the moist fabric between my legs. He gives a last brief tug to each of my nipples before his hands follow, playing at the edge of the floral-decorated lace. He runs his tongue along the center of my panties, over my clit, and he sucks me through the fabric until I let out a sound I don't even realize I'm making until I stop. Then he reaches for the lace at my hips, sliding the soaked material down and away until the cool air tells me I'm fully exposed. He laps his hot tongue several times up my center, teasing me until I shudder. And then he rises, hovering above me on his knees.

I study him, poised between my legs as he strokes his long shaft, preparing to enter me, and it strikes me again how different this feels. I have stared up at him like this a hundred times, feeling no desire whatsoever despite my love for him. Just bracing to endure whatever came next, what he wanted and would do to get off.

This feels so different. My body and mind feel different. Tuned in to my own arousal and desire, but also his—noticing the ways I react that seem to excite him, seeing his enthusiasm to arouse me. Becoming a participant rather than a reluctant spectator is completely changing how we react to each other, and I'm both grateful for it and regretful that it took me this long. Sex between two people shouldn't ever be one-sided.

Unless, of course, you're doing it wrong.

Gently, Anton brings the tip of his cock to my center, rubbing it in my juices until it's slick, and another thrill radiates through me. I *need* him inside me. I press my hips up to meet him.

He pauses, looking straight at me with a mix of lust and caution.

"Is this okay?" he asks.

I nod without hesitation, parting my lips, adding, "Yes. Please." In case he needs it to be any clearer. My whole body is alive with anticipation in a way I've never felt. Every inch of my skin is on fire, and there's a desperate urge, almost like an ache between my legs. Like *he* is all that's missing from my body.

He lowers his eyelids like he's gotten the message, and my insides surge as he positions himself, but instead of plunging directly into me, he pauses, reaches to his left, and comes back holding the rabbit. I gasp, opening my mouth to tell him I appreciate the gesture, but my insides are throbbing for *him*—his cock, hot and hard *in my vagina*. Before I manage to find words to say this, however, he places the pink silicone in my hand and presses the on button.

I look up, confused, but then he repositions himself at my entrance, his thick head pressed right up against my delicate folds, pulsing in my juices. I close my fingers around the vibrating rabbit as I think I understand. I open my legs a little wider, tilting my pelvis and making more room for him as I lower the vibrator in the same direction. He watches hungrily as it touches down against my clit and I jerk my hips in response. I run the head of the rabbit down to where he rests, getting it just as slick as his dick with my copious juices, and then I lock eyes with Anton, giving him the final go-ahead.

He thrusts his cock inside me, and my hips jut up to meet him. We pause like that, locked together at last, both of us overloaded with sensation as he fills me. The look on his face—eyes closed, lips parted in exaltation—must exactly match my own, because *this* is exactly what I needed. What that ache at my center was begging for.

Slowly, he begins to move his hips, and—so differently than ever before—I move in time with him. I am apparently so aroused the sound of us moving together is loudly wet and sloppy, but I can't focus on that long enough to feel embarrassed because his thick cock sliding in and out of me feels so freaking *good*. There is no dry chafing and pulling, no discomfort, just the most wonderful wet friction. I'm so entranced by the novelty of this sensation that I almost forget the rabbit, but Anton grabs my hand between thrusts, reminding me of the toy still humming in my grasp. He guides it down toward my glistening clit, but then leaves me to do as I please, bracing his arms on either side of me for better leverage.

I look up at him again, his face absolutely euphoric, and it's like he injects that feeling into me with each thrust. He opens his eyes to find me looking and leans in to meet my lips. Then, firmly holding his gaze with mine, I touch the vibrating rabbit down on my clit.

The effect is complete and instantaneous, electrifying a whole new set of muscles and interconnected nerve endings I had no idea existed. Heat radiates from my center, and I am suddenly so aware of every sensation—my pulsing clit, the weight of his cock filling me, my dripping arousal, and the friction of all these things moving together. Anton straightens, making room for me to guide the vibrator anywhere I need, but he doesn't slow his pace or pull back. If anything, his thrusts intensify as our eyes lock, our muscles tighten, and then with a sudden groan, he gives one particularly great thrust, and the rabbit shifts into the exact right spot. My center ignites, muscles clamping and spasming around his cock, sending heated sparks through my torso, my limbs, all the way out to my fingers—both of us yelling, clawing, moaning, until finally, together, we collapse.

CHAPTER FORTY-THREE

Her

Seth looks sharp in a gray suit, his figure lean, standing straight and confident, and so much like his brother apart from the sandy hair that I nearly do a double-take. Bruno circles, meowing at his heels as Seth serves up his morning sardine. I smile. Sharon would be glad to know her beloved orange cat is being spoiled rotten.

"Anton went for a run," he says, taking a mug from a cabinet when he sees me. He pours a generous cup of coffee and slides it across the faded yellow breakfast bar. I wrap my hands around it gratefully.

"I figured," I say, though I'm secretly relieved by the confirmation. I woke up at seven, Anton's presence all over me and the sheets, but he was nowhere to be found. He often works out early, but I wasn't sure. Had he changed his mind after last night? Decided he wanted something different after all?

I ease onto a barstool, my body a little sore, but not in an unpleasant way. Just unfamiliar. Not so much like it's recovering, but rather savoring a bit longer.

I sip the black brew, make a face, then search in the fridge for cream. "How was your night?"

A wistful smile plays across his lips. "Not bad for a weekday. Do you want details? I can remember the highlights, though names and faces might be a little fuzzy."

I blink, caught off guard by his candor. Seth is an awesome brother-in-law, and despite what he'd have some people think, he truly is a decent person. But his open promiscuity has always made me blush. "You know, I think my imagination can fill in the blanks pretty well."

He shrugs, his smile stretching into a grin. "Anyway, seems like you two had some fun of your own, right?"

My eyes widen, heat creeping into my cheeks. Can he read on my face what we did? Or did he hear us? I'm not sure what time he returned from his exploits, but the walls of this little house are paper thin. I stare into my mug, unable to meet his eyes. "Did Anton talk to you about it?"

"No. But my brother's got-laid face is pretty different from the needs-to-be-fucked expression he's been wearing all week."

Oh my God. He is probably at least picturing what we did right now, and I might as well be standing here naked in their dying mother's house. My face lights up with shame. I pour questionable-smelling milk into my coffee, taking a gulp when it doesn't curdle. But if it was poison and I died on the spot, that might be okay.

"It's good to see him happy," Seth says more quietly. "Both of you. Mom always said you two were gonna last."

This makes me pause. I remember Sharon saying that, often with a wink, before telling us some story about her one true love, Anton and Seth's dad. I feel a little pang of guilt thinking about how close we've come to *not* lasting. Maybe in part because of my messed up feelings about having sex with my own husband.

I clear my throat. "I'm glad he seemed satisfied," I say, then quickly make a bid to change the subject. "Bruno's looking good."

The cat glances up from his smelly fish breakfast and gives a hoarse meow before winding affectionately between our legs. Seth scoops him up and cradles him with zero regard for his expensive-looking suit. Bruno starts up his motor, resting his orange-and-white smudged chin on Seth's shoulder. "Thanks. Gotta keep Old Salty fat and happy for Mom."

His phone goes off in his pocket, and he takes the call, wandering out of the room with the cat just as Anton comes through the kitchen door.

My husband pauses on the threshold. He's shirtless, absolutely dripping with sweat, and judging by his expression, was not expecting to see me.

"Good morning," I say shyly.

"Morning." He grabs a bottle of water from the fridge, toweling off with the shirt tucked into his waistband. He doesn't look unhappy, but he isn't looking right at me either. I get the distinct impression he's as lost for what else to say as I am.

I rise from my stool, realizing that actions might come more easily. But as I move closer to him, my confidence wavers. Last night, I'd had the "Classic Guide" to refer to, at least in my head. With its instructions on where to look, how to touch, and how to act. It was everything I needed. Now, I'm not sure. Do I touch him? Should I speak? After a moment, he sneaks a look at me like he's thinking all the same things, and this is the push I need. I reach out tentatively, running my fingers over his heated skin. And it works. He closes the remaining space between us, warming the air around us with his body and filling my nose with a masculine, sweaty scent.

"Thought you'd sleep a little later," he says, bringing his hands to my waist—only lightly, like he's afraid to leave them there. In answer, I wrap my arms around his neck.

"I—I wasn't sure why you left." I look down, feeling stupidly insecure. I guess because he's pulled away when I thought things were better with us before.

"Just needed to run so I could think." His fingers trace lightly under my shirt, along the bare skin at my waist, sending shivers through me.

"What did you think about?"

"Everything. Mom, the Pooches, us . . ." His voice and posture are so heavy. He twists a lock of my hair around one finger, then tugs lightly. "Although mostly my mind ran an X-rated loop of replays from last night."

I raise my head and his eyes are dancing. I laugh, despite my burning cheeks, planting a kiss on his lips.

"I'd tell you two to get a room," Seth says, coming back into the kitchen sans cat. “But I’m going to work, so the place is yours. Just don’t spill anything on the furniture.”

I pull away too quickly and too stiffly—embarrassed and ashamed for *being* embarrassed all at once. Anton frowns. But then he grabs my hand, clasping my fingers possessively. Reassuringly.

“Actually, I was thinking we should head back to Denver,” he says to Seth. “Lydia’s got some big stuff going on at work.”

He squeezes my hand again, and I look at him in surprise. His eyes are bright. There’s no resentment in his voice, but I’m not entirely sure how to interpret his expression. It’s sort of . . . anticipatory.

“Oh yeah?” Seth raises a brow. “What’s going on in Poochville?”

“Well . . . at first, it was going to be an acquisition,” I say, watching Anton carefully. “But now it looks like I’ve negotiated a partnership.”

“Really?” Seth raises both brows. “Will that complicate things with the new place opening?”

I shake my head, squeezing Anton’s fingers back, growing more confident as I think over my conversation with Henry. “Not at all. It should actually simplify some stuff. Make it easier to expand while taking a lot of the burden off me.”

Seth looks at his brother. “Can’t argue with that, I guess.”

“It’s a bold move.” Anton nods, looking similarly impressed. And inside me, it feels like something’s started to glow. “Lydia’s just proving her brilliance as a businesswoman once again.”

I hesitate. “What about Sharon, though? Do you need to stay here in case—”

“Mom wouldn’t want that,” he says, though it seems like he’s choosing his words with care. “She was so proud of you. She’d want me to go with you and support you.”

Seth nods, looking resigned. “Anton’s right. I’ll call you guys if anything changes, but you can’t stay here forever.” He glances at the kitchen clock. “And on that note, I need to take off. Lock up when you leave, okay?”

He gives me a warm, brotherly hug, then forces Anton into an awkward one too.

And then it’s the two of us, alone again.

"Guess I'll see what flights are available," Anton says, taking out his phone.

I put my hand over his, forcing him to look up at me. "Are you really sure about this?"

I'm not talking about his mom anymore, or going to Denver. This is deeper, much bigger than anything the two of us have successfully handled.

"Yes." He sets the phone down, focusing entirely on me. "If you are."

I manage a nod, but I'm afraid to admit how scared I am. That I'll go home and still get the balance wrong. That things will somehow go back to the way they were. That I'll wake up one day and realize everything still fell apart.

As if he can read my mind, Anton looks at me and says, "We'll work on it together."

I don't have words. Only the warm sensation spreading through my chest, so I just press my lips to his.

"Going from sole proprietor to a partnership is a big sacrifice," he says, looking at me warily.

"It is," I say. "But I think it will be good for me on a lot of levels. You were right, I can't do everything myself. It was hard to admit that. But I want things that can't all exist together without a little flexibility."

"What do you want?" he says, moving closer.

"I want to run and grow the Pooches, but . . . I also want space to breathe. To exist outside of the businesses. I want to find some stability, more time to do things other than work, and maybe . . . maybe think more seriously about whether we should start a family." I trace the line of his collarbone with my fingers. "But most importantly, along *with* all of that, I want you. Our marriage. I've neglected it. And I want to work at least as hard at building it back up as I do on the Pooches."

"I want all of this too." He pushes my hair back, then glides his hands down my front and gives my breasts a playful squeeze. "Well, and these."

I laugh, shoving him playfully away until he comes in with a repentant kiss.

"I'm not going to deny sex is a *need* for me," he says more soberly.

"But if I've learned anything the last month or so, it's that I don't just want sex. I want sex with *you*, my wife. Lydia, you are the most important person in my world."

I look down. "I'll try to get better at it. I want to keep learning."

He catches my chin, giving me a reassuring look, which morphs into a lustful grin. "Happy to help you practice."

I giggle, but there's an uneasiness balling up in my stomach, which ends the moment a little too soon. "I'm just worried—I might still mess up sometimes."

He presses his mouth into a line. "I probably will too."

Neither of us says anything more for several minutes. I lean into his chest, pressing my cheek against his flesh, listening to the steady beat of his heart. His arms come up, around me, holding me close. Secure.

"Seth suggested—" Anton says abruptly. "Maybe we should see someone."

I take a moment, letting that sink in. Caprice had encouraged the same thing. "Like a sex therapist? I guess we could."

"I don't know." He grunts. "What does someone like that even do?"

I glance up at him. "Hopefully not watch us have sex."

His eyes flash briefly with a *very* dirty look, but then his expression softens. "Do you think talking to someone would be helpful?"

"Maybe, for me," I say slowly. I can't argue that advice from a professional might go further than some sex guide I found on the internet. "I'm still trying to figure a few things out."

He squeezes my shoulder. "Then let's do it."

I turn in his arms, and our lips come together, softly, sweetly, hopefully. For the first time, maybe in our whole marriage, rather than acting like adversaries when we touch, it just feels . . . intimate.

"I should probably shower before I get on a plane," he says, indicating the salty sheen of sweat now dry on his skin. "I forgot what it's like to run in eighty percent humidity."

Reluctantly, I let go of him and nod, taking a step toward the bedroom. "I'm going to pack—um, but maybe I'll put the rabbit in a checked bag."

"Wait." He seizes my hand, and when I look back, there's fire in his eyes. "Don't pack it just yet."

CHAPTER FORTY-FOUR

Him

LYDIA'S HEAD STIRS ON HER PILLOW. HER PHONE IS RINGING for the second time on the bedside table, and I lie next to her, waiting to see what she'll do. I've been awake for a while, but haven't gotten out of bed yet. I wanted to see if she woke on her own. And what might happen after that. It's the first Saturday in longer than I can remember that she hasn't set an alarm. I've never felt invited to just linger like this before. But for the first time, that's exactly what I want to do.

Or it was until her phone rang.

Reflexively, her hand darts out of the covers, and she answers.

"Scarlet?" her voice is groggy and sleep-laden. "What's going on?"

I roll my eyes. We returned to Denver ten days ago to find Scarlet begging for her job back. Something about making up with her boyfriend and not leaving her cat. I thought Lydia should tell her to go brush up her résumé. She is a constant source of drama. Instead, she consulted Henry, gave her a *raise,* and made her a manager.

I climb out of bed—to get us both coffee, I tell myself—keeping my back to her as I abandon the sheets and resignedly pull on underwear. I shuffle slowly down the hall, but I'm still listening.

"It actually caught fire?" Lydia's voice rises with concern.

My shoulders slump. Heartthrob jumps up from his bed, following me toward the kitchen as soon as he realizes I'm going in the direction of breakfast. I switch on the coffeepot, stir up his food, then step out onto our little patio while he eats. It's gorgeous out. Still cool because it's early, but the birds are singing, flowers are coming up everywhere, and even the trees have started leafing out. I'm reluctant to go back in. I start itching to go for a run.

Heartthrob's face appears at the door, and I let him out to do his thing, making my way back in when I smell the fresh-brewed coffee. I pull a couple of mugs from the cabinet and strain to listen. I can hear Lydia thumping around in our room, probably rushing to get dressed.

She blusters into the kitchen behind me as I pour the coffee, and I wonder vaguely if I should've put hers in a travel mug. I'm trying hard to accept the choice she's made, so I just focus on what I'm doing.

"Yes," she says, apparently still coaching Scarlet over the phone. "Well, if that didn't work, you could try removing the filter and letting it cool for a while first."

I glance at the clock, gritting my teeth. Scarlet has barely been at work an hour and she's already managed to come up with some emergency. Heartthrob whines at the door, and I sip my coffee, laying out my jogging route in my head as Lydia lets him in.

"Okay, but this is why I gave you a raise," she says in a different tone. "You're the manager. You know what to do. You can handle this."

Wait. What?

I turn, forgetting my running plans as my eyes land on her. The phone is to her ear, but she isn't dressed, ready to grab her keys and head out the door like I expected. Quite the opposite. She stands in front of me in her robe, hair down, keenly eyeing my coffee.

"Great. I'm glad you spoke with Dave. That was exactly the right thing to do. If what he suggests doesn't work, then we'll have him take it for repair." Her voice is calm, authoritative, as I hand her a steaming mug. "You've got this, Scar. I know it isn't ideal, but I have faith in you."

Lydia lowers herself to a chair and takes a sip. The robe parts when she crosses her legs, revealing such an expanse of her smooth, bare legs that I suspect she might not have any clothes on underneath.

My mouth goes dry.

"Okay. Keep me posted," she says, and then she ends the call and looks up at me.

I clear my throat, still trying to catch up to what's happening. Or maybe what *isn't* happening. I know what to expect when Lydia pulls away and throws herself into work. I'm not as sure what to do now.

"That old stand dryer is having electrical problems," she huffs.

I had guessed that was the issue. I know exactly which one she means. There are three stand dryers at Ooh La Pooch—like a tall hair dryer on wheels—used mostly to fluff up and straighten dog fur. But that one was bought secondhand when she opened the shop and has always had issues.

"Do you want me to go in and look at it?" I offer, letting my gaze drift up her bare legs, my imagination dipping beneath the edge of her robe.

She shakes her head. "Scarlet's got it. If it keeps having problems, we'll have Dave take a look on Tuesday."

My gaze shifts to her face, searching for any sign of anxiety or insincerity. Some hint that she'd rather go to her business than stay here, at home with me. But her eyes are calm. Present. Even her posture seems relaxed. She and Henry spent all last week in meetings, hashing out efficiencies and putting systems in place so Lydia wouldn't have to rush in for every little thing—there'll be some true emergencies for sure, but not as many—I guess I have been holding my breath waiting to see if their plans actually work.

"Thanks for the coffee." She shifts forward, giving me a view straight down the front of her robe.

Our eyes meet, and she smiles. The corner of my mouth rises slowly in response as my eyes trace the outline of her breasts. She is definitely naked under there, and it seems clear she wants me to know. I swallow hard. I had slipped into boxer briefs when I got up, but that's all, so the fact that I've noticed is also hard to miss.

"What do you want to do today?" I ask in a low voice. As obvious as my desire is, I need more confirmation that she's on board. That she's not just teasing me, even unintentionally.

Her cheeks turn pink as she follows my gaze down, and briefly, maybe reflexively, she goes to pull the robe closed and tighten the belt.

But as I watch, her hands go still and drop again. She leaves the fabric open, sliding her fingers along the underside of one partially exposed breast instead.

"I thought we could stay in this morning," she says quietly. "Maybe . . . go for a picnic or something this afternoon?"

I set my empty mug by the sink and stalk toward her. "That sounds nice."

Her phone is still in her hand, and she pauses a moment to tap something out on the screen. I wait, watching a small smile play at her lips as she slips it into her robe pocket. "Maybe we can talk about vacation plans," she continues. "Or even what to do with our home office."

I raise one eyebrow. She's moving on a bunch of things at once, and while I'm enthusiastic, I'm still feeling cautious.

"How about our plans for right now," I say, offering a hand and pulling her out of the chair, running my lips along the edge of her jaw.

She gives a little shiver, then tugs me down the hall toward our bedroom. She starts pulling at the knot in her belt, but I push her hands out of the way, feeling more assured about what's going to happen. As we enter our room, a last tug on the loose knot makes the two sides of the robe fall open. I trace my hands up to her shoulders, slipping the fabric down her arms and letting it drop to the floor until she's standing nude and perfect—stunning—in front of me. She moves shyly, instinctively, to cover herself, but I reach out, taking each of her hands in mine. We stand connected like this, and I can't bring myself to pull away. In part because of the energy now coursing between us, but also selfishly, because with her hands trapped in mine, I can admire each gentle curve of her nakedness longer.

Eventually I guide her down to the bed, laying kisses along her skin. This is where I used to cut to the chase when I could sense she wanted it to be over. When I didn't know what else to do. But now my mind swims with everything I've learned—from reading and podcasts, from Lydia herself.

I don't think I know my own body very well.

Would you like to?

Yes . . . I think I would.

So, I go to work. Tracing along the insides of her arms and thighs with just the warmth of my breath. Exploring the soft skin of her wrists and the back of her neck with my lips. Running my tongue along the rim of her belly button. It takes a little while, but her response becomes evident in the little sounds she makes, the way her breathing changes, and how she arches her back.

Once she seems greedy for every small touch, I let my hands move toward her breasts. Cupping them, lightly squeezing, tracing along the outside, but avoiding her nipples. The small sounds she started making become more like little moans, her hands reaching for the sheets at her sides. Finally, I let my thumb barely brush her left nipple, and she gasps. Gently, I come at it again, lightly playing and pinching until it becomes tight and hard. Then I move over to her right side, using my tongue to coax the other one out where I can play with it too. The way she showed me when we got back to Denver.

As I work every erogenous zone I have learned about, her fingers weave into my hair, grasp my neck and shoulders, and trace down along my arms. She seems to be reaching for something she can't quite find, which charges me with energy because I think I know what it is, and it's something I'm pretty sure I can give. I raise my gaze to hers, and I'm met with such a sincere level of lust it's everything I can do not to consume her right then.

I lift her lightly, positioning her higher against the pillows to make sure she's comfortable, but as I do, my forgotten phone pings and lights up on the duvet next to us. Lydia glances over at it, and I grab the device, my stomach sinking at the notification she had to have seen on the lock screen.

You have 1 unread message on Unmatched

My lip curls. I'd forgotten all about the stupid app after re-installing it to send my awkward slew of desperate messages. It hadn't crossed my mind once since Lydia showed up in Dallas in the flesh.

"I . . . sorry. I'm done with this," I say in a stilted voice, tapping the screen to delete the app immediately.

But before I can confirm, Lydia stops me, covering my hand with hers. I look up at her, heart pounding, hoping the stupid notification hasn't just ruined everything we've been rebuilding.

Her eyes are downcast, but there's a light blush of color across her cheeks. "Maybe you should check your message first."

My brows draw together. I search her face, wondering why she would ever suggest it. Until I see her mouth twitch and her eyes flash. I'm not at all sure what's going on, but this is enough to get me to breathe. Tentatively, I do as she suggests.

LONELYGIRL8

I want you to come on my breasts.

I look up, trying to gauge her expression, but she bites her lip, still avoiding my eyes.

"Lydia, what . . ." I trail off, not sure what to say. What to do. MountainMan3 and LonelyGirl8 had discussed doing exactly that during a period of utter dysfunction. I'm having a hard time resolving this directly from my wife. Her face is so red now I'm not sure how else to reply, so I type.

MOUNTAINMAN3

Why?

She retrieves her phone from her robe pocket and types back.

LONELYGIRL8

You said you'd like it.

MOUNTAINMAN3

I would, but . . .

I pause, trying to collect myself. To process this whole conversation. But before I can finish my thought, she replies again.

LONELYGIRL8

I'd like to find out why.

Now she is looking at me. And it's *my* turn to full-body blush.

"I—I don't know why," I admit softly, aloud. "When I look at you, at your body, I just . . . want to."

She stares at me, tongue tracing over her lips as she types.

LONELYGIRL8

Reason enough.

I swallow hard, my erection growing almost painful as her suggestion plays out in my head. I slide one hand around her waist, gripping her ass and squeezing, typing with my other hand.

MOUNTAINMAN3

Did you really want to be spanked?

The heat in her face shifts to her eyes, pupils widening. She makes a barely perceptible nod, but then looks down quickly.

LONELYGIRL8

I'm not sure why I want that either.

I lean down, careful not to force her to look at me, but close enough to whisper in her ear. "Reason enough."

She sucks in a low breath, then types.

LONELYGIRL8

I'm really NOT sure about "butt play."

Laughter rumbles out of my chest. "Fair," I say, laying soft kisses on her cheeks. "We can try anything you want. But nothing you aren't comfortable with."

She raises the phone to tap out a reply, but this time I stop her, covering her hand with mine.

"Maybe we should move this conversation in person," I suggest.

Her eyes flicker shyly from me back to the screen.

"I'm glad it's helped us communicate," I say, running my fingers lightly along her thigh. "But we don't really fit the user profile."

She considers this, then nods, pressing her lips to mine, sweet and soft and warm. She runs her tongue over my lower lip and speaks. "Maybe you're right. It *has* been thirty days."

"Thirty-two," I say.

She sits up, pushing me back against the pillows as she rises to her knees and swings a leg over to straddle me. I stare up at her, poised and confident in a way that makes my groin ache. I trace my hands over the curve of her hips, along her tapered waist, and cup her full, round tits.

"Would you say things have improved?" she asks.

"Yes—" I hiss as she positions herself directly over me, sliding her slick, heated center along the shaft of my throbbing cock.

She picks up both our phones, guiding her thumbs over the screens until the delete buttons appear, side by side. Then she hands mine over, and we erase the app together.

"I've got my fantasy girl right here," I say, discarding the phone in the covers.

She leans in to find my lips. "Just call me Mrs. Richie."

Heat shoots through my groin, and I can't take it anymore. I grab her hips, holding her still so I can shift my cock into place outside her entrance. Our eyes meet, and she is so clearly aroused, so consumed by a desire I know *I* put there, I almost lose it. With a single thrust, I plunge deep inside her, wet and hot, and we groan together at the shock of pleasure. Lydia takes a moment to get seated on top of me, and as she starts to move, taking control of her own indulgence, I do lose myself. In her body. In a burst of love tangled up with lust. I used to think they were two separate things, but they're more entwined than I ever thought. And now, looking up into her face as she takes pleasure from my body, I am certain we both feel it.

Lydia opens her eyes, gazing back at me with newfound heat. "Yeah. I'd say we're pretty well matched."

Thank you for reading!
Lydia and Anton's story continues in:
MISMATCHED
The Unmatched Series, Book 2

THANK YOU FOR READING!

WANT A FREE STORY?

Did you enjoy Lydia and Anton's story?
Reviews help other readers discover my books. If you enjoyed *Unmatched*, please leave a review on your favorite book platform. I appreciate it!

FREE STORY
Receive *In The Making*, the exclusive free prequel to *Unmatched*, and stay up to date on new releases and events when you sign up for Emilia Reed's newsletter:

SIGN UP HERE:
emiliareed.com/newsletter

ALSO BY EMILIA REED

The Unmatched Series

In The Making - series prequel (available *free at* emiliareed.com/newsletter)

Unmatched (Now Available)

Mismatched (Now Available)

Rematched (TBA)

Love In Training

Watch for Caprice's story coming soon!

ABOUT THE AUTHOR

Emilia Reed was raised in Upstate New York until she fell in love and fled its gray skies for the sunny Rocky Mountains. She is an author, former business owner, and recovering freelance editor. When she is not attempting to substitute couples therapy with romance novels, she spends her time obsessing over dogs and searching for the perfect coffee and ice cream pairing. Emilia lives in Colorado with her family.

You can find out what's new with Emilia Reed and sign up to get a free prequel to The Unmatched Series at emiliareed.com

Made in the USA
Las Vegas, NV
10 February 2025

17856318R10177